I0658390

RESISTANCE

Devin O'Branagan

Cornucopia Creations Press

ISBN: 979-8-9910361-0-8

Published by:
Cornucopia Creations Press

For all the members of the Resistance.

PROLOGUE

"What does my death matter, if through us, thousands
of people are awakened and stirred to action?"
– 21-year-old Sophie Scholl of the White Rose non-violent
resistance group, executed in 1943 for distributing
anti-Nazi leaflets at her university in Munich.

I never thought he would betray me. The possibility never crossed my mind. The profound shock of it still takes my breath away.

Would I do it all again? Yes, of course I would. Heroism is a family tradition, after all.

Did I help to change history? I believe what I did made a difference, but I certainly didn't do it alone. I worked with a noble group of resisters.

As I contemplate my own death, I wish I had more time to live, to love, and to grow.

And as the great unknown looms, I wonder how the hearts of my loved ones will hold my memory.

CHAPTER ONE

Erin Tavano did not believe in ghosts until the day one saved her life.

Nothing was right in her world, and probably never would be again. And like all the other monsters that had terrorized her over the past year, this one also attacked without warning. With a fierce howl, the blizzard descended from its mountain lair like a ferocious beast abruptly roused from a fitful slumber. Fifteen minutes earlier when Erin left her home in Boulder, the late-afternoon sun had kissed her goodbye. Now, on this two-lane highway where the gentle Colorado plains morphed into wild foothills, the dragon of winter swooped down, and with shocking fury attacked the car in which she and her daughter rode. Its fierce breath shook their BMW, its wicked fire lit up the black clouds that chased them, and its haunting roar taunted with sinister laughter. Large shimmering ice crystals showered down hard, as if the dragon were attacking them with its sharp scales.

Sixteen-year-old Izzy looked up into the lightning-streaked sky and said, "Whoa, thundersnow. Cool."

Erin's gloved hands tightened on the wheel. "I did not see this coming."

"Colorado weather's always been a fickle bitch," Izzy said, and then went back to the casual conversation she had been having with her best friend via FaceTime.

At that moment the dragon unleashed a small army of snow devils upon Erin and her fellow road warriors. Rising from the blanket of snow that had fallen the night before, a myriad of whirling vortexes took flight in startling fashion. A rare sight, Erin uttered a sharp gasp in response.

Izzy looked up from her conversation. "Holy hell." She turned her phone around so her friend could see. "Get a load of this, Karma."

"Wow," came the girl's breathy response.

Although strangely beautiful, the columns of swirling snow rocked the car, obscured the road, and shot a bullet of fear through Erin. She turned on her headlights and slowed her speed. As she veered right to head up a steep hill, she felt a subtle change with the grip of her tires. This stretch of road had a slick coating of ice. BMWs were built for mountain driving, and when Erin encountered treacherous conditions, she always reminded herself what the young salesman had said years earlier when he handed over the keys to her new car.

"Treat this baby with respect because chances are that someday it will save your life."

Uncharacteristically, Erin felt compelled to reach out and pat the dash. "You're a good car," she whispered, ignoring the surprised smile that crossed Izzy's lips.

Erin felt no need to explain herself. Everyone was allowed an occasional moment of eccentricity.

Through the years Erin had learned that unlike other cars she had driven, her BMW hugged the road and could be precisely controlled. And yes, there had been times when that ability to become one with the car had extricated her from dangerous situations. She had always felt safe driving it.

Briefly, a snowsquall clouded her vision, and when it passed what confronted Erin was so horrifying as to be completely surreal. As she watched, a red sedan in the oncoming lane lost traction on the downhill ice, drifted into Erin's lane, and headed directly for them in a slow out-of-control spin.

Time elongated. Erin's vision narrowed. The universe held its breath.

This stretch of road had no shoulder. To Erin's right was a sheer drop-off, guarded by only the flimsiest of reflective rails. The flat expanse to the left of the road was walled off by a row of large boulders. Oncoming in the left lane was a school bus, which at this hour was likely filled with children. Her rearview mirror showed no cars behind them.

Erin had never experienced a moment of such clarity or detachment. She understood that she had only seconds to decide what to do, and her choices were limited. She could stay in her lane, try to stop, and meet the sedan head on. That course of action would risk fewer lives than if she tried to go around the car and possibly slam into the bus. Or she could steer toward the guardrail, crash through it, and go over the side.

Her thoughts flew to her grandfather, who had to make a similar choice as a pilot in Vietnam. When his plane was hit by enemy fire he could have safely ejected, but the plane would have crashed into a village. Instead, he rode the plane in to control the trajectory and took it down into the jungle. He lost his legs, but the sacrifice saved many innocent lives.

However, Captain Conor Doyle was a hero, and unlike him, Erin was not at all courageous. And when faced with the choices in front of her now, being fiercely committed to protecting her own child above everyone else was, she realized, quite selfish. This was the first time she had faced her lack of noble character, and the shock was electric.

Erin wasn't religious so it never occurred to her to pray to God, but she did long for the guidance of her twin brother Brian, who had recently died. He was their better half in every way imaginable. He would have known the right thing to do and accomplished it fearlessly.

Erin's mother believed in all things supernatural, and Izzy embraced a philosophy that revolved around quantum physics and the multiverse. Therefore, when Brian appeared to Erin, she later decided that one of those two belief systems might explain the impossible moment outside of time and space which saved all the lives that day.

The world fell away and the only light in the darkness was a bright spotlight that illuminated Brian. Terribly handsome, he wore a tailored black tailcoat, dress slacks, and a crisp white shirt adorned with a bow tie. A classic black top hat and sleek ebony cane with a silver handle that gleamed in the mysterious spotlight completed his debonair ensemble.

The smile he greeted her with was, as always, gentle and kind.

In life, Brian had been a dancer, a skill he apparently carried over to the other side. His feet began to move with precision and grace, the tap of his shoes the only sound accompanying his performance. He executed a breathtaking series of rapid-fire taps, creating a symphony of sound. His graceful artistry seemed to convey a sense of purpose and meaning.

What struck Erin was the geometry of his movement, the spatial dimensions of the patterns he danced into being, the flow of his pirouettes. Erin wasn't creative in the classical sense, but mathematics had always been one of her gifts. With a sudden flash of comprehension, she understood exactly what she needed to do.

Brian's image faded as Erin returned to the present moment. In a series of precise turns of her wheel, she executed a dance with the oncoming sedan. Instead of trying to swing around it, she swung with it. She steered the BMW in tandem with the spinning car, gracefully mirroring its movements. A dangerous and delicate maneuver, it was akin to a skilled dancer twirling around a partner on a stage. As if they were connected by an invisible thread, the two vehicles moved with uncanny synchronicity. Gradually, the spinning lost momentum, and both cars straightened out and parted ways.

It all unfolded in only a few moments.

Erin felt as shocked as Izzy looked.

"Well done, Mom."

"That was beyond awesome, Mrs. T," Karma said though the phone.

Erin thought she heard Brian say, *"In a perfectly choreographed performance, two cars danced outside of time and space for a moment, and then returned to their respective destinies."*

Erin wrestled with a sudden urge to cry.

In the past six months Erin had lost her brother, her marriage, her home, her business, and now she had lost her mind. The absurdity of what just happened caused her to erupt with a brief outburst of hysterical laughter.

"Are you okay?" Izzy asked.

Erin wiped her tearing eyes. "I was just wondering if

I somehow might have caught my mother's insanity."

Izzy chuckled. "Grandma's type of crazy is the contagious kind and not the inherited kind, but you're like the most sane, logical, boring person I have ever known. So, I don't think you need to worry."

"Thanks ... I think?"

"Don't mention it."

Erin took a deep breath and did her best to stop trembling. Then she considered Izzy's low-key reaction to their close call. In fact, with all the horror Izzy had endured in the past year, her level of perpetual calmness worried Erin. It wasn't normal. It wasn't healthy to bury trauma. And with all her own challenges, Erin hadn't had time for many heart-to-heart talks with her lately. Maybe she should try now.

"What's going on in your life, Izzy?" Erin asked.

Her daughter cocked her head as she considered. "Well, in history I studied global pandemics, the Great Depression, the rise of fascism in Nazi Germany, and the Civil Rights Movement, but all of that seemed a long time ago in a galaxy far, far away. And yet here we are again. Coming to terms with our new reality is sucking a lot of my lifeforce."

Erin glanced at her. "The Chimera pandemic was brutal and financially ruined a lot of us, but fascism? Our government has a lot of rules now, but it restored order and stability to the country."

"At the cost of human rights. We're becoming Nazi Germany part two. You don't have a clue what's really happened, do you Mom?"

Discussions like this with Izzy were always filled with land mines, so Erin deflected. "You've been reading Teen Vogue again, haven't you? I thought that was banned for its radical politics."

"Only in this country. I read the UK edition online."

"How?"

"My mad computer skills, of course. I know how to get around the Great American Internet Wall."

Fear fluttered in Erin's stomach. "I don't want you to get in trouble."

"Can't promise that. I'm on a mission."

"To do what?"

"To fight the good fight. As the saying goes, 'The only thing necessary for the triumph of evil is for good men—and women of course—to do nothing.'"

Erin thought about her grandfather and the cost of his heroics but resisted the maternal urge to nag about risky behavior. Izzy was sixteen going on twenty-six and way too smart for her own good.

The drive from Boulder into the foothills to pick up Erin's son from her sister's ranch was taking much longer than usual. Traffic crawled.

Accompanying them, by way of FaceTime, was Karma Chen. Karma went most places with Izzy, hanging on a lanyard worn around her neck.

"Did I tell you girls that I have a job interview Saturday?" Erin said.

"What kind of job is it?" Karma asked.

"Investigative reporter for the *Boulder Maverick*."

Izzy shook her head. "What? I mean, why? Um ... *how*?"

Erin's defensive bristles rose. "I do have a journalism degree, you know."

"That you've never used."

"I was editor of my college newspaper. I submitted samples of my work with my résumé, and they want to interview me."

"Probably because they couldn't get anyone else to apply there." Karma said, then quickly added, "No offense."

"Why wouldn't anyone else want to work there?" Erin asked.

"You do know what kind of paper it is, don't you?"

Erin nodded. "Back in the day they were a subversive, underground newspaper, but like with all of us former rebels, they grew up."

Izzy burst out laughing. "You were once a rebel?"

"I turned down several solid career opportunities to marry your dad and open a restaurant. *That* was rebellion in my family."

"Point taken," Izzy said.

"But Mrs. T, since the *Maverick* stopped being all radical it's kinda nothing," Karma said. "I mean, it's small and inconsequential now. What are they going to have you investigate ... whose gardens are going to be included in the next Garden Club tour?"

"As long as I get a paycheck, I'll be happy chasing down Boulder society dames for hot leads."

"But Mom..." Izzy's voice faded, and she grew pensive.

"What?"

"Being a reporter is a crazy dangerous job these days. You haven't been paying attention to the world *at all*."

"Does she know what happened to the owners of the Bookmark Bistro?" Karma asked.

"Keith and Autumn?" Erin had recently applied for a job as a barista at the popular bookstore on Boulder's Pearl Street Mall. "I just saw them two weeks ago. Are they okay?"

"They were arrested for selling banned books," Izzy said. "The state took custody of their kids and won't tell anyone what's happened to them."

Erin's mind wasn't computing. "I don't understand. Why would—"

"Because our new government is *fascist*," Izzy said. "How many times do I have to tell you? I love you, and I know you've been dealing with a lot of horrible things, but they've blinded you to the bigger picture. Everything has changed really fast, and our country is hella scary now."

"But I watch the news and—"

"Exactly. The news. They only report what they want people to know. It's controlled by Big Brother, and you shouldn't go anywhere near it. Being a reporter is not the job for you right now. You're too good a person, and you're too naive."

Erin flinched. "I'm not stupid, Izzy."

"I didn't say you were. You're just living in the past." Izzy thrust her hand into Erin's purse, grabbed her cellphone, and swiped it awake. "What's your password … oh, wait I bet I can guess … yep, I'm in." She shook her head. "In the name of all tech things holy, how have you survived this long in the modern world?" Izzy's thumbs attacked the phone in a blur of motion. "Okay, I'm not only installing a better password, but I'm loading my favorite new rogue app that combines the best of Burner and Signal, but it's much cooler. It was designed to work around the new surveillance protocols."

"I have no idea what you're saying."

"Don't worry, I'll teach you everything you need to know to protect yourself," Izzy said.

"From fascism?" Erin asked.

"Hell yeah," Izzy and Karma replied in unison.

Erin didn't need more things to be afraid of—her life was frightening enough as it was.

The storm lightened, traffic began to flow more smoothly, and Erin breathed a bit easier. To fill the awkward silence, she asked, "What are you up to these days, Karma?"

Izzy tilted her own phone in Erin's direction so they could see each other, and then went back to performing all tech things holy.

"I'm playing my music, of course. I've started working in the kitchen at Café Paris as a pastry chef. And I'm writing a book about real life heroes." Touching the ugly scars on her face, her voice quavered for a moment as she said, "Not everyone is a villain, you know."

Erin nodded. "I do know that. My grandfather received all kinds of medals for his heroism in Vietnam."

"His story is so *awesome*." Karma quickly reined in her excitement. "I mean, seriously awful for what happened to him, but awesome that someone cared that much about others. I'd love to know more."

Erin had not seen the broken girl this animated in a long time. Perhaps visiting with Conor might help her heal. "He won't tell you the story if you say you want to put it in a book. But if you approach it right, he may share the details with you."

Izzy slipped Erin's phone back where she found it. "I'll get him to spill," she said. "I'm his favorite."

Erin laughed because it was true. They had bonded deeply over their mutual geek passion for all things computer.

"He must have been so scared," Karma said, her voice barely a whisper.

Izzy raised her phone and leveled the other girl with a firm expression. "Fear is a reaction. Courage is a decision."

"Yes. Yes, you're right." She sounded stronger.

Izzy was good for Karma.

"Speaking of decisions, where are we going to live when the bank takes our house?" Izzy asked.

Erin took a deep breath, then let it out slowly. "I don't know. I haven't figured that out yet."

The girls grew silent.

A storm roared inside Erin.

***

When they passed through the arched wooden gateway of the Paxton Homestead, it was like they entered another world. The sprawling cattle ranch set amid gently rolling hills was a picturesque spread with stunning views of the Rocky Mountains. It had been in the Paxton family for generations. After Beau Paxton's father died, Beau took over the operation, married Erin's sister, Meg, and together they had built a good life.

Beau and Meg lived in the main house and Beau's mother chose to live in a cozy stone cottage next to it. Further in, a cluster of buildings included the home of the ranch foreman and his family, a bunkhouse for the hands, and the mess hall and community room. Beyond that lay the heart of the operation—a magnificent herd of Black Angus and all that was necessary for their care and maintenance. Erin had always thought of the ranch as a modern-day Brigadoon, an enchanted village untouched by the worries of the modern world. Even the snowfall here seemed to be less than that dumped by the storm through which they had just passed. It didn't seem possible, but the difference was noticeable. To Erin, her sister's life seemed charmed.

Erin drove up to the main house and opened her car door. "Are you coming in? I'm sure Meg would love to see you."

Izzy wrinkled her nose. "No, I don't like Aunt Meg or Uncle Beau anymore."

"Because of how they acted at Brian's wake?"

"It's more than that. I don't like their politics. Their religion. Their anti-everything-sane ethic. Their whole vibe. I wish you wouldn't let Luca spend so much time alone with them. They're a dangerous influence."

Her words made Erin uncomfortable. As much as Erin didn't want to, she might end up asking her sister for a place to stay until they could regain their footing. She closed the door and settled back into her seat. "I want to understand your feelings."

Izzy shook her head. "I know your entire universe *forever* has been Dad, Luca, me, and the restaurant, but like I said before, bigger picture." Her hands flew up in a grand, sweeping gesture. "We thought the original pandemic and the chaos that came with it was bad, but when it mutated to the Chimera strain and that awful final wave drowned us, people's true colors really surfaced. That's why this country's where it's at now." She glared at the house. "I thought I knew Aunt Meg and Uncle Beau, but they turned out to be truly awful people."

Erin was taken aback by Izzy's passion. Did she even know her daughter anymore? However, it was clear that Izzy did know her quite well. She really didn't care about the bigger picture right now. Erin was in survival mode, and for that she wasn't in the least bit apologetic. "I'm sorry you feel like you do. We should talk more about this later." Overwhelmed, she stepped out of the car and slammed the door behind her with more force than intended.

Although it wasn't snowing, the cold wind whipped, and the chignon at the nape of Erin's neck started to unravel. Reaching up, she loosened it entirely, and let her long hair down. As she walked up the snow packed cobblestone path that led to the house, a flood of unwelcome feelings washed over her. She had never longed for what Meg had or for the life she had chosen, but right now she was brutally aware of the consequences of their respective choices. Erin's journey had always been ruled by passion rather than practicality. As Meg was so fond of pointing out to her, passion was invariably the path to pain. It was a cynical premise Erin had always rejected, but now she rocked with doubt.

The full wraparound porch led to a kitchen door at the back of the house. The big country kitchen was the heart of their home, and when unlocked, anyone was welcome to enter except, as the familiar sign on the door said: NO GODLESS HEATHENS WELCOME HERE. Erin, never one hundred percent sure if she met the stated criteria, let herself in. Jason Aldean sang on the radio and the scent of fresh-baked cookies filled the air.

Meg, pouring herself a cup of coffee, raised the mug in greeting. "Want one?"

Erin nodded. "Thanks."

Meg handed off her own mug and poured another, gestured for Erin to sit at the kitchen table, then sat across from her. Chocolate chip cookies beckoned from a large serving platter between them.

"Luca is still out riding with Beau," Meg said. "I expect them soon." She pointed beyond the huge picture window that graced one wall to the distant sight of three mounted horses. "He's been having a blast spending time with the men."

"I'm glad. His father's been MIA for months now." Embarrassment rose and Erin could feel her freckles burn. "Given what's happened, I get Tony not wanting to see me, but I don't understand why he's been ignoring the kids."

Meg started to say something, stopped, then replaced the unspoken words with a big bite of cookie.

Erin drank in the glorious view of the snowy hills and felt a twinge deep in her stomach. "You have such a lovely home."

Meg studied her for a few moments with her all-seeing eyes. "Luca told us that you're about to lose yours."

Erin groaned. "I wish he had let me tell you the news."

"The boy's scared."

"I am, too."

"What I don't get is why Tony let this happen," Meg said. "He needs to cowboy up. It's his responsibility to take care of his family. Instead, he's whoring around with that wetback waitress. What's wrong with him?"

Meg had always managed to push Erin's buttons, and she struggled to control her temper. "Firstly..." Her thoughts floundered. "Maria isn't illegal."

Meg studied her through narrowed eyes and took another large bite of cookie.

"And Tony has been giving us every cent he has been able to part with and still keep the restaurant up and running. It's been hard for us ... him ... to stock the kitchen, find reliable help, pay the increased rent and taxes, rebuild the customer base. Not everything is his fault." Erin knew it sounded lame, but it was the truth.

"A real man would find a way."

"He tried. He failed. Izzy believes it's Tony's shame that drove him away from us."

Meg snorted and turned her attention to the approaching riders.

A sea of silence rose between them.

Erin studied her older sister. Meg had inherited blond hair, high cheekbones, and a sturdy frame from her father, Erik Nygaard, their mother's high school fling. On the other hand, Erin and Brian came by their curly red hair, fair skin, and more graceful bodies from the mysterious man their mother called The Irish Bard, a lover she met on a brief trip to Ireland when she graduated college. Even though all three siblings were conceived out of wedlock, Meg had always lorded over the twins the fact that she knew her father's name, and they didn't. After a lifetime, Erin still found Meg's superiority complex intimidating.

"Don't you have any compassion at all?" Erin asked.

Meg continued staring out the window for a long time before answering. "I feel badly for the cows and calves crying for each other when we have to separate them. Their wails never fail to rip my heart open, even after all these years."

That revelation startled Erin and her mind dissected it. She knew that Meg and Beau had never been able to have children and wondered if that's where the crack in her sister's armor lay. "I'm sorry you haven't experienced motherhood yourself. Why didn't you ever adopt?"

"We didn't want a child conceived in sin by an unwed mother, or a child from unknown parentage." Meg reached for another cookie. "The perfect opportunity did arise once when a woman at our church died in childbirth. Her husband was worried about raising the baby on his own, so we tried to convince him to give her to us, but he decided to keep her after all." A sour expression crossed Meg's face, and she put the cookie back. "It wasn't fair."

Erin wondered what part of the tragic story she considered unfair. "I never knew that about you."

Meg chuckled. "There's a lot you don't know about me."

Brian had always joked that Meg hid her heart behind an ancestral Viking shield. It was true.

Meg's brows furrowed. "Where's Isabelle?"

"She's in the car talking to Karma."

"Karma? Oh, that broken china doll she wears around her neck. That's not healthy for either of them."

"They've been friends their whole lives, and they're good for each other. When Karma was disfigured in that attack she withdrew into a shell. Izzy's just trying to draw her back out into the world."

"Oh, Erin. Karma is *Chinese*. A good mother would put an end to that unhealthy, and possibly traitorous, behavior. What must other people think of Isabelle's bizarre antics?"

"Karma is second-generation American."

Meg huffed her bangs out of her eyes. "As if that matters."

Erin reined in her growing anger and tried to sort out a way to ask for the help she so desperately needed.

However, Meg jumped that fence first.

"You know, with your life in limbo, Luca's welcome to live with us. He's real happy here. A ranch is the perfect place for a ten-year-old boy to build character and learn what's important in life."

Luca. Not Erin or her Chinese-loving, possibly traitorous daughter. Well, that said it all, didn't it? Erin blinked back the unexpected burn of tears. "I'll figure something out so we can stay together. Thanks anyway."

A racket arose at the door and Luca, Beau, and the ranch foreman, Manny, spilled into the kitchen, scattering snow and laughter.

Luca's eyes glowed with excitement and his radiant smile widened upon seeing Erin. With great flourish he swept the cowboy hat off his head and held it to his heart. "Well, howdy there ma'am."

Erin laughed. "Where'd you get the fancy hat?"

"Uncle Beau. He said if I was going to help out around here, I needed to look the part. Gave me this cool fleece-lined jean jacket, too."

Erin caught Beau's eyes. "Very kind of you."

"He was born for this life," Beau said. "He's a natural."

Manny tipped his own hat in Erin's direction. "Nice to see you again, *Señora* Erin."

"Likewise. Luca told me that you have something to celebrate?"

"*Sí!* I, Manuel Lopez, am now a United States citizen. Beau sponsored me all the way, from getting my green card to becoming an American. I took my final oath right before Christmas. Such a happy day. I am as grateful as one man can be."

"That was awfully nice of you, Beau," Erin said.

"There's a right way and a wrong way to do things," Beau said, his voice gruff, "and Manny chose the right way. Glad to help."

Erin was surprised by the revelations this visit had uncovered. Both Izzy and Meg were correct; there was a lot she didn't know. However, the one thing abundantly clear about the Paxtons was that everything had to be by the book ... their own book.

Snow and mud-encrusted boots were removed at the door, and while Luca lunged for the cookies, the men poured themselves coffee. Then they attacked the freshly baked treats, too. Within minutes, the cookie platter was empty, and Meg swiftly replenished it with a towering pile of huge fudge brownies.

As she watched everyone dig in with gusto, it became clear to Erin why Meg and Beau had plumped up so spectacularly over their twenty-five years of marriage. Despite that uncharitable observation, Erin decided to grab two of the brownies, wrap them in a napkin, and tuck them into her coat pocket. Her intention was to share with Izzy later.

Erin stood. "We should go. I left the keys in the ignition in case Izzy needed the heater, but I'm still worried about her."

"I invited Luca to come to church with us on Sunday," Beau said. "The boy needs religious training."

Irritation shot through Erin like a bullet. Who was he to decide what Luca needed?

Luca turned around to display the back of his new jacket. Stitched to it was the name of the Paxton family church: Rocky Mountain Patriot Church. The logo was an American flag overlayed by images of a Christian cross and two crossed rifles. The motto read, *God, Guts, & Glory.*

Izzy, who was apparently savvy about the bigger picture, had said she didn't like their religion. Although Erin knew nothing about the Patriot Church, guns in the context of religion did make her uncomfortable. "Thank you, but that's not going to happen."

"Why can't he come with us?" Meg asked. "You never take him to church."

Because he's my son, not yours, and I'll raise him how I want to. She took a deep breath. "Luca's Catholic."

Beau grunted. "That's not a church. It's a nest of anti-American pedophiles. The boy shouldn't be exposed to such corruption."

A sudden surge of adrenaline flooded, and Erin bolted to her feet. "Put on your boots, Luca. We're leaving now."

Sullenly, Luca complied.

There was so much Erin wanted to say in parting, but she resisted the urge. She rushed Luca out the door before she gave voice to things she would later regret.

***

Erin's childhood home was in the far eastern part of Boulder County in the city of Longmont. The house belonged to her grandfather, Conor. Erin's mother, Kelly, still lived there. And Brian had also lived there until his horrible death from the Chimera virus. Conor had always been the family anchor. Erin hoped he would give them safe harbor now.

Izzy, who had been absorbed in texting with Karma

the entire trip, looked up as they pulled into the driveway. "Ah, so I take it Aunt Meg said we couldn't move in with her?"

"Correct," Erin said.

Luca, sprawled across the back seat, sat bolt upright. "What? I won't live here if that's what you're thinking. This place totally sucks. Besides, Uncle Beau told me that I could move in with them. That's way more cool."

Erin's fingers tightened on the steering wheel. "He had no right to tell you that. You're part of this family, and we're broken enough. The three of us are going to stick together, whatever may come."

Luca kicked the back of her seat. "That's not fair."

"Life isn't fair." Erin blinked back tears. Izzy had always been the rebel; not Luca. Why was he acting out now? "And don't ever kick my seat again. It's disrespectful. This is hard enough. Please don't make it harder." After pulling into the driveway, Erin turned off the engine and took a deep breath.

"It's been so long since we've been here," Izzy said.

The whole family had last gathered right after Brian's death. Erin had stayed away since then out of fear that she would be sucked into the dark hole that his absence left behind. And that same sense of dread flooded her now.

"I missed seeing Grandma and Papa at Christmas," Izzy said.

"Everyone agreed it would be best," Erin said. "Between grieving Brian, the fight I had with your aunt at his wake, and your dad leaving us, none of us were feeling festive."

"I miss Uncle Brian," Izzy whispered.

No one missed Brian like Erin did. They were two

halves of one soul.

"Like Aunt Meg said, a lot of good wearing that mask everywhere did him," Luca said, his voice whiny. "Nobody on the ranch wore masks, and no one there died."

"That's because during the Chimera outbreak nobody hardly ever left the ranch," Izzy said.

Luca snorted. "They knew that the whole mask thing was all about *them* wanting to control us."

"Who wanted to control us?" Erin asked.

Izzy chuckled. "Oh, you know, the same ones who were trying to control us when they created face-recognition technology. It makes perfect sense that they wanted us to all cover up our faces, right? I told you that Luca shouldn't be allowed to spend time at Aunt Meg's house."

Luca's whine shifted into shrill mode. "Yeah, and about *that*, so by the end of the pandemic most masks were clear, which just goes to show the face tech thingy was still important to them. But from the beginning *their* plan was to make us obey and be like sheep. Well, I am not a sheep."

"You've got it wrong," Izzy said. "The clear masks were really a conspiracy on the part of Big Lipstick because of plummeting sales."

Luca shook his head. "Huh?"

Erin, after successfully suppressing a scream, managed to say, "For God's sake Luca, stop whining and talking nonsense. Please be nice. I really need you to be nice right now."

Luca issued a dramatic sigh, but at least he didn't kick anything.

"Let's go in," Erin finally said, and they all spilled out

of the car.

Majestic trees of every type surrounded the simple 1960s red brick ranch-style house. Even though it was already late January, the evergreens in the front yard still twinkled with colorful Christmas lights. In the thickening dusk, they beckoned welcomingly. At least that's how Erin chose to see it. *Please welcome us home.*

Mojo, Conor's service dog, invited them inside, his tailless bottom wiggling with delight. The Australian Shepherd was part overgrown puppy and part earnest, hard-working sidekick ... depending on the circumstances. Mojo had achieved an almost Zen-like balance in life that inspired everyone in his orbit. Erin adored him.

In greeting, Luca pulled a strip of beef jerky out of his pocket. "Uncle Beau gave me jerky, Mojo. Would you like—"

Uncharacteristically, Mojo snatched it right out of his hand.

Luca laughed. "Someone hasn't been fed dinner. You want more?"

Mojo whined and Luca shared more of his bounty.

Erin slipped her coat off, hung it on a rack inside the door, and entered the living room.

Conor sat in his wheelchair staring into the dancing flames of the fireplace. Erin's first impression was that he looked simply awful. His face was drawn and pale, and when he looked up at her, his expression was wrong. Off. Haunted.

"Are you okay, Grandpa?" Erin reached out to feel his forehead; it was cool and clammy.

He waved away her hand. "I'm not sick. I'm just very ... tired."

Izzy and Luca crowded noisily into the living room, but their excited chatter came to a sudden halt when they saw Conor.

"You okay, Papa?" Izzy asked.

Conor sighed, pulled a tightly rolled joint out of his pocket, struck a wooden match on the wheel of his chair, and lit it up. He inhaled deeply. "Better now," he managed to say.

Luca pointed at a photograph of Tom Hanks tacked to the wall above the television. It had been defaced with the words SICK BASTARD, written with what looked like red lipstick. "Someone here hates Mr. Rogers?"

"Your grandma hates Hanks," Conor said. "She did that in protest when I watched *Forrest Gump* the other night."

"Why does she hate him?" Luca asked.

Conor exhaled loudly and sweet-smelling smoke filled the air. "It's all part of that QAnon Moms movement she joined. They think he tortures kids for some kind of secret elixir to make him stay young."

Luca inched closer to the photo. "It's not working, is it?"

Conor laughed. "Out of the mouths of babes."

"Hey," Luca said with indignation. "I'm no baby."

"How did Grandma become a QAnut?" Izzy asked.

Conor waved the glowing joint around absently, "Kelly has always been about magical thinking."

"How far has she taken it?" Izzy asked.

"The neighborhood war between the QAnon Moms and the Suburban Snowflakes has become fairly entertaining," Conor said.

The conversation was over Erin's head; she cared

little about politics or cults. It was the least of her concerns. "Grandpa, I need to talk to you about something important."

Brian's Siamese cat, Diva, jumped onto Conor's lap and curled up in a tight ball. Conor patted her. "Lay it on us."

Emotions rose like a tsunami and drowned Erin's thoughts. Words wouldn't come. Instead, she swiped away wild tears.

Izzy, and then surprisingly Luca, each patted her back sympathetically before settling themselves onto the overstuffed couch.

Strengthened by their show of support, Erin took a deep, shaky breath and her voice finally managed to surface. "Tony left me, Grandpa. He's been living with Maria, our head server, for a while now. The restaurant has been treading water since the first wave of the pandemic, and the harder things got, the more Tony drank. He feels like a failure and wasn't ... well he isn't the man I thought he was. We drifted apart. He found another port in the storm. We're broken. There's no fixing it now." Grief flooded her.

Conor sucked in air, and it hissed back out through his teeth. "You want I should beat him up?"

A smile broke through her storm. "Yeah, that would be fabulous."

"I'll run him down with my chair. He'll never know what hit him."

Reality resurfaced, and the moment of humor floated away. "We've lost our home, Grandpa. Even with what Tony's been able to give us, and my income driving for Uber, plus Izzy's earnings as a waitress ... well, it's not been enough. The bank is going to take the house at the end of the month and we—me and the kids—I don't know where we're going to go."

A hush fell over the room and lingered. Would he not offer to help? The hope of rescue had been the only thing keeping Erin's terror at bay.

Finally, Conor broke the silence, his voice uncharacteristically soft. "Your family will never be homeless as long as I have a roof to offer you. However, I can't afford to feed you. See, the food banks ran dry a while back. Social services aren't a thing anymore. Social Security payments have stopped, and my pension payments are erratic. Your ma hasn't worked since her New Age thingamajig closed down. And after Brian was fired from his teaching job, his gig at the gym was the only thing bringing in any steady cash. But just like your restaurant, the gym opened and closed and restricted and operated like a drunken revolving door. The price of food is astronomical." He paused and cleared his throat. "None of us have eaten well in a long time."

Realization dawned. All of Erin's self-absorbed shadows dissipated in a flash, and she really looked at her grandfather. That was why he was so frail. And her mother's weight loss wasn't the magic new diet she had bragged about. *Oh, and Brian.* Why had she ignored how gaunt he had become? She assumed it was because he had been working out too hard while training others at the gym. Was his weakened condition what had left him susceptible to the virus? Her face grew hot with shame. "Why didn't you tell me? Why didn't you ask for help?"

Conor shrugged. "We knew you were struggling too."

"You didn't ask Meg? She and Beau have a goddamn cattle ranch for chrissake."

He ran a shaky hand through his bushy white hair. "You know how they feel about us. To their way of thinking I'm just an old pothead, your ma's a crazy hippie chick who never grew up, and your brother was a flaming faggot. They have always done everything in their power to keep their distance. It just didn't seem like the thing to do."

"Omigod." Erin fought for control. "Grandpa, as God is my witness, no one in this house will ever go hungry again."

His rumbly laughter returned in an unexpected burst. "Why thank you, Scarlett." Despite the laughter, tears filled his eyes.

Luca jumped up, dug deep in his coat pocket, and withdrew a handful of beef jerky. "Take all I've got. It's real fresh."

Conor eagerly accepted the gift. "Thank you, kid." With a trembling hand, he raised a piece to his mouth.

Erin thought she was going to start sobbing again.

The food quickly caught Diva's attention, and Conor offered her a piece. She snatched it out of his hand and leapt to the top of the TV, where she attacked it ruthlessly.

"Don't act so desperate," Conor said to her. "You've been faring better than the rest of us." He looked up at Erin. "She's a good mouser."

Izzy dug through her shoulder bag, pulled out a small baggie filled with vanilla macarons, and dropped them in Conor's lap. "I got them from work. I'll get you more." She swept past him into the kitchen, where they could hear her rifling through the refrigerator and cupboards. A moment later she returned. "All that's there are a few cans of soup, some crackers, and a jug of apple juice."

Conor nodded. "That's the last of the box we got from the food bank. Uh, that was right after Christmas, I think. We made it last as long as we could."

Erin shook her head. "How could things be this bad? This is America."

Conor snorted. "In the aftermath of the worst social meltdown we've ever experienced."

Erin remembered the two brownies in her coat and retrieved them. "Take these, too. I'm going to go get some food from the restaurant, and I'll be back tonight."

"You don't need to do it tonight. Your ma found a few bucks today while sorting through Brian's things. She's headed to McDonald's now."

"That's not nourishing."

"It will be heaven, Erin. Absolute heaven. The thing about life is," he patted his leg stumps, "you don't realize what you have until it's gone, but then you learn to adjust." He gave her a sad look. "Just like you'll do, *macushla*. You and the kids can have the basement and Brian's art studio out back. Your ma doesn't want to pack away his bedroom up here yet, but she's starting to clear out his studio. Why don't you go and check out your new digs? Make a plan."

Erin was grateful for the opportunity to shed more tears away from him. He had enough of his own grief to deal with. She reached for Luca's hand. "Come on. Let's explore our new home."

***

Izzy hung back so she could have some one-on-one

time with Conor. She sat on the floor next to Mojo and pressed her fingers through thick hair to examine his ribs. Their prominence told her he hadn't been eating nearly enough.

"Papa, why didn't you tell me about the food thing? You know I could have helped."

Conor took in a lungful of smoke and held it for what seemed like forever. Finally, he coughed it out. "Isabelle, you do enough for me as it is."

Izzy used her computer hacking skills to run deep dive background checks in exchange for bitcoin, which she in turn used to buy his heart medicine on the Dark Web.

"I could always do more."

His eyes regarded her dreamily, and he stabbed the air with the glowing roach. "You, my sweet girl, are living on the edge as it is. I should never have shared my brilliant mind with you." He had been a computer engineer at IBM and introduced Izzy to all things geek.

She giggled—a reaction that was too girly for her own comfort. She preferred to resist girliness. And frills, chick flicks, and all things silly. She was a woman on a mission. "Yep, your genes are definitely the ones at play inside my particular brand of madness. I love being a cypherpunk."

He smiled, then his face fell, and he looked away. You know, your ma's got Nana's genes. Your dad's betrayal is going to break Erin beyond repair. Her heart is a big, bright bullseye, and Tony hit it square on. I'm scared for her."

Izzy didn't remember her great grandma well, but what she did recall of Nana was that she simply gushed love. And yes, that described her mom as well. Over the past several months Izzy had watched the five stages of grief unfold in her, but they hadn't manifested one at a time resolving in the coveted place of acceptance. No, Erin was still a crazy jumble of denial, anger, bargaining, and depression. "Dad's not who I thought he was, either. Maybe if I'd gotten more creative online, I could have figured out a way to bring in some more money. Then maybe he wouldn't have started drinking and everything wouldn't have gone to hell. But I guess I'm a coward, too ..." Her voice died off. She felt miserable.

Conor shook his head. "You are brave, and brilliant, and beautiful. The world has gone crazy. It's not your responsibility to save everyone."

Izzy didn't agree. With knowledge came responsibility. That's why she aspired to be a cypherpunk. The world had indeed gone crazy, and she wanted to help fix it.

"Do you hear me, girl?"

"Error 404. Page not found."

CHAPTER TWO

When Erin met Tony, he managed a pizza parlor near the campus of CU Boulder. Lightning struck and rocked both of their worlds. That once-in-a-lifetime magical connection had never died—at least for her. She joyfully sacrificed all her previous dreams in the fire of him, and together they started Tony Tavano's. Wildly popular, the Italian restaurant was known for its delectable cuisine, unique ambiance, and its charismatic gravitational center—Tony himself.

Tony was Erin's gravitational center as well, and her axis hadn't stopped wobbling in the six months since he had discarded her.

Tavano's was located on the famous Pearl Street Mall, a four-block, red-brick paved, pedestrian promenade in the heart of Boulder's historic downtown. A favorite destination for tourists, college students, and locals, it was known for its diverse restaurants, art galleries, bookstores, street performers, gardens, fountains, and lively nightlife.

Erin hadn't come to their restaurant since the breakup. Timing her visit the next morning to arrive a half hour before opening, she parked in the back alley but decided against using the employee entrance. Instead, she walked around the building and used her own key to boldly enter through the front door. It was important to her wounded pride to still assert ownership. Her mother insisted that such things would matter when they finally ended up in court, but neither she nor Tony had made any moves toward a formal divorce. The unsettled situation just added more layers of anxiety to Erin's life.

As she stepped inside, the familiarity of her home-away-from-home for the past twenty years stole her breath. So much of her life had been wrapped up in this space, and she didn't realize until now how desperately she missed it.

Tony's new woman, Maria, was setting up the dining room for lunch. She stopped and looked at Erin but said nothing. It was the first time they had encountered each other since the tectonic shift that had altered their roles. To be fair, Maria hadn't stolen Tony directly from Erin. Tony's drinking had become so severe that he had stopped coming home at night, choosing instead to pass out on the couch in the restaurant's office. Then, before Erin realized what was happening, he was living at the restaurant, leaving only to shower and change at his brother's nearby apartment. After Tony finally told Erin he was never coming home, Maria offered him comfort and a new place to stay.

At least that's how the story was told.

Steeling herself, Erin blurted out with as much bravado as she could manage, "I need to see my husband."

Maria gave her a curt nod. "He's cooking."

Erin sidestepped the other woman and walked through the swinging doors into kitchen.

When she entered, Tony looked up from the stove and greeted her with a brilliant smile. "Hi, baby."

For a moment time stood still. Heat flooded Erin, her knees turned to jelly, and hope rose.

Then that moment was shattered when his

expression turned cold, and he instantly threw up the wall that had separated them for months.

Erin blinked back tears, and her voice took flight.

Tony turned his attention to the sizzling frying pan. Their awkward silence seemed to stretch into icy infinity and Erin had no idea how to navigate the moment.

Finally, time regained its center when Tony's younger brother, Nick, crashed through the back door, his arms heavily laden with supplies. After he plopped down his heavy load, he noticed her and grinned. "Wow, what an unexpected surprise." His eyes gave her a critical once-over. "You and the kids okay?"

His warmth helped her voice finally thaw. "Not so much. The bank is taking our house at the end of the month. We're moving into my grandfather's place. He's giving us the basement."

Erin and Nick both looked at Tony, whose expression turned bleak, but he didn't say anything. Keeping his eyes averted, he grabbed a full wine glass from the shelf above the stove and took a big swig.

Dumbfounded, Erin summoned strength from the mysterious inner reservoir that had been fueling her, lifted her chin, and said, "We need help moving."

Tony shrugged. "I gotta keep things running here. Can't take any time off."

Nick regarded him with disgust. "I'll help you, Erin. Of course I will. I've got the truck and a roommate who's behind on his rent and owes me. Andy and I'll get it done."

A myriad of shifting emotions did fierce battle inside Erin. She looked around for something to pick up and throw at Tony. Then grief overwhelmed her, and she fought the irrational desire to turn to him for comfort. Instead, she moved to embrace Nick in a fierce hug. "Thank you. It means more than you could know."

He gave her back an awkward pat. "Sure. It's okay. Everything will be okay."

She pulled back and swiped away her tears. "No, nothing is okay. I found out last night that Grandpa and Mom have been literally starving. They never said anything, but they're in a desperate situation. I need food and I need it now. And I will keep needing it. It's the least you can do for us, Tony."

He nodded, and his mood abruptly shifted again. "Sure, baby, sure. Anything you want." He gestured wildly in every direction. "I just made fresh batches of meatballs, gnocchi, and Asiago potatoes. I've got lasagna with sausage, and a perfect basil pesto—we couldn't get fresh basil anymore, so Maria started this little garden." He pointed to the same type of small window greenhouse that Conor used to grow his marijuana. "There's a lot we can't find now with the food shortages and supply chain issues, so we've had to get creative. I've started making pineapple cannoli —why didn't we ever think of it before? And did you know I make gelato now?" Strangely animated, his hand gestures became a blur. "Maria found this ice cream maker at a garage sale, and I use it on the slow setting to create the most exquisite flavors: espresso, pistachio, almond, *fior-di-latte*—which is sweet cream— and *stracciatella*—which is sweet cream with chocolate shavings." He kissed his fingertips and flicked his wrist. "*Bellissimo*. I know the kids would love it. Maria also suggested—"

Overwhelmed, Erin couldn't take anymore. "Stop it!

Just stop it."

He looked at her with confusion. "What? What the hell did I do now?"

Nick shook his head. "Jesus, Tony, Erin doesn't need to hear *Ave Marias* right now." He ran his fingers through his beard. "Just tell us what you want, and it's yours."

Trembling, Erin managed to pull herself together enough to think. "Ah, I'll take the lasagna and cannoli. Otherwise, just groceries."

Nick nodded. "Let's get you what you need."

While Tony packaged up lasagna and cannoli, Erin and Nick poked around in the cupboards, the storage room, and both the walk-in fridge and freezer. Ultimately, Erin chose sacks of onions, potatoes, and carrots, a box of chicken breasts, a huge can of pineapple, several loaves of fresh-baked *ciabatta* bread, butter and cheese, a flat of eggs, several gallons of milk, and jugs of olive oil and balsamic vinegar. Finally, she snatched a bag of frozen clams for Diva.

Nick made several trips to haul the bounty to her car.

Before leaving, she said to Tony, "You may be done with me, but the kids still need you."

His dour mood returned. "They know where to find me." He downed the rest of the wine and refilled his glass to the top.

Frustration and disgust joined her emotional shitstorm. "Luca needs a father. He's getting way too close to Beau for my comfort."

"Beau's a good man."

"For chrissakes, Tony, who the hell are you? What have you become?"

"People change," he muttered.

There was so much she wanted to say. Instead, she just shook her head, turned on her heel, and stormed out.

Nick was leaning against her car smoking a cigarette.

"He's not the man I thought he was," Erin said. She couldn't come to grips with that fact, and it made her feel as if her entire life with him had been built on a lie.

Nick nodded. "He was always my hero. Not so much now."

They stood awkwardly for a couple minutes.

"It's not that he doesn't still love you," Nick said. "It's that he hates himself. And Maria? She's just a convenient distraction. He has no love to give; he just wants to get lost."

"I don't know how I'm going to survive this."

"You will. You're an amazing woman. He's a fool."

"His behavior is so strange." Erin's mind struggled to understand. "He seems happy—gleeful even—giving us stuff, but he can't be bothered to give us anything of himself."

Nick shrugged. "I don't understand it either. From the time he was a kid he was always the one taking care of everyone else. First our mother, in that miserable marriage. Then me after our folks died. You and his family. He was always everyone's rock. But now he's just crumbled into this pathetic pile of gravel." He kicked a piece of loose gravel for emphasis. "For the life of me, I can't figure it out."

"I can't come back here."

Nick flicked his cigarette away. "Once a week I make a run to the wholesaler in Denver. I'll plan to make a delivery to you on the way back. You want more of the same?"

Erin thought about it. "Yeah, except add ground beef; I'll make my own damn meatballs. More fruit if you can ... fresh, if possible. And frozen shrimp maybe? I've got to feed my kids and a malnourished family. Plus, I've got a starving dog and cat on my hands."

"I'll do my best. Tony wasn't kidding about supply shortages. There's never any guarantee about what I'll find."

"Thank you." She looked past him to give the restaurant she loved a final look and remember the priceless memories it held: the joy of creating it with Tony, the friendships born of its womb, the children they reared in its unique world, and the family it molded. Inside her, joy and sorrow did a wild dance that made her dizzy. She struggled to find the right parting words. Finally, she managed to say, "Thank you for all you've done through the years and for all you're doing now."

Nick's eyes captured hers and held them. "You're family. I will always be there for you."

Erin hoped so, but she wasn't sure any longer whom she could truly count on except herself. Her family's survival depended on her recreating herself and her own life. Finally coming to terms with that simple truth provided her with the sense of control she knew would allow her to move forward.

***

Izzy's tribe growing up had been The Pearl Street Orphan's Club. It consisted of four children whose parents owned restaurants on the mall. The thing about owning a restaurant is that it's an all-consuming time suck, and when their parents didn't have time for them, they gravitated toward each other and bonded for life.

Izzy was a year younger than Karma; Miguel was two years older than Karma, and André was almost one year older than him. Izzy and Miguel both had younger brothers, Luca and Esteban, but they weren't club members. The younger boys survived by hanging out together in the office at Tony Tavano's, which conveniently had a comfortable couch, a big-screen TV, and a PlayStation. The opportunity to scrounge all the pizza their little hearts desired from the kitchen made their worlds complete.

Karma's parents owned The Buddha Belly, a very cool hippie-themed Chinese restaurant. Grace and Tommy Chen were first-generation Americans who delighted in retro American culture—especially the counterculture of the 1960s and '70s. Psychedelic artwork covered the walls, groovy music filled the air, and traditional Cantonese-style food filled customer bellies. Grace's mother Mei Ling, a superb cook, provided traditional recipes from her home country and ran the kitchen. Grace and Tommy, decked out in their distinctive bohemian-style clothing, ran the front of the house. Their unique concept was enthusiastically embraced by Boulder's large old-time hippie community as well as the college crowd.

André Night's family owned a split-level establishment. At street level was Café Paris, a French bakery and coffee shop. His mother, a French woman named Lili Laurent, descended from family who had been members of the *Maquis*—the French Resistance—during the Second World War. The décor of the restaurant reflected that era and theme. The flag of the French Resistance and photographs of Resistance fighters were proudly displayed on the walls, French swing music danced through the house and patio, and servers donned snappy costumes designed with 1940s flair. And, of course, everyone wore jaunty berets. The ambiance was charming.

Below the café was an aptly named blues club, The Underground. André's father, the world-famous blues singer Johnny Night, had met Lili while playing clubs in Paris. The Underground became a permanent home for Johnny Night and his Midnight Blues Band, and it was *the* place to be after the sun went down.

The fourth orphan was Miguel Velázquez. His Spanish parents owned The Seville, which featured cuisine from the south of Spain. Of all their restaurants, The Seville was the most elegant and upscale. Miguel's father, Santiago, serenaded diners with his flamenco guitar every night during dinner, and on Saturdays his wife, Valentina, danced the flamenco for their guests.

What Izzy always found intriguing about the Orphan Club's history was that, even though their own busy parents always seemed somehow out of reach, the other parents profoundly influenced the individuals each of them became.

For instance, Miguel loved to hang out at Tony Tavano's. He spent endless hours in the kitchen talking to Izzy's dad about his childhood home in New Jersey. Tony had mysterious ties to the Italian mob, and although he never revealed many details about his own family, Tony could spin terribly exciting tales in his thick East Coast accent that was peppered with colorful "yos," "youse guys," and classic gangster speak.

The décor and ambiance of the restaurant also fed into Tony's mystique. Framed black and white posters of the infamous 1960s Rat Pack hung on the walls alongside sultry images of Marilyn Monroe and Angie Dickinson. Frank Sinatra, Dean Martin, and Sammy Davis Jr. crooned to diners while the staff served them with practiced deference. Miguel absorbed the entire vibe like a sponge. In his teens he started wearing snazzy suits, ties, and fedoras, and his manner became oh-so-smooth and confident. Izzy thought he was sexy as hell.

André eventually transitioned into Andrea, and influenced by Karma's parents, became the most beautifully feminine hippie Izzy had ever known. The child of a white mother and a Black father, her delicious skin tone was the perfect canvas for the body art she created, and her Afro hairstyle easily held the colorful flowers that became her personal signature. She was peace, and love, and all things groovy. Izzy adored her.

Santiago's flamenco guitar was the magical instrument that captured Karma's imagination and sparked her passion for music. From an early age she hounded Miguel's father for lessons, and in his spare moments he guided her well. Johnny Night expanded her education to include other string instruments and musical styles. Karma's skills as a musician were phenomenal.

And from the beginning, Izzy was mesmerized by Lili's family history with the *Maquis*. She learned that it was Lili's female relatives who had worked in the Resistance, and one had even died heroically in Paris while defying Nazi occupation. Over the years, Izzy adopted a personal style of dress, attitude, and ideology influenced by Lili's legacy. In many ways Lili affected her life path more profoundly than anyone besides Papa Conor.

Izzy ultimately came to the realization that the person one became in life wasn't simply due to nature or nurture. There was also the almost mystical hand of destiny involved.

Then of course there was Fate, and that bitch could be cruel. In Izzy's life, there was a clear delineation of Fate's influence. She named those life-streams the Before Time and the After Time.

The Last Perfect Day in the Before Time

For Karma's sixteenth birthday she requested only one thing: that she make her musical debut at The Seville performing with both Santiago and Johnny. The two seasoned professionals jumped at the opportunity to stage a major theatrical event for her. Johnny offered up the entire Midnight Blues Band as backup and presented her with a full set playlist, but she declined both. She said she'd rather perform just one epic song and invite her friends to accompany the three of them. This request proved problematic because none of her friends had any musical abilities whatsoever except for Miguel who sometimes accompanied his father's guitar by playing the *cajón*, a box drum used in flamenco music.

It was Lili who finally came up with the solution. She remembered that her late mother, well-known in Paris for being a disco queen, had once won a contest dancing to Santa Esmeralda's cover of "Don't Let Me Be Misunderstood." The French band had made the old blues song famous again in the 1970s by reimagining it as disco with a driving Latin beat. The original sixteen-minute version YouTube link was sent to everyone involved and they decided that they could totally pull it off because Karma's musically-challenged friends would only have to play simple percussion instruments. Johnny would handle vocals and bass, Santiago the guitar, and Karma being the musical prodigy she was, would switch between violin and guitar. Miguel added a kick pedal to his *cajón* so he could drive the song with more punch. A variety of percussion instruments including maracas, bongos, tabor drum, and tambourines were handed out to the rest of "the rhythm section"—Izzy, Andrea, Luca, and Esteban. Valentina and The Seville's dynamic Moroccan bartender, Omar Ahmed, agreed to dance the flamenco during the (hopefully awesome) percussive break. Lili, who handled the sound and lights for the Midnight Blues performances enthusiastically jumped on the new bandwagon. Izzy's parents were recruited to film the event, and her Uncle Brian, who taught theater, staged and choreographed the show. The musicians composed their own unique cover of Santa Esmerelda's cover, Johnny obtained the requisite legal permissions to perform it, and they practiced in a multitude of stolen moments until they were ready.

~

The night of the performance Izzy made it a point to take dinner to Luther Thunderhawk before the show. She had befriended the homeless Afghanistan veteran who spent his days playing trumpet on the mall, accepting donations in his open instrument case. She found him sitting in his usual place on a wooden bench near The Seville. He had long before staked out the prime location because the restaurant catered to wealthy, and generous, Boulderites.

Izzy sat down and set the big red and white checkered paper bag between them. "If you don't mind, I thought we could eat dinner together. I brought my dad's famous sausage and mushroom calzones."

Luther carefully placed his trumpet in its case, closed it, and nodded in her general direction. "Thank you and thank your father."

Luther could not make eye contact. In fact, from the time of his arrival on the mall almost a year earlier, he had never spoken to anyone until Izzy told Conor about him. Then every day for a month Conor and Mojo drove to the mall in the specially modified van Conor drove, sat with the troubled young man, and listened to the soulful music he coaxed out of his horn. Conor, in his beat-up Vietnam Veteran-inscribed cap and Luther in his equally ragged USMC cap communed wordlessly under the hot Colorado summer sun for weeks until one day Mojo, forgetting his very proper therapy dog dignity, started howling to Luther's music. Izzy was told that Mojo's singing voice was both passionate and melodic, and it inspired Luther to reach out and pet him. "You have the soul of a very confused wolf, my friend," were the words that finally shattered the thick sheet of ice which had encased him. For a week after that, Luther would only talk to Mojo. Then the following week he opened up to Conor. For the remainder of that summer the men shared the secrets and horrors that only fellow wounded veterans of war could understand.

When Izzy later pressed him for details, Conor refused to betray confidences. However, he did reveal that neither alcohol nor drugs had anything to do with Luther's struggles. It was a wicked case of PTSD, and gentle companionship was the only remedy Conor could think to prescribe. So, Izzy started bringing Luther, Conor, and Mojo lunch and sharing it with them. Eventually, Luther silently invited her into his life.

Izzy unpacked the bag, handing Luther the bigger calzone and bottle of Pellegrino, and keeping the smaller ones for herself. Between them she placed a large cup of dipping sauce and a stack of paper napkins. As she did so, she noticed he looked different. His ratty USMC cap was nowhere in sight, and his long black hair wasn't in its normal wild state but had transformed into a single, sleek braid. And his usual olive drab tee-shirt and camo pants had been replaced by decent jeans and a black Henley shirt. He looked good. "Whoa, Luther, you clean up nice."

He gave her a sidelong glance. "Out of respect for Karma. I know what this event means to her and don't want the important people coming tonight to see a bum sitting outside her venue."

Word had spread fast throughout the mall that Johnny Night had invited prominent members of the press and entertainment industry for Karma's debut performance.

Izzy was so moved by Luther's effort that she found herself at a rare loss for words. However, the silence was filled when a familiar, talkative crow landed on the trumpet case and loudly demanded attention.

"How does he always know when you've got food?" Izzy asked.

"He's my shadow," Luther said, tearing off a sizable hunk of his calzone and offering it to his friend.

The crow seized the gift, and with his black feathers reflecting a violet sheen in the late afternoon sun, flew up onto the roof of a nearby building.

"Have you named him?" Izzy asked.

"He's not mine to name."

After a few minutes of companionable silence and shared food, Luther said, "I've been listening to your rehearsals, and your band will own the night."

"You think?"

He dipped his sandwich in the marinara and nodded.

"Well, we sure have been working hard, that's for sure. I'm getting pretty good at clapping my hands and beating on things."

"Useful skills."

"It's Karma who will own the night," Izzy said. "She's so *incredibly* talented, and beautiful, and confident."

Luther nodded. "She is all that."

"And Miguel's got that same star quality. He'll shine bright tonight, too."

Luther nodded. "He's the boy I always see you ogling."

"I don't ogle." Izzy grinned. "But yeah, he totally blows up my skirt. All of us girls wanted him, but Karma got him. Who could resist her? I mean, if I were into girls, I'd be crying into my metaphorical beer right now."

"Is there a name for your band?"

Izzy shrugged. "Nah, this is a one-shot deal. Besides, Johnny is so famous he's not going to join someone else's band ... he's got a rep to protect. We're all about giving Karma's talent some exposure."

"I noticed your brother is coming out of his shell."

"I am *so* relieved he agreed to be part of this. He's super shy." She took a long swig of sparkling water while gathering her thoughts. "Luca's just like our mom —real sensitive. I'm more tough, like Dad. But I love that kid so damn much and I worry about him, you know?"

Luther nodded. "I do know that about you."

Izzy thought his skills of observation were impressive, and she made a mental note to try to improve her own. She had learned a lot from time spent with him.

"At least now that the pandemic is over, Luca's life is getting better," Izzy said. "He's back at school and finally getting into sports. Making friends outside of this weird little bubble we've been living in. It's so healthy for him."

"About that—" Luther's words were interrupted by his shadow's return. The crow landed nearby, shook his tail feathers twice—which Izzy had been told was the crow equivalent to Mojo's happy dance—then dropped something from his beak and nudged it toward his friend.

Luther set his unfinished calzone aside and picked up the gold wire earring with a red stone teardrop dangling from it. "Very nice. Thank you, I'll treasure it."

Seemingly satisfied, with a loud caw and fluttering of wings, the gift-bearer returned to his high perch.

Izzy admired the earring in Luther's hands. "Quid pro crow?"

"He always brings me something when I share my food, but he's never given me something like this."

"Crows blow me away. Is that a ruby?"

"No, better. It's a garnet. A healing stone."

"What will you do with it?"

"Clean it up and start wearing it."

Izzy's hands fluttered toward the sky. "The crow will tell the tale of the Calzone and the Stone, and his progeny will keep you under their wings of protection forever."

Izzy had meant that as a joke, but Luther responded with a solemn nod. "That's true."

Luther put the earring in the pocket of his jeans but made no move to finish his dinner. Instead, he simply stared at the ground.

"You okay?" Izzy asked.

It was a while before Luther spoke, and Izzy waited patiently. Conor had shown her the power of that approach.

Finally, Luther said, "The calm right now is an unnatural one. Everything isn't as it seems. There's a storm coming ... a terribly destructive one."

Izzy had no idea how to respond. Over the past year she had come to respect Luther's insights, some of which she thought might be related to his Native American heritage. However, Conor had told her that it was more likely due to his brokenness because when souls are crushed, they tend to see reality through different eyes.

Finally, to break the tense silence Izzy asked, "Are we talking about the pandemic? We are over it, right?"

He cleared his throat and said in a quiet voice, "I feel there is far worse sickness of body and soul ahead."

A chill seized Izzy.

"Do you still study kickboxing with Andrea's mother?" he asked.

"French *savate*," Izzy clarified. "Yes, I do, but how did you know?"

"And do you still carry that knife in your boot?"

"How do you know about *that*?" Izzy asked but didn't wait for a response. "Lili is teaching me self-defense, like her family in the *Maquis* practiced."

"Good," Luther said. "Learn all you can, while you can." He reached up and removed a chain from around his neck that held a dark green and red stone. Then he looked at Izzy—right into her eyes for the first time ever—and held out the necklace. "This is for you now. It's a bloodstone my father gave me when I was a child. It helps with courage. It's the stone of warriors."

Izzy took it reluctantly. "I can't accept this. It's too special."

"You're family to me. I want you to have it."

Izzy tried to think of something profound to say but floundered before blurting out, "In your culture this doesn't mean we're engaged or anything, does it? I mean I know you're all ripped and super-hot, but you're like twice my age."

His eyes twinkled, "No, it's penguins who give stones as engagement gifts."

Izzy grinned. "Crows and penguins, a girl can get confused with all the ritualized gifting." She slipped the chain over her head and her eyes searched deep into him. "I have nothing to give you in return."

"Just survive, Isabelle Tavano. That's all I ask for."

~

The Seville was elegant in every way. Reminiscent of traditional Spanish architecture, the walls were adorned with textured white stucco and the ceiling featured exposed wooden beams with wrought iron chandeliers. Stunning floors were comprised of polished terra-cotta and colorful mosaic tiles. Beautifully carved wooden tables and chairs filled the dining room, and there were two ornate bars—one in the dining room and one in the upstairs lounge. Wide aisles provided a spacious feel to the dining room, and one central aisle led to the front door that opened onto a patio which had as its centerpiece a gorgeous fountain.

A stage ran the length of one wall near the downstairs bar, and a raised dance floor butted up to it. A balcony ran around the perimeter of the lounge, providing a perfect place from which to watch the entertainment.

Above the dining room, the lounge overflowed with guests eager to drink homemade sangria and enjoy the much-hyped musical event from a bird's-eye view. Also perched on that balcony were Lili and Brian, who operated the spotlights and sound board from there.

Roaming the restaurant were Erin and Tony, camcorders in hand, filming the night for posterity. Izzy felt a surge of pride at how attractive they both were— her father in his snazzy suit and matching fedora, and her mother in a low-cut black cocktail dress that rocked her gorgeous figure. And it never failed to thrill Izzy to witness how their obvious passion for one another created an electrical field that seemed to affect everyone in their orbit with a contact high. She hoped that one day she would experience a love as powerful as theirs.

Tonight, there wasn't an empty seat in the house. Many familiar faces from the local community filled the room, as well as a slew of celebrities, music industry professionals, and entertainers.

Guests of honor in the front row of tables included Karma's family: Grace, Tommy, and Mei Ling.

Izzy's grandmother Kelly—all dolled up in her usual bohemian Stevie Nicks-inspired attire—sat with Conor, who tonight resembled the high-powered IBM engineer he used to be. Further down the row was the press section filled with local television personalities and their photographers. And, most notably, front and center was the Governor of Colorado and his husband. Apparently, Johnny was close friends with them.

What had Izzy been thinking when she signed up for this? Nervous as hell, she gave herself the same pep talk she had been giving to her brother. *Just have fun.*

The musicians gathered onstage. They had all worn their own signature styles of clothes, but Brian had asked them to stick to a color scheme of red, black, and white, which matched the restaurant décor and the dancer's costumes.

The rhythm section—Izzy, Andrea, Luca, and Esteban—clustered together on one side of the stage. Next to them, closer to the middle, Miguel sat on his *cajón* drum. In the center of the stage stood Karma. To the right of center was Johnny, and on the far side was Santiago.

The house lights dimmed, and Johnny approached his microphone. "Welcome everyone! My name is Johnny Night, and I'm honored this evening to be making my debut as a member of Karma Chen's Pearl Street Band. Please hang around following our performance to eat, drink, and schmooze with the musicians, dancers, and technical artists responsible for tonight's show. In my experience there is nothing more uplifting than to be in the presence of great talent. The energy of creation is the nectar of the gods, and tonight we want you to all drink deeply."

Izzy was shocked that Johnny had declared a name for the band and announced himself as a member of it. The honor it paid Karma was extraordinary. He was a class act.

For just a moment, everyone on stage exchanged glances. Karma's smile was radiant, Miguel's sexiness simmered, Johnny embodied the epitome of smooth, Santiago, who always made everything look easy, was totally chill. In the percussion section Andrea was so excited as to be practically giddy, Luca and Esteban wore mischievous smiles, and Izzy had trouble breathing. She glanced up at her Uncle Brian on the balcony, and he flashed her flamboyant jazz hands and an encouraging smile.

Izzy had watched her uncle's favorite movie, *All That Jazz*, with him countless times, so she understood the reference. Flashing jazz hands right back at him, she mouthed the words, *It's showtime*.

Miguel counted them down and his driving kick drum, accompanied by a complex rhythm of hand clapping, opened the song. Valentina had taught Izzy, Andrea, Luca, and Esteban how to perform the traditional flamenco *palmas* hand technique, a primal and visceral rhythm that established the pulse and heartbeat of the music. It set the stage for Santiago's guitar to enter the song and weave a romantic Spanish melody that danced on air.

Andrea's tambourine made its entrance, striking a sharp beat that ramped up energy and excitement, followed by Johnny's bass which added depth and resonance.

Then the spotlight captured Karma and her electric violin as she jumped into the song with an exhilarating explosion of pure, sweet sound. Her black instrument's sleek and sinuous form held an air of mystique and sophistication that mirrored Karma's own exotic style. Wearing a red satin tuxedo, with her long hair swept up into an elegant twist held in place by a diamond comb, Karma took command of the stage. Looking out at the audience she offered a brilliant smile, and in response people's own smiles widened. Some leaned forward in an unconscious effort to draw closer. Her captivating fusion of beauty, talent, and charisma justified the name Johnny had provided the band.

It was clear right then that Karma Chen did indeed own the night.

Johnny began to sing, his deep voice rich with its trademark magnetic allure, and everything came together perfectly.

Izzy had never performed for an audience and was surprised by the rush she experienced from the exchange of energy with them. The connection with her bandmates was intimate, but when that energy was shared with the crowd, it was absolutely intoxicating.

Abruptly, the vocals and melody surrendered to wild rhythms created by all the musicians. Maracas, bongos, and the tabor drum blended with the tambourine, *palmas,* and *cajón* and brought the song to a sudden shift that introduced the dancers.

A spotlight fell on Valentina standing on the elevated dance floor dressed in a long red, ruffled dress. Lifting her arms gracefully, the *castanets* in her hands added fast trills, rapid rolls, and sharp strikes to the rhythmic mix. Slowly the tapping of her heels created a percussive counterpart, and she began to twirl, her black-fringed shawl swirling in the air like wings.

The second spotlight captured Omar's commanding presence as he launched into intricate patterns of rapid-fire footwork and assertive stomps. Then slowly, in a mesmerizing display of passion and connection, they came together to dance the flamenco. Their mutual gaze unwavering, they generated a smoldering intensity that sizzled. They circled each other seductively, and as their breathtaking performance swelled to a sensual climax, they came together in a tight embrace.

The lights fell, and the room went dark.

There was a moment of expectant silence.

Slowly, the spotlight came up on Karma, who had switched to her guitar. Softly, her strings created a complex, haunting melody that was soon joined by Santiago's guitar. Together they wove a remarkably intricate and mesmerizing tapestry of sound.

One by one, the other instruments jumped in and with increasing volume and intensity ramped up the excitement until the music reached a thrilling crescendo. Brian had choreographed a move for that moment which involved all members of the band jumping up in the air. They performed the leap flawlessly as one, coming down on the downbeat which marked the energetic shift.

What wasn't scripted was that Izzy was so overcome by the moment she yelled out a tribal, "Whoop!"

Mortified, embarrassment flooded her. She looked up at Brian, who with a big grin, blew her a kiss. Then she gazed out at the audience expecting to see judgment, but instead only saw a sea of smiling faces and hands clapping in unison to the driving beat.

Even the governor smiled at her.

The shift was designed to drive the song home in an electrifying fashion. What wasn't in the plan was the most dramatic moment of the evening.

Suddenly, as if the heavens opened and the magic of Gabriel's horn pierced the worlds, the air resonated with the soaring notes of a trumpet. Standing right inside the front door of the restaurant, Luther boldly entered the concert.

The spotlights panned over in unison to capture him.

The audience exploded with excitement.

People leapt to their feet.

"Luther!" was the resounding welcome.

Wild applause filled the air.

Spectators leaned dangerously over the side of the balcony to get a better look. Others raced down onto the wide stairway and crowded together to see him.

On the main floor, admirers filled the aisles, and some even stood on their chairs to watch.

Two of the cocktail waitresses kicked off their shoes and climbed onto the bar, where they brazenly danced.

Luther—despite doing his best to live in the community but not be part of it—was known and admired by so many.

Tony raced down the central aisle toward the door, dropped to his knees, and slid into a position right below Luther where he could film his performance from that angle.

Of course Dad would do something so dramatic, Izzy thought with delight.

"Luther, my man," Johnny cooed into the microphone. "Welcome to our family."

Karma threw her head back and laughed.

Izzy was so overcome by emotion that for the first time in her life, she wept with joy.

The fact that Luther had finally accepted the band's invitation to join them freed Karma up to do what she did best. While Luther and his trumpet dazzled the crowd, Karma and Santiago jammed the most spirited —and critically acclaimed—guitar performances of the evening.

Everything about the concert was epic.

That was the last perfect day in The Before Time.

~

Luther had been correct in his predictions. The pandemic returned with a vengeance. The virus everyone thought had disappeared silently simmered and mutated until it exploded in a deadly form that proved impossible to prevent or treat. They called it Chimera. It swept the world but ravaged the United States more viciously than many other countries because a wide swath of the population stubbornly refused all reasonable mitigation measures.

Miguel died horribly, followed by Lili and Johnny. Izzy's Uncle Brian lost his fight, too. And six months after Karma's stellar musical debut she was assaulted, her face slashed and disfigured in a hate crime.

By the time Chimera grew so hot that it burned itself out entirely, panic and anger had turned the country upside down. Power was seized by an authoritarian government that used draconian measures to quell the chaos.

And those who survived now lived in The After Time.

CHAPTER THREE

"Your closet has nothing but waitress and mom clothes," Izzy said.

Erin and Izzy stood side-by-side surveying the sparse wardrobe choices Erin had for her interview at the newspaper.

A crowd of black slacks and matching vests, white shirts, blue jeans, and tee-shirts silently mocked Erin. "Well, the slacks and button-down shirt with a colorful scarf would be professional enough for a job interview. I'll worry about wardrobe after the paychecks start rolling in."

"Since you're determined to pursue this reporter gig, I can't let you go there looking boring. Not on my watch." Izzy rifled through Erin's closet until she found a long-forgotten black cocktail dress. "This will do for a start. We'll jazz it up with one of my short leather jackets ... the dark green one would make your eyes totally pop. And I've got those matching green leather lace-up ankle boots."

Erin suppressed a laugh. "Sweetheart, that's not age appropriate. Besides, the neckline is too low for the occasion."

"You should let your boobs shine; you've got great cleavage. Besides, the *Maverick* is at its heart a subversive underground newspaper run by a long-time gay activist and former rock concert promoter, a politically militant university professor, and one of Boulder's most notorious playboys. Trust me, this whole daring middle-aged steampunk thing will fit right in. Besides, we're making mothers sexy again."

Erin reluctantly held the dress up to herself in front of the mirror. "How do you know so much about the paper's executive staff?"

"Mother, mother, mother. When are you going to learn that I know everything?"

"Well, if you really do know everything, explain why they told me to leave my phone in the car for the interview."

"Because Big Brother is always listening, of course."

Erin shimmied into the dress and Izzy helped by zipping her up. "Orwellian nonsense like that is the kind of silly conspiracy theory favored by my mother."

"The secret to conspiracy theories is in knowing which are true," Izzy said. "Grandma doesn't think about them, she just feels them. If they excite her, she's all in. It's an endorphin rush. But I think about them, and research them, and trust my gut."

Erin's hand went to her own gut, which was churning. She hadn't had a formal job interview since, well, ever. She went from college to marriage to owning her own business. After Tony left her, she started driving for Uber because it was the only work she could find, but she had been hired online.

Izzy ran across the hall to her room and returned with the leather jacket and ankle boots. "Thank goodness I hadn't packed these yet."

Reluctantly, Erin tried them on and turned to the mirror once again. The reflection staring back at her looked way over-the-top for a job interview.

"You need to let your hair down and wear it wild." Before Erin could react, Izzy pulled the pins out of her modest chignon, and red curls showered her shoulders in ringlets.

Erin groaned. "I don't think so."

"Twirl. Let me see."

Erin did a three-sixty. "And these shoes hurt my feet."

"Sexy requires sacrifice, Mom."

"Whoa," Luca said from the doorway. "Are you going to a costume party?"

Erin pointed at him while glaring at Izzy. "See? What did I say?"

"Don't you think she looks good?" Izzy asked her brother.

"Well, yeah, but—" He issued a loud sigh and frowned. "Why?"

Izzy grinned. "There you go. You look like a perfectly adorable badass so, you know, go and kick it."

Now it was Erin's turn to be confused. "What?"

"Go kick that interview in the ass. Believe in yourself as much as I believe in you."

Erin snorted. "The other day you were questioning my credentials, but now you believe in me?"

"You always thought that Dad was the reason the restaurant was so successful, but—" Izzy's hands fluttered in the air, "—he's one of those unstable creative souls who, on their own, never amount to much. But you, you were the brains that built and held that business together. You're scary smart. You got this."

"Izzy's right, you know," Luca said.

Izzy nodded. "I always am."

Their sweet earnestness buoyed Erin up and kept her from drowning in a sea of self-doubt.

***

The *Maverick* offices, located close to the university in a picturesque Victorian-style home, reminded Erin of a Barbie dollhouse. Perhaps because it was pink.

As Erin approached the whimsically designed glass front door, a familiar face opened it and stepped out. Josh Jameson had been one of Denver's top TV news anchors until the new government brought in its own reporters. In fact, most of the local TV news personalities had been replaced with fresh talent who promised the strife-weary public to report honestly and in a non-divisive manner. Although Erin no longer held illusions about the fact that they were sanitizing the news, she honestly appreciated the welcome respite from relentless horror and violence. It allowed her some space to grieve all that had been lost.

As she entered, a woman unceremoniously thrust a clipboard into her hand. "They're running behind; I was just summoned. You're supposed to fill this out while you wait." Clutching a piece of paper the perfectly coiffed woman whose scent was Chanel No. 5 and tailored suit was Halston, pivoted in her stylish Gucci shoes and scurried though the conference room door, shutting it soundly behind her.

Erin glanced down at her own attire and uttered a soft moan. What had she been thinking? She didn't stand a chance in hell against the competition. It occurred to her to just leave now before she totally humiliated herself, but Izzy's parting words echoed. "Be brave. Be strong. Be badass. And remember that we believe in you."

The soft leather couch sighed as she settled into it. Taking a deep breath, she reviewed the form on the clipboard. It was a simple confidentiality agreement, stating that the interviewee wouldn't repeat anything discussed, including salary and employment benefits. Filling in the requisite blanks was easy. It was the waiting that was hard.

Despite her aching feet, Erin stood and paced. At one end of the reception area, a colorful, chaotic-looking office beckoned through glass French doors. The walls were plastered with old posters announcing big-name rock concerts and pride parades. Ruth Bader Ginsburg's poster carried the message to "Speak your mind even if your voice shakes." And Anne Frank's image said, "What is done cannot be undone, but one can prevent it happening again."

A Tree of Life Menorah with a rainbow of colored candles graced the top of an overflowing bookcase, and piles of paper tried hard to obscure the delicate beauty of an antique desk.

Erin paced.

The office at the other end of reception was furnished with expensive leather and mahogany. Simple, uncluttered, and decidedly masculine. The only decoration was a beautiful portrait on the wall of a young girl around five years old who looked strangely familiar, but before Erin could sort through crowded memory banks a doorknob rattled, a door opened, and Ms. Designer Everything stepped out.

"You're up," she said. "It seems like a boring job. I'm not interested, but good luck."

Erin nodded. "Thanks. I'm good at boring tasks, so maybe it'll be a fit after all." Perhaps it really did involve chasing down Boulder society dames for bits of juicy gossip. That she could do.

"And be prepared ... this isn't like any newsroom I've

ever been associated with," her rival said in parting.

When Erin stepped into the conference room, the thing that struck her first was the long mahogany and black leather poker table with matching chairs. That and a well-appointed bar in the corner were the only furnishings. She glanced up at the engraved CONFERENCE ROOM sign mounted on the door, to be certain it didn't say GAME ROOM, before shutting it behind her.

A good-looking man seated on the far side of the table stood to greet her. "Ian Grant, Editor." His rakish smile, piercing blue eyes, and tousled dark hair—coupled with the smoothest of British accents—oozed sexiness. No doubt that this was Izzy's 'notorious playboy.'

Erin accepted his outstretched hand and shook. "Erin Tavano."

Ian gestured first to the older man on his left. "Our publisher, Harlan Weismann," and then the woman on his right, "and I believe you know Sasha Swan."

Erin blinked as recognition instantly dawned. "Dr. Swan. This is unexpected." Sasha Swan, a journalism professor at CU Boulder, was a regular customer at Tony Tavano's. "I didn't know you worked here, too."

Sasha smiled her usual, radiant smile. "All three of us own this journalistic travesty." She nodded to the center seat across from them. "Please sit. We have a lot to talk about."

As Erin settled in, she took a moment to study Harlan Weissman. The bald man with the thick gray beard, round wire-rimmed glasses, Rolling Stones tee-shirt, and gold Star of David hanging from his neck was the likely resident of the first office she peeked into.

Looking up from the file he was studying, he gave her a curt nod. "You play blackjack?"

"I do. My brother ran a weekly game for years. Taught me how to count cards. I'm dangerous."

Harlan almost cracked a smile. "Good to know."

Sasha laughed. "I didn't know you were a card shark. Seems we have a lot to learn about each other. Also, I've never seen you in street clothes before. Interesting style you have."

"My daughter dressed me today. I'm supposedly making mothers sexy again."

"And doing a fine job of it," Ian said.

Erin took a deep, unsteady breath and wondered if this was how job interviews usually went.

"Your résumé says you haven't been associated with Tony Tavano's for almost six months?" Harlan said.

"My husband and I separated. He runs the restaurant now."

"Is the separation permanent?" Ian asked.

Every time Erin faced that question, her heart filled with longing, but her head knew the truth. "Some relationships are broken beyond repair."

"My life is a living testament to that," Sasha said under her breath.

Erin knew Sasha's personal story; it was much like her own.

Harlan leaned back in his chair and leveled her with piercing eyes. "You're an excellent writer."

Erin smiled. "Thank you. The stories I attached to my résumé were written when I was in college, but—"

"Not those. They were ... meh. I mean your more recent work." Harlan raised a fistful of brochures and shook them at her.

"Your Tavano's *Uncommon Heroes* stories," Sasha said. "I collected them through the years. They're brilliant."

"Oh, thank you. I had good material to work with." The unexpected compliment pertained to a series of biographical pieces Erin wrote about noble deeds done by employees of the restaurant and their families. It was a public relations idea Erin had conceived many years before. She published them as print brochures displayed on the restaurant's reception desk and as human-interest stories on its website.

Harlan dropped the brochures on the table and rifled through them. "It seems one dealt with your young son, Luca, witnessing homeless people digging through the restaurant dumpster looking for food. He apparently put a sign up that said, 'Please don't eat thrown away food. Just knock on our door and we'll give you something good.' And his father left the sign up and fed everyone who knocked."

Erin smiled at the memory. "Luca has a soft heart." She hesitated for a moment before adding, "He got that from his dad."

Harlan held up one that featured a photo of her nemesis. "And a beautiful young server named Maria waited on an elderly man whose date stood him up, so after her shift she bought dinner for them both and ate with him."

Erin managed to say, "Maria likes helping men who are hurting."

"And your sister and her husband convinced a shitload of other ranchers to stay silent during the public auction of a local ranch so that the owner could buy it back from the bank?"

"That's bloody amazing," Ian said.

Erin nodded. "It was. And, as the story explains, the ranchers donated money to the cause so that the purchase price could be met."

Sasha said, "I like the one about your daughter and her uncle making dozens of pizzas and hauling them up to the firefighters battling the wildfires up in the foothills during the infamous Summer of Hell. Wasn't she something like eleven years old?"

"It was Izzy's idea. She would save the world if she could."

Ian picked up a brochure and scanned it. "You had a bookkeeper named Louise who took in a young homeless girl and ended up adopting her?"

"There have always been so many homeless kids hanging out on the mall. That one had a happy ending."

"You have a lot of compassion and insight into people," Sasha said. "It shows in your writing. It also manifests in your dealing with others. I remember all too well what it felt like to be on the receiving end of that."

The first time Sasha had come into Tavano's it was late, and the regal-looking woman wearing an African-print kaftan and matching turban sat at a table in a dark corner. After ordering a glass of wine, she quietly wept until closing time. That was when Erin joined her, bearing the gifts of a bottle of wine and a sympathetic ear until nearly dawn.

"I'm told that I inherited compassion and people skills from my grandmother," Erin said. "I believe they're my greatest strengths."

"And what is your worst thing?" Ian asked. "Tell us the worst thing about yourself."

Erin had recently read enough online advice about job interviewing to know she should say something along the lines of, "I'm a perfectionist" or "I work too hard." Instead, she blurted out, "Louise ended up embezzling thousands of dollars from Tavano's, my sister and her husband are only kind to people they approve of, and Maria is sleeping with my husband."

Sasha burst out laughing, but quickly put a hand to her mouth to stifle it.

Ian cocked his head. "And why does telling us that reveal the worst about *you*?"

Erin struggled to sort out her thoughts. "I could have left you feeling all warm and fuzzy about Tavano's uncommon heroes, but that wouldn't have been the complete story. I felt the need to tell you the flip side. That makes me a rather ugly person, doesn't it?"

Harlan's smile finally cracked. "No, actually it makes you a reporter."

Ian stood. "Well then. I think that brazen bit of honesty calls for a drink. Would you like one?"

Throwing common sense completely to the wind, Erin blurted out, "Oh God, yes."

"Right, then. And what is your pleasure?"

She craned her neck to see what bottles the bar contained. "Jameson, neat."

"Ah yes, I seem to remember your maiden name was Irish, but I won't hold that against you."

Ian served Erin her whiskey, Sasha a glass of wine, Harlan a bottle of craft beer, and something that looked like a White Russian for himself.

The mood shifted, but Erin couldn't read the room. She sensed an undercurrent of something deep and dark.

"What are your politics?" Harlan asked her.

"My politics?"

"What are your thoughts about the current political situation in this country?"

"Well, I don't really have an opinion. I've been too involved in personal matters to pay much attention." As soon as she said it, Erin knew that she had blown the interview. Or maybe it was the echo of Izzy's disapproval? Whatever it was, the shocked looks on all their faces caused her stomach to flip and so she downed her drink in one gulp, appreciating the burn. She was foolish to think someone like herself would qualify for a position as a journalist. She had lived a narrow, insular existence and that choice now limited her prospects. Maybe she could eventually find a job as a server in another restaurant. People liked her and she had always made good tips. It wasn't ideal, but she would do whatever was necessary to provide for her family.

Sasha's long, elegant fingers snaked across the table and tapped Erin's confidentiality agreement. "This is a lightweight version of the real non-disclosure agreement we would like you to sign in order to take this interview to the next level."

"Next level?"

"We think you might be exactly what we're looking for, but we can't really tell you what that is until the atomic NDA is in hand."

Erin must have missed some shared secret communication between the three of them, but she didn't question her strange good fortune. "And what should I know about that particular atomic bomb?"

Harlan withdrew a document from his file and

pushed it toward her. "Because there are now big dollar bounties offered to citizens who turn in anyone who violates the new laws, threatening the signor with fines or lawsuits is generally moot. However, a disclosure that our heirs reserve the right to sue your heirs should you violate the terms of this contract is a threat with teeth."

Erin read the contract carefully. It was written in simple, but ominous, language. She took a deep breath and wondered what she had gotten herself into. "Why do I get the feeling that this isn't going to be a boring position?"

"Boring?"

"The last woman you interviewed said it sounded boring."

Ian laughed. "Oh, we knew within a few minutes that she wasn't a fit, so we told her the job was fact-checking press releases. Sent her scurrying."

Erin's mind floated back to the idea of working in the restaurant industry again. The truth was, she had applied for several positions over the past few months, but ironically her twenty years as a restaurant owner caused prospective employers to consider her overqualified.

Be brave and bold, Izzy had advised.

Erin signed the nuclear NDA.

Harlan punched buttons on a desk phone at his end of the table.

A man's voice answered. "Yeah?"

"Come down." Harlan said. "We're ready for you."

The line disconnected.

"Are there more offices upstairs?" Erin asked.

"Actually, I live upstairs," Ian said. "Our security guy

has been taking care of my daughter while we've been doing interviews."

A few moments later, the conference room door opened, and a young man came in. Erin's first thought was that he looked just like Neo in *The Matrix*: short black hair, dark sunglasses, and long black leather coat. Her second thought was that Izzy would be totally wowed by him, a complication she didn't want in their lives right now. Her third thought was that she couldn't let them meet.

"This is Dylan Kane. He's in charge of electronic and cyber security," Harlan said. "He's going to sweep you for anything that might compromise our privacy."

"Um, well I left my phone in the car, as you requested."

Dylan Kane waved a small wand-type device around Erin. "No smartwatches or any other electronics on you or in your purse?"

"Not a one."

He picked her purse off the floor and examined it anyway. When he was apparently satisfied, he said, "She's good."

Just then a young girl charged into the room and headed straight for Sasha. "Mommy, I'm bored." She climbed into her lap. Seeing Erin, she giggled and said, "Hi!"

Suddenly, Erin connected the dots. The portrait on the office wall and Sasha's daughter were the same child. They had come into Tavano's together several times. She returned the girl's smile. "Violet, it's so nice to see you again."

"*Ultra*violet," the little girl said. "Dylan said I need to be ultraviolet, which is invisible, and that I should only be around him for a little while because too much ultraviolet is dangerous."

Ian groaned. "What nonsense are you teaching my girl now?"

Dylan grinned. "Just trying to manage your demon child from Hell. Babysitting isn't in my job description."

Violet climbed off Sasha and onto Ian. "He said ultraviolet is powerful. I'm powerful, Daddy."

Ian kissed her nose. "You are indeed."

Startled, Erin looked at Sasha with sudden understanding. Ian was the philandering husband who had broken Sasha's heart. He was the unnamed man they had discussed during their marathon grief session all those years ago. Ian was the man Erin had encouraged Sasha to divorce ... *because some relationships are broken beyond repair.*

Sasha gave Erin a sad smile and a conspiratorial wink.

Erin looked at Violet with fresh eyes. Her delicate beauty was the obvious genetic blend of the stunning Black woman and the dashing white man. Violet could never, ever be invisible, no matter how hard she tried.

Or how much Dylan Kane wanted it.

Dylan swept Violet off Ian's lap and perched her on his hip. "Come on UV, let's go hone your power of invisibility."

Harlan handed him an appointment book. "We had one more interview scheduled after this one. Would you head him off at the pass and let him know we need to cancel for now? And please lock the front door before you head back upstairs."

Dylan replied with a curt nod, slipped off his sunglasses and gave Erin a frank look of appraisal, then left as he had come.

"Wow, that young man has a powerful presence," Erin said.

Sasha nodded. "An absolute dynamo. He's one of my students. He's working on a degree in photojournalism and digital media, as well as one in cybersecurity."

Erin was seriously impressed. "No wonder he's adopted Neo as his avatar."

Sasha laughed. "Definitely by design."

Ian settled back in his chair "Okay, we're going to present you with the job details and if you want to decline the position, fine. If you need to think about it, we'll understand. We only want you to proceed if you're one hundred percent committed. Okay?"

Uneasily, Erin nodded.

Ian captured her eyes with his. "In the chaos leading up to the insurrection the press was vilified, labeled the enemy of the people, and violently targeted. So many reporters were hurt or killed that the United States was ranked the most dangerous country in the world for journalists."

Erin thought of all the world's hot spots: Mexico, Russia, Ukraine, China, the Middle East. "In the *world*?"

He picked up his drink and slammed it back onto the table. It splattered, but no one except Erin flinched. "When the new regime came to absolute power, it commandeered the press and dictated exactly what we can and cannot report. Anything critical of, well anything at all really, is considered sedition and reporters are arrested … in many cases they're made to disappear."

A sense of disbelief flooded Erin.

Ian's eyes clouded and it seemed as if he wrestled

with personal demons. He clutched his dripping glass more tightly.

Sasha sighed, reached out to touch his arm, then leaned toward Erin. "We decided not to submit to tyranny and are part of a growing Resistance movement. It's no longer legal to have print newspapers, so the *Boulder Maverick* only has an online edition now. It is, of course, closely monitored. We use stringers, mostly my students, to write the daily copy and pay them fifty dollars a story. Ian edits. Dylan maintains the site. And Harlan sells advertising. That's the bones of the operation. But the meat is in an underground print version where the four of us write the real news. I won't elaborate right now about how it operates, but we have a wide circulation and it's growing."

Erin's thoughts flicked to Izzy and her fascination with the French Underground. This would have been a perfect mission for her, and she'd approve of it ... if Erin could tell her.

"We're good journalists and our stories get valuable information out there," Ian said. "We're the head, but what we've been lacking has been the heart. To truly convey the evil that is unfolding in this country, we need more stories about the people whom this fascist state is impacting. You've written beautifully about the heroes. We need that same energy and talent to reveal the victims."

Sedition ... reporters are arrested ... echoed in Erin's mind. "What exactly do you want from me?"

"We want to hire you in a dual capacity. We'll feed you stories from our network of informants. You'll write a version fit for the general public, and it'll go on our website with the rest of the pablum. However, you will also research deep and write the real story for our underground paper. It's incredibly risky and dangerous work for a reporter."

... in many cases they're made to disappear. Erin took a deep breath. "Frankly, I'm not the most courageous soul, guys."

An uncomfortable silence fell over the group, which Harlan eventually broke. "There is reward. Besides our ad revenue we have several big private donors, so we can pay extremely well. We also have a full benefits package with medical, dental, and life insurance. Of course, there is the satisfaction of doing the right thing and standing up to injustice ... if that matters to you. Frankly, Sasha is of the opinion that it would because you care about people so deeply."

Sasha added, "That you have no political bias is a plus. You'll bring a fresh innocence to the work. Your stories will carry more power. You won't be approaching it from the angle of a certain ideology, but simply of humanity."

The risk made Erin's stomach flip and her heart pound.

But the promise of excellent pay and benefits was incredibly alluring.

What kinds of stories would they ask her to write? Exactly what evil was unfolding?

Making this a better world for her children and others really was important to her. *You inherited my heart,* her grandmother had once told her. *A deep compassion like ours is an awful ache that hurts like hell and can't be ignored.*

If it was indeed true that journalists were being

killed in the United States for reporting the truth, at least if something happened to her there would be life insurance for the kids.

I'm not any kind of hero, Erin thought.

Lost in a thick, swirling fog she made her way to the bar, poured herself another whiskey, and threw it back.

Fear is a reaction. Courage is a decision, was the mantra Izzy always tried to drill into Karma.

After a few minutes the fog cleared, and she realized that there really was no other choice but to accept the mission.

Erin turned and pulled the words from somewhere within herself that she didn't recognize. "Okay, I'm in. Just point me in the right direction, and I'll give you whatever you need."

***

After the death of her parents, Andrea took over running Café Paris and The Underground. Following the attack on Karma, Grace and Tommy Chen closed The Buddha Belly and stepped in to help Andrea run her restaurant. Over time, Luther Thunderhawk slid into place as security guard and the trumpet player for the Midnight Blues Band; the resident blues band now featured Johnny's sister Ruby Night as lead singer. And eventually Izzy chose to become a server at the café instead of at Tavano's.

Roles had shifted, but the Pearl Street Orphans family bond remained.

After seeing Erin off for her job interview, Izzy headed over to Café Paris. It was her day off, but she had a plan to score more food for her family.

Business was bustling as she slipped inside and

found Andrea behind the counter.

"Good morning, sunshine," Andrea said to Izzy, then she waved at Karma hanging on the lanyard around Izzy's neck. "Good morning, starshine. The earth says hello."

Karma blew her a kiss.

"What's up?" Andrea asked. "You girls need to borrow my car again?"

Izzy shook her head. "Our days of car borrowing are over. Well, at least for now. As long as I pay for gas and insurance Grandma is letting me drive Uncle Brian's Mustang until it sells. I guess she figures me driving it around with the FOR SALE sign in the window is better advertising than it just sitting in front of the house."

"How groovy is that?"

"Pretty damn groovy. We stopped by to see if you have any day-olds I can buy?"

Andrea gestured toward the far end of the counter. "I just marked down some croissants and macarons from yesterday. A few eclairs too."

"Good, I'll take them all."

"For your family?"

"In a roundabout way." Izzy took a paper bag, and carefully wrapping each delicate pastry in tissue paper, began to fill it. "There's a farmer's market at the fairgrounds in Longmont where some vendors allow trade in lieu of cash, so I figure maybe I can trade these for some greenhouse veggies to give to Grandma and Papa. Mom wasn't able to get anything green from Dad and they need more vitamins and—"

"And chi," Andrea interjected. "Life force. Prana. Yes, they need the healing magic of photosynthesis." She waved her hand dismissively. "Just take them. It's on me. I feel majorly bummed that your family was starving practically right under our noses all this time."

Izzy nodded. "Despite the challenges in our corner of the world right now, it's nothing compared to what others are going through."

"I don't think we can see even the tip of that particular iceberg, babe." Andrea said. "There's a whole lot the man ain't telling us. Trust me. The vibes are strong on that one."

***

The old Boulder County Fairgrounds complex was in Longmont close to the Diagonal Highway that connected the city of Boulder to its eastern cousin. When the country melted down and the economy crashed, hundreds of suddenly homeless people took up residence on the grounds in a makeshift tent city and dubbed the encampment, The People's Park. Izzy heard that a private company had subsequently purchased the grounds and renovated the infrastructure into formal housing. However, the huge parking lot remained public property and hosted a popular community open-air market featuring a variety of goods and services. In fact, on this Saturday it was busier than the Pearl Street Mall or any other commercial outlets Izzy had visited lately. Recovery from the Second Great Depression had been slow.

The day was chilly, but the midday sun worked its magic and removed the bite from the air. Winter weather in the Mile High region had a reputation for being whimsical and surprisingly charming. Downslope winds tended to blow away clouds, which allowed the sun to do what the sun did best. Rapid snowmelt, low humidity, and bright skies provided an average winter daily temperature of forty-five to fifty degrees. However, sudden extreme shifts weren't uncommon, so Izzy usually traveled with a rucksack containing extra layers of clothing just in case. When she stepped out of the car and tested the Longmont air, she didn't feel the need to change a thing.

Izzy's signature style was influenced by photos on Café Paris's walls of French Resistance fighters. In winter she favored black tights, short pleated woolen skirts, knit tops, leather jackets, and—no matter the season—color-coordinated berets and custom-designed boots which held her throwing knife. That, and an expandable baton she wore in a discreet holster on her belt, were her weapons of choice. Let all the crazies strut around with their intimidating guns on display; she favored stealth and the element of surprise. Lili had been fond of saying that a person's energy introduced them even before their words did, and Izzy hoped her subtle badass vibe was intense enough to confuse the enemy and provide an advantage. As the attack on Karma had taught her, they were swimming in a sea of danger.

Izzy's purse was a cross-body bag with a thin leather strap that she could wear comfortably while active. She slipped it on, adjusted her cell phone where Karma was hanging out, grabbed the sack of pastries, and waded into the crowd.

Dodging wild kids and wandering dogs, Izzy and Karma explored. The wonderfully chaotic market swirled with proof of life in its many forms. Live music even played in the distance.

A farmer wearing a dirty John Deere cap sat on the

tailgate of his truck drinking a beer. Hopefully, Izzy made a beeline in his direction but was dismayed to find crates containing only the same root vegetables that they already had.

"Do you have anything besides potatoes, carrots, and onions?" she asked.

He issued an epic burp and shook his head. "There was cabbage and kale, but they went fast."

The girls moved on.

They saw ice-packed coolers filled with fish, and hunters hawking a wide variety of smoked meat and homemade jerky. A local dairy had an impressive display of milk, cream, yogurt, butter, and cheese. Vendors sold honey, homemade applesauce, kombucha, dried mushrooms, and kettle corn.

Vendor signs spelled out whether they were cash only or also accepted trades. Some were quite specific about what they were willing to trade for.

A heavily tattooed woman with a cigarette hanging tough-girl style from the corner of her mouth offered haircuts. Her handwritten sign said, *Tell me what you're willing to pay in Cash, Cigarettes, or Booze & I'll tell you what I'm willing to do for it.*

"I think it would be wise if she changed the wording on that one," Karma said.

"Yep, the Morality Police would have a field day trying to find out exactly what she *would* do for it."

A booth set up by the Bethlehem Lutheran Church announced itself as a drop-off center for donations of food and clothing for the needy. A queue of desperate-looking people lined up to claim whatever was donated as quickly as it was dropped off.

A table right next to them featured expensive

jewelry and watches. Some of the items were labeled as "antique" or "family heirlooms." A group of well-dressed women examined the find with an intensity that resembled hawks looking for carrion.

"I only accept cash." The scruffy man guarding the treasures had an AR-15 rifle slung over his shoulder.

"Are they stolen?" a surprisingly bold elderly woman asked.

He shrugged. "Not so's anyone would know."

In a flash of motion, wads of money changed hands, jewels, gold, and silver were snatched up, and buyers melted into the crowd.

"The haves and the have-nots in perfect contrast, right there," Karma said. "It's all so unfair."

Izzy counted the men, women, and children in the church booth queue. Ten. She had a dozen pastries. Without hesitation, she made her way down the line sharing the bounty. She offered the gifts silently, afraid if she tried to speak that her voice would crack. Overwhelmed by their gratitude, she turned and fled, her eyes burning with years of unshed tears. "It's beyond unfair," she finally managed to blurt out.

"Like Andrea said, we don't even have a clue how much bad there is."

"Did you see the expressions on their faces when I shared the pastries?" Izzy asked. "The adults, I mean?"

"It was ..." Karma paused. "They were, like at the same time, both horribly grateful and horribly embarrassed."

"That! Exactly that." Anguish filled Izzy. "I think I understand now why Grandma and Papa didn't tell anyone what was happening to them."

"Well, at least the kids were just kids. Simply

thrilled. Nothing complicated in the way they reacted."

"I have to do more to help, Karma."

"You can't save the world."

Izzy raised her phone and looked at her friend. She studied the horrible scars that mapped her face. She saw in her eyes the deeper scars that were far worse. Her own guilt rose like a tsunami. She fought for breath. "I couldn't save you," she managed to say. "I was *right there*, and I couldn't save you. I couldn't save my parents' marriage or our home. I couldn't save Uncle Brian or keep Grandma and Papa from suffering. What good am I?" She clutched the delicate Cross of Lorraine she wore around her neck. The symbol adopted by the French Resistance had once belonged to Lili—who inherited it from a *Maquis* ancestor—and the legacy it represented meant the world to Izzy. "I imagine myself as a courageous warrior fighting the good fight against evil, but what actual good have I ever done for anyone? I'm just a kid playing at being a superhero. I'm *such* a fool."

The ever-present pain and fear in Karma's eyes softened and she offered Izzy a rare smile. "I love you so much."

Izzy waited for more and when it didn't come, she sighed. "You're not going to tell me I'm not a fool?"

"All dreamers are fools. But fools are the risk-takers, the ones who take ginormous leaps of faith. And doing that requires a wild amount of courage."

Izzy considered the irony of Karma lecturing her about courage. Well, at least that was progress. "So, what do I do to help? To really help."

"We'll think of something."

"You promise?"

Karma crossed her heart.

Izzy took a deep breath to steady herself, and then they made their way deeper into the market.

"Where's the band?" Karma asked.

Izzy followed the sound until, at the far side of the plaza, the crowd briefly parted to reveal four young musicians—most of whom seemed to be around Izzy and Karma's age. Their presence reminded her of Pearl Street Mall's heyday of free concerts showcasing local bands. However, this group wasn't one she was familiar with.

"Who are they?" Izzy asked a cluster of teenagers gathered on the outer perimeter of the audience.

A boy with spiky Mohawk hair shrugged. "Don't know the name, but I know the family. The Castillos. Their dad's the Wildwind doctor." He gestured behind the market to a sign over the arched gate leading to WILDWIND TERRITORY. "Well, except for the blonde. I think she's the girlfriend of the other chick."

Izzy stood on tiptoes to try to get a better look, but there wasn't an elevated stage, and she was too short.

"Move closer," Karma said. "I hear a fiddle and earlier there was a mandolin."

Izzy put the bag of remaining pastries into her purse, then snaked through the crowd until they stood right in front of the musicians. The band was playing a country rock version of "Fat Bottomed Girls." Izzy's attention immediately fell onto the girls Mohawk had mentioned. The blonde sat behind the drums and the Latina played fiddle—and from the placement of equipment, apparently the mandolin too. Another string instrument prodigy like Karma? A wave of nostalgia rose, but Izzy pushed it down to drown alongside all the other lost dreams.

Then she noticed the guitar player. The gut punch he delivered almost doubled her over. His resemblance to Miguel was surreal. When she could think, it occurred to her that seeing him might send Karma into a tailspin, and she fought the urge to simply run away from the potential trigger. She tilted the phone to glance at her friend, but it appeared as if Karma wasn't fazed. In fact, her elusive smile had returned.

Relaxing, Izzy's attention turned to the bass player. A few years older than his siblings, he casually sat on his amp while playing and surveyed the crowd. When his gaze fell on her, they locked eyes, and she experienced his energy as a fierce swipe of a wildcat. One of her superpowers, nurtured first by Lili and then Luther, was reading people. Her instant assessment of him felt validated when he turned his head, and a neck tattoo became visible—an Aztec panther. A gang tat, perhaps? She wasn't sure but knew enough about Mexican culture to understand it was the ancient sign of a warrior.

One thing about the three Castillos that jumped out at Izzy was that each of them wore a bullet on a chain around their necks. Was that some kind of new gang sign? Unfortunately, she was sadly lacking in knowledge about gang culture. Historically in Boulder one had to be more worried about drunk frat kids burning couches on their lawns than gang violence.

"Fat Bottomed Girls" ended, but a fiddle player remained. It took a few moments for Izzy to realize it was Karma.

"Who's that? Where's that coming from?" The Latina musician zeroed in on Izzy.

"It's my friend Karma." Izzy held out her phone.

The young woman put her fiddle in its stand and walked over to accept the proffered phone. "Damn, girl, you are good."

Karma abruptly stopped playing. "Sorry. I just got carried away."

"What do you mean sorry? You should come and play with us."

"Well, I really don't get out much." Karma's voice was soft, apologetic.

The musician glanced up at Izzy, who ran a finger across her own face, tracing out the map of Karma's scars.

"Karma, my name's Rita. How'd you like to play with us right now? We do a mean 'Devil Went Down to Georgia.' Want to join in?"

"Well—"

Rita gestured to Izzy to remove the lanyard that anchored Karma to her.

Hesitantly, Izzy complied.

"Okay if I install an app on your phone?" Rita asked. "It's new tech that reduces latency while jamming online."

Izzy nodded.

To Karma, Rita said, "I'm going to hang this phone on my mic stand, facing me, and we're going to duet the shit out of our fiddles. Okay?"

Her voice stronger, Karma said, "Okay."

While Rita worked to set up and jerry rig the phone by her microphone, she leaned into the mic and announced, "My friend Karma's going to play some crazy good fiddle with us on this next tune. She couldn't be here in person, but thanks to the demon of modern technology, all hell's gonna break loose."

The crowd shouted its approval.

"Karma, meet the band." Rita picked up her instrument and used the bow to point out her bandmates. "Dante's on guitar and sings lead vocals, Rafael's on bass, and Shiloh beats the drums. Just jump in, girlfriend. Mirror me, harmonize, play counterpoint, or do whatever your heart desires. Let's have some kickass fun."

Shiloh counted them down.

Izzy held her breath.

Karma and Rita jumped into the hellfire together seamlessly.

Dante's voice was deep and smooth, and Izzy enjoyed watching him perform. Like Miguel, he had charisma.

Wild energy ignited the music and the intensity of it finally drove Rafael to his feet.

Shiloh drummed powerfully with perfect timing and delightful flair.

The band's performance filled Izzy with a jumble of conflicting emotions. Although this was an incredible breakthrough for Karma's healing, it brought back what she was and what could have been.

And Miguel. Poor, dazzling Miguel.

Bright stars Lili, Johnny, and Uncle Brian.

All the horror and loss that Izzy had never allowed herself to fully grieve crashed down.

When the song ended, Izzy felt the ground shift and her body absorbed the earthquake. Trembling, she staggered away from the stage. As her eyes filled, she blindly bounced off people like an errant billiard ball until, breaking free of the crowd, she ran. Seized by an irrational urge to escape it all, she simply ran.

A thunderous sob escaped her, and the flood of tears dammed up for years burst with wild fury. Through the madness, she thought she saw Miguel open his arms to catch her, and into them she flew. Perhaps it was her heart that had burst, and she was dead, welcomed into whatever lay beyond by her dazzling friend. So, she surrendered.

He embraced her and held on while her storm raged.

"It's all too ... awful. I ... I tried ... so hard ... to be strong for everyone," she managed to say. "I ... I ... just can't ... do it ... anymore. I—" Suddenly, she couldn't breathe. Feeling like she was drowning she gasped, struggling for air.

If I'm not already dead, I'm about to be, flashed through her mind. *And if I'm not dead, whose arms am I in?*

Dante's hand cupped the back of her head as he drew her face into his chest and tented her with his jacket. "You're hyperventilating. It'll be okay; you just need less oxygen."

Since you're suffocating me, that won't be a problem, she thought. Even though her mind understood what he was doing, her panicked body struggled to break free.

He held her tightly. "Just breathe."

As breath slowly returned, she relaxed.

"Better?" he asked.

Tentatively, Izzy emerged from the cocoon. Embarrassed, she looked up into his face but saw no judgement.

"When my mother was executed, I hyperventilated too," he said. "Some horrors are beyond bearing."

Her gaze fell to his chest and the hanging bullet. Izzy now understood. She had heard that after the execution of state criminals by firing squad the fatal bullets were delivered to immediate family members, but she hadn't believed it. It didn't seem possible that even fascists could be that cruel.

Izzy's trembling returned, and he steadied her.

"The last thing my mother said to me was, 'Here is the world. Beautiful and terrible things will happen. Don't be afraid.' So, Karma's friend, I say don't be afraid to stop being strong for everyone else. Be who you need to be."

"Izzy. My name's Izzy Tavano."

He smiled. "Dante Castillo."

She stepped away from him and tried to regain her composure. "How'd you get ahead of me, Castillo?"

"I saw you melting down, and I run faster than you."

The enormity of what just happened shook Izzy. "Holy hell, I abandoned Karma. I've got to get back."

"Can it wait? I'd like to have my dad check you out. He's a doctor and is right over there." Dante gestured to a building on the other side of a high fence. Taking a phone from his pocket he punched in a number and put it on speaker.

"Where'd you go?" Rita asked in greeting.

"I'm with Karma's friend, Izzy. Do we need to get back right away?"

"Nah, we're good. Talking music. Gonna jam some more. Take your time."

He looked at Izzy questioningly, and she nodded.

"See you in a while," he said before disconnecting.

Izzy didn't think she needed to see a doctor, but she was grateful for more time to put herself back together. Maybe she could wash her face and fix her makeup. She didn't want Karma to know about her freakout.

As they walked toward the Wildwind enclosure, Izzy replayed everything that just happened. Strangely, the thing that stood out in her mind was that Dante smelled like cedar, just like her late nana always had.

"Do you keep your clothes in a cedar chest?" Izzy asked.

He gave her a quizzical look.

"I noticed the smell while you were, you know, smothering me."

His eyes twinkled. "No, I'm just manly."

Izzy laughed. It felt good to laugh. She did it far too rarely these days.

The wire fence that surrounded Wildwind was extremely high, a sign warned it was electrified at night, and an armed guard manned the front gate. The vibe Izzy got made her uneasy.

"Is this a prison?" she asked Dante as they approached the guard station.

"Yes and no." He shrugged. "As most things are these days, it's complicated."

The guard was a heavy-set white man dressed like a sheriff from the Old West, complete with cowboy hat, boots, leather vest, fully loaded gun belt, and shiny star pinned to his chest with the name JOE etched into it.

Sheriff Joe jutted his chin toward Izzy and asked, "What's this?"

Dante put his arm around Izzy and drew her close to his side. "My new girlfriend."

A quick study, Izzy slipped her arm around Dante's waist and issued a girly giggle. She batted her eyes at the sheriff for good measure.

"For chrissake, you and your sister ain't got no shame, do you?"

Dante grinned. "None at all."

Joe fixed Izzy with a steely glare. "We don't like outsiders here, but I guess I gotta let you in. Need to see ID."

Under the new government, identification checks were commonplace almost everywhere one went, therefore Izzy didn't hesitate to display her driver's license so he could photograph it. However, she did bristle when he removed a scanner from his belt and held it in front of each of her eyes. Iris ID technology was becoming more common as well, but Izzy hated its invasiveness. The Patriot Party had risen to power in part by preaching about personal freedom, but life now was anything but free. Big Brother had come a long way since Nazi Germany, and the implications were just as scary.

After scanning Dante's eyes, Sheriff Joe waved them through the gate with a disgusted, "Go on then."

Holding hands, they walked into Wildwind Territory.

"Why his comment about shame?" Izzy asked when out of earshot.

Dante looked at her with surprise. "Well, because you and Shiloh are white, of course."

"Really? With all the bad going on in the world, he's got his long johns in a twist about interracial dating?"

"You're not from around here, are you?"

"Just down the road in Boulder."

He chuckled. "Ah, The People's Republic of Boulder, the Berkeley of the Rockies, the hippiest city in Colorado, one of the few liberal cities left standing. Trust me, that Boulder bubble won't last much longer. Boulder's about to get the *This Is the New America* memo any day now."

"I'm moving to Longmont tomorrow."

"Brace yourself for some serious culture shock."

"I'm starting to figure that out." She reclaimed her hand from his and waved at their surroundings. "What is this thing called Wildwind Territory?"

Dante gestured to a nearby park bench. "Want a modern history lesson?"

"Sure." Izzy was grateful for the chance to sit.

Dante sat next to her. A cool breeze had picked up, so he zipped his bomber jacket and stuck his hands in its pockets. "When the country melted down, Wildwind Western Wear negotiated with Boulder County to buy these grounds with the promise to give the county an equal size spread to rebuild the Fairgrounds. The deciding factor was that Wildwind agreed to deal with the homeless population that had taken this property over. By then the homeless crisis had totally overwhelmed the government and it was grateful to walk away from the chaos here."

"Well, I suppose it would be the perfect place to squat," Izzy said. "I came here years ago with a friend for a big, national dog show. The grounds have toilets, showers, all the amenities. Even formal campgrounds."

"Yes, but they also broke into the exhibit halls, barns, even administrative buildings. Eighty acres of desperate displaced people whom the authorities chose to ignore. It was a human disaster. "

"So ... Wildwind Western Wear? The newest fashion craze that features the Annie Oakley, Buffalo Bill, and Wyatt Earp clothing lines?"

Dante nodded. "It was a new company funded with big money, and it had an all-American gimmick that tied in with the whole uber-patriotic mindset. Plus, the triple W helped to set the current standard for privatizing social problems." His eyes scanned the grounds. "They renovated the buildings into living quarters and support services, added a few new buildings, and all the residents are basically owned by Wildwind. To stay, if you're twelve or older, you have to work at their new factory east of town or have a job here as staff."

"*Twelve?* What about child labor laws?"

Dante's laugh was harsh. "What about them?"

"That's horrible. Are they at least paid?"

"Everyone gets three dollars an hour, plus free housing, food, education through age eleven, onsite total medical care, and Wildwind clothes to wear."

Izzy's mind calculated. "But how can anyone ever get ahead and rebuild their lives?"

"That isn't in the company's best interest, is it?

"And if they can't work? What about the sick, old, mentally unstable people?"

"Well …" Dante's voice faded, and he closed his eyes. After a few moments he looked at her and said, "What about them? I'd like to know, too. Unless a friend or family member agrees to work their shifts for them, they're shipped off somewhere for another private company to deal with. And opting out isn't allowed because now homelessness is a crime."

The implications were staggering. How did she not know about this? "And I thought I knew everything."

He tilted his head, rubbed his whisker stubble, and sighed. "I don't think my heart would be able to handle knowing everything,"

Izzy thought about how broken his heart must

already be and agreed. He didn't have that tough, streetwise attitude that his brother and sister had. Instead, he seemed gentle and vulnerable. Reaching out, she took his hand back. "I'd like to meet your dad now."

***

Given what Dante had told her, Izzy expected the Wildwind Clinic to be impressive enough to count heavily for the company perk called "onsite total medical care." As it turned out, it wasn't impressive at all. The clinic consisted of a waiting room, an examination room, a room with multiple beds that served as the hospital, and as far as she could tell, little in the way of advanced medical equipment. Izzy thought that the whole retro-American rustic vibe Wildwind projected was way too literal in its application.

After a quick tour of the office, Dante steered Izzy to the front desk. "We'll get you signed in and then my father can check you over."

"I really don't think I need to be checked out. I'm fine now. Besides, I don't live here, and I can't pay him."

He grinned. "Oh, Dad wouldn't charge my girlfriend."

"But I'm not—"

"Just go with it," Dante whispered. "This room is monitored."

Her eyes instantly took in the overhead cameras.

"Besides," Dante said more loudly, "we're training a new receptionist. This will give her some practice."

Wildwind Clinic's reception desk was manned by two red-haired, freckle-faced children—a twelve-year-old girl named Joplin and an eight-year-old boy named

Jagger, although Jagger explained that today they were Annie Oakley and Wild Bill Hickok.

"The real James Butler Hickok was born in 1837 and died in 1876, so I am not actually Wild Bill the gunslinger, I am just wearing clothes like his today." Jagger adjusted the black felt wide-brimmed hat and then snapped his suspenders. "Clothes like his. Did you know that he was also a spy for the Union Army? A spy. And an actor. Actors and spies wear costumes so it makes perfect sense that I am, too."

It only took a few moments for Izzy to understand that the boy's flat affect, lack of eye contact, and unusual speech pattern indicated that he was on the autistic spectrum. "I didn't know that Wildwind Western Wear had a Wild Bill Hickok clothing line," she said to him. "It looks good on you."

"It looks good on you," Jagger echoed. "Joplin is really my sister and looks better in the Calamity Jane clothes than Annie Oakley ones because Calamity Jane wore pants instead of a skirt, and I am not used to my sister wearing skirts. Pants are better. Did you know that Wild Bill was shot dead while playing poker?"

"I did not know that," Izzy said.

Joplin handed Jagger a pack of cards. "Please play poker while I get our new patient checked in."

"I will play poker with myself, but I will not be shot dead because I am facing the door. Wild Bill had his back to the door when the bullet killed him. And the cards will keep me quiet so that you can check in our new patient because she does not look good at all."

"Thank you." Joplin's eyes lingered a moment on him with a loving expression, but when she turned back to Izzy, she was all business. She handed her a clipboard.

"Please fill this out and return it to me. You really do look as if you should see Dr. Castillo as soon as possible."

"Do I look that bad?" Izzy asked Dante as they walked to the row of empty chairs along the wall. They sat next to each other under one of society's ubiquitous portraits of the country's new president.

"You look beautiful except for the red swollen eyes, pale splotchy face, and smeared-all-over lipstick." His wink made his honesty a bit easier to bear.

"So, Joplin and Jagger? Their parents are classic rock fans?"

"Were. They're Chimera orphans. At the end it was just the two of them and their mother. After she died, no relatives surfaced."

That took her by surprise. Millions of children were orphaned by Chimera, but there were an equal number of adults whose children didn't survive. The newscasts overflowed with happy stories of new families created by matching up the survivors. "How'd they end up here instead of adopted?"

"Joplin wouldn't allow them to be separated and no one wanted an autistic child."

That begged the unspoken question of exactly where autistic orphans ended up, but it wasn't a conversation Izzy was prepared to have.

"Jagger told me he was eight. Why is he working here instead of being in school?"

"He's been through too much trauma, and he panics when separated from Joplin. Plus, he's not good in chaotic environments. This seemed like an ideal situation for now."

Izzy wondered about what might be ahead for them. "If I understood what you told me earlier, when he turns twelve, he's got to work or she's going to have to take on two jobs so he's not sent away?"

Dante nodded.

"Damn." Izzy didn't want to think about that either so turned her attention to filling out the intake form. When completed, she returned it to Joplin, who stuck it in a manilla folder and escorted Izzy into the examination room.

"Take off your coat and have a seat on the exam table," Joplin instructed. "Oh, and if you have a cell phone or smart watch give them to me, and they'll be returned when you leave."

Izzy found that fascinating. "I don't, but why do you do that?"

Joplin shook her head. "Duh? Because this is a room that should always be private. Dr. Castillo insists on it."

"He's right. No worries, I left my phone with Dante's sister and—" she raised her arms "—no smart watch."

Joplin's eyes narrowed, and Izzy thought she might insist on a full body pat down. Instead, the girl issued a dramatic "harrumph," turned on her boot heel, and strutted out the door with her fringed suede skirt swishing dramatically in her wake.

Izzy hung her coat on the back of a chair, spent a few minutes double-checking the room for cameras or electronic bugs, then sat on the table as instructed. "Fascinating," she whispered. It was always validating when others shared your personal paranoias.

Dr. Carlos Castillo came in and shut the door behind him. He had the same short dark wavy hair and sexy cleft chin as his sons. And like Dante, his vibe was gentle.

Izzy instantly liked him.

He extended his hand to Izzy to shake. "I'm Dante's father, and he tells me you're his friend. Please call me Carlos."

"Nice to meet you, Carlos."

"We no longer have a nurse at the clinic, but would you be more comfortable if I asked Joplin to come in while I examine you? Usually my daughter assists me, but she's off today."

Izzy shook her head. "Nah, I'm good, thanks for asking. Honestly, I really don't think an examination is necessary at all, but Dante insisted. I just sort of melted down, and I'm totally over it now."

"I see." He spent a few moments reviewing her intake sheet. "When's the last time you saw a doctor?"

"Since the Before Time. We can't afford health insurance anymore."

"I see. At least allow me to check your vitals? It won't take long."

Izzy sighed with resignation. "Okay, if it won't take long."

Like Dante, Carlos had a nice smile, and it put her at ease. He shined a penlight into each of her eyes, placed a pulse oximeter on the middle finger of her right hand, then wrapped the blood pressure cuff around her left upper arm and inflated it. "How's your diet?"

"Better than that of a lot of people right now."

"Any problems you're aware of you'd like to ask me about?"

"Not that I can think of."

After recording the equipment readings, he listened to her heart and lungs, took her temperature, palpated her neck, looked at her throat, checked her reflexes, and then did a second blood pressure reading.

"Hmm," he said.

"Hmm is nothing you ever want to hear your doctor say."

"That is true, young lady." Carlos sat on the chair and scribbled some notes in her chart before fixing his full attention on her again. "High blood pressure is rare in teenagers, unless they're overweight, have a poor diet, or experience prolonged stress. I'm guessing your issue is stress."

"Holy hell, I have high blood pressure?"

"It's pretty high."

"There's a lot to be stressed about."

"Yes, there is. What are we going to do about it?"

Izzy's hands fluttered in front of her as if she were trying to conjure something. "So ... thinking here ... uh, my best friend Karma is a Buddhist. Maybe she could teach me to meditate?"

"Good plan. Do that." He stood, unlocked a white metal cabinet, and withdrew a small, brown tincture bottle. "Why don't you try this, too? It's CBD oil. It reduces blood pressure, alleviates stress, and is useful in PTSD disorders."

She regarded it with distaste. "No, I realize marijuana is still legal, but I don't do drugs. I like to keep my mind sharp."

"It's hemp-derived CBD. It won't get you high. I promise." He wrote some directions on the label and handed it to her. "Unfortunately, the clinic has very few medications, and what we do manage to obtain is usually old, expired, and rarely useful. Our lack of proper funding combined with supply chain problems have been disastrous for us. I've learned to prescribe off-label, find acceptable substitutions, improvise. Please give it a try; I've seen it help others. No charge."

"Whoa, wait a minute. I thought good medical care was one of Wildwind Western Wear's many perks?"

Carlos issued a deep belly laugh. "So they would like the world to think. The company does the bare minimum across the board. The clothes? Factory rejects. The food? The company sends sacks of beans, cornmeal, and oats to the kitchen. That's all. Education? No licensed teachers and only books that are approved by the government and filled with dangerous propaganda. Shelter? Yes, but it's rudimentary. The people here are warehoused with little to no privacy or dignity. And they're paid slave wages. Even I am poorly paid for my position, but I can't turn my back on my patients. I won't."

Izzy's heart and mind raced. She had been looking for a way to really help others, and this need—which she could totally fill—just presented itself out of the blue. Taking a deep breath, she tried to decide how to word her offer. Even if the walls didn't appear to have ears, one could never be too careful. Buying anything via the Dark Web was an illegal act. Even accessing the Dark Web was forbidden. "So, um, Carlos, I have some connections in the pharmaceutical industry and am able to get my great-grandfather his heart medicine despite the shortages. Is that something you could use here? Or something else, perhaps?"

"Seriously?" He sat up straighter. "Are you serious? We desperately need insulin. Antibiotics, too."

"I can get both."

"Are the prices exorbitant?"

"I trade services. There wouldn't be a cost to you. If you just write down exactly what you need, I'll do my best."

"But how could this be?" His expression of hope turned to one of concern. "I wouldn't want you to do anything that might get you in trouble."

Izzy managed a casual laugh. "I'm *so* not a risk-taker. No worries there. Really." She clutched the vial of CBD in one hand, while her other hand clutched the Cross of Lorraine. So what if her stress level skyrocketed? Warriors had to push through obstacles all the time. She would summon that wild amount of courage Karma had mentioned and take a ginormous leap of faith.

***

Before leaving, Izzy used the restroom to repair her makeup. She washed and dried her face, then reapplied powder and lipstick. That's all she ever wore. Her eyelashes were naturally dark and thick, so she didn't need mascara. The powder kept the shine away. And the lipstick was part of her *Maquis* persona. Hitler had famously hated red lipstick, so during the war Allied women proudly painted their lips with it as an act of defiance. For Izzy, it represented her solidarity with all the women who had ever fought fascism.

On her way back to the lobby Izzy took a wrong turn and ended up in a strange hallway. There, at the far end she discovered a makeshift shrine where a red candle burned in front of a woman's photograph. A handwritten sign identified her as *Carmen Castillo, MD, who lived and died in service to others*. The red candle was telling—the color of blood, it was the modern symbol of Resistance. Although Izzy didn't know the details of this woman's sacrifice, it still inspired her. "Help me be brave, too," she whispered.

"There you are." Dante said, coming up behind her. "I figured you must have gotten lost."

"Is this your mother?" Izzy asked.

"Yes."

"She was beautiful."

"Yes, she was."

"Someday I'd like to hear her story."

"Someday I may tell it to you."

On their way out of the clinic, Izzy stopped to give Joplin and Jagger the last two pastries she had stashed in her purse. Their delight fueled Izzy's fire and her commitment to do all she could to help ... no matter the cost.

CHAPTER FOUR

Moving day was more gut-wrenching than Erin had expected.

"Are you okay?" Nick asked her, then immediately held up his hands in a gesture of surrender. "Dumb question. Let me rephrase. What more can I do?"

They stood alone in the empty living room.

Erin blinked back tears. "Can you and Andy take the kids with you on this last load? I ..." Her voice cracked. "I'm going to clean the house before I go."

"Why? Tomorrow, the bank takes it. Let them clean the damn thing."

"It's not a *damn thing*. It was our home."

He flinched at her harsh tone. "Yes, yes it was. Sorry. Thank you for sharing it with me. Thank you for helping to raise me. I haven't said it in a long time, but I love you, Erin. Marrying you was the best thing my brother ever did."

She swallowed a sob. "And I love you, too. You were a joy to raise, and you've become a real good man."

Nick grabbed her in an awkward hug. Then he walked out of the house to join the others, quietly closing the door behind him.

Erin knelt and placed her hand on the hardwood floor, feeling the familiar grooves and knots beneath her fingertips. On their first night here, this was where she and Tony danced to celebrate the remarkable life they had built together. This was where she had taught her children to take their first steps, where birthday parties were held, where lives unfolded.

She glanced up at the painting that hung above the fireplace. Her brother had painted it for them as a housewarming gift. It featured a quote from Kahlil Gibran: *Your house is your larger body. It grows in the sun and sleeps in the stillness of the night; and it is not dreamless.*

Erin wondered if this house had fashioned its dreams around her family as they had fashioned their dreams around it.

Standing, she walked to the master bedroom, a sacred temple where love was celebrated and babies were created. They had never made love casually, but always with great passion. In the emptiness she heard echoes of their joy. She still didn't understand how that powerful bond had broken but knew she would never recover from its loss.

Erin cleaned the house with tender care. Then she removed the painting Brian had given them and put it in her car. The last thing she did before leaving was to write on the whiteboard in the kitchen, *This house was a home.*

***

Izzy had lobbied hard for the right to claim Brian's old art studio behind the house as her own. The basement of Conor's home had two bedrooms, a bathroom, and a large family room. And since Brian's old bedroom upstairs was still occupied by his ghost, the art studio was the only option for a third bedroom. Erin had considered giving the basement to her kids and taking the studio for herself, but she felt Luca was too troubled by Tony's abandonment to risk him feeling she was also abandoning them. Add to that Izzy's desperate desire to have her very own "computer cave," and the decision was made. Erin fixed up the family room just like their old living room, put what wouldn't fit inside the house in a storage shed out back, and they settled into their new life.

That evening while the kids were watching TV, Erin felt the pull to visit Brian. The truth was that she had never truly processed her grief. He died just as her marriage had melted down and there hadn't been enough space within her heart to deal with both losses at once.

She stood in the doorway of his room, every muscle and nerve in her body resisting the desire to cross the threshold.

Kelly reached around her and flipped the light switch on.

Erin jumped. "For chrissake Mom, you startled me."

"You need to go all in. Immerse yourself. You two shared a womb for nine months, and you're still connected. It's not healthy that you've walled yourself off from what happened." Kelly gave Erin a push across the threshold and closed the door behind her.

Kelly Doyle had never been gentle, and subtlety was an art she never bothered to master.

The room had been preserved as a shrine, and the intensity of Brian's presence knocked the breath out of Erin. She stumbled to his bed, and just as her knees gave out, the soft mattress became her landing pad. She closed her eyes, and she remembered.

~

The last time they spoke to Brian, before he was put on the vent, was via iPad. His physician, Dr. Cohen, held the pad for him while the entire family crowded around Conor's laptop in the dining room.

"I wish I could be there with you," Kelly had managed to say, her voice tight. "But the bastards won't let any of us in."

Brian tried for a smile but failed. His soft voice rasped. "Ah, Ma, it's okay."

"Are you going to die?" Luca asked.

"Nope. I'm strong as an—" Coughing stole his voice.

"Your uncle is an athlete. He'll be just fine," Kelly said. "It's just the flu, nothing to worry about."

Brian managed a wan nod.

Dr. Cohen's grunt sounded disgusted.

"Doctor, have you checked my brother for AIDS?" Meg asked. "Isn't there some kind of special pneumonia that AIDS patients get? You know that he's gay, right?"

Brian's startled eyes flew to Meg just as Dr. Cohen tilted the pad toward his own face.

"Your brother has Chimera, not influenza, HIV, or Pneumocystis pneumonia," the doctor said. With a huff, he turned the iPad back to face Brian.

Meg's husband snorted. "There ain't no such thing."

"I'll be okay," Brian murmured.

No one knew Brian better than Erin did, and despite his words, she saw the fear in him. "Get out. Everyone just get out now, and let me talk to him alone."

The family looked at her with surprise.

Conor nodded. "I love you, Brian. You're the son I never had." Tears rimmed his eyes as he swiveled his wheelchair toward the living room. "Come on. Let them be. Twins and that super special bond, you know."

Izzy kissed her fingers and pressed them to the computer screen. "Come home soon, Uncle Brian. You promised to teach me to dance."

Love radiated from his eyes.

Kelly shook her head so fiercely that red curls escaped from the tight bun on her head. "Don't believe that doctor, son. To them, it's all Chimera."

Erin sighed. "Let us be, Mom."

Kelly's eyes shot fire as she stormed out.

They were alone.

Erin steadied herself. "Talk to me."

A cough seized him and didn't seem to care if it ever let go. Finally, he managed to say, "I feel ... in my soul ... I'm going to die." He paused to catch his breath.

Erin had the same feeling. They had been connected since they had been conceived. Maybe even before then.

"I can deal with that," Brian said. "It's the dying alone part that scares me."

Erin's stomach somersaulted, but she focused on her heart. "My dear baby brother—"

He held up four fingers. She had been born only four minutes before him.

"You'll never be alone, Brian. We're half of each other. Your blood runs through my veins. Your heart beats with mine. And after?" She shrugged. "Our souls will always be connected. You know that's true."

"I love you fiercely, Erin."

Then coughing and gasping stole him away from her.

"We have to sedate him and intubate now," Dr. Cohen said. "Gotta go."

"Wait!"

The pad captured his worried eyes.

"Don't let him die alone," she whispered.

The iPad bounced and his face came in and out of focus. A door opened and closed. Then the good doctor returned.

"He will absolutely not die alone. You have my word."

~

Grief sliced through Erin like a sword cleaving her in two. She grabbed one of the pillows off the bed and covered her face to muffle her sobs. When a semblance of control returned, she steered her memory to the wake they held for him right here in this room. The Chimera virus had set the country on fire, the scientific community was advising against public gatherings, and the family was divided as to how to proceed. Ultimately, Conor made the decision that only the family would gather to celebrate his life.

~

Brian had the largest, brightest bedroom in the house. Sunlight streamed in through the bay windows and reflected off a copper urn that rested on the window seat. Standing guard next to Brian's ashes was Diva, and the regal Siamese cat glared at everyone in turn. Erin felt the chill of blue-eyed reproach. Maybe it was their fault. Cowardice, apathy, defeat, denial. When Chimera exploded, everyone was so exhausted by what had come before that too many people just pretended it wasn't happening and let it rip.

"That cat sure looks pissed," Beau said.

Erin glanced at her brother-in-law standing casually in the doorway leaning up against the jamb. He wore dirty jeans and dusty boots, but at least he had shown enough respect to remove his cowboy hat. Meg stood next to him, having also refused to sit down. She always followed his lead.

"Nope, Diva isn't a happy catster. What do you expect?

Uncle Brian was her world." Izzy, sitting on the floor, tried to coax Diva to her lap.

Unblinking, Diva glared at her and whipped her tail from right to left.

Mojo moved to Izzy's side instead.

"Okay then." Izzy pulled a folded piece of paper from her pocket. "I have a eulogy kind of thing I want to read."

Erin sat on the bed sandwiched between Kelly and Luca. Luca leaned into her. "I wish Dad would have come."

At the thought of Tony, yet another wave of tears threatened, and she swallowed hard. "Me too. Brian adored him."

Izzy smoothed the paper out on her knee and cleared her throat. "Uncle Brian read Kahlil Gibran to me a lot and I found this in a book. It's from, On Death.

'For what is it to die but to stand naked in the wind and to melt into the sun?

And what is it to cease breathing, but to free the breath from its restless tides, that it may rise and expand and seek God unencumbered?

Only when you drink from the river of silence shall you indeed sing.

And when you have reached the mountain top, then you shall begin to climb.

And when the earth shall claim your limbs, then shall you truly dance.'"

A sob escaped Kelly, and Erin slipped a comforting arm around her shoulders.

"That was perfect, Isabelle," Conor said. "Just perfect." He swiveled his wheelchair to face one of the many paintings that graced the walls. It was of two terribly sexy men dressed in matching purple tuxedos, tango dancing. "When Brian painted this one, he told me that the men

in Argentina danced the tango together as far back as the 1860s. Women were scarce, and they wanted to polish their skills to woo what women they could. The whole queer tango thing emerged from that history."

"Jesus Christ," Beau mumbled.

Kelly stiffened. "Did you ever see him dance? He was brilliant."

"Ah, no ma'am, I never had the pleasure." His sarcasm was thick.

Meg pointed to a painting of Jesus kissing a naked man who resembled Brian. "I always thought that one was utterly sacrilegious. Now he's gone, I think we should burn it." In a flash, she moved across the room and yanked it off the wall.

Equally fast, Erin flew from the bed and met her there. She reached for the painting. "You'll do nothing of the sort. Only you would see something ugly about it. Don't you understand he was making a statement about being loved by God just as he was?"

Meg shoved her backwards. "And can't you see that glorifying perversion is evil?"

Meg was the older sister, the practical mother figure who tried to raise her siblings with as much normalcy as possible because Kelly was a bohemian free-spirited wild feather floating on wind currents that only she could understand. Erin had always tried to be respectful and obedient to her, but after forty-three years it was too much. It was just all too much. In a fit of defiant rage that rose from stormy depths, Erin slapped Meg's face hard.

Meg dropped the painting and gasped.

Mojo emitted a sharp bark.

Erin snatched up Brian's glorious work of art and clutched it to her chest.

Beau moved protectively to Meg's side. "What the fuck, Erin?"

"Get out," Conor said, waving at Meg and Beau. "Both of you, just get out of my house. Your sanctimonious bullshit isn't welcome here."

Meg pointed a trembling finger at Erin. "Brian always said I was the house cat, and you were the wildcat. You just proved him right. You're unfit to be a—" She paused and threw Luca a meaningful look. "You are unfit … period."

With great flourish, Beau ushered his wife out of the room and out of the house, the harsh slamming front door his final obscenity.

"She's always been jealous that you had children and she never could," Kelly said, seemingly unmoved by all the drama. "I'd watch my back if I were you."

Erin's knees weak, she sank to the floor and leaned up against the wall, the painting still firmly in hand.

"Uncle Brian told me once that if anything happened to him, he wanted us to keep his paintings," Izzy said. "So why don't you keep that one, Mom."

Erin nodded. "I'd like that. Yes, I'd like that very much."

"Each of us should choose one," Kelly said. "I know I'd love to have the queer tango guys hanging over my bed. My dreams would be oh-so-wild."

Visions of sugar plum fairies dancing in her mother's head lifted Erin's mood. "What about you, Luca. Do you want one of your uncle's paintings?"

"Yep, the two guys riding the horse. I don't care if it's two guys together on it, I just like the horse. Uncle Beau lets me ride his horses and it totally rocks."

"The rocking horse, it is. Homo subtext notwithstanding," Kelly said. "Isabelle?"

Izzy stood and claimed the painting of Neo, Trinity,

and Morpheus from The Matrix. "This definitely speaks to me. I'm a red pill kind of girl."

Kelly looked at Conor. "Daddy?"

He chuckled. "When Brian first reimagined the famous Times Square VJ Day kiss between the sailor and the nurse it ticked me off. It wasn't so much that it was a man kiss, it was because he made one guy Army and one guy Navy. I mean, no self-respecting ground pounder is ever going to smooch a squid."

Izzy grinned. "You're very strange, Papa."

"Why yes, I am. My ma said I was a changeling."

"So, Uncle Brian being a fairy did come honestly," Izzy said.

Conor's rumble of laughter shook the residual tension out of the air.

Erin glanced at all the colorful Gay Pride paraphernalia scattered about the room and gestured toward the photograph of Brian's boyfriend, Mark. He had been one of nine gay men fatally shot by a Patriot at a Pride Parade in Denver a year earlier. "When Mark was killed, Meg told Brian that it was God's punishment for their sin of homosexuality. Brian told her that while Mark bled out in his arms that horrible day, he sang 'Somewhere Over the Rainbow' to him, and the profound love they shared in those final moments was not human, but most definitely Divine. Then he proceeded to sing the song to Meg. As far as I know, it was the first time our Ice Queen sister had ever been moved to tears about anything. That moment of compassion didn't last, but maybe someday it'll return."

"Brian was quite a man, and most certainly loved by God," Conor said.

Erin's stomach once again turned over. She was in so much pain she could barely breathe, and a moan escaped *her.*

"Don't be mad at Meg," Conor said. "She's just never known what to do with all of us. I'm a pothead, your ma's a free spirit, your brother was out and proud, and you threw away all your career opportunities to marry a hot Italian. To her, we're just a bunch of wayward children and she's the only adult in the room."

"I'll never forgive her for being so horrible today," Erin said.

"What would Brian say about that?" Conor asked.

Erin thought about it. "He'd have never gotten mad at her in the first place. He was the better half of us."

~

And he was. Erin hugged the pillow to her chest. "I miss you so damn much," she whispered.

Exhausted, she dozed. In that liminal space between this world and the next, Brian appeared to her. Stepping out of the fog of her consciousness he looked robust, healthy, and more dynamic than ever. His smile dissipated the shadows, and his words pierced her shroud of grief. "I never left, it's just that you can't see me anymore. But I can see you and the future you're going to create. And even though right now you can't understand why everything is unfolding as it is, there is a reason. You, my dear sweet older-by-four-minutes sister, are going to change the world."

***

Erin started her new job at the *Boulder Maverick* the next day. A heady blend of nervous and excited, she did her best to exude confidence and hoped she was at least somewhat convincing.

Ian and Violet greeted her as she arrived.

"Violet's nanny is running late, so we're going to give you the grand tour and get you settled in. Then Dylan will see to your press pass and equipment."

Erin had been told they would provide her with a phone, laptop, and everything she would need. She imagined it all would be properly set up and vetted by their resident security expert.

Ian hoisted Violet up onto his shoulders, and she happily pointed out all the notable features on the tour.

"The kitchen has lots of great snacks," was apparently the most exciting feature.

Beyond the offices Erin had already seen, a hallway led to the back of the beautifully renovated house where the small kitchen, restroom, three offices, and an enclosed sunroom were located.

"Sasha also has an office at the university but uses the one here for everything related to the paper. The middle office is Dylan's, and this one will be yours." Ian directed her to the smallest of the three. "It used to be our copy room, but we've moved the equipment down to the basement and fixed this up as best we could for you."

Although small, Erin thought it was delightfully cozy with its antique rosewood rolltop desk and matching chair upholstered in rich brocade. The ornate Persian rug and Tiffany lamp provided the finishing touches that sucked her right into its charm. "It's amazing. Someone put a lot of effort into its transformation."

Ian nodded. "That would be Sasha. She wanted you to be happy. She's quite fond of you."

"The feeling is mutual." Erin reached into her purse,

110

pulled out a small, framed family photo, and put it on her new desk next to a vase of aromatic white roses.

"Your children and your husband?" Ian asked.

"My children and my brother."

He studied it for a moment. "Your daughter is stunning. She's going to break a lot of hearts."

Erin smiled. "That's a foregone conclusion. When Izzy was seven, she asked me, 'Do I have to fall in love someday?' I told her no she didn't. She replied, 'Good because I have stuff to do.' And I think that best sums up her modus operandi in life."

"Do you think her resolve will hold?"

"I believe she's too passionate a soul to never fall in love," Erin said. "I just hope that when it happens, she doesn't lose herself."

"Did you lose yourself when you fell in love?"

"No, actually I found myself."

"And now?"

Erin thought about it for a minute. "Now it's time to recreate myself."

"Dylan!" Violet was the first to notice his arrival.

As Dylan stepped into the office, the two of them bumped fists. "What's up UV?"

"Maisie Mae is late."

He took off his sunglasses and regarded Ian with a look of barely restrained panic. "I've got way too much to do today to watch her."

"Maisie Mae had an appointment with her solicitor … something about Henri's will. She'll be here soon."

"Maisie Mae is an unusual name," Erin said.

Violet nodded. "She's from Louisa."

"Louisiana," Ian corrected.

"That's what I said and it's why she talks so funny.

And she gives me chicory and sugar banayaya."

"*Beignets*," Ian said.

"And she knows ghosts and has pretty masks and a big stuffed alleygate."

"Alligator."

"She sings to bouncy music, too."

Erin laughed. "Wow, there was a southern-born Mary Poppins practically in my own backyard all this time and I never knew?"

"Life is strange that way," Dylan said. "So, are you ready? I've got classes this morning and need to get you outfitted now."

Erin tucked her purse into a cubby beneath the desk. "Eager to get started."

"We'll leave you to it then," Ian said.

Violet waved as they left.

Erin waved back. "She's a doll."

"Reminds me of my kid sister."

"What's her name?"

"It was Olivia. She didn't make it."

There had been so much death that *I'm sorry* had become a trite response. "I lost my brother."

His eyes met hers. "Maybe the work they hired you to do will make people care about each other again. Maybe next time they'll make more of an effort to keep one another safe."

The full weight of their expectations dawned on her for the first time. "I'll do my best."

"That's all anyone can ask." He gestured toward his office. "Let's do this."

Dylan's space was filled with computers, photography equipment, and electronics of all types. He closed and locked the door behind them, took off his sunglasses and coat, and settled in. Removing three pairs of eyeglasses from his desk drawer, he set them on his desk.

"Choose one," he said.

"But I don't need glasses."

"These you'll need. Pick the one you like best." He gestured to a mirror on the wall.

Erin tried on each pair and discovered the lenses were clear and not corrective. After several minutes of indecision, she settled on frames embossed with a delicate ivy design that were the same shade of green as her eyes. "What do you think?"

Dylan studied her. "Yeah, they look like they belong on you." He waved her over to stand in front of the wall. "I'm going to take the photo for your press pass with you wearing them, so they won't be questioned. They're equipped with a video camera and a microphone."

"Is that legal?"

"Depends on your definition of legal. Smile."

She put on her best waitress-dealing-with-disaster smile. It was a practiced skill.

He took a few shots with his camera, then gestured for her to sit in the chair in front of his desk. "Colorado is a one-party consent state for recording conversations. Plus, there's a journalist exception if taping occurs while investigating a newsworthy event. So, as long as you don't film people naked, technically you'll be operating legally. However, under the new government, ultimately it decides what's legal. No one in power follows the letter of the law anymore. They all seem to just make it up as they go. Everything's risky nowadays."

"That's comforting."

"I take it you're not an adrenaline junkie?"

"Nope. Not me. Not at all."

He grinned. "Too bad. Some of us grew up playing at being spies. The fantasy was exciting."

"My childhood fantasies were more Disney than James Bond."

"And did you ever find your Prince Charming?"

"Yes, but then he turned into a pumpkin."

"Better him than you." Dylan sat behind his desk and studied her for a moment. "Your hair. Can you rein in some of those curls, tuck them behind your left ear, and tap the tip of the eyeglasses arm once?"

She did as he asked and felt a slight momentary vibration.

His fingers danced across the screen of a smartphone on his desk. "You've activated it. Now do the same thing, but on the other side."

That time she didn't feel anything. "No vibration?"

"You just shut it off."

"It's that easy?"

He nodded. "There's a memory card inside them, but I've also set it up to stream to a hidden app on your phone. And that will back up to the cloud where it'll be heavily encrypted."

She removed the glasses and examined them. There was no obvious camera lens or any indication of their capabilities. "How likely am I to be discovered?"

"The technology is well-shielded enough to be undetectable by standard RF detectors. It would take really sophisticated equipment such as a TSCM device to reveal it, and it's unlikely you'll encounter many situations with that level of security. But use your judgement whether to use them or not."

Erin didn't understand everything he said, but she got the gist of it.

"Of course, for usual circumstances you can record interviews on the phone." He handed it to her. "This is the only phone you'll ever use while on the job. Leave yours at home. I've set this one up with all kinds of encryption and security protocols."

Erin's head was reeling.

"Are you a good photographer?"

She nodded.

"This phone has a decent camera. On stories where higher quality pictures are needed, or where you shouldn't be alone for whatever reason, I'll accompany you as photojournalist."

"I'd like that."

"Last but not least is that you need to set a strong password for the phone and your new laptop."

Her recent dressing down by Izzy flashed through her mind. "According to my daughter, my password savvy is lame and predictable. Can you set one for me?"

"How good are you at memorization?"

"I was a waitress for twenty years. I remember *everything*. It's a blessing and a curse."

He grew pensive. "Yeah, memories can be both of those things."

Erin's heart broke for him. There were so many walking wounded among them. Ian's unusual behavior the day she was interviewed elbowed its way into her mind. "Out of curiosity, who did Ian lose?"

"Ian? Oh, his brother. He was a reporter, too. Came over from England for a visit and happened to be here when our government came tumbling down. Chased the story and uncovered more than the powers that be wanted told to the world. Was going to file the story when he got back to the UK. Ian put him on a plane to return home, and he disappeared. Gone. Poof. Just like that."

"He was a British citizen?"

Dylan nodded.

"How could they get away with that?"

"How do they get away with any of it?" He looked at his watch. "We've got to wrap this up. I'll have the press pass for you after lunch. And I'll walk you through how to charge the spyglasses, access its app, and transfer the data. Also, now that we have an official photo, use it to register yourself with the State as a reporter so they can monitor your work because the First Amendment was murdered by the Second Amendment and its well-armed militias."

The bitterness in his voice startled her. "Forgive my ignorance, Dylan, but I don't recall an all-out civil war happening. Surely, I couldn't have missed that."

He shook his head. "Tactically, what they did was brilliant. Elected officials abruptly changed parties and declared themselves members of the new Patriot Party. New laws were strategically passed, voting rights were suppressed, a truly awful man was elected president, the constitution was suspended, and human rights were upended. And while all this unfolded, states whose officials resisted had their leaders assassinated by various militias, mobs rioted, martial law was enacted, and just like that—" he snapped his fingers, "—the bad guys won. A lot of people died, but the press was suppressed so it was all underplayed. The fact it all happened during the worst of Chimera helped the new government cover up a lot of its crimes. And here we are

116

now."

"And here we are now," she whispered, a sense of unreality overwhelming her.

He tossed her a set of keys. "These are for the front door, your office, and your filing cabinet. Always guard the fort well. We've got a war to win."

Erin understood the truth of that better than she had even an hour earlier.

After he created the passwords on her new phone and laptop, she returned to her own office, booted up the computer, and as she was familiarizing herself with it heard a loud knocking. Following the source of the noise, she found a woman standing outside the sunroom pounding on the back door.

Erin opened it. "May I help you?"

"I'm Maisie Mae Marchand. Who are you?"

So, this was the famous nanny. Erin had expected a colorful New Orleans-style Voodoo queen. Instead, with her diminutive size, conservative dress, and thick Southern drawl, Maisie Mae was Sally Field in *Steel Magnolias.*

"I'm Erin Tavano, the *Maverick*'s new reporter."

"Tavano as in Tony Tavano's Italian restaurant?"

"Yes, my family owns it."

"Well, aren't you just a lucky girl? Welcome to the Maverick family." Maisie Mae giggled, reached out, and gave Erin a big hug. "I'm late. Where's Violet?"

"I believe she's with Ian up front. Ah, do you usually come to the back door?"

"Sometimes. I live right next door. There's a gate between the yards, and back doors are so much more neighborly, don't you think?" She slipped an arm around Erin's waist and gave her a tight squeeze.

Erin nodded politely. The little woman's exuberance was rather overwhelming.

Maisie Mae lowered her voice and leaned into her. "Are they paying you well? Harlan holds the purse strings around here, you know. Don't let him Jew you down on salary. He's loaded."

Startled, Erin wasn't sure how to respond to the offensive pejorative phrase. After a moment, she simply said, "I have no complaints."

"Well, that's good to hear, sugar. You just never know what to expect from those people, do you?"

Those people? Erin didn't know where this conversation was going, and honestly didn't want to find out. She disentangled herself from the woman's clutches. "Would you like me to tell Ian you're here?"

"No need. Charmed to meet you, I'm sure. I just know we'll be *great* friends." With that, she flounced away.

"Not looking promising," Erin muttered to herself, and then continued to explore the features of her new computer. It was a bit more state-of-the-art than she was used to, but perhaps Izzy could provide her with some guidance.

Shortly, with much flourish and fanfare, Violet and Maisie Mae left, and then Ian poked his head into Erin's office.

"Harlan and I are ready for you now."

She grabbed a notebook and pen and joined him in the hallway. "Do I need to lock my office door?"

"No, I locked the back door after they left, but I'm glad you asked. We're extremely cautious about security. Do lock it up when you're not here. What worries me more than someone breaking in is the casual curiosity of people who come through here. People like Maisie Mae, for instance. Delivery people. Even Violet. Someone who simply might notice something they shouldn't. We try hard to make sure that never happens."

Erin considered the nosiness Maisie Mae had already demonstrated and the ever-curious nature of children. The security protocols seemed prudent.

Harlan was waiting for them in the conference room. A freshly brewed pot of coffee on the bar set the tone for a more businesslike meeting than the first one Erin had experienced, which was a relief. Part of her had worried about the company's professionalism. She was counting heavily on this venture working out as hoped.

After everyone had filled their cups and settled in, Harlan got right down to business.

"We call the underground version of our paper *The North Star*, in honor of the 19th-century newspaper that championed the rights of oppressed people. It seemed fitting. Ian's byline is Veritas, Sasha's is Libertas, Dylan's handle is The Webmaster, and I'm Forbidden Fruit ... once you study the paper you'll understand why. Published weekly, it's printed here on a press we have in the basement and disseminated via a system of small independent cells. Each of us gives a substantial number of copies to one person, who in turn gives them to five people they trust, each of whom hands the papers off to five more trusted people, and so forth. We do it like this in case someone is caught with the illegal materials. It limits exposure."

The approach reminded Erin of the clandestine cell network of Resistance fighters in the Second World War. "Is there any kind of electronic version?"

"Not yet," Ian said, "although Dylan really would like to publish on the Dark Web. Our concern lies in the very nature of that beast. Bad players. Computer geniuses on a par with our own. Dicey as hell."

"What will my byline be?" Erin asked.

"We'd like you to publish under the name White Rose," Harlan said. "Are you familiar with Sophie Scholl and the White Rose resistance group in Nazi Germany?"

"Actually I am. My grandmother raised me on stories of heroic women. Heroism was kind of a family theme." Erin connected the dots. "Oh, White Rose wrote and disseminated leaflets about the German atrocities."

Ian smiled. "And the White Rose was formed by a professor and five students at the University of Munich. Many of our people are university students inspired by Sasha."

"I'd be honored to publish under the name," Erin said. "However, I have a question. If I openly research a story and we publish the politically correct *Maverick* version of it, then won't writing an unvarnished version of that same story lead directly back to me if it's discovered?"

Harlan nodded. "That's a risk. For *North Star* stories, feel free to change names and identifying details as best you can, but disclose you are doing so. Feel free to serialize the stories so they're spread out. Use your creative judgment and trust your intuition."

Erin's coffee turned bitter in her stomach. "You do realize that Sophie, the professor, and the other four White Rose core members were all arrested and executed?"

Ian tried for another smile but wasn't quite able to pull it off. "Yes. Well, let's all try not to meet that same fate, shall we?"

**

"This restaurant sure is popular tonight." Erin had arrived home to find everyone crowded into the kitchen watching Kelly cook. Even Mojo sat at attention next to Conor, watching every move Kelly made.

"As long as the tips are good, I'll be happy," Kelly said. "Except Diva's. Waking up to a disemboweled mouse on my pillow is more than enough thanks for one lifetime." Everyone had heard her scream that morning.

"Are you sure it was a gratuity?" Izzy asked. "Diva's kinda bitchy. It might have been a statement about the new pet food you're serving."

Kelly tapped a large simmering pot with her ladle. "Clams, chicken, potatoes, carrots, eggs, olive oil. What's not to love?"

"For a cat maybe everything besides the clams and chicken?" Luca said.

"Well, Mojo's thrilled with it and I'm sure Diva is too. They need all the nutrition they can get."

Erin's stomach growled. She hadn't eaten lunch. "Is that what smells so good?"

Kelly opened the oven door and displayed its contents. "That and meatloaf and scalloped potatoes."

"When did you start cooking traditional mom food?" Erin asked. When they were young, Kelly fed her kids tofu, alfalfa sprouts, fried dandelions, yeast sprinkles, spirit-infused sun tea, and all things New Age. If it hadn't been for their grandmother, Erin was certain they would have died from malnutrition.

"I am a woman of many talents. Now sit and tell us

about your first day as a reporter."

Erin had to displace Diva to claim the only available chair. "It was busy. I spent the day in the office becoming familiar with the lay of the land, and I was given a list of initial assignments as well as a lot of reading material to study. It's not going to be a boring job, that's for sure."

Izzy curled her lip. "Did you really wear your waitress uniform today?"

Erin glanced down at the black slacks and white shirt. "Well, at least I didn't wear the vest and apron. But you do bring up a point. Mom, do you have any clothes I can borrow until payday?"

"Not unless you want to go in looking like Stevie Nicks. I mean, it works for me but would it for you?" Kelly's bohemian signature style was extreme. "Besides, I'm not sure if my clothes would fit you. You inherited my mother's big breasts, and I got my father's small ones."

Everyone looked at Conor.

He shrugged. "I don't have man boobs; I've just got a muscular chest from compensating for not having legs."

"Mother had some gorgeous suits," Kelly said. "What did you do with them?"

Conor reached out to Mojo and rubbed his ears. "After she died, I couldn't look at her clothes every day in my closet, but I didn't want to get rid of them either. I put them in her big cedar chest. If Erin wants to go through it after dinner, I'm good with that."

"Thank you, I will." Erin recalled that her grandmother always looked smart and professional. It might be the perfect solution.

"Well, since we're all here, I have a dilemma to

discuss," Izzy said. "Dad wants to see me on my birthday. When we were moving, Uncle Nick told me that Dad wants to close the restaurant Sunday night and fix me dinner. Just the two of us. No Maria even. Just us."

That stole Erin's breath. What did this mean? Was it a first step towards Tony trying to reunite the family? He never closed the restaurant on high traffic nights. "That's a big deal," she managed to say.

Izzy's expression looked pained. "You wouldn't mind?"

"Why would I mind?"

Izzy bit her lip. "I feel like if I do it, it's kinda like choosing sides."

Erin's heart ached for her children. "There aren't any sides here, Izzy. I'm thrilled he wants to spend time with you. And seventeen is an important birthday. It's the threshold of being an adult. You should go."

"He didn't invite me?" Luca's voice quavered.

"I—" Izzy stopped and threw a panicked look in Erin's direction.

Erin had no idea what to say to alleviate Luca's pain. In many ways their children had been hurt more deeply by Tony than she had. Couples always lived with the tacit understanding that one might betray the other. However, a child never expects to be betrayed by a parent.

Conor said, "As a man, I can tell you that when it comes to emotional situations, sometimes we need to take baby steps. Your dad has a lot to be ashamed about. Maybe he's only able to make amends to one of you at a time."

Luca's face reddened and he swiped away tears. "Dad's a big baby, all right. Like Aunt Meg says, 'he's not any kind of man.'"

Erin didn't think she could hate her sister more than she did at that moment. "Meg is wrong."

"Please don't cry, Luca," Izzy said. "I won't go if it upsets you."

Kelly slammed a cabinet door shut. "Oh, good grief. Isabelle, you go. Luca's sadness is not your responsibility. Luca, it's okay to cry. Tony *is* a man, and Meg can be a real bitch. And now all of that is settled, let's eat dinner so I can go join my fellow QAnon Moms for tonight's big mission."

Grateful for a change in topic, Erin asked, "What's your mission?"

"We're meeting outside of Suburban Snowflake Stella Preston's house to bang pots in protest."

"In protest of what?"

"Stella's a nurse and runs low-income vaccination clinics around the county. Vaccinations are pure evil. They're all about making Big Pharma money and they contain nanobots that the Global Elite use to control the masses."

Erin almost laughed. "You actually believe that?"

"It's true. You should write a story about it."

"Did you know that Hitler was an anti-vaxxer?" Izzy asked.

"See? He wasn't all bad like they want you to believe."

"Kelly, stop that kind of talk." Conor's disapproving tone didn't seem to faze her.

Erin knew Stella. Many years earlier, Stella and Kelly had been close friends. "You do know that Stella's autistic granddaughter lives with her now, right?"

Kelly stabbed the air with her index finger. "Exactly!

124

Vaccinations cause autism, so I can't understand why she's such a champion of them. It's completely insane."

"Actually, the preservative in childhood vaccines that might have contributed to autism hasn't been used since 2001," Izzy said.

"That's just what they want you to believe."

"Do you know that autistic people are usually super sensitive to loud noise, and it can really scare them?" Izzy asked.

"That's not my problem," Kelly said. "It's my right to bang pots wherever I want to. It's a free country."

"But it's a mean thing to do."

"So what, Isabelle, you're *woke* now?"

Izzy's hands fluttered in the air like they were trying to capture just the right words. Finally, she said, "No, Grandma, I was never asleep."

***

After dinner, Erin joined Conor in his bedroom to sort through her late grandmother's clothes.

Erin had always presumed the large cedar chest that sat at the foot of his bed contained bedding, but it was filled with the remains of Ginger Doyle's life. Besides the carefully folded clothes, it contained photographs, handwritten journals, bundles of love letters Ginger and Conor had exchanged during the war, souvenirs of their wedding, and childhood memories of their only child.

Conor sat next to Erin as she explored the chest's contents, seemingly taking pleasure in revisiting the past.

Mojo sat next to Conor, alert to every detail of their treasure hunt.

"All the good genes in this family come from Ginger," Conor said. "Even when Alzheimer's stole her memories, she never forgot the love she had for us."

"I remember," Erin said. "And I remember she always had a glow about her, like she was filled with sunshine. I figured it was related to how religious she was."

"Let me tell you a secret about Ginger. She never really was all that religious. She was more of a mystic than anything else. She hated the hypocrisy and politics of the Church."

"Did her employer know that?"

Ginger had been an administrator at a Catholic church for decades.

He laughed "She was never shy about speaking her mind."

"Kind of like her daughter?"

Conor's smile faded. "No, nothing like her daughter. Ginger didn't have a selfish bone in her body."

Erin thought about her mother's religion of selfishness. "Why is Mom like she is?"

Conor spent a few minutes lighting a joint and partaking of its gifts before responding. "I sacrificed my legs because I decided that the lives of the women and children in that village were more important than my own. Ginger sacrificed her youth and beauty to care for a man with no legs. Your ma saw the struggles we endured as weakness, instead of strength. Somewhere along the way Kelly decided she would always put herself first, which she equates with being strong."

"So, she never fell in love, never married, never cared about anyone more than herself or made herself vulnerable in any way."

"Tragic, isn't it? She missed out on so much."

Inside Erin something stirred. All those jagged, broken pieces of her own heart slowly began to coalesce. She realized that despite the heartbreak of losing Tony, she would go through it all again to have had the experience of their big love.

Conor sucked in another deep cloud of smoke, held it, then let go. "And I think that all this QAnonsense she's into gives her a sense of meaning that her own life lacks. It makes her feel special."

"I wondered what you thought about her conspiracy theories."

He chuckled. "Well, I do understand the mindset which allowed that kind of thinking to become so widespread. It really began with my generation. Our involvement in 'Nam exposed some of the rot at our country's core. Once that was revealed, it became easy to believe the worst. Belief in an absolutely corrupt Deep State grew from some real seeds." He rubbed Mojo's ears. "In fact, I would say that there is a grain of truth in most every conspiracy theory out there. Big Pharma is a giant fire-breathing dragon of Capitalism, but it's done a hell of a lot of good, too. There are pedophiles everywhere, but that kind of evil isn't exclusive to any particular group. There is a Global Elite of the wealthy and powerful, but are they a demonic cabal responsible for all the problems in the world? Of course not."

Erin thought about it in relation to now. "What do you think about our new government?"

Conor reached up and touched the eagle patch sewn on the front of the Vietnam Vet cap he often wore. "An eagle needs two wings to fly. Like a plane, it operates on a system of checks and balances to keep the main body aloft. Our new autocratic government relies on one very dark, heavy wing. This country is doomed if that doesn't change."

"And how can that change?"

Conor shrugged. "That's a tough one, but I do find a lot of similarities between what went down in Germany during the Second World War and what happened here. One third of Germans supported Hitler and the Nazi Party, one third of Germans opposed them, and the final third simply wasn't paying attention. If the blind segment of that population had truly understood what Hitler stood for and the atrocities the Party was committing, I believe good would have prevailed over evil much sooner than it did." He waved his hand toward the window. "Despite all the selfish, mean, and stupid people in the world, I think they're outnumbered by people who care, are kind, and who can use their brains. In our country, only a third of Americans supported this new fascist government. Roughly a third opposed it. And the other third simply wasn't paying attention. If only we could make them pay attention now, it might help to turn things around."

Erin felt intense shame that she was a member of the clueless third, and she considered the job she now had. "Grandpa, I need you to make me a promise. If something happens to me, and Tony doesn't step up, I don't want my kids raised by Meg or being unduly influenced by Mom. I want you to make sure that doesn't happen."

His eyes narrowed. "What exactly do you think is going to happen to you?"

"I think being a journalist is a dangerous profession. I just need your assurance that my kids will be raised with love."

"You're asking a lot from an old cripple."

"Well, this old cripple has a really big heart."

He took a deep breath. "I'll do my best, *macushla*."

She hugged him hard. "That's all any of us can do."

***

Despite the many years since Ginger Doyle's suits had been worn, they needed very little care to make them ready for Erin. She hung them up, steamed the wrinkles out, and they were good to go. The cedar scent that the material held smelled better than her own perfume. And they fit her perfectly, which she hoped might be some kind of cosmic sign. Unlike her grandmother, Erin wasn't a woman of strong spiritual faith. Nor did she possess her grandfather's courage. Could that faith and courage still manifest through their shared genes and buoy her up in the days ahead?

Erin's brother had inherited those noble genes. Knowing that gave her hope.

"Please help me do this right," she whispered in prayer to her twin. His presence was always with her.

After the clothes were tucked away in her own closet, Erin turned on the radio to drown out the television show the kids were watching in the family room. Then she propped herself up in bed, unlocked her briefcase, and booted up her laptop to study all the material she had received that day.

On her laptop she reviewed the list of assignments that Ian had given her:

1. ICE has opened a new detention center, which a press release describes as a state-of-the-

art facility. Visit it and report on it for the *Maverick*. Try to interview detainees and write a human-interest story for *The North Star*.

2. An elementary school in Weld County has recently adopted the new Patriot education model that will soon be the standard for all the schools in the state. Also, a source tells us that an oil company is fracking dangerously close to the school. Seems like plenty of material here for both papers.

3. Pastor Christian Tobias of the Rocky Mountain Patriot Church just announced his intention to run for Congress. Stories for both papers? Source that might be helpful: Maisie Mae Marchand just put a bumper sticker on her car in support of the pastor's new political campaign.

Note: Press releases for 1-3 attached.

4. Also, feel free to chase your own leads and write stories as you see fit. Anything you deem might be of interest to our readers.

PS. Harlan is counting on you to be the next rock star he gets to promote, so go forth and shine! (No pressure...)

"Nope, no pressure. None at all," Erin said, a renewed wave of anxiety rising within.

Erin had also been given a stack of *North Star* newspapers to read so she could familiarize herself with their layout and style.

Studying them, she learned that Ian's Veritas stories centered around politics and the suppression of the free press.

Sasha's Libertas focused on civil rights issues, as well as the rise of Christian Nationalism and its fostering of the white supremacist movement.

Dylan's Webmaster instructed readers about accessing and navigating the Dark Web and circumventing the Great American Internet Wall that the new government had erected.

And Harlan as Forbidden Fruit wrote stories about the new world of underground entertainment. His columns revealed where all of that which was now forbidden could be found: performances by exotic dancers and drag queens, concerts with music deemed immoral, showings of banned movies, and libraries filled with banned books. His stories were written in some sort of code to protect the entertainers and curators involved should a paper be intercepted by authorities. Apparently, the underground movement had developed its own language and geography. Erin's mind reeled from the discovery of this entire secret universe she had known nothing about.

She was so engrossed in reading that she didn't hear Izzy come in.

"What the hell?" Izzy plucked Erin's press pass from her open briefcase. "Since when do you wear glasses?"

"Since when don't you knock?"

"I did."

Erin's mind stumbled. "Well, my boss decided I looked more like a journalist with glasses on. They're just plain glass."

"You are the *worst* liar I've ever known." Izzy zeroed in on the glasses inside the briefcase. Before Erin could stop her, she snatched them up and gave them a thorough inspection. "Spy glasses? Mother, mother, mother. What have you gotten yourself into?"

Erin leapt to her feet and shut the bedroom door. "Izzy, please—"

"*The North Star?*"

Too late Erin tried to cover the pile of newspapers with a pillow.

"I read that paper, Mom. I especially love The Webmaster's column."

"How did you find it?"

"Some very interesting people hang out at Café Paris." Izzy grinned. "Holy hell, I always wondered if it was the underground version of the *Maverick*. I mean, it totally fits."

"Oh, dear God." Erin felt tears threatening and struggled to hold it together. Taking a deep breath, she sat on the edge of the bed and gestured for Izzy to join her.

Izzy's smile vanished and she sat. "Are you okay?"

"No, I'm not okay at all." Erin's voice broke. "I can't express how awful it is that you figured this out."

"Don't worry, I won't tell anyone about you and," Izzy's hands fluttered, "it."

"Don't worry?" Erin tried to calm her internal storm. "First of all, you shouldn't be reading that paper. If you were found in possession of it, you could be arrested."

"And you could be killed for writing it. I have a friend whose mother, a doctor, was executed by firing squad for breaking one of the new laws. Do you know after that happens, they send the bullets to the family? I don't want your bullet, Mom. I don't think you understand how evil this new government is."

Erin's emotions grew more turbulent. "I'm starting to."

"Why are you taking such risks? You, of all people?"

"Well, I took the job because of the pay and benefits, but now that I understand what's at stake, I want to do something to help."

"But I'm the fighter. You're the lover. You've got no useful clandestiney skills. You can't even tell a lie convincingly."

"Clandestiney isn't a word."

The tension broke.

They looked at each other and both burst into laughter.

Izzy flopped onto her back.

Erin did the same. "You, my sweet girl, have guts and mad martial skills. You're a genius cypherpunk and on a passionate mission to save democracy. All I've got going for me is that I'm a good writer. If that's the only strength I bring to the fight, it'll have to be enough."

"What can I do to help?"

Erin propped herself up on one elbow. "Mostly just don't ever tell a soul. They made me sign a pretty scary non-disclosure that not only affects me but also our family."

"Of course I'll never tell. You've got my word."

Erin considered the situation from all angles. "I really think I should tell my bosses right away that you figured it out."

"Why would you do that?"

"Think of it like a *Maquis* Resistance cell. The members can deceive the entire German army, but if there's not integrity among their own ranks what's the point?"

"Well yeah, but I don't want you to lose your job."

"Trust me. It's the right thing to do."

"Okay, then I support your decision. What else can I do to help?"

Erin thought about it. "They want me to write a story about the pastor of that church Meg and Beau go to. He just announced he's running for Congress. What do you know about him?"

"That's sure horrifying. He's the one who started the whole 'Be a Bounty Hunter' campaign."

Erin drew a blank.

Izzy shook her head. "You haven't seen the commercials?"

"Educate me."

"It glamorizes the turning in of people who are violating the new laws and offers large bounties as rewards. The commercials feature sexy cowboy and cowgirl bounty hunters. The bounties start at ten grand and go up from there depending on the seriousness of the crime. Donations to his church by the rich and powerful fund the payments. I'm sure he'll make it the centerpiece of his political campaign and take it national."

"Yes, that is truly horrifying."

"What else can I do to help?"

Erin thought about it. "They want me to chase my own leads. What happened to your friend's mother might make a good story."

"Not yet. It's a new friendship and I don't know all the details. But I am learning some awful things about Wildwind Western Wear and their work camp, their use of child labor, and the mistreatment of employees."

"That sounds promising. Please just start

documenting your discoveries, and I'll take it from there."

Izzy giggled. "And if you get hard up for stories, there's always the war between the QAnon Moms and the Suburban Snowflakes. Lots of exciting material there to work with."

Erin knew she was joking but actually liked the idea. What she had so far learned about QAnon worried her, and a deeper dive into how the cult impacted human lives was something she'd like to investigate.

Izzy took Erin's hand and squeezed. "We'll make a good team."

"Yes, we will."

"I apologize for underestimating you, Mom. I'll work at becoming your biggest cheerleader if you promise me that you'll be careful. We lost Dad. We can't lose you, too."

Izzy's belief in her meant more to Erin than she ever imagined it could, and she struggled for the words to express that gratitude. Finally, she simply said, "I promise I'll be careful."

Erin hoped it was a promise she could keep.

CHAPTER FIVE

"Come on, hurry up." Getting Luca out the door proved more challenging than Izzy had bargained for when she volunteered to drive him to his new school. In Boulder, their mom had driven him every day, but with her new schedule she couldn't do it anymore. So, Izzy offered to make sure he got there each morning as long as someone else picked him up. Yesterday she had registered him, and he spent his first day there. Today he didn't want to return.

Luca sat slumped at the kitchen table wearing a sullen expression and repeatedly kicking the table's leg. His breakfast still sat on his plate.

"Why didn't you eat?" Izzy asked. She had made the fried potatoes and scrambled eggs from their limited supplies, then sprinkled it with as much grated cheese as they could spare to add some extra zing. Everyone inhaled it, including Mojo. Even Diva gobbled up the eggs and cheese.

"It's yucky. I want Cocoa Puffs or pancakes with maple syrup."

Izzy tamped down her irritation. "Even if we could find some Cocoa Puffs, we can't afford them right now. Or maple syrup. We have to make do with what we've got."

"It's what I eat at Aunt Meg's house. She's got a special place where she buys all the good stuff. Why can't I live with her? This whole thing just sucks."

Izzy pulled out a chair and sat next to him. "Mom and I need you. We love you, Luca." She wanted to ask him if he loved them, too, but was afraid of the answer. Kids just didn't get what really mattered in life.

"And I hate school here. I want to go back to my old school."

"Starting a new school is always hard. It'll get easier when you make friends."

"I don't want new friends. I want to go back to my old life when Dad loved us, and we were all together, and we were happy." His eyes brimmed with tears, and he gave the table another wicked kick.

Her heart ached for him. "Maybe that will happen one day, but for now this is our life. Please let's just make the best of it."

"Nothing's changed for you. You don't have to go to school, and you get to go to back to Boulder every day and hang out with your friends."

Izzy took her GED in lieu of her senior year, and she worked at Café Paris. It wasn't exactly her old life. "Look, you have to go to school. Them's the rules, kiddo."

"Why? When I grow up, I want to work on Uncle Beau's ranch. I don't need school for that."

"Well—" Her mind struggled to think like a ten-year-old. "Why don't you focus on studying really hard now so you can get your GED as soon as the law allows, and then you'll be free to be a cowboy if that's still what you want."

The ice thawed a bit and he looked at her for the first time all morning. "What do you want to do with the rest of your life? Work on the mall?"

She shook her head. "I wanted to go to college, but that's not in the cards anymore. We don't have the money, and scholarships and student loans are no longer a thing. I don't know what I can do."

137

"But if we had money again, you could go to college and be happy?"

"I might be able to go to college, but I'm determined to be happy now."

"Good luck with that." He stood and shuffled toward the living room.

Frustrated, Izzy set Luca's plate on the floor for the animals and grabbed his lunch box off the counter. She had packed it with carrot sticks and a sandwich made with last night's meatloaf and some *focaccia* flatbread Uncle Nick had scored for them. Since he hadn't eaten breakfast, she added a big hunk of buttered *ciabatta* and a small Tupperware container of canned pineapple. And she made a mental note to buy some day-old pastries with today's tips for his breakfast tomorrow.

"Goodbye!" Izzy shouted before they left, but the only response was Mojo's happy yap from somewhere unseen.

"Papa's in the shower, and Grandma left when Mom went to work," Luca said.

Izzy made sure to lock up the house, they piled into the Mustang, and headed to Luca's school.

Not far from home, at a busy intersection, Izzy saw a redheaded Stevie Nicks walking around, dodging traffic. Startled, she pulled over to get a better look.

"Is that Grandma?" Luca asked. "What's she doing?"

"Oh no. Yes, it's Grandma and she's doing something not very nice."

"What?"

Izzy's brief inner debate about whether she should tell Luca was won by the side that hoped he would learn a lesson. "You probably don't remember, but a few years ago Grandma's dog, Blarney, got away from her and was hit by a car in that intersection."

"And died?"

"Yes, and it totally devastated her. So, she built a little roadside memorial to him, which was a sweet thing to do. But then, in one of her more loopy moments, she decided that Blarney's spirit was hungry. That caused her to undertake daily missions of throwing all kinds of food into the intersection right where he died, which caused other animals to be hit by cars because they were lured into the street. Now because she's got food again, I guess she's back at it."

"Why doesn't she just put the stuff by the memorial?"

"Something about appeasing his spirit at the exact spot of his death." Izzy shrugged. "You know Grandma. All the neighbors tried to get her to stop, but she insisted it was a free country and it was her right."

"Well, she's not wrong."

"Really? You think that?"

He didn't answer.

"Grandma's best friend at that time was Stella—"

"Snowflake Stella?"

"—and Stella's cat was killed there—"

"Well, she shouldn't have let the cat out."

"—and Grandma still wouldn't stop, and that ended their friendship."

"What's your point, Izzy?"

His obnoxious tone shocked her. "My point is that bad things happen when people are selfish. There's no upside to it."

"How very snowflake of you."

Izzy struggled hard to not lose her temper. "Who teaches you to think and talk like that?"

"Uncle Beau and his crew have zero patience with snowflakes. Real men follow their own consciousnesses and to hell with everyone else."

"You mean conscience?"

He slouched down and kicked the dash. "Whatever."

A wave of anger rose up and crashed down hard. "Don't you *ever* kick Uncle Brian's car again."

He crossed his arms and turned away from her.

"Wait here." She turned off the engine, stepped out of the car, and slammed the door much harder than she should have. After her grandmother had driven away and the coast was clear, Izzy ventured into the street and picked up a half dozen small pieces of chicken. Surprised to see the memorial still standing and well-tended after all these years, she deposited the food there and returned to the car.

"You gonna do that every day?" Luca asked.

She put her seatbelt back on and started the engine. "I don't see how I can."

"Then why do it at all?"

"Sometimes the only good you can do is that which is right in front of you. Every little bit of kindness adds up in the grand scheme of things."

Luca snorted.

They rode the rest of the way in silence.

When they arrived, Luca grabbed his lunchbox and backpack, and left without a word.

Izzy rolled down the passenger side window to tell him goodbye, but he didn't respond.

In his haste to get away from her, he ran into another boy and tripped. Scrambling back onto his feet he shouted, "You stupid gimp, stay out of my way," then he shoved him and disappeared into the crowd. His victim, who had a leg brace and wore an elbow crutch, lost his balance and fell to the ground.

Horrified, Izzy jumped out of the car and raced to his side. "Are you okay?"

The boy pushed himself into a sitting position. "It happens a lot. There's a bunch more bullies than there used to be."

Holy hell, her brother was a bully?

As Izzy helped him to his feet, she calculated he was probably a year older than Luca. His backpack had the name Ryan Stephens stenciled on it.

"Ryan, I'm so sorry. There's no excuse for what he did."

Ryan struggled to find his balance. "My dad says I've got to be tough if I'm going to survive. He says the world doesn't like people who are different anymore. He sounds scared when he says that, so I'm tough because I don't want him to worry."

Izzy's heart broke for both of them. "I'm so sorry."

"It's okay. I'll be okay. Thanks for the help." He shrugged his backpack onto one shoulder and hobbled away.

Izzy stood for a long time watching the crowd of children disappear into the school. After they left her alone, she looked up into the big, empty sky and asked, "What is happening to us?"

The Big Empty gave her no answers.

***

When Erin arrived at work, she found Ian in the kitchen making tea. "I need to talk with you and whoever else is here," she told him.

"Now?"

"Yes, it's important."

"Right." He finished adding sugar and milk to his cup, then gestured for her to follow him into the conference room. From there he made an announcement over the intercom, asking everyone in the office to join them.

The timing worked out well, as Harlan, Sasha, and Dylan were all there. Within minutes, everyone had gathered around the poker table.

"The floor is Erin's," Ian said. "She called this meeting."

Erin experienced a moment of panic, wondering if she should have opened this can of worms. However, there was no turning back now. "So, I have a wicked smart daughter and she figured out what we're up to in about thirty seconds last night. Izzy walked in on me in my bedroom, noticed the press pass, knows something about spy glasses, and saw the stack of *North Star* newspapers before I could hide them." Erin took a deep breath and looked at Dylan. "She reads the paper and is a big fan of your work, by the way."

Besides a muttered "bloody hell" from Ian, no one said anything for what seemed like an eternity.

"No lock on your bedroom?" Sasha finally asked.

Erin shook her head. "We just moved a few days ago and everything is still unsettled."

"How old is your daughter?" Harlan asked.

"She'll be seventeen on Sunday, but her IQ and emotional maturity are light years beyond most adults I know."

"Please tell us about her. Help me assess our security risk," Dylan said.

Erin hesitated for a moment because she didn't

want to betray any confidences which might endanger Izzy. However, she had to make them understand. "For most of Isabelle's life she's been on a mission from God to save the world from fascism. I'm not exaggerating in the least. Her mentor growing up was a woman whose family was part of the *Maquis* in the French Underground. Izzy's an expert at French *savate*—both the kickboxing and the baton defense—and knows more about the state of the world than I ever will. She's a computer genius—calls herself a cypherpunk—and there's nothing about that world she doesn't understand. Her great-grandfather, who was an engineer at IBM, nurtured that side of her from the time she was old enough to sit at a computer. He was also a war hero, and Izzy is determined to emulate that energy." She paused long enough to try to read the room but couldn't. Like all good reporters, they listened to her story impassively. "If it would help to know, I can tell you that she's nothing like me. In every good way possible, she takes after her dad who most of his life was incredibly strong, courageous, and honorable." Erin wanted to tell them more about Tony's history, but that was a confidence she would never betray. "I'm not sure what else to say, except that she gave me her word she'd never tell anyone, and her word is absolute gold. Also, because of her life choices, she understands exactly what's at stake. I felt I owed it to you to let you know because we're a team."

"Your honesty is appreciated," Harlan said.

"She's sixteen. How is it that she reads *The North Star*?" Ian asked.

"She works at Café Paris on the Pearl Street Mall. Apparently, someone she knows from there shares it with her."

"A lot of CU students do hang out at Café Paris and downstairs at The Underground," Dylan said. "Makes sense."

"Does she have to sign an NDA now?" Erin asked.

Harlan chuckled. "She's not old enough to sign a binding contract." He threw up his hands. "Don't worry about it. I trust Dylan to monitor the situation and let us know if we need to address it further."

Erin wasn't sure how to interpret that comment, but instead of asking, decided a wait-and-see approach was prudent.

"Well, now that's settled shall we get on with our day?" Ian said.

As they were leaving the conference room, Sasha asked Erin, "Are you coming to our poker game on Thursday night?"

She shook her head. "I'm not in a financial position to play poker right now."

"We don't play for money," Ian told her. "It's more of a strip poker type of thing."

That was horrifyingly unexpected. "What?"

Harlan laughed. "Not literal strip poker. More psychological strip poker. The stakes are the opportunity for the winner to ask anyone at the table a pointed question. Kind of our take on truth or dare. It's all about bonding. Usually quite fun too, except when these two—" he gestured to Ian and Sasha "—were in the throes of their nasty divorce."

Sasha laughed. "Those were interesting times."

"But we made it through," Ian said.

"Probably worse for wear, but yes we're still here," Sasha said. "We start at seven, if you want to come."

Erin thought it might be helpful to attend a bonding event, especially after the bombshell she just laid on them. "Unless work interferes, I'll be here."

"What story are you chasing first?" Harlan asked.

"I'm going to start with the ICE center."

"Take cigarettes and chocolate," Ian said. "Trust me, I was a war correspondent. If you have an opportunity to interview any detainees, that's the best way to thaw the ice. There's a box of each in the kitchen just for situations like this. Help yourself."

"Thanks, I will."

"I've got some advice, too." Dylan said. "The man in charge of that center, John Yates, isn't a nice guy. Be careful."

"Can you elaborate?" Erin asked.

"I could, but I think it's better if you figure him out for yourself. I don't want to influence the direction of your investigation."

Well, that's unsettling, Erin thought. *And so it begins.*

***

When Izzy arrived at work, she sat in her car for a few minutes to collect herself, then decided to call Conor.

"I'm sorry to ask for your help already, Papa, but, well, I need it."

"Lay it on me. We old folks like to feel useful."

She took a deep, shaky breath. "Today, when I dropped Luca off at school he was rushing and tripped over the crutch of a boy named Ryan. Maybe it was embarrassment, but he totally lost it, called Ryan a gimp, and pushed him down. It was ugly."

"And you want me to talk to him because I'm disabled too, and it might give him some perspective?"

Izzy hoped she hadn't offended him. "Something like that, I guess. He does love you."

"Sure, I'll pick him up today and give him the talk."

The fact that Luca had been a bully still felt unreal to her. "I know you can't really teach someone to have compassion, but even if we can tone down his bad behavior it's a start."

"Well, he's been hurt, and acting out isn't unusual for a kid his age."

Izzy thought about that. "I really think Uncle Beau is a big part of this new Luca. It scares me because he's so damn vulnerable."

Conor was quiet for such a long time that Izzy checked her phone to make sure they were still connected. Finally, he said, "People of Beau's ilk need to have things their way, and in their world the ends justify the meanness. It is truly unfortunate that he's become the father figure in Luca's life."

Anxiety flooded Izzy's internal server, and worst-case scenarios involving Luca manifested as a series of frightening pop-up windows in her mind. "We need to troubleshoot this, Papa."

"Hopefully, we'll be able to reboot and put an end to the loop he's stuck in."

Izzy wanted to believe that. The thought of her baby brother crashing was too horrible to bear.

***

Izzy entered Café Paris via the back kitchen door, and the magnificent smell of fresh-baked bread enveloped her in a comforting cloud.

Karma and her grandmother, Mei Ling, arrived every morning at three and baked until the café opened at seven. Karma, who still resisted being in the presence of everyone but those in her close circle, went home at seven and Mei Ling worked until three in the afternoon as chef. It was the same role she had filled at The Buddha Belly, except with French cuisine instead of Cantonese. Like Izzy's dad, Mei Ling was an artist and her food a thing of beauty.

It had taken a herculean effort to convince Karma to return to the world at all after the violence she endured. Luther was the one responsible for helping Karma cross that bridge by offering to pick her up and take her home. Every day. Seven days a week. A cot in the corner of the kitchen allowed him to sleep while the women worked. He told them that his years in Afghanistan taught him to sleep anywhere but remain alert enough to awaken if trouble arose.

Luther was one of Izzy's favorite people.

Andrea ran the front of the house and practically lived there herself. Passionately embracing that which her parents had so loved was her panacea for pain.

Survivors of tragedy clung to whatever life preservers they could find.

Andrea, behind the front counter, winked at Izzy in greeting. "Anything you want to share?"

"Um, nothing in particular. Why?"

"No new, special man in your life?"

"There's never been a special man in my life, new or used."

Andrea turned toward the mirror on the wall and readjusted the floral bouquet in her hair. Being the boss now, she exempted herself from wearing the mandatory beret. Her flower child roots ran deep. "Well, some cute-sounding dude called earlier to see if you'd be in today. I'm consumed with wonder and curiosity."

The only remote possibility could be Dante, but Izzy was certain she hadn't told him where she worked. "It's a mystery."

Andrea squealed. "I love mysteries, especially when they involve men."

Izzy laughed and put on her apron. "What do I need to know about today's specials?"

"We were able to get bacon and blueberry preserves today. It's like Christmastime around here right now."

Izzy's mouth watered.

"So, specials. Hold onto your cute little beret, babe. We've got blueberry crepes with honey-sweetened whipped cream, as well as a vegan version sprinkled with powdered sugar. Then there's a fully loaded breakfast croissant with cheese, eggs and, wait for it ... *bacon* for all the wicked carnivores."

Izzy felt dizzy.

"And finally, the *pièce de résistance*, quiche Lorraine."

"Be still my heart," Izzy said.

"I know, right? When we were young would we have ever thought food would get us so turned on?"

"The innocence of youth." Izzy couldn't wait until her midday break. One of the perks of the job was a free meal every shift. She glanced at the clock on the wall and began an internal countdown.

"Luther's here," Andrea said. "You want to get his breakfast?"

Every day after taking Karma home, Luther would go to the small apartment he now rented, shower and change, and then return for breakfast. Izzy often wondered when he caught up on sleep, but she chalked it up to him being a superhero.

In the kitchen Mei Ling was already putting together a plate for him; she possessed a kind of psychic Luther radar. The tiny woman adored the loyal guardian who protected her granddaughter.

As did they all.

Mei Ling handed Izzy a large platter that had all three of today's specials on it.

The amazing sight mesmerized Izzy and she stood frozen.

"Hurry." Mei Ling made urgent hand gestures. "Shoo."

"Yes, ma'am."

Luther sat in a special booth near the front door which a big sign announced was RESERVED FOR SECURITY. Given how bad things became on the mall during the riots, patrons seemed to appreciate his regular presence.

Izzy set the plate down in front of him. "You sure are the teacher's pet."

He grinned. "Jealous?"

"Oh, yeah."

His laughter was a thing of beauty. As was the eye contact he now made. Life had fully returned to him, and he wore it well.

"Coffee?"

"Please."

As she was filling a cup at the coffee pot, Andrea came up to her and whispered, "The new man you don't have is here. He asked me which section was yours."

"What man?"

"Neo."

"Who?" Izzy turned and scanned the room until she saw a young man seated in the far corner of her section who looked just like Neo from her beloved *Matrix* movies. "Neo?"

Andrea flashed jazz hands. "That's what I said."

"Pinch me."

Andrea happily complied.

Izzy flinched at the wide-awake pain. "Ow."

"I aim to please. Now go tend to your very groovy mystery man. I'll cover for you with the boss."

"Thanks. She can be *such* a bitch."

Andrea responded with another sharp pinch.

As Izzy walked away, she blew Andrea a kiss.

After dropping off Luther's coffee, Izzy picked up a menu, walked up to her stalker's table, and handed it to him. "Hi, I'm Izzy."

He took off his sunglasses and studied her with an intense gaze. "Hello, Izzy."

Something about him unsettled her, like she was momentarily unplugged from reality. However, she managed to point to the handwritten insert inside the menu. "We have some awesome specials today."

He studied it. "How's the quiche Lorraine?"

"I've never had it. The mushroom quiche we usually serve is wonderful, but the special has, you know, *bacon*."

She probably said it with a bit too much excitement because he laughed. "Bacon makes everything better. I'll take it."

"Coffee?"

He slipped off his long coat. "Hot tea. I work with an Englishman, and he introduced me to it. Although in these uber patriotic times I do worry about not leaving it consigned to the bottom of Boston Harbor. Are you okay?"

She was staring at the press pass he wore around his neck. "My mother works for the *Boulder Maverick*."

"I know. I came in because I wanted to meet you." He extended his hand to shake. "Dylan Kane. I work for the paper as photojournalist and handle cybersecurity."

Now she knew why she felt off; her spidey sense had been trying to alert her to danger. She shook his hand. "Izzy Tavano, but I guess you knew that."

"Your mother talks about you a lot."

Just this morning, I bet. She reached for his press pass and examined it. "What, no glasses, Kane?"

He raised an eyebrow. "Glasses?"

She smiled. "Yeah, your whole Neo vibe isn't complete without those sunglasses."

His look of surprise confirmed Izzy's suspicion that this was a test of her ability to hold secrets.

Gotcha, she thought.

"You like *The Matrix*? Erin mentioned you're pretty savvy about all things cyberspace."

Izzy did her best girly giggle. "Aw, moms tend to exaggerate. But yeah, I love that movie. That and *Casablanca*." She gestured to a poster on the wall advertising their monthly showing of the classic movie at The Underground.

"I'm surprised that one hasn't been banned yet," Dylan said. "I guess they've blacklisted *Schindler's List* now. Someone told me there's an underground showing of it somewhere. You wouldn't happen to know where?"

Of course she knew. She'd read about it in Forbidden Fruit's *North Star* column. "Can't say that I do. I try to stay away from anything illegal. This country's way too scary right now." She batted her eyes innocently.

Dylan grinned, and she got the sense that they

were done dancing. He pointed to the *Casablanca* poster. "What's that full moon showing all about?"

"You haven't heard about our monthly tradition yet?" She put her hands on her hips and gave him a mock-disgusted look. "Just what kind of newspaper man are you, anyway?"

He bowed his head. "I accept your disdain with shame in my heart."

The ice had broken, and Izzy was happy to relax and just be. "Remember the midnight showings of *The Rocky Horror Picture Show* where everyone would dress up as characters from the movie, sing along with the music, and shout out the famous lines? Well, we do that with *Casablanca*. It's epic. You should come."

"That actually does sound like fun." He picked up his sunglasses and shrugged. "Whatever would I wear though?"

"Anything 1940s elegant. Except no Nazi uniforms. Those are totally *verboten*. But if uniforms are your thing, we do allow people to dress as the policeman, Captain Renault. Although he starts off as kind of a bad guy, in the end he chooses to side with the Resistance."

"And you enjoy that movie because it's about fighting fascism?"

"Of course, but it's about so much more." Her hands fluttered in the air as she captured her thoughts. "It's about the downside of trying to remain neutral —in love or war. It takes place in December of 1941, which was when Japan bombed Pearl Harbor. America had remained neutral in the war until then, but *that* sure turned out to be a fatal error. I mean, they never mention Pearl Harbor in the movie, but the symbolism is clear. When evil tries to destroy good, you simply *must* choose a side. And Ilse tries to remain neutral in her love for two men, but although you can choose duty over love, you can't ever deny what's in your heart. That movie is *such* a brilliant take on the fight for love and glory." Her impassioned speech left her breathless. And a little embarrassed.

However, it didn't seem to bother Dylan. "You are absolutely delightful, Izzy Tavano."

"Um. Okay." She picked up the menu. "Quiche Lorraine and hot tea it is." Her face burning, she scurried away.

"You're blushing," Andrea said.

"No, I'm not."

"You like this Neo."

"No, I don't."

"Keep telling yourself that."

The mature woman she was, Izzy stuck her tongue out at Andrea and escaped into the kitchen.

Later, as she was standing at Luther's table refilling his coffee cup, Dylan passed by on his way to leave. "Goodbye, Izzy. It was a pleasure."

"Bye Kane. See you at *Casablanca*?"

"If not, we'll always have Paris."

She laughed. That was one of her favorite lines in the movie.

After he put on his coat and walked out, Luther said, "You have goosebumps."

She looked down at the gooseflesh on her arm. "No, I don't."

"And you have a tell, you know," he said. "I saw his press badge. Whenever you're attracted to a guy you call him by his last name."

"No, I don't."

"I think you do it to establish emotional distance because relationships scare you."

"No, they don't." Desperate to change the subject, she noticed the large, thick manilla envelope in the corner of the table. "Is that what I think it is?"

He nodded and handed it to her.

Casually, she accepted delivery of her copies of the latest issue of *The North Star.*

CHAPTER SIX

The new U.S. Immigration and Customs Enforcement Detention Center had been built in Weld County, in a rural area fifteen miles east of Longmont. Even before the Patriot Party seized the country's reins, Weld County had been ultra-conservative. Now, while Boulder County desperately tried to hold onto its liberal roots, Weld celebrated itself as the Wild Wild West. County Line Road marked the border not just between counties, but at times it seemed Boulder and Weld were two entirely different countries. Erin found it fitting that ICE would establish a major presence there.

Weld County, which stretched from the Denver metropolitan area to the Wyoming border, was the richest agricultural county in the United States east of the Rocky Mountains. Besides abundant corn, hay, and wheat, its fertile plains supported a multitude of cattle, poultry, and dairy farms. Oil and natural gas production added to its lucrative use of the land. The 2.5-million-acre county had a formidable presence in the state, but in the years leading up to the insurrection Weld campaigned to secede from Colorado to distance itself from the state government's progressive policies. That effort failed. However, in 2019 the county did declare itself to be a Second Amendment sanctuary.

Now the entire nation was a Second Amendment sanctuary. And now, of course, there was no further need for Weld to divorce its home state.

When Erin made the appointment to go inside, no restrictions prohibited her from bringing in a phone or other electronics, so she felt that wearing her spy glasses would be safe. Even so, the sprawling complex surrounded by high fencing topped by wicked-looking razor wire did a good job at intimidating anyone in its shadow, which Erin supposed was the plan. It had her properly spooked.

John Yates held the title of Special Agent in Charge of the center, which turned out to be involved with more than detention.

As Erin took a seat in front of his desk, she was struck by his casual, easy-going manner. Based on Dylan's warning, she had expected an overtly villainous creature. She guessed that he was about forty-five years old, but his blond hair and pale blue eyes gave him a more youthful appearance. His smooth voice carried a slight Texan accent. He wore slacks and a matching vest with shirt sleeves rolled up and collar open. However, the expensive Bulgari watch and diamond-studded Bulgari wedding band didn't quite fit the puzzle.

"Is this strictly a detention center?" Erin asked. "I was surprised to see two signs outside: one for US Immigration and Customs Enforcement, and one for Homeland Security."

John took a sip from a black coffee cup that had the word *Patriot* embossed on it in gold. "ICE is part of DHS and has two bureaus. ERO—Enforcement and Removal Operations—is what most people associate with ICE. But we also have Homeland Security Investigations. HSI deals with criminal and terrorist activities that threaten the homeland. At this location we've combined both ICE and HSI under one roof as we move forward with a more expansive directive than we've operated under in the past."

Based on information in the press release, Erin's preliminary research had been strictly ICE-related, so she decided to start with that. "I understand that this detention center was seeded with detainees from Texas?"

"Our facility in Texas was overcrowded, so we contracted with a private company to build and run this new one. When this location opened, we brought our prisoner overflow with us. Overall, this operation is a hybrid of the government partnering with the private sector, and we've got big plans." He settled back in his chair and flashed a warm smile. "My wife and I find that we like living here so far. It's more appealing than Texas. The mountain views astound, don't they?"

Erin nodded and gestured toward the framed photograph on his bookcase of a pretty young woman and a child who appeared to be around five years old. "Your wife and son?"

His smile faltered. "Yes, but our son was killed in a car accident not long after the photo was taken. An illegal from Mexico who didn't understand our driving laws here caused the accident. No license, no insurance, no clue. They do it all the time. Wild animals with no concern for others. That's what led me into this work. I'm on a personal mission to send them all back. Every last goddamn one of them." The sudden edge to his voice and flash of ice in his eyes spoke volumes.

Erin struggled to find adequate words. "What a horrible loss. I'm so sorry."

He looked at the family photo, and his voice softened. "Kyle's death nearly destroyed my wife. It's been a rough road. I'm determined to do all I can to make things better."

"A new start in a new home is a good beginning."

He didn't reply.

"Do you have other children?"

"We tried for a long time after Kyle's murder, but Lisa's finally pregnant. Yes, we have a good new beginning."

Erin noted his use of the word murder. His rage was deep.

"Let's continue," he said.

Erin removed her phone from her purse. "May I take a photo of you for the story?"

"Of course." He offered her camera a charming smile.

"Is it okay if I record our interview?"

He nodded. "We want an accurate reporting."

Erin set the phone on his desk and pressed the record button. As a backup, she also surreptitiously tapped into action her spy glasses. "So, over and beyond the facts and figures included in your press release, what would you like to tell me about this facility?"

He leaned forward with his elbows on the desk, steepled his hands, and captured her with his eyes. "We're closing the borders. A new policy is being signed into law that completely changes our immigration policy. No more refugees will be accepted, no more asylum or sanctuary offered ... no more new citizens, period. It's time to lock out all the worthless trash and focus on Americans." His smile returned, but it wasn't as warm as it had been. "Every single person in our detention centers will be returned to their own countries, no matter how pitiful their tales of woe. A veritable army of new ERO officers is headed this way and will sweep Northern Colorado to round up all the illegals, detain them here, and then send them home."

Erin considered that plan of action and stated the obvious. "Well, there certainly are a lot of farm workers here illegally." She didn't mention all those who also worked in the restaurant and hospitality industry.

He sat up straight and pointed at her, his fingers cocked like a handgun. "Boom." The imaginary gun fired, his hand tipped back, and he blew away the phantom smoke.

"And what happens with this facility once that army of yours completes its mission?" she asked.

"As our population of illegals decreases, we'll be transitioning into a good, old-fashioned debtors' prison —the first of many across this country. The bankruptcy laws are being changed and we're going to start holding American citizens accountable for their debt. If they can't find a way to pay, they'll have to work it off while in custody." John chuckled. "A hell of a lot of those farmhand jobs will be available to fill."

Erin tried to wrap her mind around everything he had told her. "Excuse me, but what is the connection between people holding debt and Homeland Security?"

"The financial well-being of this country is implicit in its security. Part of our new directive is to strengthen the foundation of this nation. The legal system is being completely revamped. We will no longer prop up the weak, lazy masses looking for a free ride. No more welfare state. In this new society only the strong shall survive. The slogan for our new American plan is, Make America Strong."

Erin considered her own recent financial struggles and those of so many others impacted by the pandemic and other unforeseen tragedies. "But what about people who get in trouble through circumstances outside their control? That's not about being weak or lazy but about misfortune."

"Well, Mrs. Tavano, that's what family is for. There was a time not too long ago in this country when people took care of their own. That's an ethic we need to return to. And if a family can't or won't step up, then the state will step in. Mark my words, in a few short years this country will be the strongest and most healthy nation in the world."

And the most heartless, Erin thought. "These new laws are ... monumental. And quite a surprise."

"A lot of changes are being made with very little fanfare to avoid the inevitable resistance that change brings."

"Then why are you telling me this now?"

"We've just been given permission to go on the record. It's *a fait acompli*. A done deal. Protests—even if they were still allowed—will accomplish nothing."

Erin glanced at his jewelry again and wondered who this man really was. A simple government employee? Doubtful. He projected a type of dynamic energy usually associated with significant prestige and power. That stray thought captured her imagination and led her down an unexpected rabbit hole. Could he represent some new division of Homeland Security? If she had to put a label on her sudden suspicions, it would be in the realm of Izzy's worldview—an elite force analogous to the Nazi SS. That idea stole her breath, so she took a moment to study her notes and regain her equilibrium before proceeding.

"I presume armies of ERO officers will be fighting this battle nationwide?" she asked.

John nodded. "And we've recruited tens of thousands more Border Patrol Agents to prevent the crossings in the first place. They'll be directed to shoot to kill, blow up the boats, take down the smuggler's planes. Hell, most of those who are sneaking in are criminals, terrorists, and cartel members anyway. Killing them won't be a loss to humanity. No more playing nice. This country won't allow itself to be taken advantage of by the rest of the world any longer. At DHS our sacred mission is first, foremost, and always to protect the homeland."

Erin's mind raced. "And this expanded directive you mentioned that involves HIS?"

"Besides our stated mission to take on TCOs—Transnational Criminal Organizations—and terrorist networks, we're now authorized to take out of play all manner of internal threats to the homeland. Enemies of the state, anarchists, deviants—those who foment rebellion in any form. No one will be allowed to impede the fulfilment of our divinely ordained patriotic vision."

It took a beat for Erin to find her voice again. "Well, I feel like I've just received the scoop of the century." It seemed there would be no need to write a sanitized version of this story for the *Maverick* and the truth for *The North Star*. She could just lay the truth bare. "I will have to fact-check my story, of course. Would you please refer me to some key members of the new government who can corroborate what you've told me."

John's animated face froze, and the affronted look he threw at her reinforced her perception of his importance in this new American hierarchy. After an uncomfortable silence, he said, "You're not the type of reporter I expected from an insignificant community newspaper."

"No matter what publication we write for, good journalists always fact-check."

"I see." A tight smile cracked his icy expression into a mosaic of sharp shards. "I'll have Eve, my secretary, put together contact information for you. While she does that, why don't you relax and take a cigarette break." He gestured to the pack of cigarettes peeking out of the pocket of her suit jacket. "We have an outdoor recreation area on the women's side of the facility that you may use. I'll have someone show you the way. However, please leave your phone behind. I don't want any photos taken of our prisoners. We need to protect their privacy."

Two simultaneous thoughts passed through Erin's mind. One was that after leaving today she would have to immediately connect with Dylan to make sure her phone hadn't been compromised, and two was that she doubted they remotely cared about anyone's privacy.

And those thoughts led her to wonder exactly what they did have to hide.

***

The women's outdoor recreational area was simply a large fenced-in area on the west side of the complex; just a few concrete benches scattered atop a concrete slab. After Erin's interview with John Yates, it didn't surprise her that no creature comforts were offered.

The day was cold, but clear, and the rank smell of a nearby dairy farm tinged the air. The only person outside was one woman seated on a bench in the far northeast corner, huddled up against the main building.

RESISTANCE

As Erin approached her, the woman's eyes fell first to her press badge and then the pack of cigarettes. "I trade you my story for cigarette."

Erin glanced at her very pregnant stomach and pulled a Hershey's chocolate bar from her shoulder bag. "How about this instead?"

"I take that, too."

Erin laughed at her boldness and sat down. She handed over the chocolate but not the cigarettes.

"You Americans make me crazy always acting like you know what best for everyone. Here they treat me like I am fragile as butterfly wing. My *babusya* smoked every day, and her babies were strong. Ukrainian women are more strong than anyone. We had to be." She held out her empty hand and waited.

"But if they don't want you to smoke, I'd hate to get you in trouble so maybe—"

"The cameras not show this corner. It called blind space. I find this out from guard when I said I wished for somewhere to be alone. The guards, they like me and tell me things. Everyone here try to make me happy."

Erin scanned the yard and took note of the strategically placed mounted cameras. Against her better judgement, she handed over a cigarette and a book of matches.

The woman lit the cigarette, inhaled deeply, and exhaled the smoke with a contented sigh. Handing the matches back, she introduced herself. "Sofia Kostenko. You ask questions now, reporter Erin."

Erin smiled at Sofia's self-assured, bossy manner. "Do they treat everyone here nicely, or just you?"

"Just me. They say the big man here worry because I am going to have baby. Everyone want to keep him happy."

"His wife is pregnant, so maybe he's sympathetic to the cause."

Sofia grunted. "Good woman. She train him well."

Erin studied her, trusting the glasses to record a complete picture. Sofia's sky-blue eyes and long, golden hair shone with classic Eastern European beauty. She was stunning. "Are you alone or is your husband here as well?"

"No husband. No one."

"How long have you been in ICE custody?"

"Since—" she paused to look down at her belly, "almost nine months? I not know for certain. Time means nothing here. When ICE first took me, I was sick with Chimera. For many, many weeks ... maybe months ... I was in infirmary. All big blur of memory. Then when prisoners move here, I come with."

So, Sofia had been relocated as part of the overflow prison population John Yates spoke about. Erin dug a notebook and pen out of her bag. "Please tell me your story."

Sofia took another long drag of smoke and exhaled it in rings. "When Russia invade in 2022 most of my family die. I want to stay and get revenge, but I more want to get my sister Anna to safe place. We escape to Poland. I made stupid—" she slapped her forehead "—stupid mistake of trust. Woman told me she was part of team to settle refugees, and we went with her in car. She gave us food and water, and next I knew we woke up in strange place with other girls and women. We were not rescued, we were took by traffickers. Ended up in America and both forced to do sex work. Anna only fourteen." With a trembling hand she swiped sudden tears off her cheek and then caressed the delicate gold cross that hung around her neck. "I escape and find help, but when we go back Anna and others gone. Stupid me."

Erin wanted to tell her she was brave, not stupid, but those words felt hollow. Instead, she said, "I can't imagine your pain and how frightened you must be for Anna."

Sofia seemed surprised by Erin's compassion. From inside a small Bible on the bench between them, she withdrew a photograph of a girl. "Anna Kostenko."

Erin took the photo and studied it. The Kostenko sisters didn't share the same coloring, but their high cheekbones and bow-shaped lips were identical. "She's lovely."

"You take picture and find. I not know when I get out of here, and nothing matter more than finding Anna."

From what John told her, Erin knew that when Sofia was released, she would be immediately sent back to Ukraine. "Have they told you what will happen to your baby?"

"What will happen?"

Erin felt she had worded that wrong. "Do you want to keep your baby, or because of the circumstances surrounding conception will you give it up?"

Sofia's eyes narrowed. "Give baby up? What the hell you talking about? I love my baby." Her free hand cradled her belly protectively. "No one take my baby from me."

Once again Erin felt as if she had stumbled. "I thought because you were raped maybe—"

"Rape has nothing to do with my love for baby. My

babusya was born from rape by Russian soldier during the Holodomor. She was family and loved much. The enemy bastards can take many things from us, but not our love for family."

"I'm sorry ... I didn't mean ..." Erin's voice died along with her words. She was making a mess of this.

Quite deliberately and with eyes fastened on Erin's face, Sofia crushed the glowing ember on the end of her cigarette with her bare fingers. "You Americans are weak and gutless. Even this whole new government of yours—" her arm swept the air around them "—is like America trapped in loveless marriage with itself. No honesty, no promises kept. Country of bullies and the bullied. I do not like it here. I want to get Anna and take her and my baby home."

Erin didn't want to ask the question, but felt it was important. "What if your sister is dead?"

Instead of responding with anger or indignation, Sofia said, "Oh, I know Anna is alive because she does not talk to me. The dead, they talk to us. We Ukrainians know that. We always know that. You not hear your dead?"

Erin thought of Brian and the dream she had of him the night she dozed in his bedroom. "Yes, my brother might have spoken to me once. Mostly, I talk to him."

She cocked her head. "Do you listen for him?"

Erin's eyes burned. "No, I don't suppose I do."

"You should try. You might have surprise." Erin tried to hand Anna's photograph back, but Sofia refused it. "I told you to take and find her."

Erin didn't need it but couldn't explain that her glasses had recorded it. "I'll make a copy and return it to you."

"You do so." Sofia handed the dead cigarette butt to Erin and stood. "You sit here and look at beautiful mountains and think about how good it is to be alive. With life there is hope." Picking up her Bible, Sofia went back inside the prison.

Shaky, Erin felt as if she had collided with a great force of nature. Obediently, she stared at the glorious mountains in the distance. From this far away, she could see a wide expanse of the Front Range, and its beauty did make her feel alive and hopeful. Strange that. She imagined Sofia sitting here day after day mining that hope.

"Incredible view, isn't it?"

Erin started at the woman's voice. Guiltily, she slipped the dead cigarette butt into her coat pocket and stood to face John's secretary.

Eve handed her an envelope. "Here are the names and numbers you requested, and here is your phone back. Please let me know if you require anything else."

"Thank you." Erin slipped the two items into her purse.

"You're Brian Doyle's sister, aren't you?"

"Why yes. You knew him?"

"I worked with Brian at the high school. I was a teacher, too. We were horrified to hear of his death. I am so sorry."

Erin studied the woman, trying to remember when they might have met. "Why did you leave teaching to work here?"

Eve lowered her voice to a near whisper. "Because if I had stayed, my secrets might have been discovered, and I would have been fired for the same reason Brian was."

Brian had been fired for being gay.

"And you're not nervous they'll find out here? I think that would be a more frightening prospect."

"Here I don't have a cadre of neurotic parents poking around in my personal business looking for another human being to demonize, so my odds of flying under the radar are better. Also, I think given the way things are shaping up, I might be of more use here. That's worth the risk." She smiled. "I included my personal cell number on that list I gave you. As I said, please let me know if you require anything else."

***

"BREAKING NEWS: Disaster struck the *Boulder Maver*ick tonight when a diabolical, card-counting cub reporter wiped out all the senior journalists. When asked to comment on her dirty deeds, she said, 'Don't hate me. I needed to boost my confidence somehow.'" Erin raised her celebratory glass of Jameson. "*Sláinte!*"

Ian raised his White Russian. "I'll double your entendre, and raise you my deepest, darkest secret."

Sasha, Harlan, and Dylan raised their drinks.

"*L'Chaim*," Harlan said.

"Well done," Sasha said.

"We were warned," Dylan conceded.

Erin eyed the big pile of poker chips on the table in front of her and laughed. "I could get used to winning, but to be more sporting, next time we do this maybe we should play seven card stud instead. I've never been able to card count in that game."

"It's a deal," Ian said. "Now the time has come to claim your winnings. You can ask each of us one question and we must answer truthfully, but please be gentle."

Erin didn't have a desire to pull anyone's covers; she just wanted to get to know her new colleagues better. "Then I guess I'll ask everyone the same question: why did you choose journalism?"

"Oh, thank God for an easy one," Ian said with obvious relief. "My big brother was a war correspondent and I wanted to follow in his dashing footprints. Thought it would be glamorous, sexy, and exciting. It wasn't." He downed his drink and gestured to Dylan.

"Red pill/blue pill," Dylan said. "I always wanted to escape the propaganda and know the truth. I'm good with the investigative aspect of the business, but I'm a shit writer. I do rock the camera though. Photojournalism and cybersecurity both speak to my crazy creative soul."

The way he lit up made Erin think of Izzy. Passion for their chosen paths simply oozed out of both of them. It was charming. "Sasha?"

"Family tradition. My grand aunt was a reporter for *The Pittsburg Courier* and covered the Civil Rights Movement in the sixties. Her sass and courage were the stuff of legend. I always wanted to channel her spirit."

"What a legacy." Erin wanted to know more but would save that conversation for a later time. "Harlan?"

Harlan grimaced. "Oh dear, my path was way more complicated. Where to begin?" He rubbed his shiny bald head for a few moments while he pondered. "Well, I followed my own family's tradition and came to CU to study law, but then my community suffered its own pandemic." He tugged on his beard. "Oddly, those times were eerily like these times. Charismatic conservative figures like Jerry Falwell, Pat Robertson, Anita Bryant, and the whole Moral Majority nutjob choir preaching hate toward the gay and lesbian community. Accusing us of being pedophiles. Demonizing us for AIDS, saying it was God's punishment for our wicked, wicked ways. The civil rights that we did have were lost, and we became an underground community that had only each other to rely on." He took a deep breath and slumped in his chair. "But I digress. So, one bitterly cold night I was walking home from the campus library, took a shortcut, and literally stumbled over a guy I knew who was lying in a snowbank. I thought he was dead. I was able to wake him up, but he asked me to leave him there. He said he had full-blown AIDS, his family rejected him, and he wanted the simple and relatively painless death of freezing rather than a long, agonizing, and lonely death from the plague. But I couldn't ..." He faltered. "I couldn't honor his wishes. Carried him home. Cared for him while he endured the long goodbye. Held him as he died. Paid to have his body cremated and returned his ashes to the earth because his own family wouldn't even do that." Harlan's eyes filled with tears. "I often wonder if I should have just left Danny in the snow because he ended up suffering something fierce. Then I remind myself that at least he died knowing he was loved. Maybe there was a measure of healing in that for him?"

Erin handed him a clean cocktail napkin. "Please don't go on. I didn't mean to ask something that would cause upset."

He wiped his eyes, then waved his hand in dismissal. "No, just bear with me. I haven't talked about this in forever, and it does weigh heavily."

Dylan stood, grabbed a fresh bottle of craft beer from the bar, and set it—along with a shot of apple brandy—in front of Harlan. As he retook his seat, Erin noticed that he, too, appeared shaken.

Harlan threw back the shot, chased it with the beer, then cleared his throat. "My apartment became a hospice center for people with AIDS who had been abandoned by everyone else. In those days little was known about the disease, and those who developed it were treated like lepers. I dropped out of school, and with the help of the remarkable lesbian community, started fundraising to support my efforts. Began staging community rock concerts to make money. That led to bigger concerts and bigger bands. Along the way I submitted stories to various publications to bring attention to our cause, but few were published. Eventually, I started the *Maverick* to feature stories other papers wouldn't touch. And here we all are."

"Wow, I never knew," Dylan said. "How could I not have known that?"

Sasha reached out and took Harlan's hand.

"This man is the heart and soul of us," Ian said. "And, Harlan Weismann, I am honored to be part of what you created."

Erin nodded. "Likewise."

Harlan waved the napkin like a flag of surrender. "Let's move on. How about you, cub reporter? Why journalism?"

Erin considered. "Well, I suppose, like Dylan, I felt it was important to separate truth from lies. My mother has always lived in a fantasy world, and it was a rough way to be raised. I wanted to be the clear voice of truth but then gave it all up for love. Then love gave up on me. And I find I have come full circle."

"Your first story is damn impressive," Ian said.

Erin's stomach fluttered with pleasure. She had just filed the ICE story, and it was the first feedback she had received. "Thank you. There's more I hope to uncover. I have a source on the inside—it seems members of the Resistance are more prevalent than I imagined. And I've started researching John Yates. You were right about him, Dylan."

"Do you need help with that?" Dylan asked.

Erin shook her head. "I've got it covered, but thanks."

Dylan raised a questioning brow. "Oh, you do, do you?"

They exchanged knowing glances. Izzy was Erin's ace in the hole.

"What's next?" Ian asked her.

"After Maisie Mae brings Violet back tonight, I've been invited over to her place for homemade pralines and authentic New Orleans chicory coffee. I'm hoping to learn more about Pastor Christian Tobias of the Rocky Mountain Patriot Church."

"It might be helpful to know some background on Maisie Mae, if you're interested?" Sasha said.

"That would be great. Everyone filters truth through the lens of their own experience."

"Off the record?" Sasha asked.

Erin nodded. "Of course."

"Last year, her husband Henri died. They had no children and were a sunshine-filled world unto themselves. When hyperinflation led to banks collapsing, Henri lost his job in the financial industry. Their savings went fast, and their house was about to be foreclosed." Sasha paused and grew pensive. "Henri committed suicide and made it look like an accident.

See, he wanted her to get the life insurance that would save the house and set her up for the future."

"How do you know it was suicide?" Erin asked.

Sasha took a sip of her wine. "He left a suicide note for her. She brought it to me, and I advised her to burn it. I told her that if she showed the authorities, it would mean that Henri had made his great sacrifice for nothing. We burned that letter together."

Shocked, Erin looked at everyone else around the table. Their expressions told her that they already knew the truth and were waiting for her reaction. How *did* she feel about that? After a moment of reflection, she found the words. "His love for her was extraordinary." Then Erin thought about Harlan's history. "I guess that, in the end, all that really does matter is love."

***

The large Victorian house that held the *Boulder Maverick* offices was elegant. In contrast, Maisie Mae's smaller Victorian house was as kitschy as kitschy could be.

The exterior had been painted in Mardi Gras colors of green and purple, with gold decorative trim. Inside, the parlor looked like Carnival on Bourbon Street.

Crowded and vibrant, strings of purple and green lights illuminated a wild variety of wall-mounted masks; the Venetian masks, feather masks, jester masks, masquerade masks, animal masks, skull masks, and comedy and tragedy masks resembled a gallery of intriguing, mysterious revelers. Bowls heaped with colorful bead necklaces were scattered throughout the room, and multicolored feather boas wound around the staircase banister that led to a balcony which overlooked the parlor.

Two flags hung from the balcony: the City of New Orleans flag with its distinctive three golden *fleurs-de-lis*, and the flag of the Rocky Mountain Patriot Church with its logo of the American flag overlayed by images of a Christian cross and two crossed rifles. The motto embossed on it read, *God, Guts, & Glory*.

A display of happy photos featuring Maisie Mae and Henri stretched across the mantel of the ornate fireplace, and basking in the warmth of the cozy fire was the largest stuffed alligator Erin had ever seen, its glass eyes glittering with maniacal glee.

"If you sit on the alligator, it roars," Maisie Mae told her.

"I imagine Violet loves that," Erin said, choosing instead to sit on the plush loveseat next to her hostess.

Maisie Mae tossed a handful of necklaces to her. "All of our ... *my* guests are welcomed with necklaces and the greeting *laissez les bons temps rouler!* That means 'let the good times roll.'"

Erin hung the long strings of beads around her neck. "Thank you. This solves the mystery of why Violet is always wearing these. I see why she loves it here."

Maisie May giggled. "We have so much fun together."

The coffee table was already set with refreshments, and Maisie May picked up the thermal carafe and filled two distinctive coffee mugs on which New Orleans jazz bands were depicted in glorious detail. "Aren't these cups wonderful? The artist is Guido Borelli."

Erin accepted the mug offered to her and examined it. "His work is so unique."

"You just can't drink authentic chicory coffee out of any old mug. Doll it up with the steamed milk and sugar if you want. Some people find plain chicory bitter."

Erin did as she suggested and was delighted to discover she liked the woody-flavored beverage.

"I made these fresh today," Maisie Mae said as she offered Erin a praline.

The sweet, creamy, nutty confection caused Erin to utter some obscene moans, which seemed to please her hostess. "Wow," was all Erin could manage to say.

Maisie Mae clapped her hands and giggled again. "I'm happy you like it."

Erin marveled at the woman's childlike manner.

"Now you need to ask me all about my Pastor Christian. I'm so excited you're writing a story about him."

Erin set the coffee mug down and pulled her phone from her purse. "May I record our interview?"

"Why of course. Oh, I hope you use my name in the paper so Pastor Christian will read it and find out how much I love him. The church is so big and so many people go there that I don't think he even knows who I am."

Erin wondered how anyone could overlook this unique woman. "Well, let's begin with why you started attending the Rocky Mountain Patriot Church. What drew you to it?"

Maisie Mae fondled the wedding ring she still wore. "Well, when my beloved Henri died, I fell deep down in the well of sadness. Even with all the happy pills the doctors fed me, I wasn't sure I wanted to go on living. Sasha was really kind to me and taking care of little Violet helped—I love them both so much—but it wasn't enough. Then a friend, Franny Campbell, invited me to go with her to church services."

"So, you haven't been attending the church too long then?"

"Just a few months, but oh my, that Pastor Christian just stole my heart and soul." Maisie Mae's face looked rapturous. "He's so handsome, and dynamic, and God's truth simply flows from his lips like sweet honey."

"What's special about his message?"

"I suppose it's that he has eliminated the nasty Jewish Old Testament from our worship. He had the divine inspiration and courage to break from tradition and call it out for what it is."

Erin had never been religious, but she knew that the Old Testament was an integral part of Christianity. "And what does he say it is?"

"That it's simply full of vile, disgusting things. All manner of wickedness: orgies, idols, incest, rape, sodomy, and even bestiality. Did you know that Solomon married hundreds of women who worshipped at the altars of perversion? It even contains instructions on how to sell your daughters into slavery. And their cult of circumcision, well that's just sex abuse of children—a total travesty that they've imposed on our society today. That's why pedophilia has become the curse of American culture. My goodness, those Jews are a nasty bunch. Mercy me, there is absolutely no place for them in Christianity. They shouldn't even be part of our society."

Erin was at a loss for how to respond. Finally, she said, "But Jesus was a Jew."

Maisie Mae looked appalled. "No, no, no. Jesus is the son of God and God is no Jew. That's why the Jews murdered Jesus ... because he came to try to change all their evil and wickedness."

Uneasy at all the implications of her words, Erin glanced up at the flag. "Why does the church's logo include a gun?"

Maisie Mae reached into the big pocket of her housedress, pulled out a small handgun, and cradled it in her lap. "Because having guns is our God-given right as Americans, of course. Isn't this baby pretty? I bought it right there at the church and learned to shoot there, too. The pastor's wife, Miss Bethany, she teaches a self-defense course for all the ladies. It's so much fun."

Fun? Erin's thoughts raced to Violet. "I presume you keep that gun locked up when Violet's here?"

"Of course not. How would I protect her if I did that?" She reached out and patted Erin's knee. "But don't you worry your pretty little head about any accidents. I keep the gun safely tucked away in my pocket when she's around. I am a soldier in God's army and must be armed at all times. Have you heard the Rocky Mountain Patriot Church's theme song?"

Still stunned, Erin couldn't find her suddenly elusive voice, so she simply shook her head.

For a little woman, Maisie Mae belted it out with gusto.

"Onward Christian soldiers, marching as to war,
With the cross of Jesus going on before.
Christ, the royal Master, leads against the foe;
Forward into battle see His banners go!"

She applauded herself. "Isn't it perfect? We're not just Christians who are soldiers, we're Pastor Christian's soldiers."

Wow. Erin took a deep breath and reminded herself she was a journalist. "And please tell me why you think Pastor Christian Tobias would make a good congressman?"

"Because he's a man of God, and he understands that the Jews have been controlling us. He's vowed to set us free."

Erin swallowed hard. "Can you elaborate?"

"They're filthy rich—there are hundreds of billionaire Jews—and with great money comes great power. The Rothchild and Soros families? Bloomberg, Zuckerberg, Spielberg? Controlling the banking, news, internet, and entertainment industries, which in turn has controlled our lives and our minds." Maisie Mae's eyes shifted from warm to ice cold, and she patted the gun. "Henri would be alive right now if they hadn't crashed the banks for their own sinister purposes. But things are changing now, and Pastor Christian is going to be a big part of getting rid of those evil creatures."

A wave of nausea rose in Erin. "May I use your restroom?"

Maisie Mae pointed to an archway toward the back of the room. "Sure, sugar. Through there and to your left."

Erin barely made it to the toilet before she lost the contents of her stomach. As she knelt and tried to control a second bitter wave, her mind filled with horrible thoughts. Chief among them were that Violet was in danger, that her own sister was a proud member of this church, that truly awful things were unfolding in plain sight, and that Izzy had been right about everything all along.

***

Brian Doyle's most cherished possession was the 1967 Mustang Fastback that he had restored himself. The classic muscle car was red with a black interior, had bucket seats, a wooden steering wheel, and had been his pride and joy. Izzy was sure there were all kinds of wonderful features under the hood too, but those specs were beyond her comprehension. All she knew was that one of the biggest surprises of her life was when her grandmother said that Brian appeared in a dream and told her to pass his legacy on to his niece. Kelly handed Izzy the title at her birthday breakfast that morning.

"You sure did score today," Karma said. She was in the car with Izzy via FaceTime; the phone's lanyard hung from the rearview mirror. She had spent the entire morning with Izzy and her family as they celebrated.

"Thank you for your gift," Izzy said. Karma had written a song for her, and this morning was its debut performance. "It was freakin' fabulous."

"I recorded it and sent you a copy."

"You should record an entire album of your music," Izzy said.

Karma instantly deflected. "Were you happy with Luca's gift? I picked up on some less than enthusiastic vibes."

Aunt Meg and Uncle Beau had helped Luca purchase the retractable Smith and Wesson baton. "I loved the baton—it's much better quality than the one I've got—but I wasn't happy about him pushing for me to teach him how to use it. I don't trust him to use any kind of weapon responsibly. You know, the whole bully thing."

"Hopefully, it's just a stage he's going through."

Izzy wasn't too sure about that. "Papa said he denied pushing Ryan at school. He flat-out lied. When I see Dad tonight, I'm going to tell him that he really needs to step up and do the parenting thing again."

"Maybe you should ... oh, never mind."

"No, go ahead," Izzy urged.

"Well, it's been what, over six months since you've spent any time with your dad? Maybe you should just be present to him instead of criticizing? Just provide an open space for the two of you to reconnect. No agenda."

Izzy grinned. "That's very Buddhist of you."

"Buddha did kinda rock the wisdom." Karma had recently been studying the deeper aspects of Buddhism with Mei Ling.

The subject of religion, any religion, made Izzy uncomfortable, but she was glad Karma had found comfort in hers. "Thank you for the advice. You're right, as usual. I'll try to be cool."

Izzy found a parking space in the packed lot outside of the farmer's market. This was the first Sunday she had been here, and it seemed even busier than it had been on the Saturday she had visited. "Do you want to come in with me?"

"Oh no, I think you should have some alone time with Dante. I know you *really* like him."

Izzy's stomach fluttered. "I'm not saying you're right or wrong, but doesn't that make you feel strange? I mean, he's so much like Miguel wouldn't it make you uncomfortable if I got to know him better?"

Karma smiled. "Dante is nothing like Miguel. You and I saw Miguel through totally different eyes. I fell in love with Miguel's essence, not his charisma. When you really get to know Dante, you'll understand what I mean."

Even though Karma was only a year older than Izzy, she was eons wiser.

Izzy blew Karma a kiss, they signed off, and Izzy

texted Dante to let him know she had arrived. He responded that he would meet her at the front gate of Wildwind Territory.

"You again?" the familiar, surly guard said in greeting.

"I'm shameless," Izzy replied, flashing what she hoped was a dazzling smile.

"Jesus Christ on a cracker." His handheld gizmo scanned her eyes, and then he buzzed the gate open.

Dante was there to meet her. He slid his arm around her and said in a low, sexy voice, "Hiya, baby."

Grumpy Guard sneered, turned away from them, and stalked back into the guard station.

Dante winked at her. "Angry people will always find something to be angry about. It makes them happy." He released her. "It's good to see you. You said you had something for my dad? Barring emergencies, Sundays are his day off. Hopefully, I can stand in?"

Izzy nodded and gestured toward the medical office. "I'd prefer to talk in there where we can have some privacy."

Dante led the way, unlocked the front door, and ushered Izzy inside. Then they each set their phones down on the front desk and went into the examination room where she fervently hoped there really was no surveillance.

"Did your dad tell you that I promised to bring some medicine?" Izzy set her large shoulder bag on the exam table and withdrew a half dozen big, pharmacy-sized bottles of Amoxicillin and a cooling case filled with insulin pens and vials.

Dante gasped. "No, he didn't." He examined the bounty. "What the actual hell?"

"I have connections. I wanted to help."

"But this must have cost a fortune. You didn't tell me you were independently wealthy."

She chuckled. "If only. No, I traded some computer services for them. My source is legitimate. I can't really elaborate, but it's quality stuff. My great-grandfather uses medication from the same place."

Dante regarded her with wonder. "You have no idea the lives you just changed. This is a true miracle."

And that right there was what Izzy didn't like about religion. Useful miracles didn't haphazardly shower down from a place called Heaven. People helping each other was the true stuff of miracles. "Glad I could help."

"You have no idea," he repeated. "Thank you so much."

"Let me know when you need more."

"Really? Wow."

"Do you have a refrigerator for the insulin?"

That seemed to snap him out of his gratitude stupor. "Yes, of course." He unlocked the closet door where there was a small dorm-sized refrigerator. After he put the insulin inside, he returned Izzy's cooling case. Then he placed the antibiotic bottles on top of the fridge and locked the closet back up.

"Well, this is a banner day for the Wildwind Clinic," he said.

"If the clinic isn't open today, why are you here?" Izzy asked.

"I'm here every day to tend the gardens."

"Gardens?"

"I didn't tell you about them? Oh, you've got to let me show you."

He ushered her out of the clinic, and while he was

locking it up Izzy saw Joplin and Jagger kneeling by the fence trying to pet a dog who was on the other side.

Izzy gestured toward them. "Don't they ever get to leave here?"

"I take them out whenever I can," Dante said. "But I don't like them wandering around unsupervised. There are some truly awful people out there."

Izzy knew that to be terribly true.

Joplin noticed Izzy and ran up to her. "Hi, Isabelle Tavano. You look a whole lot better today than the last time I saw you. You were pretty hideous then."

"Yes, I was, wasn't I?"

"You must be feeling better?"

"It's been a good day."

Joplin cocked her head. "What made it good?"

"Today is my birthday, and the people I love made it special for me."

"Did you get nice birthday presents?"

Izzy didn't want to brag about all the amazing things she received, but she did say, "My friend Karma wrote a song just for me. It was beautiful."

"'Where words fail, music speaks,'" Joplin said. "That's a quote from Hans Christian Anderson."

"It's a wonderful quote," Izzy said.

Joplin looked at her brother, who was still engrossed with his canine friend. "Music speaks to Jagger when words can't."

Izzy's heart ached for their struggle.

"Well, I've got to get back to him," Joplin said. "You kids go on and have fun now."

As she ran away Izzy laughed. "She's like twelve going on thirty."

"She has to be," Dante said.

Izzy felt her eyes start to burn but pushed the sadness back ... she'd never live it down if she got all hideous again. "So, your gardens?"

"My secret gardens," he said with an air of mystery. "Come right this way, my lady. My magical lair awaits."

Izzy followed him all the way to the back of the medical building. "It doesn't seem nearly this big from the inside."

"Ha! In its advertising, Wildwind Western Wear describes the medical center as being as big as this entire building, but three-quarters of it was just an unused storage area. I took that over and behold my magnificent feat." He unlocked the back door and ushered her inside.

The sight that greeted them took her breath away. There were rows upon rows of vertical shelves containing all manner of vegetable and fruit plants in various stages of maturation. The multicolored lights scattered throughout the hydroponic gardens and the sound of trickling water lent an almost mystical quality to the scene. As Izzy wandered up and down the rows of foliage, cool moist air carried the sweet aroma of basil, the sharp scent of peppermint, the earthy smell of tomatoes, and the sweet fragrance of Concord grapes.

"It's incredible," Izzy said. "I could totally imagine fairies living here ... you know, if fairies were a thing."

"I told you it was magical."

The gardens contained herbs of all kinds, a myriad of leafy greens, bell peppers, cherry tomatoes, green onions, celery, strawberries, and even some flowers. An integrated trellis system supported the growth of cucumbers, snow peas, grapevines, and other climbing vegetation.

"You did all this?"

"I constructed it with Rafael's help, but yeah, it's my baby. This is the future. I wanted to get a degree in urban farming—Cornell University has a great Controlled Environment Agriculture program—but, well, our country exploded and blew that dream to hell."

"Do you sell the produce at the farmer's market?"

He shook his head. "It's just for the people here. Wildwind provides them so little nourishment I had to do something to supplement it. It's amazing how much can be grown with limited resources. The water's recycled, the lights are LED, the space is maximized. If this technology were used inside a building the size of one big box retail store you could produce what 700 acres of conventional farmland can. Plus, it's organic, safer, and can be transported more quickly to the consumer. Like I said, it's the future."

"You sort of glow when you talk about it."

His smile widened. "Yeah, I've found my bliss."

"Does Wildwind mind you doing this for its people? It doesn't seem like a caring institution."

"They've seen it and brought it up in a meeting with my dad, but he told them it's part of a comprehensive nutritional program he's implemented to keep the workers healthy. As much as they want to keep the peasants needy, they also want them to be productive. And it's not costing the company much money. So, for now, I guess I have Wildwind's indulgence."

"Why all the different colored lights?"

"That's the art of the science. Different plants benefit from different wavelengths at different times in their growth cycle."

"I'm seriously impressed, Castillo."

Dante took Izzy's hand and led her to a section of strawberry plants, picked one of the large berries, and offered it to her.

She bit into the sweet, juicy fruit. "Omigod, this is delicious."

"Let me harvest some for you as a birthday present." He pulled a small bag from his jacket pocket.

"No, I don't want to take them from the people who live here."

"I insist. Please accept the gift; consider it from all of us."

Izzy didn't want to be rude. "Just a few then."

When he handed them to her, he did so with reverence. Izzy figured that for him this was akin to sharing treasure, and she accepted it accordingly. "Thank you. I'll enjoy them so much. I can't even remember the last time I had fresh strawberries." She gently placed the precious gift inside her shoulder bag.

Dante cleared his throat. "Ah, so, I wanted to ask if I could take you out sometime. Dinner or a movie maybe?"

Startled, she blurted out, "You mean like on a date?" then immediately followed with, "I don't date."

Disappointment washed over him. "Okay. I get it."

Izzy saw that he had misunderstood and reached out to touch his arm. "Really. I don't date ... anyone. I have, um, well I have issues."

He took a deep breath. "I see."

Izzy's mind raced; she really did like him. "How about ... why don't you, Joplin, and Jagger come over to my house sometime? I can make pizza. I make good pizza. And we could watch a movie. Maybe a western for Jagger? My brother's ten, and he wants to be a cowboy when he grows up, although he is going through a real dickhead phase right now, but maybe Mojo, Papa's service dog, would make up for Luca being an unmitigated jerk." Izzy knew she was rambling, but the more she painted the picture, the more appealing it became to her.

Dante's smile returned. "That would be great."

Relief flooded her. "Really? Next Sunday afternoon?"

He nodded. "The timing would be ideal. Sundays are hard on the kids. With no work or entertainment, the day is long for them."

"We just moved in with family, so I've got to ask permission, but I'm sure it'll be okay. I'll text you?"

"I look forward to it."

Izzy felt a little bit giddy. "Okay then." She gestured to the door. "I'd better head out. I'm having dinner with my dad tonight and need to go psych myself up. Haven't seen him in a long time and Karma tells me I've got to be all serene, just like Buddha."

"I'm sure there's a story there for another time." He opened the door. "Let me walk you to your car."

They were near the outskirts of the public market when Izzy saw them, and the shock kicked her in the gut. Gasping, she grabbed Dante's arm and abruptly swung around to face him.

"What?" he asked.

"Those two guys behind me wearing white cowboy hats."

Dante looked over her shoulder. "Yeah, what about them?"

"They're the ones who attacked Karma. Well, the

shorter one held me back while the taller one tackled her and slashed her face. This is the first time I've seen them since."

"You're sure?"

Izzy was having trouble breathing, but she managed to nod.

Dante slipped his hand behind her neck and drew her into his chest. "Breathe." As he had the last time she hyperventilated, he enclosed her inside his coat until it passed.

After she regained control, she stepped back. "What am I going to do?" The world was spinning, and her knees trembled.

"Do you realize who they are?"

Confused, she shook her head.

"That's Nash and Billy Tobias, Pastor Christian Tobias's sons. Every Sunday after his church services, the pastor comes here with a bunch of his family and nutty disciples to drum up support for his political campaign."

"Holy hell."

"Yeah, Hell's where the entire family should be. They're awful people."

"What am I going to do?" she repeated. "Are there any cops around? They need to be arrested."

"Do you have proof it was them? Was it filmed? Other witnesses?"

She shook her head. "It happened inside her parent's restaurant after hours. Everyone else was gone. Karma and I were leaving, and they pushed their way in. It was brutal. It was the stuff of nightmares ... which we both still have. I have panic attacks—obviously—and Karma can barely leave her house. We're poster children for

PTSD. We need resolution."

Dante looked into her eyes for a long time. Finally, he said, "Our world is different now, Izzy. There is no justice when it comes to people like that. And, frankly, it could go very badly for you. They're powerful and dangerous." She started to protest, but he placed a gentle finger on her lips. "Just hear me out. If there's anything at all that can be done, I know the person you need to speak to. My sister's girlfriend, Shiloh, lives with her grandmother, Julia Bainbridge. Julia used to be one of the top criminal attorneys here in town. She's a big deal. Well connected. And really good people. If you want to talk to her, I'll put you in touch."

Izzy trusted him. "Okay."

"Now, do you have the strap for your cell phone with you?"

Izzy nodded.

"Put it on and set the phone to record video. We're going to walk right past them and see if they recognize you."

It only took a minute for Izzy to defeat her inner demon of fear, but the battle was intense. She had once spoken to Luther about how the attack on Karma had weakened her own innate courage, and he told her that strength came from fighting for what a person believed in. That weapon was much stronger than all the knives or batons she could possibly wield, and she invoked it now. Taking her cell phone from her pocket, she slipped the lanyard over her head and set the phone to record. Then she took a deep breath but couldn't get her feet to move.

Dante grasped her hand. "I got you."

His support gave her a surprising surge of

confidence, and this time her body cooperated with her mind.

Together they walked toward Nash and Billy. When they were just a few feet away, the taller one pointed at her. "Well, lookee there, Billy. It's the ch-ch-chink lover. How's your commie girlfriend?"

Izzy stopped and turned to face him. "Not as pretty as she was before you cut her up." She hoped to goad them into a confession, but instead they responded with raucous laughter, Nash gave her the finger, and then they simply walked away.

Dante squeezed her hand. "That was good."

"Not good enough."

"It's a beginning."

***

The handwritten sign on the door of Tony Tavano's read, *Closed for a private party*. When Izzy unlocked the door and stepped inside, the sight of the empty restaurant with a candlelit table set for two made her heart ache for all that had been lost. Then when Tony swept her up in a tight hug and whispered, "*Carissima*," her Buddhist-inspired serenity disappeared in an instant. Finally, when he drew back and gave her a look of pure love, it undid her entirely.

"How are you?" he asked.

"I'm just all kinds of emotional right now."

A sad smile crossed his face. "If it helps, I am too. Thank you for coming."

"Thank you for inviting me."

He gestured toward the waiting table. "Please, sit. I made all your favorites."

"All of them?"

He shrugged. "Best I could with what I had to work with. Sit, I'll be right back."

Izzy settled in. She couldn't remember the last time she dined in the front of the house. In the past, she usually ate at the little employee table in the kitchen, at the picnic table outside behind the restaurant, or while watching TV with her brother in the office. This room was elegant, or as her father referred to it, "snazzy." And the retro music fit that same description; Frank Sinatra's smooth rendition of "Fly Me to the Moon" floated from the speakers and caressed the air around her. She relaxed. In a strange way, she felt like she had left this place as a child and returned as an adult.

Tony came back to the dining room carrying a large, food-laden tray that he placed on a nearby stand. One by one he covered their table with a multitude of dishes. "Antipasto—I couldn't get true prosciutto, but I found a ham and put an Italian glaze on it. Caprese—I grew the basil leaves right here myself. Crispy pan-fried polenta with pesto—I finally was able to get cornmeal, so I ordered an extra twenty-five-pound sack for you to take home. Here's my famous pan-fried gnocchi in brown butter sauce, some fresh-baked garlic bruschetta, and an exquisite tiramisu for dessert." He placed a small stack of clean plates on the table and sat down across from her.

Izzy marveled at the feast before them. "Wow."

Tony poured sparkling Pellegrino into two champagne glasses and raised his. "To my beautiful seventeen-year-old Bella. Happy birthday."

She raised her glass. "*Salute.*" It was not lost on her that he wasn't drinking liquor. For that gift, she was immensely grateful.

Tony watched as she filled a plate with a little bit of everything. "I've missed cooking for you."

"And I've missed your cooking," she said. "Andrea and I were just talking about how much food means to us now that we can't always get what we want when we want."

He gestured toward the kitchen. "Food has always been important to us and people like us. It's been our life. Our identities. Our livelihood. Our creativity. The way we show our love."

That was true, Izzy realized.

"You're working for Andrea now?"

Izzy nodded. "I serve breakfast and lunch, Monday through Friday. It's easy for her to find college students to work the night and weekend shifts."

Tony raised his hands palms up in a gesture Izzy knew him to make when he was dealing with something inexplicable. "Lili and Johnny gone so fast. It's still hard to believe. How is Andrea doing?"

Izzy thought about it. "She puts on a brave front, but I know her too well. Losing her parents absolutely destroyed her."

He silently crossed himself. "I know that feeling."

Izzy knew that he did.

"I heard Santiago and Valentina sold The Seville and went back to Spain."

"After Miguel died, well ..." Izzy shrugged. "It's been especially hard on Luca because Esteban was his best friend."

He took a deep breath. "Luca? Your mother? How are they?"

Izzy had expected him to ask about them but hadn't decided how she should respond. After all, he could check directly if he really wanted to know, but he had completely ignored all three of them for over six months. The pain of that shared heartbreak was so profound she couldn't even begin to articulate how any of them were. She wanted to throw their anguish in his face, demand answers, call him out for his callousness. But selfishly she also wanted to enjoy the gift of his attention and not push him away. So, she simply said, "Mom found a job as a reporter, and Luca is enrolled at his new school."

Her response appeared to relieve him; it was as if he had been braced for battle. "Good. That's good."

Izzy wanted to ask what was going on inside of him. She wanted to know how he could live with himself. What was his heart feeling? How could he have walked away from the big love he had and so easily fall into another woman's bed? Instead, she asked, "How's business been?"

Tony shrugged. "Better. We're not even close to where we used to be, but yeah ... slowly getting better." He loaded up an empty plate for himself and dug in.

They both ate in silence for a while.

"This is wonderful," Izzy finally said.

His smile returned, stronger than before. He lifted his glass and tipped it toward her. "Your birthday. Did you get some fun gifts?"

"Fun? Well, Papa scored a free pass to a quantum computing webinar for me. He arranged it through an old friend of his at IBM. And—" she reached into her pocket and pulled out a beautiful, pearl-handled flip knife "—Mom gave me this." She pressed a button and a sharp Damascus steel blade instantly flipped up from inside the handle.

"Whoa."

Izzy laughed. "It's good for self-defense."

"You still have that throwing knife in your boot?"

Izzy closed the pocketknife and put it away. "Of course."

"I remember when Lili bought that for you. She asked for my permission since you were so young. I asked her if you could be trusted with it, and she said she would trust you with her life."

Startled, Izzy caught her breath. "Really? She said that?"

Tony nodded and his expression radiated pride.

Izzy couldn't imagine a higher compliment from her mentor. "Thank you for telling me."

He cleared his throat, took another sip of water, and put his glass down. "To that point ... on the subject of trust ..." He faltered. "Your mother always told me that I could tell you the truth when I felt you were ready." His hands massaged the air as if he was struggling with an unseen foe.

Izzy's spidey sense kicked into play, and she braced herself for something bad. Pushing her plate away, she folded her hands on the table in front of her and waited. Being with her father reminded her how often she, too, spoke with her hands. Keeping them purposefully still now helped her to remain centered.

Finally, Tony took a small package off the chair next to him and handed it to her. "I'm giving you the gift of my trust."

The small gold box had a white ribbon tied around it. With a profound sense of trepidation that wasn't at all rational, Izzy opened it. Inside there were two items: a Catholic rosary made of exquisite pearls and glistening gold, and a folded, yellowed newspaper article. Gently, so as not to ruin it, she unfolded the article and laid it flat on the table. The first thing that jumped out at her was the photograph—the man looked like her dad and the woman looked like an older version of herself. The second thing that grabbed her attention was the headline: *Local Family Killed in Mafia Bombing.* Below that the lede read, "Latest victims of Philadelphia mob wars include a six-year-old child." Izzy's eyes flicked up to the name of the paper: *The Philadelphia Inquirer.*

"What the hell, Dad?"

"Just read it," Tony said, his voice uncharacteristically soft.

She struggled to focus.

Yesterday morning, a car bomb exploded at the home of Vincenzo Moretti, a reputed captain in the Philly Mafia. Killed in the explosion were Vincenzo, his wife Isabella, and their sons, sixteen-year-old Antonio, and six-year-old Nico. This is the first time a bomb has been used in a local, high-level mafia hit since mob boss Philip Testa was killed by a bomb on his South Philly doorstep in 1981.

There was more, but Izzy couldn't get past the first paragraph. Feelings of unreality and harsh reality wrestled for control of her mind, and she found refuge in the strangely calm limbo between them. She looked at her father. "Apparently, you're not dead."

"Depends who you ask."

Izzy shook her head. "Moretti? Are you in witness protection? And what about the story I grew up believing that your parents were killed in a car accident? Oh, and Philadelphia? You always said you were from New Jersey." A hint of anger reared its ugly head at her edges. She felt foolish because she had honestly believed that her father's mysterious mob-related past was a total façade. It had never occurred to her to believe his jokes, innuendo, and tall tales. She always thought it was just about selling the restaurant brand.

Tony pointed to the article. "Every Sunday we went to church together, but that day Nick had the flu. I offered to stay home with him. Ma gave me her rosary and told me since I was going to miss Mass, I should use the time to pray. The garage was attached to the house. When the bomb went off—" his hands rose up and mimed an explosion "—it took out the whole place. Nick and I were in the back bedroom but managed to climb out a window. There had been rumors about a vendetta against us because one of my father's soldiers accidentally killed family members of a rival he was ordered to hit. I guessed that the bomb was supposed to settle the score. Scared, I took Nick up to our treehouse at the back of the property, and we hid there all day. That night I snuck out and went to my mother's brother, Gino, the underboss my father answered to. He fixed it that the police would report we were all killed. Otherwise ... well vendettas are always carried out, no matter how long it takes. My uncle gave us all very public funerals, got Nick and me new identities— Tavano was your great-grandmother's maiden name, a part of the family tree still in Italy. He gave me a suitcase full of money and two tickets to Denver. Although the ID made me eighteen years old, I had just turned sixteen three days before it all came down. I had to become a man overnight."

Izzy stared at him, her mind trying to process all of

it. "But the colorful stories you tell. Why bring up any of it again?"

He shrugged. "At his age, Nick couldn't keep everything secret that he should have. So, over the years I incorporated the stuff he blurted out into a semblance of reality. He didn't remember Philly, but he remembered the amusement parks at the Jersey Shore. He blocked out the explosion, but remembered our parents died in the car. He had overheard a lot of conversations between our dad and uncle talking about the family business. If I had tried to deny his memories it might have brought more attention to us than just going along with him like it was no big deal. It was a matter of life or death. It still is, Bella. *Capiche*?"

Yes, she understood all too well. "Who else knows?"

"I straightened Nick out when he became a man. I told your mother before she married me. I don't know who my uncle told, but of course it wouldn't be many people."

"Why are you telling me now?"

"A couple reasons. One is that a vendetta can span generations, so you should know, to protect yourself. I wasn't too worried because the mob lost a lot of strength due to relentless prosecution, but with the way our country's changed, it's growing again—the remaining roots have been watered and fed Miracle Gro. It's like how Prohibition basically created the American mafia as we came to know it. All those things that the new government has outlawed, and its dismantling of the FBI ... let's just say the mob is taking advantage of this time in history."

"Is there mafia here in Colorado?"

"The Denver branch of La Cosa Nostra was always

affiliated with the Five Families and the Chicago Outfit, but it lost steam over the years. It, too, has been reborn."

"Is your Uncle Gino still alive?"

Tony nodded.

"Are you two in touch?"

"He regularly checks on us to see if we're okay or need anything. He adored his sister."

She thought about the struggles they endured that caused the breakup of their family. "Couldn't you have asked for help when things went bad for us? So we didn't have to lose our home? So our family didn't have to fall apart?"

He shook his head. "I didn't want dirty money to buoy us up. When I was a kid, I didn't have a choice. It's different now. It wasn't an easy decision." He patted his heart. "That's part of why I'm so tore up."

Anguish consumed her. "But you could have saved our family!"

"Bella." His reprimand was gentle, but clear.

Her father's ethical stance was right, of course. Izzy was embarrassed she had even considered such a thing. Trembling, she stood and walked it off, then sat back down. "You said there were a couple reasons you told me now?"

"I suppose the other is selfish. I just want you to understand me better. I've lost your respect, and I may never get that back, but I want you to know that I always tried to be a good man and take care of my family." His voice broke. "I failed."

"But why did you leave Mom? We could have survived all this together."

"Ah, your mother is too good a woman for someone like me. I knew that from the moment we met, but God how hard I fell into love with her. Still love her more than life itself, but she deserves a man and if a man can't provide for his family, what good is he?"

"Omigod, Dad, that kind of thinking is so archaic."

He hung his head, and when he finally looked up, Izzy was horrified to see that he was crying. She had never seen him cry before. "It's how I was raised," he said. "It's who I am."

"And who you are is also the love of Mom's life, just as she is yours."

His tears turned into sobs, but he managed to say, "Love isn't always enough."

"Aren't you the one who always said, *amor vincit omnia*?"

That made him cry even harder.

Izzy wanted to help him but didn't know what to do. How could one person make another see their own beauty? Tonight, she had finally seen what an amazing, broken, beautiful soul he truly was. She went to him, took his hand, and pulled him up into her arms.

"Life is so damn messy, isn't it?" she said. "But in the midst of all this chaos, please know how proud I am to be your daughter."

Izzy held him until his tears were spent.

***

When Izzy returned home that night, she found her mother and brother in the basement family room watching *Wildwind Western Wear Presents*, a weekly family-friendly drama shown on one of only three networks still allowed to broadcast. The all-American, white-Christian, seriously wholesome drivel always made her feel nauseous. She had no idea how anyone had ever survived the 1950s.

Izzy sat in the recliner, leaned back, and stretched out. "I brought home lots of leftovers if anyone's interested. Dad also sent a big bag of cornmeal and half a glazed ham."

Erin and Luca, sitting at opposite ends of the couch, both looked at her expectantly.

"How did it go?" Erin asked.

"It was emotional, but good." Izzy took a deep breath and averted her eyes. "I did find out some news. I guess as part of his redemption tour, Maria is no longer in the picture. He let her go. She's moved somewhere far and away, and Dad's living with Uncle Nick now."

"Does that mean we can be a family again?" Luca asked.

The eagerness in his voice felt tragic. "Life isn't that simple, Luca. You'll learn that lesson as you get older."

"It's not fair."

"Life's not fair." Izzy said.

"Is it about money still?" Luca asked. "Maybe I could ask Uncle Beau to help. If we had more money, we could get our house back and—"

Erin cut him off. "As Izzy said, life isn't that simple."

"Seems to me that adults just like to complicate things."

"You're not wrong," Erin said gently.

"Did Dad give you a birthday present?"

Izzy nodded. "His mother's rosary."

"You received a wonderful gift," Erin said. "That rosary means the world to him."

"He told me all about its history."

Erin smiled. "Good. That was his story to tell, and I'm glad he finally did."

"What are you going to do with a stupid rosary?" Luca asked. "You don't even go to church."

"I'm going to treasure it," Izzy said.

Luca rolled his eyes. "Did he ask about me?"

"Of course he did. I told him you'd started your new school and were doing well. When I was leaving, he said he's going to invite you for dinner on your birthday."

Luca kicked the coffee table. "That's like forever from now."

Izzy loathed his new kicking thing and wished their mother would do something about it. "Give him a break. Like Papa said, men sometimes need to deal with their emotions by taking small steps."

Luca snorted. "Yeah, right. Did he even ask about Mom?"

Izzy had debated all the way home what to say about that. Her eyes captured Erin's anxious ones, and she knew she had to tell the unvarnished truth. "He loves you, Mom. He loves you like I've never seen anyone love anyone. This whole thing has been about him not believing he's man enough for you anymore. It goes back to—" her hands invoked the winds of time "—how he was raised."

Izzy watched Erin's face as she processed a kaleidoscope of emotions. When sobs once again shattered the night, Izzy's heart broke for her.

And so, apparently, did Luca's. He scooted down the length of the couch and gathered her into his arms. "Don't cry Mom, please don't cry. It'll be okay. I'll be the man of the family now. I'll take care of you. I'll take care of all of us. You don't need to cry anymore."

Until that moment, Izzy had not shed a tear. However, she was unable to resist the poignant tide any longer.

CHAPTER SEVEN

Erin made an appointment to meet with Annie Ambrose, a teacher at the elementary school that was the state's flagship for the new Patriot education program. Patrick Henry Primary School was in Weld County, a few miles south of the new ICE facility. Erin's intention was to tour the school, interview Annie, and then swing by the prison to return Sofia's photograph.

Annie's father was one of Dylan's professors and the source for the secondary story Erin planned to investigate—recently a hydrofracking facility was erected dangerously close to the school. Because of his connection to the story, Dylan teamed up with Erin for the first time.

A brutal winter snowstorm hit the area early that morning, and by afternoon the roads were treacherous to navigate. However, Dylan owned a rugged Jeep Wrangler that he swore would meet any challenge they encountered, so he drove.

On the way, Erin used the opportunity to talk to him about Maisie Mae. "I told both Sasha and Ian about the gun she carries, and neither of them seemed concerned. What the hell?"

Dylan gave her a sidelong glance. "Their lack of concern might be because they both carry guns, too. We all carry."

Shocked, Erin had no idea how to respond.

"America is the Wild West now, and if only the bad guys carry weapons, how are the rest of us supposed to protect ourselves and those we love?" Dylan asked. "For the Patriot nutjobs, it's about power. For the criminals, it's about control. For us, it's about survival."

Erin started to protest the insanity of it all, but then she thought of Izzy. Even Izzy carried weapons for self-defense.

"Before everything changed, when there were laws governing the use of weapons, there was at least a measure of checks and balances." Dylan shrugged. "But now it's a free-for-all. No licenses needed. No restrictions about concealed carry. No personal weapons of any kind outlawed anymore." He laughed mirthlessly. "It's all about freedom and nothing about consequences. It's a truly shitty time to be alive in this country. A total hellscape."

A quote from Shakespeare came to Erin's mind. "'Hell is empty, and all the demons are here.'"

"It sure seems like it." He looked at her again. "If you want a gun, I'll help you pick one out and train you on it."

"No. Yes. I don't know. Let me think about it."

"Fair enough."

Erin tried to think about it, but her brain short circuited. She needed to change the subject. "In the meantime, let's talk about fracking for gas and oil."

Dylan nodded. "Before the new government came into power, Colorado had over fifty thousand active wells, and almost half of them were in Weld County. In fact, locals started calling it Welled County even back then. I couldn't even guess how many wells there are now—there's been a veritable stampede of oil and gas companies. Licensing and inspections are lax of late because big money's involved. And the danger is real."

"I remember a house exploding not far from here in

2017 because of fracking. People died."

"They said it was from a leaking gas flowline. Besides accidents like that, there have always been issues about toxic releases and health hazards. Professor Ambrose told me that he's scared for his daughter and really worried about the kids. Apparently, this new fracking operation was built only about one hundred feet away from the school."

"So close? Is that even legal?"

He let go of the wheel for a moment to throw up his hands. "What's that got to do with *anything* these days?"

The Wild West indeed.

***

Larger than the school, the sprawling fracking complex took up as much space as six football fields and contained a dozen wells. Erin had pulled what public records she could find on Stanwyck Petroleum's newest project but reviewing them hadn't prepared her for the visual impact of the massive site which—according to permit dates—was built in record time.

The tall red and white drilling rig towered high above the vast array of hydraulic fracturing equipment, sand and chemical storage tanks, above-ground pipeline system, generators, compressors, monitoring stations, trailers, and outbuildings. Entirely surrounded by chain-link fencing, the operation was indeed shockingly close to the school grounds.

They pulled into Patrick Henry's parking lot, donned their press badges, and Erin slipped on her spyglasses. When she stepped out of the Jeep, the stink in the air made her gag. "Dear God, how does anyone stand the smell?"

Camera in hand, Dylan slammed his door shut and pointed to a man standing right on the other side of the fence by a row of storage tanks. "Let's find out." He raised his arm and waved. "Excuse me? Can we ask you some questions?"

As they approached the fence, the young man turned and gave them an easy smile. "Depends. Who are you and what are your questions?"

"Reporters for the *Boulder Maverick*," Erin said. "We're here to do a story on the new school curriculum at Patrick Henry, but I was just about knocked over by that god-awful smell. Is it usually that strong?"

"Nah, it's the cold inversion today." He finished writing something on his clipboard and stepped closer to meet them at the fence. The nametag on his dark blue winter coveralls said Jack Williams, a black skull cap covered his ears, and his bright red face indicated he'd been outside for a while. "It's colder than a witch's tit and the air's heavier than a fat woman's ass— no disrespect ma'am, but that's what everyone's saying around here today." He tapped his green hard hat. "I'm a rookie and am learning to fit in with the guys." His laugh was hearty, his breath a fluffy cloud in the bitter cold.

Dylan's camera captured the moment.

"The inversion is keeping fumes close to the ground," Jack said. "It doesn't happen often."

"How can you stand it?" Erin asked.

"You get used to the smell, but the cold out here is a wicked witch on these long shifts." Jack stuck the clipboard in the crook of his arm and slapped his gloved hands together to warm them up. "It's so cold today the generator that powers my shack keeps turning itself off, and my lights and space heater won't stay on. I've got to figure a solution before dark or I'm gonna freeze to death tonight."

There was a sweetness about him that Erin liked. "Definitely don't let that happen. Thanks for taking time to talk, but you go on and take care of yourself. Slay that witch."

Jack's smile was bright. "Yes, ma'am." He turned and trudged away from them through the thick snow. In the still air he could be heard softly singing the song, "Ding Dong! The Witch is Dead."

Erin laughed. "He's like an overgrown kid, isn't he?"

"A kid with a dangerous job." Dylan gestured toward the school. "Now let's go meet the real kids and find out what kind of danger they're in."

***

Patrick Henry Primary School had bars on the front, glass doors. There were also bars on all the windows.

"You gotta wonder if the bars are to keep the bad guys out or the kids in," Dylan said.

They stood outside waiting for Annie to respond to his text and unlock the doors. It was three o'clock, classes were over for the day, and she had stayed late to supervise the students who were in detention.

Erin pointed to the words painted on the wall in the front hallway. "I'm not sure what this Patriot school model thing is all about but being greeted every day by 'Give me liberty or give me death!' would have spooked the hell out of me when I was a kid."

Dylan took a photo of Patrick Henry's famous motto through the front door bars. "It'll be an ironic shot," he said.

Annie was young and hugely pregnant. She also wore a pistol in a shoulder holster. The dichotomy of that image startled Erin and made her thoughts jump from Annie to Maisie Mae to everyone she worked with at the paper. All this societal change had been happening while she was lost somewhere in time and space. Her own naivety caused yet another wave of shame to flood through her, but she quickly swam to the surface and introduced herself to the teacher with as much confidence as possible.

Annie's handshake was firm and her smile bright. "Pleased to meet you, glad you came." Her smile widened when she greeted Dylan. "I've heard a lot about you from my dad. He thinks you're pretty cool."

"He's my favorite professor," Dylan said, then added an aside to Erin. "Don't tell Sasha."

"Do you mind if I record our interview?" Erin asked.

"Feel free. Everyone else is." She gestured to a wall-mounted camera. "But let's talk in the classroom. I can't leave the kids alone too long."

They followed Annie not far down the hall to a classroom that held twenty students, all seated at individual desks with their hands clasped in front of them. Their ages ranged from about five to eleven, Erin marveled at how well-behaved even the youngest seemed but was also dismayed that they were here at all.

"Why are such young children in detention?" Erin asked.

Annie perched on the edge of the teacher's desk at the front of the room. "Discipline is taught from the jump here. The school board takes it very seriously." She picked up a wooden paddle. "Corporal punishment is also practiced, and yes, even on the very young." She made a subtle hand gesture—her thumb and middle finger made an O and then she flicked it open.

Casually, Dylan held up his fist and flicked his index finger up, then looked at Erin. A slight smile played on his lips.

It took a moment for Erin to understand what was happening. When it hit her, she gave Dylan a slight nod of acknowledgment. Annie's father taught American Sign Language, which Dylan was taking to fulfill his language requirement. Technically, it appeared as if there would be two simultaneous interviews happening today. Erin glanced at the camera mounted above the chalkboard at the front of the room. The All-Seeing Eyes, along with imposing portraits of the president, seemed to be everywhere she went lately. It unnerved her.

"Kids, this is a newspaper reporter and a photographer who are going to do a story about us," Annie said. "Isn't that exciting?"

Some of the children mumbled, "Yes, Mrs. Ambrose." Most remained stoically silent. One little boy —who appeared to be about eight—shouted, "No!" and covered his face with his hands.

"Cody, stop acting out," Annie said. "That's what landed you here in the first place."

Erin walked over to him and knelt by his desk. "What's wrong, Cody?"

He pointed at Dylan and started to cry. "Don't let him take my picture."

Dylan hung the camera strap around his neck and held up empty hands. "I won't if you don't want me to."

For some reason, that made Cody sob harder.

Erin reached out and took his hand. "Why don't you want your picture taken?"

"Because ... then everyone ... will know. My ... dad ... will ... be ... so mad." Taking a deep breath, he added, "My butt hurts enough."

Erin squeezed his hand. "I'm sorry you're in pain."

Cody abruptly stopped crying and looked at her with surprise. A moment later, he launched himself into her arms. "I'm so scared," he whispered.

"Cody, we don't hug in school," Annie said.

Erin glanced at her and noticed—out of sight of the overhead camera—that she was frantically signing.

A little girl with Down syndrome who sat next to Cody jumped to her feet and squeezed her way into Erin's arms. "My butt hurts, too."

"Laura, we don't hug in school," Annie said, her voice betraying a hint of sadness.

Sadness and fear. Erin felt it permeating the room. Her eyes swept the faces of the other children. Puffy red haunted eyes stared back at her, and she resisted the urge to comfort each one of them.

"It's okay," Erin whispered to the two children in her arms. "You're stronger than you know. You'll be okay." Reluctantly, she released them and walked away, wishing she believed her own words.

"Is there a school counsellor?" Erin asked Annie.

She shook her head. "The school board has decided to prioritize academic achievement, not student's emotions."

Erin decided that the hardest thing about being a reporter was not speaking one's own mind. Abruptly switching gears, she pointed to the poster on the wall of the Christian Bible's Ten Commandments. "I've not seen that in a schoolroom before."

Annie nodded. "It's standard in this program. Every day the children must recite them after saying The Pledge of Allegiance and The Lord's Prayer."

"But what if the children are Buddhist, Muslim, Jewish, or atheist?" Erin asked.

"The official line is if they don't like it, they can move to a country where their religion is prominent. And if they're atheists, they can go to Hell."

Startled, Erin almost burst out laughing, but Annie's face told her that she wasn't joking. She wondered what her fingers were telling Dylan.

Erin gestured toward the large red box mounted on the wall beneath the American flag. The label said, *Bleeding Control Station.* "And what's that?"

"From the third grade up, students are taught to deal with medical emergencies. They learn to apply pressure bandages and tourniquets, cover the injured with the space blanket that's inside the box to prevent shock, and even perform CPR. Many wouldn't have the strength to do CPR on an adult, but they could help the other children."

Erin's eyes slid to the gun Annie wore. "Are you required to carry that?"

"Yes."

All the pieces fell together, and scenes from a horror movie played out in Erin's mind. She wondered how a young child could deal with an extreme emergency well enough to be effective, and how devastating the guilt would be when they failed to save their teacher or best friend from dying of gunshot wounds.

If this was the future of public schools, it horrified Erin to think about Luca having to attend.

"Curriculum?" Erin asked. "Please tell me how the board has designed that."

Annie nodded but didn't immediately reply. She pulled her long blond curls into a pile on top of her head and secured them in place with a sharpened pencil. Picking up a file folder from her desk, she fanned her face. "Wow, it's hot. Are you hot?"

Erin shook her head. "No, I was thinking it was a bit cold in here. Are you okay?"

Annie patted her stomach. "Probably just me." She cleared her throat. "Okay, so curriculum. From primary school through high school, academics have been pared down to the basics: reading, writing, and arithmetic. The textbooks are government issued, and approved reading materials are all Christian based. The arts and sciences are no longer taught, except band is still allowed because that supports the sports teams—sports are encouraged because of their focus on physical fitness and competition. Traditional gender roles are emphasized, so home economics has made a comeback for girls, as have shop classes for boys." She paused and put her hand on her forehead.

"Are you okay, Annie?" Dylan asked.

"Just a bit dizzy." She took a deep breath. "In high school there will no longer be any college prep; the kids will be taught practical trades instead. Boys will choose a course of study in professions such as carpentry, electrical, plumbing, and car mechanics. Girls will learn service industry and clerical skills. In the higher grades they'll begin offsite apprenticeships—on-the-job training."

"But what about students who want to go to college?" Erin asked.

"They'll have to go to private schools. One would presume if their parents can afford to send them to college, they can send them to private schools to be prepped."

Erin's mind raced to try to find an alternate path for Luca as soon as possible. This entire concept was just not acceptable.

"I noticed the girls are all wearing dresses," Dylan said. "Is that part of the traditional roles nonsense?"

"You're not supposed to say that part out loud," Annie whispered. She tried to stand up but sank back down onto the edge of the desk. "Oh, I don't feel so good." She reached out to them with both hands. "Please help me to the bathroom."

Erin and Dylan each took one of Annie's arms and helped her up. Supporting her, they headed to the door.

"Cody, you're in charge," Annie said.

"Me?" Cody asked.

"I'm trusting you to take care of things while I'm gone."

Cody sat up straighter and swiped the tears off his face. "Yes, ma'am. You can count on me."

Erin marveled at Annie's style. To teach in this hostile environment and still be kind was admirable.

They walked Annie across the hall to the teacher's lounge and into the women's bathroom. Once through the door, Annie shook them off. "I'm good. I just needed to get you in here because it's the only damn room in the entire school with no surveillance. We women insisted on it."

Dylan pointed to the portrait of the president that hung on the wall. "Even so, you still appear to be under his eye."

Annie looked at it with disgust. "The man who would be king." She rubbed her belly. "I don't want Hope to grow up in a country where tyrants like him rule."

"Working on it," Dylan assured her.

Annie nodded. "Okay, we need to make this quick. Get your camera ready." She turned on the sink's cold-water faucet, and the water started a fitful flow punctuated by loud coughs of air. She removed several wooden matches from her pocket, struck one against the tile, and held the flame to the water. The water ignited like a torch.

Erin stepped back, but the flames quickly died.

Annie did the demonstration again with another match.

Dylan's camera and Erin's eyeglasses captured everything.

Annie turned to face them. "I've worked here for years. Because the school is rural we're heated by propane and get water from a well, and the quality of that water is regularly tested. Before the fracking began our water's methane level was barely negligible. Now the levels have skyrocketed." She took a clear drinking glass off the counter and filled it with tap water. It bubbled as if it were a carbonated drink. She handed it to Erin. "Smell it."

Erin did and recoiled. It smelled like what the air outside had when they arrived. And she noticed a greasy film on the top. "What the hell?"

"The list of toxins in the water is lengthy." Annie pulled a flash drive from her pocket and handed it to Dylan. "The latest report's on there—don't ask me how I got it. See, the way fracking works is by injecting water mixed with sand and a toxic brew of chemicals deep into the ground to fracture the shale, which then releases natural gas or oil. But it also releases methane and radon, and not all the chemicals they use are recovered. We can't drink the water here anymore; we have water coolers now for that. But everyone is still washing their hands with it. Headaches, bloody noses, and strange rashes are the norm. And besides all of that, I've got it on good authority—also documented on that thumb drive—that a lot of safety protocols at the site have been bypassed for expediency and maximum profit. There's no government oversight anymore—it's been sacrificed in the name of freedom. I'm scared for all of us. I know the press isn't allowed to tell the truth these days, but my dad told me he thought you might have helpful connections. Please help us." Sudden trembling revealed the depth of her desperation.

Erin reached out and embraced her. "Yes, we have connections, and we'll do everything we can to help."

After a moment, Annie relaxed and pulled away. "Thank you." She took a deep breath. "Okay, we need to get back in there. Those poor kids have another hour of misery to endure. Working here is a nightmare. Honest to God, the apocalypse isn't some far off revelation. It's here and now, and no Divine Second Coming's going to transform this mess into Heaven. We've got to save ourselves."

At that moment, Erin thought of the perfect title for her *North Star* article. *American Apocalypse*. Nothing could describe it better.

***

Fifteen minutes later, Erin and Dylan finally stepped outside the school. The late afternoon temperature had plummeted even deeper, and the air was eerily still. Erin had experienced winter weather inversions often, but never in a rural setting. It was like Earth was holding her breath. In the greater silence, the lesser sounds were more pronounced. Halfway to the Jeep, Erin stopped and listened. She heard a quick burst of Jack's hearty laughter, while wisps of men's conversations danced around her like ghosts. Vibrations deep beneath her feet rose as a hungry growl, and bright flames shooting from the fracking pad's flare tower roared like an angry dragon. She found this remote corner of the world both haunting and ominous.

"You okay?" Dylan asked.

"I'm ..." She faltered. "I'm wishing we'd gotten to this story sooner. I feel a sense of impending doom."

"I feel the ticking of that tock, too, but I couldn't pin Annie down until now. I understand that she wanted to schedule it after she had collected all her evidence, and at a time when she would be the only adult here." He shrugged. "But we're on it now, and we'll make it our priority."

"Yes, but ..." Her voice died off.

"But?"

"What good can we really do? Isn't *The North Star* about the long game? Trying to reveal to those who will listen what's really going on?" She threw up her hands in frustration. "How will that help these people now?"

Dylan looked around nervously. "Sound travels far in this kind of weather. Let's talk in the car."

"Sorry. Yes, of course."

They climbed into the Jeep, Dylan turned on the engine, and he cranked the heater. "I know that the reason you told Annie we had connections was to give her some hope, but the truth is that we do have connections of all kinds. The Resistance movement is growing, and members aren't only found in liberal counties like Boulder. In fact, universities are probably the most fertile ground, and UNC in Greeley is ground zero for Weld County. One thing I'm sure of in my soul is that Gen Z will ultimately be this country's salvation."

Erin appreciated his youthful enthusiasm but didn't share it. "How can college students up there do anything to help the situation down here?"

"Maybe if we get these reports about the water quality and site violations to them, they can figure out a way to anonymously get the data into the hands of the parents of the students that go here. Given that Greeley's the county seat, clever members of our Underground network could easily access their contact information. I mean, even radical Patriots don't want their kids to get sick or die."

"That's actually a really good idea."

"You sound surprised." He slipped on his Neo sunglasses and gave her a cocky smile.

Erin shook her head. "You're such a character."

"I do try."

"By the way, what was Annie signing?"

"Her first comment was about corporal punishment. She said it was terrible. I responded that I understood. The remainder of her comments were a slew of bad words followed by a slew of *very* bad words. She's so not on board with any of it." He shifted the car into gear. "Where to?"

"I'd still like to swing by the ICE facility if that's okay? It's not far."

Dylan plugged the location into his GPS, and they

slowly headed out.

Despite bouncing around on the snow-packed country road, Erin managed to dial Eve's number. The contact list Eve had provided included two phone numbers for her: a direct office line and another listed as a "safe cell phone." She called the direct line.

"Eve Cooper."

"Hi, Eve, this is Erin Tavano from the *Boulder Maverick*. I'm in the area and wanted to return a photo to Sofia Kostenko."

"Oh, hello Ms. Tavano. Sofia Kostenko? A photo?"

Erin thought she heard John Yates in the background say, *Speaker.*

"Yes, she gave me her sister's photo," Erin said. "I believe Sofia felt I could perhaps help locate her."

"Well, um, Sofia Kostenko is no longer here."

Eve sounded as if she was now talking over the speaker. Erin immediately followed suit so that Dylan could hear. Something felt off.

"What do you mean she's no longer there?" Erin asked.

"Sofia has been sent back home to Ukraine."

"Really? So suddenly?"

A male voice mumbled something in the background, and Eve said, "Yes, she wanted her baby born there, so we expedited her release."

Even though their conversation had been brief, Erin didn't believe having her baby born in Ukraine would have been more important to Sofia than finding Anna. "But what about her sister?"

"Ah, I'm not sure that—"

The sky exploded with light, a shock wave slammed the Jeep, deafening thunder rocked the air, and the spinechilling shriek of a banshee pierced the worlds.

It took Erin a moment to realize that the scream was her own.

"No!" Dylan yelled. "No, no, no."

Looking out of the back window, Erin could see that the blast from the fracking pad had erupted into a hellscape of raging fire. As she watched, another explosion—this one from the school—sent a huge fireball into the sky.

Burning debris pelted the Jeep as Dylan struggled to control it.

Eve's panicked voice cut through the chaos. "What's happening?"

Dylan slammed on his brakes and fishtailed on the ice, but he managed to turn the car around.

"Call 911," Erin told Eve. "Explosions at Patrick Henry Primary and the fracking site next to it."

"Tell them to hurry!" Dylan shouted.

"Tell them there's a roomful of children," Erin added before the phone slipped from her trembling fingers.

They hit a wall of black, acrid smoke and Dylan killed the engine. He leapt from the Jeep, and Erin tumbled out after him.

Choking, they stumbled toward the school, but the intensity of the heat created another wall. Despite that, Erin could tell that Dylan was determined to push on. She grabbed his arm, but he shook her off.

The fire's angry roar combined with the panicked shouts and agonized shrieks of oilmen created a cacophony of disorienting sound. However, within that discordance, no human sounds escaped the school. All the windows had shattered, and flames—greedy for oxygen—billowed out every opening.

Years earlier, Erin had witnessed a residential propane tank explosion set off by wildfire; it reminded her of this inferno. Everyone in that house had died.

Despite the apparent futility of rescue, Dylan seemed intent on his mission to try. He charged toward the flames as if he really believed he was as invincible as Neo, but Erin couldn't allow him to sacrifice himself in vain. She gave chase, but he was faster. In a desperate attempt to stop him, she reached out and grasped the long, leather coat that billowed in his wake. Yanking with all her strength, she managed to pull him off his feet. Losing her own footing on the ice, she went down hard behind him. He kicked at her and tried to stand up, but she refused to let go. Then another blast from within the school erupted to fully consume its bones and shower them with flaming pieces of its body.

Embers struck Erin's face, but the glasses she still wore shielded her eyes. The ones that landed on her back and legs found purchase and their bites sparked terror. Dylan, protected by his long leather cocoon, turned his attention to her and quickly beat out her flames with his bare hands. Then he rolled her onto her back, so the ice and snow smothered the heat. Throwing himself on top of her, he defended against the final rain of fire. As soon as the assault lightened, they scrambled to their feet and retreated to the shelter of the Jeep.

Dylan ripped off his sunglasses and threw them onto the dash. Erin noticed his blistered hands and opened the car door to gather a ball of snow for him to hold.

Neither spoke. Erin looked into his weeping eyes and saw reflected in them her own horror and grief. The screams of the approaching emergency vehicles gave voice to the despair neither could express.

Erin prayed to a God she didn't understand for the lost souls of the apocalypse.

***

That evening Erin sat in bed propped up by a mountain of soft pillows and tried to process everything that happened. She had allowed her mother to medicate and bandage her burns, and her grandfather had convinced her to share a joint to help with the pain. Now, she nursed a glass of Jameson to assuage the grief.

As Erin replayed the afternoon's events, she tried to sort out everything the first responders had said. They mentioned the cold inversion keeping fumes trapped on the ground, a pooling of gas, and a generator that might have sparked. Jack Williams had been among the twelve gas workers killed, but the fire chief pieced together a series of events that seemed to revolve around him. And they did surmise it was the propane tank exploding that decimated the school. She made a mental note to follow up with the team of investigators.

Erin thought of Dylan's heroics, and her heart ached for his anguish. When she had made the decision to stay onsite and cover the story, he instantly switched gears and handled it like a pro. He said, "We owe it to those who died." Today had shown her what an extraordinary young man he truly was.

Then she remembered the strange conversation with Eve. Glancing at the clock, she decided it wasn't too late to try reaching her via the safe cell phone number.

Eve answered on the first ring. "Hello?"

"It's Erin Tavano."

"I've been hoping to hear from you. Are you okay?"

Erin was sure she'd never really be okay again. "So you know, my cell phone is safe, too."

"Good."

"What really happened to Sofia?"

"Off the record?"

"I'd like it on the record, but I will protect you as my source. And it won't be published in the *Maverick*."

After a moment, Eve said, "Okay, that'll work." There was a longer silence. "Sofia's dead."

Erin had trouble processing the words. "What?"

"The story I was told when I came in to work the other morning was that Sofia's baby died shortly after birth, and so she committed suicide overnight by hanging herself in the bathroom."

"Do you believe it?"

Eve chuckled. "Did you *meet* Sofia?"

"Yeah, there's no way that woman would kill herself."

"She was a spitfire. I kinda crushed on her."

Erin could see how easy that would be. "Are you sure she's dead?"

"I saw the body. They were still clearing the scene when I arrived."

"And the baby?"

"Never saw the baby. I was told his body was in the infirmary."

"Why the story about sending her back home?"

"It's less messy, and you're press. I was being coached."

"I heard."

Another silence. "Listen, Erin, about today's tragedy, you need to know something. I was privy to an upper echelon meeting earlier this evening. It was hastily called to deal with the fallout about the explosions, and it involved top government officials. They're planning to blame this on an act of sabotage by the Resistance."

Erin caught her breath. "They know about the Resistance movement?"

"They even coined a new name to use for us in the mainstream news. Antipats. It stands for anti-Patriots."

Erin took a big swig of whiskey. "Well, this is just great. It makes everything a whole helluva lot harder."

"It's just the beginning of a major us-versus-them campaign. They will announce that the Rubicon has been officially crossed, that we have declared war on the state, and are all guilty of treason."

"The irony is rich."

"And Erin, the fact that you were there today was mentioned. Please watch your back."

Erin downed the rest of her drink, relishing the burn. "Maybe I will get that gun after all," she said more to herself than Eve.

"What?"

"Nothing. Never mind."

"This new government is pure evil," Eve said, her voice shaky. "I just found out that our detention center is also being set up as a prison for political prisoners. I think Gitmo might pale in comparison to what's planned here. I recently overheard discussions about torture and execution methods that would make the Nazi SS proud."

Erin thought it prescient that she had gotten an SS vibe off John Yates. "It must be horrifying to work there."

"You have no idea. But because I hear things, I can be useful to our cause."

Erin poured more whiskey. "My daughter has a saying. 'All that is necessary for the triumph of evil is for good women to do nothing.'"

"Then it's a good thing we're good women."

Erin raised her glass to salute her fellow Antipat, and her daughter, and all the good women. "It's an honor to serve with you."

CHAPTER EIGHT

Many of the houses in Old Town Longmont were built in the late nineteenth and early twentieth centuries. The styles of homes were diverse, ranging from Tudor Revival to classic Victorian. But one that had always fascinated Izzy was the whimsical Queen Anne, which seemed as if it belonged in the middle of a fairytale. Painted in vibrant gemstone colors, it had gingerbread trim, decorative shingles, stained glass bay windows, a turret, and a tall round tower capped by a conical roof. The tower rose through a wrapped corner porch that featured intricately carved columns and spindles. A matching spindle fence surrounded the yard, which in the summer always came alive with magnificent gardens featuring flowers that bloomed in the amethyst, ruby, sapphire, and emerald shades of the house itself. Growing up, whenever Izzy would pass it, she imagined a Disney princess lived there. As it turned out, the princess who lived there was a lawyer named Julia Bainbridge, and Dante had arranged a meeting so Izzy could ask for guidance about bringing charges against Nash and Billy Tobias.

Izzy arrived at noon on Saturday, and Julia's granddaughter Shiloh ushered her inside. The interior of the house was as delightful as the exterior, with bold colors, stained glass panels set into ornate wooden doors, and a myriad of Art Nouveau influences in furnishings and decorations.

One of Izzy's favorite memories was Lili dragging her to a gallery on the Pearl Street Mall to see a

Toulouse-Lautrec exhibition. Among his most famous pieces were the Art Nouveau posters he had created for the Moulin Rouge cabaret in Paris. Lili bought Izzy a framed print of a can-can dancer, and it remained one of her most cherished possessions. Walking into this house stirred bittersweet memories of Lili, all that she had given Izzy, and all that she and the world had lost when Lili died. She had still not been able to truly process the death of her amazing mentor and friend.

Julia Bainbridge was another dynamic woman. Unlike Izzy's grandmother, Julia didn't dye her gray hair with henna or dress like a decades-old rockstar icon. Nor was she a typical conservative businesswoman who had a short, practical haircut and wore boring clothes. Instead, long silver hair fell in ringlets over her shoulders, the tight black turtleneck and slacks hugged a youthful figure, and a string of cream-colored pearls with matching earrings added an understated touch of class to her look. Most importantly Julia oozed self-confidence, which Izzy always found a sexy quality in people. She wished she knew the secret to possessing more of it herself.

Despite all the obvious trappings of upper-class chic, Julia's eccentricity manifested in the fact that she was smoking a cigar.

Izzy settled into a chair across from the burgundy velour sofa where Julia and Shiloh sat. A nearby fireplace was alive with flames; the heat felt good, and a hint of woodsmoke mingled with the sweet cigar smoke to pleasantly scent the air. Izzy slipped out of her leather jacket and did her best to relax.

Julia gestured to a tea service on the coffee table. "Would you care for some jasmine tea?" In harmony with the surrounding décor, the antique ceramic tea set was fanciful—the handles resembled a peacock, and hand-painted feathers decorated the pot, cups, sugar bowl and delicate cream pitcher.

Izzy gratefully accepted the offer and poured herself a cup of the fragrant brew.

"So, you are a Tavano, as in Tony Tavano's Italian restaurant and Erin Tavano the journalist?" Julia asked.

Izzy nodded, surprised that her mom's byline was already being noticed.

Julia's eyes twinkled. "I admire your mother's work, but maybe I'm seeing things through white-rose-colored glasses."

Izzy choked as the tea went down the wrong way. How could this woman possibly know that Erin Tavano was also White Rose? When she could finally breathe, she said, "Excuse me?"

"Don't panic, my dear. Her secret is safe with us."

"I don't know what you mean," Izzy insisted. She hadn't fallen for Dylan baiting her, and she wouldn't allow anyone else to trick her into betraying secrets.

The hint of a smile danced on Julia's lips. "As you wish." She tapped the ashes of her cigar into a standing ashtray designed like a red poppy resting atop a gracefully curving stem. "One of the reasons I know certain things is that I'm a newspaper woman from way back. While I was in law school, I edited the *Harvard Civil Liberties Law Review*. After graduation, I returned to Colorado, sat for the bar, and became licensed to practice law. However, I ended up accepting a position as a reporter covering the legal beat for the *Rocky Mountain News* in Denver. I fell in love and married a lawyer named Rex Bainbridge who worked in the paper's legal department. When I became pregnant with Shiloh's mother, we both quit the paper and moved here to start our own law practice, which we ran together until Rex's death. However, back in the day when I reported on civil rights I became friends with Harlan Weismann, and we're still close. I've even contributed guest columns to his paper under the byline, Agent 99."

"And would that be the *Boulder Maverick* or …?" Izzy let the sentence hang. Working in the Underground was a complex dance of caution, suspicion, deception, and knowing who to trust.

"The North Star."

Izzy issued a sigh of relief. "What types of stories have you written for the paper?" She felt she should recognize Julia's handle but couldn't quite place it.

"Pieces about some of the work we do. For instance, when our country fell into the dark pit of Hell, Shiloh and I started a bounty hunting operation. We go after deadbeat parents for child support. The new government doesn't make any effort to enforce child support warrants anymore. The warped logic seems to be that if people know the authorities will eventually go after the money, it will somehow encourage abortions. So, we hunt down who we can and bring them to justice. Our agency also works to collect monies owed the custodial parent."

Recognition dawned in Izzy. "Oh, of course. I have read your columns. I didn't make the connection. Agent 99?"

"A character from an old TV show," Julia said. "She inspired me when I was a girl. Helped me to understand women could do anything they set their minds to do and do it with class and style. The series, a spy satire, was called *Get Smart*."

Izzy racked her brain. "Wasn't there also a *Get Smart* movie a while back that—"

"We don't talk about the movie," Shiloh said solemnly.

Izzy laughed. "Copy that. What about you? Do you use a code name, too?"

"When I need to be a ghost. Mine's Lady Pinkerton, the first female detective in America. Her real name was Kate Warne, but she came to be known as Lady Pinkerton. As part of her undercover work for the Pinkerton Detective Agency, she discovered a plot to assassinate President Lincoln before his inauguration." Shiloh extended her legs and knocked her cowboy boots together. "I gotta thing for classic Americana."

"Dante told me that you were born and raised on a ranch up near Greeley?" Izzy said.

"Yep, and I can shoot, and use a lasso, and ride a bucking bull. It gave me a bunch of useful skills to apply to my current line of work."

In these dark times, they needed to have mad skills to do the job they had chosen. Izzy wished she had figured out her own career path already, but it was still nebulous. She was a work in progress.

"Dante said you had questions for me about prosecuting a crime?" Julia said.

Izzy set down her teacup, pulled out her phone, found a recent photo of Karma, and handed it to Julia. "This is my best friend, Karma Chen. Her parents owned The Buddha Belly in Boulder. After hours one night, Nash and Billy Tobias—Pastor Christian Tobias's sons—broke in and did that to her. It was during the month of riots when the meltdown occurred over Chimera, and it was a hate crime. I was the only witness; there were no cameras that recorded it, but it was them. What can we do about it?"

"Ah, Pastor Christian Tobias, the lord and master of that other bounty hunter operation," Julia said, her sarcasm thick. After a long moment, she shook her head and gave Izzy a sympathetic look. "Legally, there's not a damn thing you can do."

A surge of anger rose in Izzy, but before she could throw it, Julia held up a hand.

"I know it's not what you want to hear, Izzy, but Christian Tobias is a rich and powerful man. It would be dangerous for you to go after him openly, and what it would put Karma through at this point would be awful. *Legally*, there is no recourse. But that doesn't mean there's nothing that can be done."

Izzy's heart pounded, but she forced herself to take a deep, calming Buddhist-inspired breath. "I'm listening."

Julia handed Izzy back her phone. "To protect my license, I can't advise you to do anything illegal. However, unofficially I might suggest you look into your magic bag of computer tricks and see what you can pull out."

Buddha left the building. *What does this woman know about me and my online activities? How could she possibly know anything at all?* "I have no idea what you mean."

"My source has suggested you're quite talented at spinning virtual webs, and if my information is correct, please consider how best to tangle up a man like the pastor. I would think, hypothetically speaking of course, that if he were to lose his money and reputation, his power would vanish like a clever magician's trick."

Izzy's mind raced as she considered possibilities. "If that were to happen, would we be able to prosecute his sons?"

Julia shrugged. "A lot depends on, well, a lot. All we can take is one step at a time."

"But—"

Julia held up another silencing hand. "Please consider the end game we are all working toward. It isn't to ultimately be able to simply maneuver within this new, convoluted system. The goal is to change it. To take back our democracy."

"And if you ever need any help with any of your battles, don't you hesitate to ask us," Shiloh said. "We're fighting the same war."

Izzy was grateful for the offer. Her network was growing. However, she was still flustered about who Julia's source might be. Dante had no idea she was a cypherpunk. As far as she was aware, the only ones who knew were Papa, her parents, Karma, and Luther. Luca might have overheard conversations, but it didn't seem likely he would have understood. Based on what her mother had told her, the only person she knew with anything close to her own skill set was Dylan. His cyber savvy, combined with what her mother might have shared, could have allowed him to do a deep dive into her secret life. "Do you know Dylan Kane?" she asked Julia.

"Of course—our very own Webmaster. I wouldn't have revealed myself to you about my guest columns if he hadn't assured me that you already knew about *The North Star*." She gave Izzy a cryptic smile. "The dance we perform is a delicate one, isn't it? It's easy to slip up, and in this execution-happy society we now live in, the price of rebellion can easily be fatal."

Izzy wondered about the Castillos. "Are Dante, Rita, and Rafael working in the Resistance, too?"

"That's not for us to say," Shiloh said.

Izzy nodded. "Understood."

"Do you use a cover name in your work?" Julia asked.

Izzy hesitated sharing her secrets, but Lili had taught her that in the clandestine world close-knit cells operated on a high level of trust. Forging those intimate bonds was critical to success. "Online, I'm known as Maquis."

A slow smile crossed Julia's face. "Perfect."

Shiloh's phone dinged with an incoming text, and she pulled it up. "We have a sighting of Austin Palmer. He's at the Moose Lodge competing in a pool tournament."

"Excellent," Julia said. "Would you like to come with us on an apprehension, Izzy?"

She found that invitation strangely exciting. "I'd love to."

"Then follow us in your own car," Julia said. "When we capture him, we'll have to take him to be booked, and you'll probably not want to tag along with us for that."

That wasn't true. Izzy wanted to learn everything she could about the whole process, but she didn't push. "Lead on."

***

The Moose Lodge was at the north end of town, tucked away on a side street behind the commercial district. Izzy followed Julia's black Aston Martin and parked near it on the north side of the building. Shoving her wallet and cell phone into her coat pockets, she locked the Mustang and stepped out. From a distance, the dark windows of Julia's car camouflaged the fact that there was a wire partition between the front and back seats, but Izzy took note of it when she bent down and peered inside.

"You two beguiling young girls lure him out here," Julia said as she leaned up against the car and lit a new cigar. "Granny will slap on the cuffs."

Shiloh pulled up a photo of Austin Palmer on her phone for Izzy. "This is who we're looking for."

Izzy examined the image of the good-looking guy. He appeared to be around thirty years old, had short shaggy brown hair, and a neatly trimmed beard and mustache. A large scar bisected his left eyebrow, and another one creased his top lip. It was his eyes, however, that gave Izzy pause. They were deep, dark, chilly pools.

"The bartender, Roxy, is our informant," Shiloh said. "She works part-time at several bars in town and is one of our most reliable sources."

"Okay," Izzy said taking a deep breath. "Let's do this."

The Moose Lodge was a private club that required a membership card at the front door, but the patio on the west side of the building where smokers gathered had its door propped open. Izzy and Shiloh walked through that door into the packed pool hall.

Inside, the heavy smells of sweat and liquor fogged the air, Luke Bryan sang about country girls shaking it for him, and Izzy followed Shiloh's confident stride as she stepped into the bar to the right of the hall. As Izzy's eyes scanned the rooms, she took note of how many heads turned to follow Shiloh—her long blond mane, sorrel-colored cowboy hat and boots, sun-kissed beauty, and Levi-hugged curves probably had a lot of them hoping she would shake it for them. Rita Castillo had great taste in women.

Rowdy patrons filled the bar, watching a hockey game on the big-screen TV. A heated argument from fans of both teams raged about who was at fault in a fight that had broken out on the ice. Obscenities flew back and forth with growing intensity until the bartender yelled at them to settle down.

Stepping up to the bar, Izzy and Shiloh were greeted by the bartender, a middle-aged gal with a pile of copper hair on top of her head and a pendant with her name engraved on it hanging around her neck. "What can I getcha?"

"A bottle of Bud Light," Shiloh said.

Izzy didn't really want anything, but figured she needed to blend in. "I'll have plain seltzer with lime, please."

Roxy jutted her chin towards Shiloh. "Need to see your ID."

Shiloh pulled her driver's license from the back pocket of her jeans and handed it over. "I'm twenty-two."

Roxy took a moment to study it—her amber eyes flicking from the photo to Shiloh's face—then handed it back and prepared their drinks. If Izzy wasn't already aware that they knew each other, she would never have guessed. A delicate dance indeed.

When Roxy placed their drinks on the bar, Izzy pulled her wallet out, but Shiloh stopped her. "I got this." She took some bills from her jeans and handed them over. "Keep the change."

Roxy ran the register and then tucked the extra

money away, but not before Izzy saw there was a hundred-dollar bill folded into that tip. So, that's how informants were rewarded. In this tough economy, it was likely a strategy that greatly encouraged the trading of tips.

Shiloh's eyes swept faces in the bar, then she gestured for Izzy to follow her into the pool hall. People clustered in groups around the eight tables that were in play. Mixed teams of men and women competed against each other, some wearing hats, shirts, or jackets displaying team names: Ball Busters, Smooth Strokers, The Chalking Dead, Balls Deep, Cue Anon, and All Balls Matter. They were a colorful crowd.

High-top tables and bar stools lined the walls and bright lamps dangled above the pool tables. Izzy followed Shiloh but was the first to see Austin Palmer, so she stepped in front, took the lead, and casually led Shiloh toward their prey.

Seated at one of the tables in the far corner, Austin's attention shifted from the game unfolding near him to the blond beauty walking his way. As the women approached, he stood and offered Shiloh his stool.

Despite the way he treats his baby mama, he can sure play the gentleman when he wants to, Izzy thought with disgust. Drink in hand, she leaned up against the wall next to Shiloh.

"Thanks," Shiloh said, settling in. "There's not an empty seat in the house."

"I haven't seen you before." Austin picked up his beer bottle and used it to gesture toward nearby tables. "You here to watch a friend play?"

"Nope. My granny's a member of the Women of the Moose auxiliary. She had to drop something off, so we—

me and my friend—came with. Thought we'd check out the action while we wait." She stuck out her hand. "I'm Shiloh, and this is Izzy."

He shook her hand and nodded to Izzy. "Austin. Are you two from around here?"

Shiloh took a swig of her beer. "Greeley. We came down to stay with Granny 'cause she was sick for a while."

"Sorry to hear that, but glad you're here."

"Your team winning?" Izzy asked.

"We're kicking it in the ass."

"You're up, Austin," a woman said.

He put down his beer and then leaned close to Shiloh while reaching around her to grab his pool cue. "Don't leave while I shoot. I'd like to get to know you better."

"I'll be right here," Shiloh said, her voice flirty.

It was everything Izzy could do to keep from rolling her eyes.

After he walked away, Shiloh turned to her and whispered, "It's not just a job, it's an adventure."

Izzy laughed.

Austin's baggy shirt said his team was called Breaking Bad. It suited him. A big man, he exuded a tough-guy energy. He didn't play with finesse but attacked the balls aggressively with forceful strokes and powerful follow-throughs. He moved around the table purposefully, showing little hesitation between shots, successfully sinking the balls one after another. It didn't take him long to run the table.

"Wow," Izzy said.

Shiloh glanced up from her phone where she had been texting and nodded.

Austin strutted back to their table, his feathers puffed out with pride.

"Damn impressive," Shiloh said, raising her bottle to salute him.

He grabbed his own bottle and used it to gently kiss hers. "Thanks for noticing."

A sore loser on the opposing team cursed at Austin.

Austin's eyes narrowed and a wicked smile played at his lips. He turned to the man and said, "The only mother I do that to is your mama, Paulie boy."

Paulie started to charge Austin, but his friends held him back.

Izzy winced at the men's childish behavior.

"Asshole," Austin muttered, then turned back to Shiloh with a smile that morphed back into charming. "Now, where were we?"

"I was about to tell you that Granny just texted to say she's almost done."

"No, no, no," Austin said. "You can't leave so soon. How about sticking around a while, and I'll drive you two home later?"

"I'm good with that," Shiloh said. "Izzy?"

She nodded. "Sure, I'll be happy to chaperone. I know how wild you get after a couple beers."

Shiloh batted her eyes at Austin. "She's not wrong."

"Next beer's on me," he said with a slow, sexy wink.

Shiloh sent a brief text, and then she and Austin settled into a private conversation.

Izzy's attention was captured by a heated political debate between two women at the next table. One, a self-declared Patriot, insisted all LGBTQ people should be flat-out executed for the good of society, and the other woman argued that wasn't the Christian thing to do. The Patriot accused her of being a woke whore. Face slaps and hair-pulling ensued until their men pulled them apart.

"But what would Jesus do?" the woke whore asked before her partner urged her to walk away.

"Her kid's gay," a man explained.

"I said what I said," the hater insisted.

The argument in the bar, the anger over a lost pool match, and the women's ideological fight made Izzy think about a lecture Lili had once given her. It had been after a long day of violent protests on the Pearl Street Mall. The two of them had gone for a walk under the late-night sky to assess the damage done to their home turf.

"Avoid tribalism," Lili had told her. "The tribal mind creates us-versus-them, which leads to all things bad. It doesn't elevate life ... it destroys it."

Carefully, they navigated the red brick pedestrian walkway littered with the discarded trash of the day's pandemonium: banners, flags, medical masks, random sports team caps, smashed candy, empty beer cans, broken glass from shattered windows, used tear gas cannisters, dried puddles of blood. It had begun as a protest about reinstated mask mandates because of the emergence of the Chimera virus and devolved into a riot over politics, religion, sports rivalries, and even the fact that Skittles candy was advertised to taste like a rainbow. Izzy couldn't understand why people always seemed to revel in being angry. It was like if there wasn't a reason, they'd invent one and others eagerly jumped on that new bandwagon.

Lili asked, "Is one religion right and the next one wrong? Is one sports team good and the other bad? Is one nationality better than another? I was French, but now I'm

American. Technically, I switched tribes, but I'm still the same person. Underneath all the trappings, we're always the same."

In the dim light, Izzy stumbled over a messy stack of discarded protest signs that encouraged people to rebel against the Democratic and Republican parties and support the new Patriot party.

"And don't get me started about political tribalism," Lili said. "In approaching that multi-headed hydra, simply ask yourself which head supports life, and which suppresses it, then do the right thing within that context. Ignore the loud voices and listen to your heart."

Listen to your heart and trust your gut were constant messages in Lili's lessons.

"There was a time when people needed tribes to assure survival. Today people join tribes to try to give their lives meaning." Lili stopped walking and gestured to the full moon overhead. "They gravitate to them like tides gravitate toward the moon. But, ma belle, *what gets lost in the chaos of that high tide is life itself, which is infinitely deep and the source of all of us. Make your choices based on what serves that, and not what serves you because you're just one drop in the sea. My own path could quite simply be described as* joie de vivre—*joy in life. I find my strength there, and I hope you'll choose to do the same."*

Izzy had thought about her mentor's words often but had never really grasped their full meaning until now.

Shiloh's phone dinged as a text came in. "Uh oh. Granny's car won't start." She looked at Izzy. "We gotta go out and help her."

Izzy nodded. "Yeah, she's still fragile. We should make sure she gets home okay. Maybe we can come back another time?"

Austin took the bait. "Let me take a look at it. I know cars."

Shiloh's smile dazzled. "Why, that's so sweet of you."

Austin retrieved his jacket and put it on. "It's probably something simple. Maybe she just flooded it." His voice sounded hopeful.

Izzy set her drink on the table, and they headed toward the door.

"Don't be long," a teammate shouted after him. "We're up next."

Austin looked back over his shoulder and winked. "Don't wait for me."

"You dog," one man said, and lurid laughter echoed.

Izzy cringed. This dog deserved everything that was coming to him.

They stepped outside and passed through the small group on the patio.

"Someone get lucky?" one of the smokers asked.

"Don't trust him, ladies. He's a pig." The woman with the warning found an instant place in Izzy's heart.

Austin said, "Ignore her. Some women just can't handle rejection, which is something I'm sure neither of you two lovelies have ever had to face."

Izzy walked behind the two of them as they made their way to the north side of the building, which was the most remote of the parking areas and where only a few cars were parked.

The day had warmed a bit, and the snowmelt was at the dirty, messy stage. Izzy did her best to avoid slush puddles while keeping a close eye on their prize. No one had coached her about her role in the unfolding events, but so far she thought she had improvised her part pretty well.

"If she's frail, why would she park way over here?" Austin asked.

"She's got a real fancy car," Shiloh said. "I think her heart would give right out if anyone dinged it."

When they rounded the corner of the building and Austin saw the Aston Martin SUV, he whistled. "Hot damn. Yeah, I can see why she's protective of that baby. Is that a DBX?"

Shiloh nodded. "It's a DBX707. Zero to sixty in three point one seconds. I think she wanted to be James Bond in another life."

"Jesus, that's what, almost 250K?" Austin looked at Shiloh and his smile widened. "You say you're from Greeley, huh? Let me guess. Oil money?"

Shiloh giggled like the schoolgirl she wasn't and tossed her blond hair coquettishly.

Meanwhile Julia's gray head bent over the open hood with no badass cigar in sight.

"Granny Jules, this is Austin, and he says he knows cars," Shiloh said. "Why don't we let him take a look?"

"Okay, honey." Julia's voice sounded shaky and feeble. Shuffling, she stepped back. "I sure hope you can help, son. This is my baby."

"I'll do my best, ma'am." He leaned in and peered at the car's mysterious depths. "Did the engine turn over when you started it, or was it—"

In one smooth move, Julia manifested a set of handcuffs and Shiloh grabbed his arms, yanking them behind him. While Julia went to slap the cuffs on him, she said in a formidable voice, "Austin Palmer, we're bounty hunters. You're being taken into custody on an outstanding warrant for—"

Only the left wrist was captured by the cuffs when Austin exploded. "What the hell?" He spun around fast, hitting Julia in the face with his left fist; the open cuff smacked her cheek, and blood burst from the gash. Then he shoved both women hard onto the ground. His right hand disappeared under his shirt and emerged holding a .38 Special. He aimed it at Shiloh's head. "So, you played me, bitch? Well, that was your last game."

His hand shook as his thumb moved to cock the gun.

Izzy didn't think about trying to be a hero. She didn't remember her spectacular failure when Karma had been attacked. She didn't consider her identity as a righteous member of the new Resistance movement. She only thought about the preservation of life. Without hesitation, Izzy grabbed the collapsible baton from its holster on her waist, whipped it open, and slammed it down onto Austin's right wrist.

Austin howled in pain as the gun flew.

In the next instant, Izzy's foot swept Austin's legs out from under him sending him sprawling onto the ground. Then to steal his breath, she kicked him in the ribs.

Julia scrambled to capture his gun.

Shiloh tackled and flipped him, then snapped the loose cuff onto his right wrist.

Austin moaned. "My wrist is broke."

"Better your wrist than my head," Shiloh cooed.

An outburst of applause and laughter came from the smokers who had peeked around the building to see what was happening.

"Well, look at that. Austin got his butt kicked by a couple girls and an old lady," one of the men said.

"Whatever he did, I'm sure he deserved what he got," a woman added. Her cell phone camera clicked. "Gonna text this to all your victims, you ass."

As Shiloh pulled Austin to his feet, she looked at Izzy with a brilliant smile. "Damn girl. That was spectacular."

Izzy felt Lili's presence. "*Vive la vie*," she replied.

Long live life.

***

Izzy had tried to refuse the one-hundred-dollar bill that Julia gave her. "I didn't do it for a reward," she told them.

"Then help someone else with it," Julia replied. "In the cosmic sense, money is just an exchange of energy, and this balances the scales. Do with it what you will."

By the time Izzy arrived home, she had decided to give it to her great-grandfather. As harsh as his life had been this past year, she was sure he would put it to good use. She found him sitting with closed eyes in Brian's bedroom. Liquid sunshine flowed through the south-facing bay window, splashing his face, and falling into a warm puddle around his wheelchair.

Mojo welcomed Izzy into the room—his tailless bottom wiggling with wild abandon—and she knelt to give him a big hug. All the new, nourishing food had helped the handsome Aussie regain weight. Even his hair was thick and lustrous again.

"What are you two doing in here?" Izzy asked.

Conor opened his eyes. "Communing with the dead."

Izzy settled down cross-legged on the floor, and Mojo lay next to her with his head nestled in her lap. His sky-blue eyes looked up at her with adoration. "You're the goodest of good dogs," she told him.

"Yes, he is," Conor said. He cleared his throat. "We're in here because I had a lucid dream last night of Brian. I asked him why he'd come, and he said to give me a gentler warning than the banshees were inclined to do."

Startled, Izzy took a deep breath and tried to steady herself. Unlike her grandmother, Papa wasn't inclined to flights of fancy. On the contrary, he was a scientist and the most solid rock in their family, so Izzy chose her words carefully. "And what do you think your dream meant?"

"Just what he said. There's a death on the horizon." Conor shrugged. "I presume it's me."

Izzy had trouble processing his words. "It could have just been a dream."

"There was a different quality to it than a usual dream. I was aware I was dreaming. That's only happened once before, and it was when Ginger came to me after her death." He smiled. "She was young again, and her mind was back in all its glory. I think she came to help me deal with my grief."

Papa had seen both Nana and Uncle Brian? "So, you believe in ghosts?"

"No. Yes. Not exactly." He chuckled. "You're looking at me like I'm crazy."

Despite herself, she cracked a smile. "Well, crazy does run in the family."

"To answer your next question, yes, I do believe in life after death. Energy can't be destroyed; it merely changes form."

"So ... ghosts."

"Semantics. Think back to your earliest, clear memory in life. Remember that innate sense of self

—the 'I' that you experienced yourself to be? It's still the same, isn't it?" He didn't wait for her to answer. "But physically you're not the same person as you were then; every atom in your body has changed. Emotionally and mentally you're completely different, too. But your consciousness of self has never changed. It's the only constant in life. I believe that core energy is what survives death. Following the first law of thermodynamics, it merely changes form."

His simple explanation of dying was easier to grasp than Grandma's complex theory involving astral planes, spirit guides, angels, and demons; or Dad's talk of Purgatory, Heaven, and Hell; or Karma's descriptions of the three death bardos and scary hungry ghosts. However, Uncle Brian's supposed message made no sense whatsoever. "Why would you die, Papa? Are you sick? Is there something you haven't told us?"

"No, but who else could he have meant?"

Izzy thought back to earlier in the day and wanted to tell him that it could more realistically be her who would die next, but she didn't want him to worry. She waved her hands around the room. "Were you able to commune?"

"Nope. Not a psychic bone in my body, but I thought I should at least try."

Ever since Izzy had dinner with her father she had been thinking about his mother's strong religious faith versus her own skepticism. "Do you believe in God, Papa?"

Conor nodded. "Not in a churchy sense, but from my scientific perspective, yes. I am in awe of creation and do see the fingerprint of intelligent design." He studied her for a moment. "What about you?"

Izzy struggled to put feelings into words. "I've been running a search on that my whole life. There's ... there's just so much bad in this world, you know?"

"I do know that." He fell quiet.

She waited.

Finally, Conor said, "Ginger believed that this world is the battleground of good versus evil, and that we each possess the free will to choose a side in that fight. Her logic spoke to me."

It spoke to Izzy, too. She might not be traveling the road she had expected to walk in life, but the light guiding her was bright. Pulling the hundred-dollar bill from her pocket, she handed it to him. "I got this as a tip and wanted to give it to you."

"Why?"

"Because I love you."

He grunted.

"I'm sure there are things you need," she said.

Conor tried to hand it back. "This is thoughtful, but your ma gave me a nice chunk of change for rent from her first paycheck, and with the food your family contributes, I'm good. Really good."

Izzy shook her head and refused to accept it. "Then do something wild and crazy with it. Please. It would mean a lot to me."

"In that case ..." He folded and tucked the bill into his shirt pocket. "How about I take you and Luca out to dinner? Erin's at her office working on that explosion story, and Kelly's at an emergency QAnon Moms meeting. There's a new seafood joint in town called The Cod Father. I heard that it has an all-you-can-eat fish and chips buffet on Saturday nights."

Izzy burst out laughing. "The Cod Father?"

"Yeah, their slogan is 'Luca Brasi sleeps with the fishes.'"

Izzy laughed harder. "No!"

Conor grinned and shook his head. "No, but it should be."

"Or 'Just when I thought I was out, they pull me back in,'" Izzy said laughing so hard she doubled over.

"Now, that's a good one," Conor said. "You think like a restaurateur."

"It's in my blood. I'll never escape it." Izzy wiped her eyes and pulled herself together. It felt good to laugh that hard. More importantly, it was wonderful to see Papa laugh again. And Mojo, experiencing a contact high, jumped up, bounced around, and yapped like a puppy. Diva, who had been hiding somewhere, bolted out of the room, her fur puffed out like a *Star Trek* tribble.

"I'd love to go, Papa. Thank you for the invite."

"Speaking of Kelly's emergency meeting, did you tell her that birds aren't real? That they've all been replaced with Deep State drones for the purpose of spying on us?"

"Oh no," Izzy said, laughter bubbling up again. "Guilty. I didn't think she'd take it seriously. I mean it's from a satirical conspiracy theory group that emerged years ago to poke fun at all the crazies."

"Kelly, God love her, is too crazy to grasp the finer points of satire."

"I'll remember that. Oh, how I wish I were a tiny, fluttering spy on their wall recording all the drama at that meeting."

"They're probably planning the wanton destruction of all the bird feeders in town," Conor said. "You need to try to convince her it was a joke."

Izzy nodded. "Will do. The thing about Grandma is that she means well. She really does believe she's on a holy mission."

"She does mean well, but how the hell did she get that absurd? It must have been a recessive gene from her mother's side. Ginger was of British stock—the same people from whom Monty Python and the Holy Grail emerged."

"I support that theory," Izzy said.

"Good, now we've got that settled, go find Luca and let's get this show on the road."

Izzy was more excited to eat fish and chips than she wanted to admit. Something so readily available in the Before Time, had become so hard to afford in the After. As she thought about the impracticality of someone opening a restaurant during the present financial and supply chain crisis, a seafood restaurant actually made sense. Fish was plentiful in Colorado and potatoes were locally grown, as was the cabbage which they likely used to make coleslaw. She imagined that finding lemons and tartar sauce would pose the greatest challenge.

The restaurant business was indeed in her blood; her mind always drifted to the practical side of operations.

The way Luca chattered non-stop on the way to dinner signaled his excitement, too.

Izzy's heart was full.

The Cod Father was in a small 1930s-style bungalow on a street that bordered the commercial district in Old Town Longmont. Several historic homes on the street had been converted for business use. Strings of small blue and white lights draped the outside of the building, and hurricane lanterns hung from eaves on the front porch. The ambiance was cozy and inviting.

It was twilight when Izzy, Conor, and Luca exited the van and made their way up the slick, slushy sidewalk to the front porch. There wasn't a wheelchair ramp, but the front porch was only a few inches off the ground. With a little help and a lot of skill, Conor was able to maneuver his chair up onto the porch. Luca opened the front door and held it while Conor tried to enter the dining room, but it wasn't wide enough to accommodate him. He tried repeatedly to negotiate the door until his chair became stuck, wedged between the jambs.

A young man standing behind the host station ran over to them with a panicked expression. "What the hell are you doing?"

"I'm trying to come in," Conor said. "My family and I want to have dinner."

The host—his nametag said he was Michael—looked at him with scorn. "Obviously, you're not going to be able to do that."

"Isn't there another way in?" Conor asked. "A handicapped access?"

"No, now please leave. You're blocking the door."

Izzy, standing behind Conor, couldn't believe what she was hearing. "What about ADA regulations?"

Michael put his hands on his hips and regarded her with a haughty expression. "What about them? The Americans with Disabilities Act was repealed. This country is no longer mandated to indulge the weak and useless members of our society. Our mission is to build a strong nation. Haven't you read the new Constitution?

You need to leave *now*."

"Papa?" Luca's voice mirrored Izzy's shock.

Michael looked past them toward the walkway. "There are *ambulatory* guests coming. Get out of the way."

"This isn't fair," Conor said.

Michael sneered. "I've already been through this with others of your kind. Take your crippled ass somewhere that cares. Just get out of here, you worthless old bum."

Izzy and Luca gasped as one.

"How dare you talk to him like that," Izzy said.

"Papa's not a bum," Luca said.

Conor tried to back his chair up, but it was wedged in at an odd angle. Izzy tried to help but seemed to make it worse.

Michael said through gritted teeth, "Out of the way kids. I've had to do this before." With that, and with strength which belied his slight physique, he grabbed the arms of the wheelchair, pulled it up and straightened it at the same time, and then shoved it backwards with a mighty thrust.

"No!" Izzy shouted, trying in vain to stop the runaway chair. With horror, she watched as the wheelchair bounced off the porch, turned, and tipped, spilling Conor onto the sidewalk.

"Papa," Luca cried, running to his side.

Izzy pushed through her shock and raced to help.

Conor's hat had flown off and a wide scrape on his forehead oozed blood.

Izzy knelt. "Are you okay?"

"No, I'm not okay. Get my wheelchair upright for me."

As Izzy did his bidding, she glared at Michael. "You son of a bitch, you hurt him."

Michael shrugged. "I really don't care. Just get him out of here."

Conor floundered in the cold, dirty slush while trying to sit up.

Luca started to cry.

The family who had been approaching the restaurant hurried to help. The burly man grabbed Conor under his arms and easily lifted him into the chair that Izzy held steady.

"I can't believe what I just saw," the woman said. "What's happening to people?"

"Cruelty is the point," Izzy said. "Being bullies, making others feel small, it makes them feel big."

The couple's little girl grabbed Luca's hand. "Don't cry. It'll be okay," she told him.

Her words made Luca cry even harder, his sobs harsh and loud in the otherwise still evening air.

Conor settled into his chair and tried to wipe the blood and muck from his face. "Thank you."

"Is there anything else we can do to help?"

Conor pointed to his hat that lay on the ground. "Could you hand me that?"

The stranger bent to retrieve the Vietnam Veteran cap and did his best to wipe it off. Handing it to Conor he said, "Thank you for your service."

Conor grunted, nodded, took the hat, and put it on.

"Let's go, Peter. I don't want to eat here after all," the woman said.

As they all turned away from The Cod Father, Michael shouted after them, "Sure, side with the cripple. See where that gets you in life."

Out of respect for the family that walked them to their van, Izzy resisted retaliating with the string of obscenities that ran through her mind like ticker tape. Instead, she asked, "What can we do to stop the madness?"

"Resist," Peter said.

***

After they returned home, Conor and Luca retreated to their respective rooms, and Izzy searched until she found a first aid kit. Then she knocked on Conor's door.

"Come in," was the muffled reply.

Izzy found Conor in his chair at the foot of his bed. Mojo stood on hind legs, his nose sniffing every square inch of his person apparently trying to determine exactly what adventure he had missed.

Izzy held up the kit. "I came to tend your wound."

"Thank you."

Izzy stepped inside, and thinking he might want to talk about his humiliation in private, closed the door behind her. She opened the kit and carefully cleaned his forehead abrasion with alcohol, then medicated it with Neosporin. While applying the bandage she glanced down to see him looking at her with a distinct twinkle in his eyes. "What?"

A grin flirted with his lips. "So ... do you think Luca learned anything tonight?"

"What?" Then the truth zapped her like a stun gun. "You staged that?"

"I've been in a wheelchair most of my life. When have I not been able to judge the width of a door?"

Her mind floundered. "But how did you know you'd be treated that way?"

"The others of my kind he referred to? Well, some of us share our stories with each other. We have a brotherhood of the rolling gimps society thing going on."

Shock knocked Izzy off her feet, and she sat down hard on the big cedar chest. "You could have been seriously hurt."

"I've gotten pretty good at falling through the years."

Izzy considered how devastating the experience had been for Luca. "Yes, I think Luca learned a lot tonight. I don't believe your sacrifice was in vain." Papa's capacity for heroism seemed limitless.

He nodded. "Good. Then it was worth it."

Izzy gestured to his missing legs. "Was that worth it?"

"If you're asking if I'd do it again, yes."

"What went through your mind when it was happening?"

Conor rubbed Mojo's ears. "Not much really. If I had thought about it too hard, I might have wimped out. There was just this one moment of clarity when I understood that the lives of all those women, children, and old people were way more important than my own little life."

"Were you scared?"

"I was more regretful. It saddened me that I wouldn't see Ginger or Kelly again."

"And right before the moment of impact, what did you experience?" Izzy wasn't sure why it suddenly mattered so much for her to know all the details, but it did.

He chuckled. "Honestly, my last thought was,

'Damn, this is gonna hurt.' And I wasn't wrong."

"Why did you flinch when that man tonight thanked you for your service?"

"You noticed that, did you?"

"I'm a good noticer."

Conor bent down and kissed the top of Mojo's head. "It's a perfunctory saying that tends to rile vets from 'Nam." He paused and stared into the distance.

Izzy felt she had touched a raw nerve. "I'm sorry, I didn't mean to—"

He cut her off. "No, it's okay. Those were dark times, and they still cast shadows inside me, but bringing light to it does sometimes help. When we returned, we weren't welcomed. We were called baby killers, spat on, and treated as pariahs. The anti-war movement was in full swing, and we were the enemy even though almost none of us served because we wanted to. Most were drafted. Hell, even the VFW didn't welcome us —because it had technically been a 'police action' we weren't even considered veterans of war. GI benefits were sparse. There was virtually no support system to treat our PTSD. We served in Hell, and we returned to Hell. And all that for a war that made no goddamn sense. So, yeah, being thanked for our service now feels hollow."

Izzy's heart ached for him. "I didn't know."

"Not many do anymore."

"I'm sorry you got hurt tonight."

Conor's eyes turned away from the past and returned to the present. He smiled at her. "Sometimes in life you're willing to get hurt to help someone you love, and other times just because it's the right thing to do. In the end, it's not really about you, *macushla*. You do what your heart asks you to do, no matter the cost."

***

Later that night Erin came to visit Izzy for the first time since she had taken up residence in Brian's old art studio behind the house.

Izzy answered the knock and quickly ushered her mother inside, out of the cold. The gas pot belly stove kept the studio comfortably warm, so Izzy took her coat and hung it on a hook by the door.

Erin's movements were stiff and slow. It was obvious that her burns were painful.

"Sit on my bed. It's soft."

"Did I interrupt anything?"

"Karma and I were talking and getting caught up, but she had to go anyway so it's perfect timing," Izzy said. "Can I get you something to drink? Dad gave me some Pellegrino for my birthday. I've got lemon and plain."

Erin gave her a tired smile and nodded. "Lemon sounds good."

Izzy removed a small bottle from the mini refrigerator, opened it, and handed it over.

"I didn't know Brian had a fridge out here," Erin said. "Nice."

Izzy settled into her soft leather desk chair and stroked its arms. "I kept that and this chair. Plus, there's an awesome built-in sound system out here, and Grandma let me keep his entire music collection—which is as colorful as he was. She donated everything else, including all his art supplies, to the YMCA. I guess art has been cut from public schools, but there's still a program there."

Erin looked around. "This is great. I'm glad you have your own space."

It was small, but Izzy's bed, nightstand, dresser, and desk fit perfectly. She was especially happy that it had a roomy closet and its own little bathroom. "Did you get into the doctor today about those burns?"

Erin shook her head. "Dylan and I spent all day working on the story—there were so many layers to it. We finally got both stories, *Maverick* and *North Star*, filed about an hour ago. I'm hoping maybe I can go to urgent care tomorrow." She shrugged. "I should have let the EMTs look at me onsite, but I wanted to use the opportunity to interview witnesses before they were silenced by the powers that be."

Izzy noticed her mother's red swollen eyes. "And how is your heart handling everything that happened?"

Erin took a long drink from her bottle, then shook her head. "Not well. And Dylan, well he's totally wrecked. I'm really worried about him. He lost his little sister during Chimera, and all those children ..." Her words died off.

"Does he have family here?"

"No, his parents sold their house and moved to California after Olivia's death. I guess it was too painful for them to stay. Apparently, Dylan lives alone in an apartment near campus."

"You should give me his phone number," Izzy said. "Casablanca Night is right around the corner. I mentioned it to him once, but maybe I can give him a nudge. It would do him good."

Erin's puffy eyes widened in alarm. "You've spoken to Dylan? How? What? When?"

"Where and why?" Izzy laughed. "You are *such* a

newspaperwoman."

"And a mother."

"He came into Café Paris after you told him I knew what you guys were up to and sized me up. He tried to trick me into betraying secrets, but I'm way smarter than he is."

That didn't seem to placate Erin. "He's twenty years old."

Izzy scratched her head. "Hmm. And how many years older than you is Dad?"

"That's not the point."

"Exactly three years, Mother. If it makes you feel better, my new friend Dante is coming over tomorrow, and he's only nineteen."

Erin sighed. "Actually, that doesn't make me feel any better at all."

"Chill. I'm not interested in anyone romantically. I'm on a mission and can't afford to get sidetracked."

Erin set her drink on the nightstand, took her phone from her pocket, and sent a text to Izzy's cell. "You win, but only because I've really come to care for Dylan, and I think you might be right about Casablanca Night. You've got a good circle of friends, and he needs friends right now. I get the impression he's very much a loner."

Izzy saved his phone number. "I'll do my best to help."

"Speaking of helping, have you had time to finish your research on John Yates yet? I had an extremely disturbing discussion with his secretary last night."

Izzy reached for a file folder on her desk and opened it. "There's lots of disturbing stuff about this guy's history, but there is also something very weird about his wife's pregnancy." She removed computer printouts and handed them over.

Erin reviewed them, then shook her head. "I'm sorry, I'm tired. What am I looking at?"

"That's Lisa Yates' recent online purchase history. Check out the purchases from Babybump. It sells fake pregnancy prosthetics."

"What?"

"It's a thing. Their website says it supplies high quality fake pregnant bellies for film, TV, theater productions, and ... wait for it ... private clients."

Erin sat up straighter. "Why would she need that?"

"I also found charges on their credit cards from a fertility clinic in Texas. I mean, what is she trying to do—some kind of positive thinking, body memory manifestation, if she pretends then-it-will-come thing?"

"Did you find information about a son of theirs being killed in a car accident?"

Izzy handed over copies of newspaper articles. "It was horrible."

Erin's face paled and she began to tremble. The papers fell from her hands. "Dear God, I think I know what's happened. If I'm right, they have done something monstrously evil."

Izzy retrieved the printouts. "What?"

Erin's words came in a breathless rush. "I think it's possible that when Sofia lost memories of time spent in the infirmary that she may have been drugged and then impregnated by John. And when her baby was born, they killed her and took the child as their own. It explains so much."

"Wait ... Sofia's dead?"

"She supposedly committed suicide after her baby

died. My source saw Sofia's body, but not the baby's."

Izzy struggled to wrap her head around her mother's wild theory. However, Lili had taught her to respect gut feelings. "Well, if you think so, then we need to find proof."

"We'd need to compare the DNA of Sofia, John, and the baby," Erin said.

"Even if we could get some from John and the baby, Sofia's gone. The only thing you have of hers is that photograph, but could her DNA still be on it?" Izzy sorted through her memory banks. "Isn't there something called touch DNA?"

Erin's eyes looked past Izzy. After a moment she snapped her fingers and said, "The cigarette. I gave her a cigarette and she returned the butt to me. She said they didn't want her smoking because of the baby." Erin jumped up and searched the pockets of her coat. "What did I do with—" She started to pace back and forth in the tight space. "Oh God, I didn't throw it out, did I?" She stopped and pointed at Izzy. "I think I may have put it in the ashtray of my car. I need to go look—" She headed for the door, but then turned around and sat back down. She pulled out her phone again. "Your room's secure, right? Oh, of course it is. It's only ten on a Saturday night, it's not too late to call, is it? No, of course not." She attacked her phone with a seeming vengeance.

Izzy had never seen her mother so hyper. "Calm down. We'll figure out—"

A woman's voice came over the phone's speaker. "Hello?"

"Eve, this is Erin. I've got you on speaker and am not alone. We're with my assistant on a safe phone in a secure location. Can you talk?"

"Okay." Eve's voice sounded cautious.

"John and Lisa's baby—do you know if it's been born yet?"

"Why, yes. He came early. Can you believe they named him Kyle, after their dead son? If you ask me that's beyond morbid."

"Listen to me carefully, Eve. I think that might be Sofia's baby, but I need proof before I can pursue the story. Are you willing to help me obtain some DNA samples from John and Kyle? It's a huge risk for you, so if you say no, I'll completely—"

"Whatever you need from me, I'm in. Something about this whole thing has felt hinky to me. I'd really like to know the truth."

Erin looked at Izzy, as if for help.

Izzy thought about TV shows she had watched. "DNA can be obtained from blood, hair, and saliva," she said. "A drinking glass, a baby bottle, and a pacifier might work. Urine has it, so maybe a wet diaper? Um, does John chew on his pens? Lick envelopes? Ever cut himself with his letter opener?"

Eve jumped in. "He's got a coffee mug at the office that he uses all the time. He also keeps a comb in his desk drawer. And I've been helping Lisa plan a baby shower because she doesn't know many people around here yet. It's scheduled for tomorrow at their house, and I guess it is supposed to go on as planned. I was told that Lisa bounced back from the birth quickly."

"I bet she did." Erin muttered.

"Do you happen to know what they did with Sofia's belongings?" Izzy asked. "Her hairbrush alone could be a DNA goldmine."

"I already asked about that because I thought if her

sister ever surfaced, she'd at least want her Bible and that cross she wore, but I was told everything had been disposed of," Eve said. "However, I'll see if I can find out anything more. I'll gather everything I can and be back in touch."

"Please be careful," Erin told her.

"I always am."

The phone disconnected.

Erin visibly wilted. "If we're right ..." Tears spilled and gathered in the dark circles beneath her eyes. The toll of the past two days was evident in every aspect of her being.

"Have you eaten any dinner?" Izzy asked.

"What?"

Izzy stood and grabbed Erin's coat. "Go get ready for bed. I made fried chicken and pasta salad for dinner, so I'll fix you a plate and bring it down. While you're eating, I can go out and search your car for that cigarette butt."

A panicked look crossed Erin's face. "What if it's not there?"

"We can try using the photo. And if that doesn't work, then we get a sample of Lisa's DNA and compare it to the baby's. It won't prove Sofia's the mother, but at least maybe we can prove Lisa isn't." Izzy thought about the copy she had made of Sofia's photo. She intended to do a deep dive on the dark side of the web in search of Anna but had been putting it off because she didn't want to visit human trafficking sites. It was a Pandora's Box of horror she was scared to open. "You know, if I can find Anna, I think her DNA could be used to identify a family relationship to the baby."

Erin stood and gave her a feeble nod. "Where do we

even get DNA tested? And wouldn't permissions need to be obtained first?"

Izzy figured that Julia might have DNA lab testing connections related to child support issues. If not, places could be found on the Dark Web. "I've got it covered. I know people."

Erin put on her coat. "Have I told you lately how amazing I think you are?"

"If I'm amazing, it's because of my own DNA cocktail."

Erin opened the door but hesitated and turned around. "I'm scared that you're getting in too deep. I could never live with myself if anything happened to you."

Izzy considered everything that had transpired in the previous ten hours. She had discovered that she really did have courage. And Papa had shown her the true face of heroism. Then there were the insights gained into the nature of death. She was no longer scared of anything. "Mom, if something happens to me, it's not on you. This is the path I've chosen, and whatever comes, I'm good with it. I really, truly am."

And of that, she was certain.

CHAPTER NINE

The Doyle's home was different from the other 1960s ranch-style houses in the neighborhood. When Conor returned from Vietnam in a wheelchair, he and Ginger renovated it in more ways than those needed for physical accommodation. Acknowledging that their mutual healing and marital survival would require many levels of dedication and hard work, they made changes designed to transform their minds and spirits as well.

To increase natural light, brick had to be cut away to enlarge windows and the roof modified to install skylights. Hanging plants, a small rock fountain, and stunning hickory floors invited even more nature inside. One entire wall in the living room became an entertainment center that featured carefully curated music and books, a complex sound system, and a large television. Outdoors, they replaced the high-maintenance grass with an abundance of trees and installed wide boardwalk paths, raised gardens, and a spacious, covered patio off the dining room. Dog-friendly zones throughout the backyard were landscaped with carpets of clover and creeping thyme.

The changes were made over time, and along the way their marriage also transformed into a thing of beauty. The light of their love suffused the home with an inviting warmth that still lingered.

Dante, Joplin, and Jagger arrived for Sunday dinner right on time, and Izzy was caught off guard by how excited she was to welcome them. All of them. The realization hit her that this was more than a casual meal; somewhere along the way she had welcomed them into her heart.

As they stepped inside, Joplin uttered a little gasp, Jagger's eyes widened as he looked around, but Dante's attention was entirely on Izzy and his smile made her way too happy.

Dante handed over a box of candy. "Thank you for inviting us to your home."

It took a long moment before Izzy's mind accepted what she was seeing. "Holy hell, Godiva chocolates? Wherever did you find these? This is beyond incredible. This is a feat of supernatural proportions. This is amazingly ..." She grasped for just the right word, couldn't find it, and settled on, "Charming."

He laughed. "Well, charm does loom large in my legend."

Izzy managed to rein in her wild enthusiasm enough to say, "Please hang your coats on the stand, kick off your boots, and come meet everyone." Clutching the box of chocolates tightly to her chest, she led them into the living room.

Conor sat in his chair next to the warmth of the fireplace. At his side, Mojo danced in place with excitement. Company in this house was a rare treat for him.

Izzy performed introductions.

Dante shook Conor's hand. "I'm glad you made it home, sir."

Conor's eyes flitted to Izzy as if to ask, *Did you coach him?* She hadn't and offered a slight headshake. Conor tugged on the brim of his cap and smiled. "Thank you, son. I'm glad I did, too."

Joplin studied his wheelchair. "What happened to you?"

"Plane crash."

"And you survived?"

"Sometimes we survive things we never imagine we could have."

Joplin gestured toward Jagger. "Yeah, we know all about that."

Jagger, who had been ignoring Conor, seemed fixated on Mojo.

Conor issued a soft command and Mojo approached Jagger, sat down in front of him, and raised one paw.

Jagger didn't hesitate to high five him, and for the first time since Izzy had been in the boy's presence, he cracked a tentative smile.

Kelly emerged from the kitchen and sized the two children up. "No one told me you had red hair and freckles. Are you Irish?"

"Our family was Scottish," Joplin said.

"Next best thing I suppose."

"Aye, and ye've got it backarts, but at least nayther of us is English," Joplin said with an impressive Scottish accent.

Delight spread over Kelly's face. "Oh, I like you. We're going to get along just fine."

"I hope so," Joplin said, a hint of wistfulness in her voice. "It's weird, but you look a lot like our mom." Joplin reached into the pocket of her Calamity Jane pants and pulled out a tattered wallet. She withdrew a small photo and handed it to Kelly.

Kelly studied it for a long moment. "Your mother was much more beautiful than me."

Curious, Izzy reached for the photo. Except for the

red hair and retro-hippy clothing, the young woman in it looked nothing like Kelly. However, that Joplin had wanted to make a connection between them, spoke volumes.

"It's the only picture we have of her," Joplin said. "After Mom died, the landlord put all our stuff at the curb, and everyone took everything. When the cops came, we just had what we were wearing."

The picture was cracked and ragged. "I'm a computer wiz," Izzy said. "Before you leave today, let me do my magic and repair the photo. I can also make a copy for Jagger." Her intention was also to scan it into her computer and later run some online searches to see if she could uncover any more pictures that might have survived the Great American Internet Cleansing.

"Oh, we'd like that," Joplin said.

Luca burst in from the basement and walked up to Jagger. He tipped the cowboy hat he wore in greeting. "Howdy."

Izzy hoped this wasn't a prelude to ridicule. She had told Luca that Jagger was really into cowboys.

Jagger tipped his hat in return. "Howdy."

Luca gestured toward Jagger's costume. "Cool outfit."

"Cool outfit," Jagger echoed. "No matter what else Wild Bill Hickok wore, he always had on a wide-brimmed black hat like this and not one like that." He pointed to Luca's hat.

"My Uncle Beau gave me this because I work on his ranch sometimes. He wanted me to blend in." Luca took his cell phone from the back pocket of his jeans and pulled up a picture to show Jagger. "See? This is me on a horse named Fancy."

Jagger looked at the photo. "A horse named Fancy."

"Speaking of your aunt and uncle," Kelly said, "when I picked you up today, I snuck into their library and found a DVD set they have of that old TV series called *The Young Riders*. It's about the Pony Express and when Wild Bill rode with them. Thought you boys would enjoy watching it after dinner."

"Wild Bill Hickok never really rode with the Pony Express," Jagger said. "That's a myth."

"Really?" Kelly asked. "Well, then let's pretend he did and enjoy it anyway. I pretend all the time about a lot of things because it's fun."

Izzy suppressed a smile. That explained a lot.

"And while I was there, I also stole a jar of maraschino cherries from their obscenely well-stocked bar and made a pineapple upside down cake for dessert. I even stopped by the farmer's market this morning and got fresh cream so there's whipped cream to go with it."

"Did you steal that, too?" Luca asked.

"No, smarty pants, *that* I bought."

Izzy knelt next to Conor and whispered, "Why's Grandma being so nice all of a sudden? Is her mercurial retrograde?"

Conor chuckled. "Despite her preferred wonkiness, she is her mother's daughter."

Izzy stood and handed the precious box of chocolates to Kelly. "Dante brought this. It'll make a nice extra treat to go with dessert."

Kelly's expression mirrored what Izzy imagined had been her own upon discovery of such an extraordinary treasure. "Do you possess magical powers?" she asked Dante.

"No, ma'am. My brother's a truck driver and just did

a run to Mexico. I asked him to bring back something special for today."

Kelly smiled. "Charming."

"That's exactly what I said." Izzy felt vindicated about her use of the archaic word. Apparently, it was a family thing.

"Well, the pies will be out of the oven soon," Kelly said. "Table's already set. So, relax for a while. Izzy made both cheese pizza and sausage and pepperoni pizza."

Joplin's eyes grew wide. "Meat? Wow. We never get meat. Well, except when Dante sometimes takes us out to McDonalds."

"Is that right?" Kelly cleared her throat. "You know what? We also just happen to have some salami and Italian glazed ham courtesy of my son-in-law. I'll put together an antipasto platter to accompany the pies. We could all use some fattening up. It's been a long, hard winter."

Izzy could have sworn Kelly was teetering on the edge of tears. Would surprises never cease?

"Wow," Joplin said again after Kelly scurried back into the kitchen.

Luca, Jagger, and Mojo settled down together on the couch, scrolling through photos on Luca's phone. Dante sat on the fireplace hearth and fell into deep discussion with Conor about the state of the world. And Joplin approached Izzy, reached out, and gently touched her hair.

"I haven't seen you without your beret before. Your haircut is cute. Do you think you could maybe cut mine to look like that?"

Izzy's choppy bob-style hairdo was courtesy of Karma, but she felt certain that the kindness would extend to this child. "My best friend does my hair," she said. "I'll ask her if she'll do yours, too."

"Thanks." Joplin ducked her head and self-consciously patted her own hair. Long and curly, it was pulled back into a severe ponytail secured at the nape of her neck by a rubber band.

The girl's obvious unease caused Izzy to see her in a different light. She wasn't a twelve-year-old child casually sporting an unflattering hairstyle and ugly clothes; she was a budding young woman who had zero guidance on how to blossom. Izzy grasped her hand, then led her down the hall and into the bathroom. Flipping on the light, she faced Joplin toward the mirror. "In the meantime, let's try something new."

Izzy wrestled the rubber band from tangles, then used her grandmother's hairbrush to brush them out. Gathering the wild locks, she drew them high onto Joplin's head and secured them with a scrunchie. Pulling a few ringlets free, she tugged them down to frame her face. "There. What do you think?"

Joplin picked up a hand mirror and examined Izzy's handiwork. Tossing her head, her long ponytail bounced like a tassel. "It's pretty."

Izzy agreed. Such a simple thing made a world of difference. She dug around in the fishbowl filled with scrunchies and chose a half dozen colorful ones. "Take these for now, and I'll talk to Karma about us going over there soon for a makeover." Another thought occurred to her. "Speaking of makeovers, Karma's grandmother is almost exactly your size and when the family owned The Buddha Belly restaurant, they bought her an entire wardrobe of funky cool clothes because that was the uniform. But she was too old-fashioned to even consider them, so they all wound up in the attic. I bet we could get the boxes down and find you some fun new things to wear, if that appeals to you?"

Tears welled in Joplin's eyes, and she nodded. After an awkward moment, she said, "Sometimes it's hard to breathe, you know?"

Izzy perched on the edge of the sink. "I can't imagine what you've gone through."

Joplin swiped her damp cheeks. "Mom got the virus and survived the worst of it, but she wasn't the same after. Became super weak. Had trouble thinking right. Her job fired her, and we couldn't get help because everyone needed help, so there wasn't anything left for us. Mom kept giving me and Jagger all the food, and one morning she just didn't wake up."

Izzy gasped and reached out toward her with sympathy.

Joplin stepped back and tossed her head, her expression defiant. "I don't want anyone's pity. I'm tough. And, yeah, I know I could have been adopted right away, but I couldn't abandon Jagger. In life you gotta do what's right, not what's easy."

"I don't pity you, Joplin. I admire you."

Joplin looked down at her outfit. "Jagger told me that Calamity Jane is famous for saying, 'If a girl wants to be a legend, she should just go ahead and be one.' Yeah, right. Like I can become whatever I want in life." She uttered a rueful laugh then looked at Izzy with a fierce expression. "And I've got something else to say. You're the first girl I've ever seen light Dante up, so don't hurt him or I'll hurt you."

Startled, Izzy had no idea how to process the moment.

Joplin raised her finger and shook it at Izzy. "I mean it. I'm a badass you know."

Izzy had an irrational urge to laugh, but behind Joplin's attitude there was a hint of raw fragility that stopped her cold. Did Joplin have a crush on Dante? If so, it was incredibly noble of her to want to protect him from romantic disappointment. Izzy's respect for this young woman was growing by leaps and bounds. "I know you are, and I will do my best to never hurt Dante."

Joplin nodded. "Good. See to it you don't." And with that she flounced out of the room, her curls fluttering in her wake like fragile butterfly wings.

***

After leaving the urgent care clinic, Erin intended on heading home to join the family for dinner and meet Izzy's new friends; however, she received a text that changed everything. It was from Eve: AS SOON AS YOU'RE IN A SECURE LOCATION, CALL ME.

So much strangeness had happened that Erin was no longer sure if her car was secure. She tried to think of the nearest remote area and came up with Golden Ponds Park. Located off one of the busiest roads in town and deceptively small-looking, it consisted of almost ninety acres, four ponds, and miles of walking trails.

Shortly after leaving the clinic Erin parked in the nature preserve's lot and made her way to a place she knew well—a wheelchair accessible fishing pier where Conor used to take the family. Unfortunately, there were too many people around, so she hiked further in until she reached a wooden bridge that crossed St. Vrain Creek. The area was abandoned, but Erin walked to the middle of the bridge before calling Eve's number.

It wasn't Eve who answered. "Erin? Don't hang up. Eve's been arrested. This is her cousin, Katie."

Erin experienced an immediate multi-level panic attack. Was this a trap? Could Eve's safe phone have been compromised by the government? If it was true that Eve had been arrested, was it Erin's fault because she had asked her to collect DNA? If Eve had been arrested for that, what hope was there for any of them to come out on the other side alive? Trembling, she cautiously asked, "What happened?"

"Eve lives with me and my husband. Last night she came home from hosting a baby shower for her boss and was getting ready for bed when the Morality Police showed up. They arrested her for degenerate and deviant behavior."

"What?"

"Best I could suss out, someone at the baby shower outed her. It wasn't one of the people Eve had invited but was a guest of Mrs. Yates." Katie emitted a shaky sigh. "Before the madness, most in the gay community were open. It's coming back to bite a lot of them in the ass."

Disbelief drowned Erin. "What will happen to her?"

"I've heard they are putting them into conversion camps. That's all I know."

How is this possible? "I'll do everything I can to help," Erin managed to say.

"Eve said you were a reporter working with the Resistance, so your help could be invaluable. I don't know what you've been working on with Eve, but right before my husband let the police inside, she gave me a sealed shoebox and told me to be sure to pass it onto you

ASAP. I've arranged a drop."

"A drop?"

"I'm in the Underground, too. The box is waiting for you at the farmer's market here in town. Go to the Honey Farm booth and tell them you're there to pick up your order of Queen Bee Honeycomb. They're expecting you. God speed, Erin. Stay safe."

And with that, the call abruptly ended.

***

Izzy decided she had never made more perfect pizza pies in her life. Or maybe it was the company that made them taste so good. For some unfathomable reason she was truly content for the first time in years.

"How is it that you mastered such a perfect Scottish accent?" Kelly asked Joplin. She offered her a second helping of the antipasto. "Was your immediate family from Scotland?"

"No, there's a boy who lives where we do who has all the *Star Trek* DVDs. He plays them in the common room. Scotty's my favorite character. I mean, he's got the cool accent, but he also always pulls off miracles. Can fix anything even when he doesn't believe he can. I want to be just like him, except not with, you know, ship engines."

Kelly lit up. "Oh, we're a big Trekkie family. Daddy was an original fan back in the day."

Conor nodded. "I've always enjoyed science fiction, but *Star Trek* was so far ahead of the real-world scientific curve. In the sixties the show foreshadowed personal computers, iPads, cell phones, blue-tooth devices, video calling, and so much more. It was remarkable, really."

"And I always related to Counselor Troi because I,

too, am beautiful, psychic, a free spirit, and comfortable with nudity," Kelly said without a trace of irony.

Eager to stop her grandmother from possibly elaborating about how both women were sexually liberated, Izzy asked Jagger, "What about you? Which character do you like best?"

He grew pensive. "Like best? I like Data because he wants to be human."

"And you?" Dante asked Izzy.

That was easy. "Seven of Nine. She escaped the collective and eventually became an anarchist committed to defending the oppressed. She proved that resistance is *not* futile. My kind of gal."

Dante gave her a searching look, and Izzy wondered what he was thinking.

"Well, I'm excited that Worf became a bounty hunter in the *Defiant* comic book series," Luca said. "Bounty hunters are the bomb."

"Bounty hunters are the bomb," Jagger echoed.

Izzy thought about the work Julia and Shiloh did and was inclined to agree. Then she noticed that the stereo was playing a familiar song. "Is that 'Don't Let Me Be Misunderstood?'"

Conor nodded. "It's the original by the queen of blues, Nina Simone."

"I've never heard another version besides the Santa Esmerelda one that our band played," Izzy said.

"I love blues, so this was my favorite," Conor said. "Ginger was into British Invasion Bands, so she liked the Animals' cover better."

"Elvis Costello's take on it rocked," Kelly said.

"Lady Gaga killed it," Joplin said.

Everyone became quiet and listened.

After a while Jagger said, "I'm just a soul who is misunderstood."

Izzy looked at him with surprise. Was he simply echoing lyrics or making a statement about himself?

Jagger's eyes met hers for the first time, and that hint of a smile she'd seen earlier returned. Then he did something extraordinary. He winked at her.

The unexpected force of their connection ripped open Izzy's heart. These two orphans living in a seemingly hopeless situation had the kind of courage and grit she only dreamed of possessing.

The urgent desire to do something to help them overwhelmed her.

She found it hard to breathe.

A moment later, a plan emerged from the Deep Web of her unconscious. It was as if a complex algorithm suddenly converged into a flawless solution, and a cascade of clarity flooded her mind like perfectly executed code.

Then a surge of fear threatened a system overload.

Finally, Joplin's words emerged from the cache of memory and grounded her.

In life you gotta do what's right, not what's easy.

***

Izzy punched Dante in the arm. "Did you really say, 'charm looms large in my legend?'"

He grinned. "I heard that line once and always wanted to use it, but no one ever called me charming before."

Izzy unlocked the deadbolt on her door, entered a complex pin code on a separate smart lock, then used her fingerprint to open the door's handle.

"I see security is important to you," Dante said.

"You have no idea." Izzy opened the door and ushered him inside. "Welcome to my computer cave."

While the family gathered after dinner to watch *The Young Riders*, Izzy had invited Dante to join her in the mission to repair Joplin's photograph.

They hung their coats on hooks inside the door and set their snow-encrusted boots on the hearth in front of the pot belly stove.

Dante's attention flew to a framed poster on her wall of Woody Guthrie. The famous 1943 photograph depicted the folk singer with his guitar, on which he had painted the words: *This machine kills fascists.* "That's interesting." He gave her a quizzical look.

"Mark, my late uncle's boyfriend, was a folk singer in the same vein as Tracy Chapman, Leonard Cohen, and Bob Dylan. He idolized Woody Guthrie because he used his music to speak out about systems of oppression. Mark also knew that as a cypherpunk one of my missions in life is to defeat fascism, so he gave me that to go with this." Izzy held up her laptop. A sticker on it read, *This machine kills fascism.* "The bitter irony is that it was fascism that killed Mark." Izzy set her computer down and choked back an urge to cry. "He was such a sweet man. He was ... excellent."

"You're a cyberpunk?" Dante asked.

"Cypherpunk."

"Is that a hacktivist?"

She shook her head.

"So, more your garden-variety hacker?"

"I won't say that I don't dabble, but it's not my main jam."

"I'm not sure I'm getting it."

She gestured to her bed. "Have a seat, and I'll tell you a story." After settling into her desk chair, she did her best to explain. "Back in the ancient of days when the internet was young, an anti-establishment group of rebels formed the gang of cypherpunks to write code. Worried about the role of government in the new technology, their focus was to create encryption to protect personal privacy online. In the Before Times, my goal was a career in quantum cybersecurity. Quantum computers will have the ability to break all encryption protocols, and preventing quantum-era cyberattacks will be critical. But now my immediate mission is the same as that of the original gang."

He looked at the painting Izzy had inherited of Neo, Trinity, and Morpheus from *The Matrix*. "And I imagine you're also intent on scaling the Great American Internet Wall?"

Izzy, not wanting to reveal too much about her illegal activities, framed her answer cautiously. "Few even try to scale that wall anymore. The consequences if caught are far too dire."

"That they are." Dante gave her another one of his intensely searching looks. "Let me share a story of my own." He tilted his head and rubbed his whisker stubble. "My mother was executed for performing two abortions. One was for an eleven-year-old named Abby who had been gang raped before ending up at Wildwind. The other, Stella, was a woman with an ectopic pregnancy in the process of rupturing when she saw Mother. Stella would have died without the abortion, but as it turned out, they executed her alongside my mom."

Izzy couldn't find the words to express her sense

of horror. Finally, she dared ask, "What happened to Abby?"

"Abby's in prison and scheduled to be put to death when she turns sixteen. Her mother was also arrested, but they delayed her execution long enough to finish raising Abby. In prison. You know, family values, and all." He uttered a mirthless laugh. "I believe that cruelty is the actual point."

"How did the authorities find out?"

"The nurse who worked in our clinic turned our mother in for a bounty. See, there are bounty hunters like the kind you and I know, and then there are bounty hunters like those we hope never to meet."

"So that's why there's not a nurse at the clinic now?"

Dante nodded. "My sister left her job as a paramedic to take the job. We're trying to keep everything we can in the family."

Izzy thought about the bad boy vibe his brother gave off. With his intensity, there had to be more to his story than being a truck driver. "And what about Rafael? Is Lady Godiva the only thing he runs across the border?" Shock at the boldness of her question reverberated through the room, and Izzy immediately regretted crossing such a sensitive line. "I'm sorry, I shouldn't have—"

He held up a hand to silence her. "No." He glanced at the poster of Woody Guthrie again. "I think it's time we had that discussion. We seem to be on similar paths."

The tension between them was charged with fear, and for good reason. The betrayal of his family had resulted in death. Izzy's own secrets could prove deadly. This was the new reality in which people like them floundered, trying to find a way to forge connections while also trying to survive.

"Both Rafael and Rita work in the Underground running pregnant women who need abortions to safe houses where they can be helped. There's a sophisticated network now. It's well organized, but unbelievably dangerous. And after they outlawed birth control products, Rafael started smuggling them in from Mexico. It's utter insanity what's happened here." He shook his head. "It makes no sense."

"Do you work with them?"

"I'm on a different mission. I'm with a Resistance cell that's trying to uncover what's happening to all the people the government is disappearing. The homeless who can't work, the elderly who have no family to care for them, the disabled, those they label as deviant, and people who rebel against the status quo. The mystery is deep and dark and needs to be brought into the light."

"No matter the cost," Izzy said.

"No matter the cost."

Izzy understood that level of commitment. She opened her desk drawer, pulled out the hundred-dollar bill that Papa had insisted she take back, and handed it to Dante. "I want you to take this and open a bank account for Joplin and Jagger. I have a plan to set them up financially, and I'm going to need them to have that account."

Worry splashed across his face. "Is this plan of yours something that will put them in jeopardy?"

"Not at all."

"What about you?"

Izzy thought about what her grandfather had taught her. "It's not really about me, is it? You do what your heart asks you to do, no matter the cost."

CHAPTER TEN

On Monday morning, as soon as Erin arrived at work, Harlan called her into his office. Gingerly, her burns still causing grief, she stepped into his chaotic space.

Seeing her obvious discomfort, Harlan stood from behind his desk, raced over to the Victorian-style love seat that sat in one corner, swept piles of papers onto the floor, and urged her to sit. "Oh, my sweet white rose, you've been to Hell and back, haven't you?"

Grateful for a soft place to land, she sank onto the velvet cushion. "I haven't quite made it back yet."

He sat next to her and patted her hand. "I wanted to talk to you about the stories you filed over the weekend."

Anxiety mixed with Erin's pain. "Are they okay? We worked so hard on them."

"They were perfect. I wanted to tell you I believe that when the day comes we don't have to hide anymore, the piece you wrote for *The North Star* will win awards. The way you captured the humanity within the horror was remarkable. Richard Price once said of great writing, 'You don't write about the horrors of war. No. You write about a kid's burnt socks lying in the road.' And you, my dear, can tell a story like no other journalist I've ever worked with."

Erin's vision blurred behind a veil of tears. "I wish there wasn't a need to write about kids' burnt socks. Dammit, Harlan, we need someone to rescue us from the madness. It's all gone too far."

"Right now, we need Clark Kent more than

Superman."

Erin's thoughts turned to Eve. "What do you know about gay people being arrested for deviant behavior? One of my sources was taken into custody this weekend."

Harlan's eyes widened. "I've heard rumors, but that's all. Here in Boulder, we've been somewhat shielded so far from much of the insanity."

"Why do you think that is?"

He took some time before answering. "It's logical to me that they would want to establish a new baseline of normal in the rest of the state before taking on the last bastion of liberals. Delaying enforcement of all their new laws here could be a strategy to minimize public scrutiny and resistance."

"Why do people hate others who are different?"

Harlan barked a harsh laugh. "A question for the ages."

"It's all about tribalism," Izzy said from the doorway.

"Izzy?" Erin hadn't been expecting her. "What are you doing here?"

"I need to talk to you and Kane. It's important."

"Okay." Erin struggled to her feet. "Harlan, this is my daughter, Isabelle. Izzy, this is my boss, Harlan Weismann."

Harlan stood and shook her hand. "Do I know you?"

"We've seen each other at several Casablanca Nights."

"Of course, I remember you now. My husband and I love going to those."

"The full moon's right around the corner. You should come." Izzy grew animated. "Oh, you should bring the whole office. I've invited Kane and think it'd be good for him, you know, after what he's just been through. Plus, of course, the whole spirit of resistance thing that Casablanca champions. I work there and can reserve a big table for all of us. What do you think?"

Erin tried to intervene. "Izzy, this isn't a good time to—"

"I think it's a fabulous idea," Harlan said. "I'll make it a work assignment. I'll devote an entire issue of *The North Star* to Boulder's very own subversive Paris Underground, and each of our reporters can write stories based on their own areas of expertise."

Obviously self-satisfied, Izzy didn't hide her gloat.

Harlan squeezed Erin's hand. "Go on, then. It seems you have urgent business."

As they walked to Erin's office, Izzy pulled a prescription bottle from her coat pocket. "You forgot your Percocet at home. Figured you'd need it."

"I didn't forget. I have that interview with Pastor Christian Tobias today and want a clear head."

"If you're distracted by pain, you won't be much good anyway. Take a pill."

Erin chuckled. "Yes, ma'am."

"Glad we got that settled." Izzy looked around. "Very cool office."

"I'm happy here. I really am."

"As it should be. You deserve all good things."

Sometimes Erin didn't think she deserved a daughter as good as Izzy.

***

Izzy had so much to say that she didn't know where to begin. She sat down across the desk from her mother, while Dylan stood leaning against the closed door with arms crossed. His vibe wasn't the same as the last time she saw him. Recent events had cast shadows.

"There's something that you need to know before your interview with Pastor Tobias," Izzy said. "His sons, Nash and Billy, are the ones who attacked Karma."

Erin's face paled. "What?"

"I ran into them at the farmer's market a while back. They recognized and taunted me. A friend referred me to a local bigwig attorney who said that because there's only our word about it, any attempt to pursue charges would be useless. She also cautioned me about awful repercussions if I tried because of who their dad is."

"Wait," Dylan said. "What exactly did these guys do?"

"It was a hate crime. Nash cut up my best friend's face while Billy held me back." Her hand shaking, she pulled up a photo of Karma on her phone to show him.

"Jesus Christ," Dylan muttered.

Izzy drew a quavering breath. "Yeah, well, as much as the pastor would probably preach otherwise, good old JC had nothing to do with it. I've researched the family and something I discovered is that both boys have applied to join the new elite Firing Squad Corps. With their father's influence, it's a given that they'll be accepted. And with their lack of even the slightest shred of decency, I can't imagine what they'll be capable of after that. I tailed them one day and was horrified to see that the bumper sticker on Nash's pickup says, *Save a deer, shoot a queer.*"

"You shouldn't have followed them, Izzy," Erin said. "What were you thinking?"

"I'm thinking a lot of things that you're not going to like, but I need your help." She looked up at Dylan.

"Especially yours."

He stood a little straighter, and his shadow lightened. "What do you need?"

"I've tried hacking into the Rocky Mountain Patriot Church computers, but they have some serious dark side sorcery going on there because I can't get in and—"

"Maybe I can," Dylan offered.

"No offense, Kane, but if I can't, there's no way you can. What I need is for you to figure out a way to clone the pastor's cell phone when you're there today."

"Why?" Erin asked. "What are you looking for? What are you trying to do?"

"See, here's the thing. That man's social clout comes from running a megachurch and being a charismatic kind of guy, but his growing political power comes from the bounty hunting operation he runs. Buckets of money are donated to fund it by people who love to hate and have a morbid need to be part of punishing others. Blood lust gone wild. It's their entertainment, kind of a modern version of the Roman Colosseum spectacles. If all that money was suddenly to be, oh I don't know, *embezzled* by the good pastor, it would shoot him down more effectively than The Squad could."

A silent pall fell over the room.

Finally, Dylan said, "Let me get this straight. You want to frame him for embezzlement, so you need to be able to access his financial information to do that. And we're hoping his cell phone will provide you the data to get that done?"

"Bingo." Izzy braced for a mom explosion, but Erin just sat silently staring at her.

"And what is your plan for all that money you abscond with?" Dylan asked.

RESISTANCE

"A major chunk of it will have to go to an offshore account in his name that I'll leave crumbs for the investigators to follow. Ergo, his evil deed will be uncovered, he'll be disgraced, and his entire kingdom will fall into rack and ruin. But I do have a plan for the rest of it to help a couple orphans I know. It involves some complicated money laundering and a GoFundMe campaign, but like I said, I have a plan."

Erin threw up her hands. "Izzy, I know you're good with computers, but how can you possibly expect to pull this off without getting caught?"

"Because I'm not just good, I'm great. You have no idea what I'm capable of."

"I'll do it," Dylan said. "Cloning his phone is child's play."

"No, you won't." Erin said in her best mom voice.

"Try and stop me," Dylan said, sounding like a petulant child.

Izzy burst out laughing at the crazy dynamic between them.

"This isn't funny, young lady."

The fear in her mother's voice startled Izzy. "You're right. I'm sorry. Look, I know it's risky, but if we have an opportunity to slay the monster, don't we at least have to try?"

"I didn't raise you to risk your life hunting monsters."

"No, but here we are."

After a moment Erin said, "It seems that heroism is becoming a family tradition."

Izzy thought of Papa's sacrifice. She considered her mother's surprising courage. And she realized how privileged she was to follow in their footsteps.

***

The house named Redemption was located north of Boulder and west of Longmont on two hundred and eighty rugged acres. Nestled within the embrace of towering pine trees and built of native sandstone, the sprawling ranch-style home hugged the natural contours of a hillside and merged seamlessly with the wild terrain. Together, Erin and Dylan slowly ascended the graceful, curved stone stairway that wound its way to Pastor Tobias's front door.

"I know a lot of good Christians," Dylan said. "But the ones who ignore what Jesus actually stood for really piss me off."

Erin thought of her grandmother, who walked the talk of core Christianity. "Is your family religious?"

"Yeah, and so am I. The thing about Jesus that people tend to forget is that he was a rebel, which I find relatable. Sasha is the chaplain of a non-denominational campus ministry, and I attend her services. She has an amazing way of making his teachings relevant, you know?"

That revelation stopped Erin in her tracks. "Sasha is an ordained minister?"

He chuckled. "Sasha's a gem of many facets. She found her calling because of her grand aunt's association with Martin Luther King and the influence he had on their family."

"Impressive. I really do need to get to know her better."

"She's one of the best people."

When they finally reached the top of the stairs, Erin rang the doorbell and the opening measures of

"Amazing Grace" sounded from within the home.

"Redemption and 'Amazing Grace,'" Dylan said. "I'm sensing a theme."

She nodded. "It fits with what I know of his history."

Dylan's eyes swept the surroundings. "I expected to see flags flying. American, Presidential, and Patriot Church flags, but apparently, he likes to keep his personal profile low."

"That's at odds with the flamboyant image we've heard about," Erin said.

Dylan gripped the camera that hung from his neck. "I'm eager to capture honest images. I'm good at that."

"Yes, you certainly are."

Bethany Tobias answered the door. Erin had seen photos of the pastor's wife, but none had done justice to her untamed beauty. Long, tousled hair the color of wheat, honey-colored eyes that flashed fire, and a simmering confidence projected impressive primal energy. Nothing about the woman appeared polished, including the well-worn Levi's, simple tank top, unbuttoned faded flannel shirt, and the small pistol causally tucked into the waist of her jeans.

"Are you armed?" Bethany asked in greeting.

Startled, Erin said, "Of course I'm not."

Bethany looked at Dylan.

"Of course I am."

Bethany grinned at him. "You'll fit right in, but you," she gave Erin a meaningful look, "you definitely need to cowgirl up." She turned and walked away. "Come on, then. He's waiting for you."

They followed her through the spacious, rustic house. The most impressive architectural feature was the abundance of enormous windows that invited the breathtaking landscape indoors. Coupled with hardwood floors, soaring open-beam ceilings, a surprising rock waterfall, and the massive stone fireplace, it was not just a stunning home but a natural sanctuary. Cowboy-themed paintings and bronze sculptures by Frank Remington and Charles M. Russell added a touch of quiet elegance to the unique, Western ambience.

Bethany led the way to the pastor's private office, introduced the journalists to her husband, and then left them alone.

Seated behind a simple, knotty pine desk, Pastor Tobias stood and shook hands with each of them in turn. "Welcome to Redemption. Please call me Christian." He gestured to the two leather chairs across from him. "Have a seat and let's get to know one another."

Pastor Christian Tobias was another sexy human who radiated charismatic confidence. Erin was surprised by the fact it really was confidence and not arrogance that colored his personality. Detractors had characterized him as a slick con man, and even if that were a true assessment, he didn't display even a hint of artifice. Within minutes of small talk and pleasantries, she was completely disarmed by his charm.

Finally, Erin adjusted her special glasses and pulled out the special cell phone Dylan had given her to use for the interview. "May I record this?"

"Go right ahead."

As Erin put the phone on his desk, she took note that his own was also there and so placed hers close to it. Then she glanced at Dylan.

"Do you mind if I take candid shots, sir?" Dylan

asked. "Or would you prefer we wait and shoot more formally after the interview?"

The pastor waved his hand. "Just do what you do best. Actually, I'm surprised that the *Maverick* is running a story about me at all. Until recently, wasn't it an alternative press run by advocates of Boulder's colorful counterculture?"

"Times change," Erin said carefully. "People change. Didn't you start out as a hard-drinking rodeo star who was often arrested for fighting?"

His lips twitched. "Point taken."

"Above all, the paper's committed to sharing news with the Boulder community," Erin said. "And you are big news."

"God and country are the big news. I'm just a mouthpiece."

From her purse, Erin pulled out a small notebook that contained her list of questions. "To that point, I'd like to start by asking if your given name really is Christian? My research indicates you were Chris until you became a pastor."

"Fair question. Yes, it was the name my parents gave me, but I hated it and insisted on using Chris until I found my calling. It seems as if there was an element of predestination involved."

"And please tell me about how you transitioned from your own colorful past to who you are now," Erin said.

His brilliant smile shined its light. "The love of a good woman set my life straight, and God set my soul on an unexpected path. I stopped riding at rodeos and started ministering to the cowboys. It was a slow transformation until the pandemic, and that's when I settled down and started the Rocky Mountain Patriot Church. God set fire to my words, and it was during those turbulent times that the church became what it is now."

"It truly was miraculous how you went from preaching in a barn to holding the reins of a megachurch with thousands of members in such a short amount of time," Erin said. "You must have had significant financial backing?"

He nodded. "My message is important and important people took notice. When all hell broke loose, it became imperative to issue a rallying cry, and swift action was taken. We managed to secure the Larimer County Fairgrounds and Events Complex for the church, and the rest is history."

Erin wondered about the identity of the powerful people who were able to obtain that prime location along the heavily traveled stretch of Interstate 25 which linked Denver to Cheyenne. The large arena had been famously used by sports teams and rock stars, and it was an impressive venue. However, her intuition told her that wasn't something she should ask. The safer route would be for her to find a covert way to discover that information. "And what is so important about your message?"

"Our identity as American Christians needs to be claimed. It's been a muddled mess for centuries, all mixed up with Rome, Africans, crazy cults, PC bullshit, and of course, the Jews." A sour expression shifted his energy to one not as charming.

Erin steadied herself. From what Maisie Mae had said, his beliefs were ugly. "Yes, I've spoken to one of your parishioners who mentioned you have excluded the Jewish influence in your church. Could you elaborate?"

"The very fact that the Jewish religion has been mixed up with ours for millennia is beyond ridiculous. The Jews killed Jesus. Do you know your Bible?"

"Somewhat."

He gestured to the Bible in the corner of his desk. "It's all right there. Pilate washed his hands of responsibility for Christ's blood after the crowd —the Jewish crowd—demanded that he be crucified. Pilate only wanted to flog Jesus; it was the Jews who wanted him dead. So, how did they end up any part of the Christian religion? Make it make sense. They are the enemy; they have always tried to undermine our religion and our country, and it's time for their influence to be eliminated entirely."

Erin struggled to maintain her composure. "Why do you deem Jews a danger?"

"Up until now they've controlled everything. Their money is behind all that's bad in this country. Jews were the greedy money lenders in the Bible." As he spoke, his tone shifted from personable to preacher, and the room seemed to grow colder. "The only time Jesus lost his temper was with them, and they haven't changed since that time. He showed us how to treat them, and we shall overturn their tables and drive them out as well. And if they won't leave, we *will* eliminate them because as the Book of Revelation tells us, the Antichrist is Jewish, and they are the synagogue of Satan."

A shiver caused Erin's body to tense, and the pain from her burns resurfaced. Taking a deep breath, she forced her mind to focus on his message. She was familiar enough with the Bible to know that what he said was a misstatement of verse, and there was so much she desperately wanted to say but knew the *North Star* story would have to be her voice. However, there was one point she wanted to bring up before moving on to discuss his political aspirations. "What you have been describing is White Christian Nationalism."

A slow smile crossed his face, but it wasn't reflected in the chill that seized his eyes. "You say that like it's a bad thing."

At that moment, Dylan captured a starkly honest image of Pastor Christian Tobias.

***

The full moon rose, and The Underground's Casablanca Night commenced.

The blues club, which usually had a low-key ambiance consisting of dim, moody lighting, a few cozy vintage sofas scattered among wrought-iron bistro tables and chairs, and exposed brick walls decorated with photos of legendary blues artists, now throbbed with exotic Moroccan spirit.

Vibrant, jewel-toned tapestries covered the walls, smoky wisps of myrrh-scented incense danced in the air, and the potted palms scattered throughout the room added tropical elegance to the evening. Ornate lanterns graced the tables, their flickering candles creating a mesmerizing play of light and shadow. Near the bar several roulette tables entertained guests who traded their Monopoly money winnings for temporary henna tattoos, Turkish coffee, freshly baked Moroccan pastries, and Moroccan-spiced falafel.

Most notably, however, it was the music that set the mood for the evening. Karma, costumed in a whimsical outfit straight out of the Arabian Nights, agreed to join the house band for a performance of Andalusian music before the movie began. She had only agreed to the public appearance because her enchanting harem costume included a colorful veil that partially shielded her face. The club's cocktail waitress, Jaya Kumar, came up with the idea and offered to dress the same way in solidarity. It was a moment of inspired, compassionate genius.

The large VIP table Izzy had arranged held a prime location in the middle of what was usually the club's dance floor, and she designated it for Erin's coworkers and her own close circle of friends. Two empty chairs at one end of the long table displayed memorial signs for Lili Laurent Night and Johnny Night. Erin sat at the opposite end, flanked on one side by Izzy and the other by Dylan.

Although they were just settling in, Dylan had already begun shooting photos of the gathering crowd, and Erin was encouraged to see a return of his smile. She was also impressed with his classic 1940s noir detective costume: a tailored suit, trench coat, and snazzy fedora hat. Of course, Dylan had long before proven himself to be comfortable with cosplay.

On the other hand, Izzy's dress was completely out of character. In fact, it was the first time in years that Erin had seen her daughter in anything other than her signature badass outfits. She wore a surprisingly feminine white Grecian-style silk jersey evening gown decorated by gold lace appliqué that matched her strappy sandals. The shoulder pads connected the overall style to the 1940s, but the delicate drape with its classical elegance remained timeless. Besides Lili's ever-present Cross of Lorraine that hung from a golden chain around Izzy's neck, the only hint of the teenage girl she knew and loved was when the slit up the right side of the skirt parted enough to reveal a thigh holster containing her trusty throwing knife.

Erin had never attended Casablanca Night before. For the occasion, she found a green satin, bias-cut gown in her grandmother's trunk. It was more reminiscent of 1920s or '30s fashion, but it hugged her figure perfectly. And she had spent an uncharacteristic amount of time styling her hair using pin curls to try to capture a retro 1940s look.

You remind me of the sexy redheaded Hollywood siren, Rita Hayworth, Harlan had told Erin when she arrived that evening. So, she figured she did something right.

Dylan aimed his camera at Lili's and Johnny's memorials and took a photo. "Johnny Night is the famous singer, right?"

Izzy nodded. "After they both died from Chimera, I started this tradition to honor the family. Lili's ancestors were members of the *Maquis* in the French Underground, and that legacy became a big part of her own identity. With that in mind, they created Café Paris and named this club The Underground."

"Oh, Erin once mentioned you had a mentor. It all makes sense now." Dylan looked around the club. "Casablanca Night is all your doing?"

"It was my idea, but Omar helped me put it together." Izzy pointed out the bartender dressed in a fitted white Kaftan and red velvet fez hat. "Omar's Moroccan and he knew how to capture the legit Casablanca mood. And The Underground's house band, Ruby Night and the Midnight Blues, handles the entertainment end of things. Its crew runs the movie equipment, and the musicians will play songs from the movie live during the showing. The price of the tickets covers the costs of staging the event, but that's about all; it's never been about profit. Really, it's just a huge labor of love for all of us."

Dylan studied Izzy for a moment, then raised his camera and took her picture.

She appeared flustered. "Please don't use that in the article. I ... I like to keep a low profile."

"Oh, I didn't take that for the paper. It's for me."

"What? Why?" Izzy shook her head and waved at him dismissively. She glanced past Erin, then leaned toward her and whispered, "Look, because of what we're, you know, *doing*, our survival isn't guaranteed. So, I want to ask for your help in having one really special night." She reached out and placed her hand over Erin's. "Please Mom, put everything else aside and let's just have one perfect night together. For me."

In that moment, Erin knew. She didn't have to turn around and see who had captured Izzy's attention and what was being asked. Her blood knew, and she felt the heat rise.

"No Izzy—"

"Please?"

Izzy's expression embodied an intensity of desperation that Erin had never witnessed in her. "Okay, just for tonight. And for you." However, Erin was honest enough to acknowledge it was for herself as well. Maybe it would help to heal some of the pain.

"May I join you?" And there Tony was, dashing and debonair in his signature 1950s gangster-inspired pinstripe suit, vest, and matching fedora. He also wore a hesitant smile and—despite the tough-guy East Coast attitude and accent—oozed the same type of sexy vulnerability he had demonstrated when he first asked Erin out decades earlier.

And like that moment so many years ago, Erin's pounding heart drowned out her thoughts. Scrambling for words to say, a famous line from *Casablanca* came to her rescue. "Of all the gin joints in all the towns in all the world, you walk into mine."

His smile strengthened. "Imagine that."

Izzy stood. "Here, take my seat."

Tony slipped into her chair next to Erin.

"Dad, this is Dylan Kane. He's the photographer who works with Mom, and we're going to go play roulette now."

"We are?" Dylan asked. "Oh, why yes, we are. Nice to meet you, sir." Dutifully, he got up, accepted Izzy's hand, and allowed her to lead him away.

Erin laughed. "Subtle, isn't she?"

"Our girl is many things, but subtle ain't one of them. Is that her new guy?"

"No. She's still determined to never *ever* fall in love."

"That would be such a tragedy. Love is what gives this—" his hands made a grand, sweeping gesture, "— whole damn thing meaning."

Erin agreed. Love in its many forms was the only proof she needed to affirm the reality of the soul. Everything else was, to her, only hopeful myth and fairytale.

Tony's intense eyes captured hers. "There's something I gotta say while we have a minute alone. I'm sorry I hurt you, baby. So damn sorry."

Erin had been longing to hear those words.

Just those words without excuse or explanation. She harbored no illusions that the apology would heal the betrayal, but it did create a bridge. She reached out and took his hand. "I've been thinking a lot about the love and the pain we shared and have come to the realization that despite everything, even knowing our end, I would do it all over again to have had the experience of you."

In response, his fingers intertwined with hers. He said nothing, but his radiating love carried the magic that had always united them. To Erin, it was a connection of pure lifeforce that never failed to make her feel powerfully alive and centered. Basking in it now, she felt refreshed and renewed, and for that she was grateful. However, the healing was for her and not them. Some things just couldn't be fixed.

Gently, she withdrew her hand.

A subtle nod of his head conveyed his understanding, then a look of anguish crossed his face. "Do you think … is it because of what I did that Bella doesn't want to love anyone? My betrayal of you? I've been such a horrible example of what a man should be."

Erin shook her head. "She's not afraid of being hurt. She talks about just wanting to stay on mission —her mission to save the world—but it's far more complicated than that. I think of it as hormonal interruptus. She was just becoming a woman when the pandemic hit, and socializing stopped. Then there was so much death to contend with. And now all the new laws that ban birth control have made intimacy something to be feared."

"Right? They don't even allow birth control inside of marriage." He pointed to his own lap. "Not even vasectomies? What's that all about? What's gonna happen to an entire generation who can't simply surrender to the joy of lovemaking?"

Erin's thoughts strayed to the powerful passion they had shared, and she needed to change the subject. "How did you get away from the restaurant?"

"Nick's covering the back of the house tonight, and I have a new head server running the front." He gave her a guilty look. "She's a mature woman. Reminds me of my mother."

"Good."

"That she reminds me of my mother?"

"That's she's old."

They shared laughter for the first time in far too long.

Omar approached their table carrying a large tray heavily laden with bottles of champagne and non-alcoholic sparkling apple cider. On his heels was Jaya, her own tray filled with champagne glasses.

"For the table, courtesy of Forrest Kennedy who is killing it at roulette tonight," Omar said in greeting. Then he noticed Tony. "The reclusive Tony Tavano is making a social appearance on the mall? How the hell are you, man?"

"Better than I deserve; here let me help." Tony stood and steadied the tray as Omar lowered it onto a collapsible stand.

"You're looking mighty sharp in your fine suit," Jaya said in greeting.

"And you make a dazzling harem girl. Good to see youse guys found a new home here when they closed The Seville." Tony grabbed a few of the bottles and worked alongside Omar to open and place them around the long table. "Forrest Kennedy, as in the Boulder bazillionaire?"

"The big, Black, *beautiful* Boulder bazillionaire," Jaya said as she distributed the glasses. "He's quite a charmer."

"Forrest is my boss's husband," Erin told Tony.

"Really? I want to hear more about this job of yours." Tony took a moment to slip both Omar and Jaya sizable tips before sitting back down and giving Erin his complete attention. "Are you happy working there?"

"I am. I really am."

"I've read your stories. They're—" his hands worked the air to as if capture the right word— *"remarkable.* I'm so glad your talent has been given wings."

She wondered if he had seen her work in *The North Star.* "Exactly which of my stories have you read?"

"All of them."

"All of them?"

He leaned into her and whispered, "Even the gutsy ones. Your courage takes my breath away."

"How did you know they were mine?"

"How could I not know your voice? Your talent sings in a way that only yours can."

A rush of pleasure flooded Erin. Among the things she had loved most about him was how thoroughly he knew her. He listened when she spoke, he saw her when he looked, he understood her when she laid bare her soul. The multitude of ways they connected without touching was the most erotic part of their romance. So many aspects of their relationship had been foreplay.

"Do you get *The North Star* from Izzy?" Much to her intense dismay, Erin had recently discovered that Izzy was one of the paper's covert distributors.

"No, from Luther." He looked at her with alarm.

"You mean Izzy's involved with that, too? That's playing with hellfire, Erin. I know she fantasizes about fighting fascism, but the danger is real." He shook his head and waved his hands. "No, I won't allow it. I don't put my foot down about much with the kids, but she has no idea how risky—"

Erin grabbed his hands in midair and held them tightly. "It's too late. She chose her path even before I was faced with that same choice. And she does know the risk. She's not a child anymore."

Angrily, he shook away her grasp. "Is that why she said this might be the last opportunity for us to be together? I thought she was just being dramatic to play peacemaker. What's really going on?"

Erin thought about the hellfire in which both she and Izzy danced but didn't want to elaborate. "As you said, these are dangerous times."

His expression shifted from anger to defeat. "I've fought so hard my entire life to keep my family safe, and now this."

"Izzy inherited your courageous heart, Tony. Please don't be mad at her. Be proud of her."

"I'm proud of you both. I feel scared and helpless, but very proud."

The overhead lights dimmed, a bright spotlight swept the crowded room, and an announcement came over the sound system. "Fifteen minutes until the movie begins. Please take your seats and prepare to celebrate the Resistance."

"Mr. T?" Karma touched Tony's shoulder. "Is that really you?"

Tony stood and swept her into a warm embrace. "My sweet Karma. It's been too long."

"You look just like Miguel in that suit," she said.

He tugged on the brim of his hat. "He always did like my style."

Karma blinked away sudden tears. "God, how I miss him. The only comfort I feel is that he didn't live to see me like this." She gestured toward her face. "I'm so ugly now."

Tony shook his head. "Oh, you know nothing about a man's heart. He loved you. *You.*" He reached up and unhooked her veil from its delicate, golden clip.

Her hand shot out to stop him, and he froze. After a moment of staring into each other's eyes, she nodded and allowed him to let the veil fall to one side.

Using his thumb, he gently caressed her scars. "*Sei bellissima.* You are beautiful and nothing so superficial as this could ever change that. I bet Miguel is looking at you from Heaven, smiling and saying, 'She'll always be mine.' Because that's how a real man loves a woman, and Miguel was all man."

A soft sob escaped her. "Yes, Mr. T. I guess I will always be his."

Tony raised her chin so that her eyes once again met his. "Love is stronger than death. Hold onto that." He rehooked her veil. "And I hope someday you'll see yourself as everyone who loves you does."

She grabbed Tony and hugged him hard.

"Don't bogart that hug," Andrea said, stepping in to grab one of her own as soon as Karma released him. "The grooviness of men in suits cannot be overstated."

Andrea wore a fringed black skirt slit up one side, a red bare-midriff sequined tube top, stiletto heels, and a glamorous wide-brimmed black hat decorated with a red dahlia.

Tony spun her around to get a good look and whistled appreciatively.

She giggled. "I bet you say that to all the girls."

"Only the sexy ones." Tony gestured to the room. "You've done a good job with the club and café. Your parents would be so proud at how you stepped up."

"I couldn't have done it without help from Karma, her family, Aunt Ruby, Luther, and of course, Izzy. She's always been my cheerleader. She's one cool chick."

"The coolest," Tony agreed.

Andrea looked past him at the table. "I see beverages are taken care of, but there aren't any Moroccan spiced nuts. I created my own version with honey, cinnamon, ginger, chili powder, and black pepper. Sweet and heat, with savory notes. I'll go grab some. You're gonna dig it."

The secret love language of restauranteurs.

"What?" Tony asked Erin when he sat back down.

Erin realized her admiration for him was showing. "You have such a gift for making people feel special. It's your best thing."

He gave her a suggestive smile. "Oh, I can think of something I do better."

Heat rushed into her face. "Well, there is that."

The table began to fill up. Izzy and Dylan returned and sat next to each other. Luther slid in beside Tony and then Karma sat by his side. Harlan and Forrest in their matching white tuxedos and bow ties claimed their places. Sasha, resembling an African princess, and Ian, doing his best imitation of James Bond, were a commanding presence together.

Erin introduced Tony to her coworkers, and despite the sordid details they knew about the Tavano's marital scandal, they were gracious and welcoming.

Andrea returned bearing gifts of spiced Moroccan nuts for all.

Sasha and Ian seemed to be having an enjoyable time in each other's company and radiated affection.

"They're a good-looking couple," Tony said.

"Well, they're a couple like we're a couple," Erin said. After a moment, she added, "Broken."

"And, like us, still obviously very much in love," Tony said.

Erin's thoughts turned to all the star-crossed lovers around them. Sasha and Ian still loved each other despite their relationship being unfixable. Karma had lost Miguel. Omar was a playboy who would settle down with Jaya if she would have him, but Jaya was crazy about Luther. However, Luther only had eyes for Yanah, the Midnight Blues' bass player. Unfortunately, that dynamic Navajo woman was on a spiritual quest which allowed no room for romance. And Andrea was in love with the band's drummer, Travis, who was a recovering redneck Texan unable to accept his mutual feelings for her. So much tragedy and heartbreak. If love was what gave the world meaning, as Tony believed, why did it cause so much pain?

But at least Harlan had his Forrest. Theirs was a love story with a happy ending despite all the challenges they must have faced along the way. The fact that at least some of them made love work gave Erin a glimmer of hope that there was light at the end of her own dark tunnel.

***

Izzy felt practically giddy with excitement, especially since both of her parents were there to witness her creation. She was eager to see their response and hoped for their approval.

She handed each of them a laminated cheat sheet of all the audience participation points. "In case you have an irresistible urge to jump in," she explained. "Oh, and there's one spot where Ilsa tells Rick to kiss her as if it was the last time. Everybody is supposed to grab someone nearby and kiss. So, feel free to fully experience the moment."

She was pleased when her dad winked at her but unnerved when Dylan availed himself of some pocketed breath spray. The thought of kissing him was at once exciting and terrifying. Life was so damn complicated.

Luther studied Dylan from across the table for a moment, then reached out to shake his hand. "Luther Thunderhawk, Izzy's friend and bodyguard. I'm extremely protective of her and thought you should know that."

Dylan accepted his hand. "Understood."

Tony patted Luther on the back. "Well done, my man."

Dylan whispered to Izzy, "You have good friends."

She rolled her eyes. "It's a blessing and a curse."

Luther stood. "Well, my work here is now done, so I need to join my band for tonight's performance."

"Be sure to break a leg," Izzy called after him, a bit too enthusiastically.

Eager to change the subject, she pointed to the spotlight that continued to sweep the room. "In the movie, the spotlight was a constant reminder to the people in Casablanca that they were always being watched. As, of course, are we." She gave Dylan a cheat sheet and then handed them to Sasha, who kept one and passed the rest down the table. "Oh, and something only briefly mentioned in the movie that might interest you is that the anti-fascist leader of the Resistance, Victor Lazlo, got in trouble with the Nazis because he dared to publish the truth about them in newspapers. Then when they put a stop to that, he continued to publish 'scandal sheets' about the enemy out of his cellar."

"Whoa, I didn't catch that when I saw it before," Dylan said. "Well, as my favorite journalism professor is so fond of saying"—he winked at Sasha—"'fear of reporters is fear of the truth.'"

"'There can be no higher law in journalism than to tell the truth and shame the Devil,'" Sasha said.

Izzy thought about the Devil in Patriot clothing, and how history seemed to be repeating. "One of the things I really love about *Casablanca* is that when it was made, no one knew who would win the war. In fact, at that time the allies were losing. The entire project was brave and daring. Something to keep in mind even though it appears that we, too, are losing right now."

"We will not lose," Dylan said.

Izzy liked his attitude. "As Lazlo says to Rick, 'Each of us has a destiny for good or for evil.' We simply *must* fight the good fight against evil, or what does our humanity even matter?" She looked up and noticed Tony's eyes tearing up. "Dad?"

He cleared his throat. "Earlier I told your mom I was proud of you, but that was an understatement. Tonight, I'm seeing you more clearly; the young woman you've become. Your courage and indomitable spirit shine, Bella."

"Well, I am your daughter, after all."

He raised his glass to kiss hers. "Here's looking at you, kid."

***

The movie experience was all Izzy wanted it to be.

Every time one of the film's famous lines was spoken, the audience shouted it out.

When a member of the French Underground identified himself to Lazlo by revealing his Cross of Lorraine, many in the club flashed their own crosses to those around them.

When the seemingly amoral prefect of police, Captain Louis Renault, said human life in Casablanca was cheap, they all booed and hissed.

When the "kiss me as if it was the last time" moment arrived, most everyone found someone to lock lips with. Throwing caution to the wind, Izzy grabbed Dylan by his silk tie and pulled him into an epic kiss that excited her far more than she wanted it to. And she noticed that her parents also shared a moment of passion. She hoped it wouldn't really be their last time.

Ruby Night in her elegant satin suit took on the role of Sam from the movie, playing the piano and singing along with him. She and her band performed "It Had to Be You," "Knock on Wood," "Heaven Can Wait," "I'm Just Wild About Harry," and the classic "As Time Goes By."

The band's guitarist, Catalina Alvarez, transformed into the film's cabaret singer, and with her acoustic guitar and powerful soprano voice, the live version of "Tango Delle Rose" became a thing of beauty.

Of course, the most iconic musical moment of all was the scene in the bar when German soldiers sang their military anthem, "Die Wacht am Rhein," and the club's patrons drowned them out in a show of defiance by singing the French national anthem. Tonight's patrons stood in solidarity and also sang "La Marseillaise." Izzy had provided the lyrics in English for everyone, but some, like her, had made the effort to learn them in French. When the song ended and everyone shouted, *"Viva la France!"* Izzy was moved to tears. It had nothing to do with being French and everything to do with standing up to tyranny.

At the movie's end when Humphrey Bogart's Rick said to the new member of the Resistance, "Louie, I think this is the beginning of a beautiful friendship," Izzy's desperate hope was that this tradition she created, which began as a celebration of past resisters, had birthed some modern-day resisters as well.

Because they needed all the help they could get.

***

Following the movie, the party began in earnest.

"Let's go forth and mingle," Harlan told his reporters. "Find meaningful stories. It's what we do."

Erin didn't want to go to work; she was enjoying Tony's company too much. And it seemed as if Dylan wasn't eager to leave Izzy's side either. Erin sensed the simmering attraction those two felt for each other and struggled to tuck away her maternal concerns for review another day. She was sorting out all those feelings when the house lights abruptly came up and a microphone on stage screeched. Then the man's voice that came over the sound system caused her stomach to bottom out.

"Pay attention," Special Agent John Yates told the

crowd. "This is a raid by Homeland Security. Everyone will provide our agents their identity information, and then peacefully leave the premises."

Erin noticed scores of Homeland Security agents in their signature dark jackets and baseball caps blocking the exits and infiltrating the club.

John continued, "As of tonight the movie, *Casablanca*, has been added to the list of banned entertainment because it promotes rebellion and social disobedience. Where is the owner of this establishment?"

Both Andrea and Ruby, who were now seated at the VIP table, stood. However, Ruby spoke first. "I am. Ruby Night."

"No, actually I am," Andrea said. "Andrea Night."

John descended from the stage. "So, which is it? The records I have contain conflicting information."

Andrea stepped forward. "When I inherited the club after my parents' death, I wasn't old enough to be issued a liquor license, so temporary ownership transferred to my aunt. However, last month I took full legal possession and control."

"Oh, Andrea, you really shouldn't—" Ruby said, but Andrea interrupted.

"If anyone's going to get in trouble for this, it should be me."

John walked up to Andrea and typed something into his iPad. Then he noticed Erin. "Well now, if it isn't ace reporter Erin Tavano. Fancy meeting you here."

Erin gestured to those seated at her table. "All the reporters from the *Maverick* are here. We're covering Casablanca Night for our readers. It's become quite a popular local entertainment event."

John chuckled. "And it takes all of you to write a story about it?"

"We're covering it from various angles: social, economic, historical, human interest. All our unique specialties. We're going to do a series about how the businesses on the mall are recovering from the pandemic and subsequent riots." Erin was winging it; she hoped that knowing members of the press were in attendance might somehow help the situation for all involved.

John's iPad beeped and his attention returned to it. "I just ran the history of this club, and it appears that the original owners, John and Lili Night, had one child and the birth records indicate it was a boy named—" He looked at Andrea with disgust. "You're André?"

"Andrea," she replied.

"Right." John's hand darted between Andrea's legs, and he squeezed hard.

Andrea screamed.

Erin gasped.

Everyone at their table stood.

"At least you've still got balls," John said. "Let's see what else you've got." In one swift motion, he ripped off her tube top.

Andrea shrieked and tried to cover her breasts.

Erin saw Izzy reach for her hidden knife, and filled with horror, lunged to stop her. However, Luther— who had been headed toward Andrea—was closer and quickly pinned Izzy in his arms.

"I couldn't protect Karma. I have to protect Andrea," Izzy said as she struggled to break free.

"Stand down!" Andrea ordered them. "You have others to protect ... both of you. I got this. I am my mother's daughter, after all."

John laughed. "You're all so pathetic. And you, *André*, mock our God." He slipped his pad inside his jacket, removed handcuffs from his pocket, and cuffed her.

"Why are you arresting her?" Sasha asked.

"*He* is an abomination but still has the equipment he was born with, so we'll fix him. Undo all the evil this boy has done to himself." John yanked the hat off Andrea's head, threw it to the ground, and stomped on it. "André Night will be deSatanized."

"DeSatanized?" Sasha asked. "What the hell are you talking about? You can't do this." Her arm swept the crowd. "Everyone's recording what you're doing, and word will spread about your cruelty. I'll personally make sure of it. I will take your evil ass down."

"There's nothing wrong with cruelty when the cause is just." John used his pad to take her photo, and then typed in some commands. After its beep, he took a moment to study the screen. "So, Sasha Swan, Professor of Journalism and co-owner of the *Boulder Maverick*, did I just hear you threaten me? Why, yes, I did." He gestured to a nearby agent. "Take her."

Wave after wave of horror crashed down on Erin. Would he arrest Izzy next for having spoken out?

Harlan walked over to Andrea. He removed the coat of his tuxedo, draped it over her shoulders, and buttoned it.

"What do you think you're doing?" John asked.

"She's just a human trying to be. I'm affording her some dignity." Harlan's voice was gentle.

John strode to Harlan and struck him hard across the face.

Blood from his split lip splattered across the white coat, but he barely flinched. "Survive, Andrea, and know you aren't alone."

"Oh, for Christ's sake." John shoved Andrea toward the agent who had cuffed Sasha. "Take them both." Before walking away, John turned to Erin. "You and your merry band of Antipats haven't seen the last of me. Say your prayers and walk softly because I've only just begun to clean up this wicked town."

CHAPTER ELEVEN

Erin didn't want to bring Izzy to the office meeting the next morning, but she had been desperate to attend. As it turned out, no one at the *Maverick* seemed to mind. Perhaps they understood that Izzy felt tremendous guilt because Casablanca Night had been her creation, and she wanted to help put things right.

Besides Izzy, there was another guest. Erin had never met Julia Bainbridge before, but apparently everyone else knew her—including, strangely enough, Izzy.

"Julia occasionally freelances for *The North Star*," Ian told Erin. "She's also our attorney. After our company meeting, we're going to try to figure out how to get Sasha and Andrea released from custody."

Erin wondered if this was the attorney Izzy had mentioned consulting with about the Tobias boys. The terrain of the Underground seemed to be filled with many crossroads.

Everyone filled their coffee cups and took seats around the poker table waiting for Harlan to call the meeting to order. However, for the longest time he simply sat in silence.

"Are you okay?" Dylan finally asked him.

Harlan sat up straighter and took a deep breath. "At one point in *Casablanca*, Rick asks Victor Lazlo, 'Don't you sometimes wonder if it's worth all this? I mean what you're fighting for?' and Lazlo replies, 'You might as well question why we breathe. If we stop breathing, we die. If we stop fighting our enemies, the world will die.' The truth is that we've been so focused on what's happening in our own country I think we've lost sight of the global expansion of authoritarian governments. It's like a rapidly spreading virus—the newest pandemic. The world is at a tipping point and that's why we absolutely must not stop fighting. Our humanity demands it."

Ian slammed his coffee cup down onto the table. "Bloody hell, Harlan. Sasha's been arrested, and everything the paper does moving forward is going to be scrutinized and dissected to use as ammunition against her. Against all of us. We can't take that chance. We must kill *The North Star* now, before it's discovered."

Harlan gave him a look of infinite compassion. "You've lost so much. First your brother, and now the mother of your child has been taken away. But what else can we do? We. Must. Not. Stop. Fighting."

"We have to find another way," Ian insisted.

"*Radio Londres*," Izzy said.

"What?" Harlan asked.

"Radio London. It was a radio show in French broadcasted by the BBC for years during the war and directed to Nazi-occupied France. The Free French ran the show. They used it to counter German propaganda and to encourage the French people to revolt against the occupation. It also was the way they sent coded messages to the French Resistance."

"You want us to do a radio broadcast?" Ian asked. "The airwaves are as closely monitored as the internet is now."

Izzy shook her head. "Not radio, but recordings. There are so many things we could do with that. They could be dropped into the Dark Web. I could get them posted to YouTube channels outside this country. We could save them on CDs to hand out just like we distribute paper copies of *The North Star*. Properly produced, they would be much harder to trace back to us than the paper is."

"That's a stroke of genius," Julia said. "It could actually work."

"It would *totally* work," Dylan said. "When they began banning our music, college students across the country started an underground network to share what we still had. We can't access the songs online anymore, so we returned to old-fashioned CDs. They're recorded and then passed along what we call the Highway to Hell. We could get our recordings to universities everywhere on that highway. Do you know what an impact that would have?"

Harlan smiled for the first time that morning. "Your underground music-sharing network is called Highway to Hell after the AC/DC song? That's surprisingly clever."

"Gen Z, man," Dylan said. "Never underestimate us."

"This feels right, and I am a music promoter at heart. The show must always go on." Harlan looked around the table. "But who would be our recording artist?"

"Mom," Izzy said.

Erin didn't want to do it. "No."

"Why not?" Izzy asked. "You're good. I've heard some of the tapes you made. Grandma played them for me."

"What are we talking about here?" Ian asked.

"When I was in college, I took a few classes in broadcast journalism," Erin said. "But I am by no means an expert. My delivery lacks the requisite pizzazz."

Izzy shook her head. "It certainly does not. You were good. We could work together. I can engineer the recordings. Mask your voice. Make them untraceable. I honestly do think it would be safer than what you're doing now."

Harlan nodded. "It's settled then. I knew when I hired you that you were star material."

"Wait, I—" Erin was interrupted by wild pounding on the locked front door.

Sitting closest to the lobby, Erin could see it was Maisie Mae and Violet, and she went to let them in.

Maisie Mae burst into the office, and with Violet in tow, charged into the meeting room.

"Violet?" Ian opened his arms to her.

The sobbing child raced to Ian and scrambled onto his lap.

"We just saw on the news that Miss Sasha's been arrested," Maisie Mae said. "Why didn't you tell us?"

Ian groaned. "I didn't think it would hit the news so quickly."

Maisie Mae rubbed her cheeks with shaking hands. "She threatened a Homeland Security officer. That's going to get her killed. They're going to kill her now. You know they are."

Violet screamed.

Ian tried to comfort her. "Hush Violet, that's complete rubbish. Maisie Mae is wrong. Don't listen to her."

Harlan stood. "There's no reason to panic. We're working on a plan to get her out."

The frantic woman pointed a trembling finger at him. "This is all your fault. She was working on a story, wasn't she? Doing your bidding?"

Erin approached Maisie Mae and placed a gentle hand on her back. "We were all there watching a movie and—"

She shrugged Erin off. "Don't you dare cover for him. That's what's wrong with this country. Everyone's always making excuses for them."

Erin stepped back. "Them?"

Maisie Mae shook her fist at Harlan. "Sasha's going to die and leave Violet motherless, and it's all your fault. You people are poison and always kill the most beautiful flowers."

"Mommy's going to die!" Violet's sobs turned into wails.

"You're upsetting Violet and need to leave, Maisie Mae." Ian said. "And don't ever come near my daughter again."

The woman's face instantly drained of color. "No, you can't take Violet away from me. She's all I've got."

Ian embraced Violet more tightly. "Get the hell out of here."

Maisie Mae studied each of their faces in turn, then pulled a gun out of her pocket and pointed it at Harlan. Her arm no longer shook, and her voice was strangely calm. "Jew bankers took away my Henri. Now the Jewish media overlords take away my little girl, too? You're evil. All of you people are evil." Before anyone could react, she pulled the trigger.

Thunder drowned out the screams. Suddenly, Erin's entire world telescoped to the flood of blood that soaked Harlan's shirt as he fell backwards. A sense of unreality overcame her, and time shifted. At once, she saw Dylan race to Harlan's side, Ian drop to the floor with Violet tucked protectively beneath him, and Julia duck under the table. Only Izzy remained seated, the laser focus of her eyes on Erin. Izzy's intensity snapped Erin out of her fog, and it occurred to her that even though several other people in the room were likely armed, the safest solution to this ticking bomb would be if it could be diffused.

Erin stepped closer and once again gently placed her hand on Maisie Mae's back.

The woman looked at her with pleading eyes. "You understand that I had to do it, right?"

Erin forced herself to smile. "Yes, I understand."

Maisie Mae lowered the gun. "It's us or them. Jews are the Antichrist."

"That's what Pastor Christian told me, too," Erin said.

"Do you think I'll get a bounty? Is there a bounty paid for killing Jews?" Her voice was an eerie monotone. "I could sure enough use the money."

"I'll give Pastor Christian a call and ask him to give you one," Erin said.

For a moment, Maisie Mae seemed confused. "A call? Oh, I forgot you know him now, too. I heard you even went to his house. Is it nice?"

"He and his wife have a lovely home."

Maisie Mae nodded. "They're lovely people."

Erin reached for the gun. "Is this the gun that you got from Bethany? She offered me one, too. Can I see yours?"

Maisie May looked down at the gun as if she just remembered it was in her hand. "Will I get in trouble with the police?"

Julia slowly approached Maisie Mae and offered her

a business card. "I'm Sasha's attorney. Would you like me to represent you, too?"

Maisie Mae accepted the card and stared at it. "Where is Miss Sasha?"

"Denver Women's Correctional Facility. I could arrange for you two to be together."

"Can I see your gun?" Erin asked again.

"It's a nice gun," Maisie Mae said, but made no move to hand it over.

Erin considered trying to wrest it from her hands, but the woman's finger was still firmly on the trigger. As irrational as she was acting, Erin wasn't sure how best to proceed.

Izzy was suddenly at their side. "I'm Erin's daughter, and she's told me a lot about you, your church, and your very cool house. She said you believe all us girls should have guns to protect ourselves. Is yours the kind of gun you think I should get?" She held out an open hand.

Izzy's boldness terrified Erin.

Maise Mae studied Izzy's face. "I imagine the world's a dangerous place for pretty girls like you."

Izzy nodded. "My best friend was assaulted right in front of me, and I wasn't able to help. It's a guilt I'll carry for the rest of my life."

Maisie Mae's eyes clouded over, and she cocked her head. "I can hear my Henri, and he's telling me that you're speaking God's honest truth." She gasped. "This is the first time he's spoken to me from over yonder since he went that way. How can this be?" She looked at Izzy again. "It's because of you, isn't it? You must be one of the special souls." Slowly, almost reverently, she placed the pistol in Izzy's open hand. "This is a good gun, child. Use it to stay safe."

"Thank you, ma'am, I will." Grasping it tightly, Izzy stepped away.

The sound of sirens rose in the distance.

"I dialed 911 right away and left the line open," Izzy said. Her voice, so steady until now, wobbled.

Julia's hand cupped Maisie Mae's elbow. "Let's go into another office and wait for them."

Meekly, Maisie Mae complied.

Izzy knelt to comfort Dylan, who cradled Harlan's head in his lap. Harlan's eyes stared at them unseeing.

Ian raced from the room with a hysterical Violet in his arms.

Erin made it to a chair before her legs and heart finally surrendered to the horror. As she wept, she thought about Harlan's earlier words. *If we stop breathing, we die. If we stop fighting our enemies, the world will die.*

As much as Erin wanted to throw in the towel because of the apparent futility of trying to defeat evil, she knew that surrender wasn't an option. What then would be the point in living?

As Erin listened to the sounds of sirens growing closer, she heard a familiar voice. It caused her to wonder if in death's shadow the veil between worlds thinned. Maisie Mae had apparently heard her late husband affirm the truth of Izzy's words, and at that moment Erin was certain she heard Harlan say, "The show must go on."

***

"Why am I even here?" Luca asked Izzy. They were at Harlan's home where his friends and family had gathered following his burial. "And why did they plant the guy right away? And why aren't you all broken up like Mom is?"

Izzy struggled to be patient with his incessant whining. "You're here because Mom needs your support. In the Jewish religion, funerals generally happen within twenty-four hours of death. And I am broken up, but one of my superpowers is the ability to hide it." She handed Luca a plate and steered him toward the impressive buffet. "Food like this is hard to come by these days, so please enjoy it and try to be nice to the rest of us. We're all having a very hard time."

Ian and Violet were in line ahead of Luca.

"Is this your brother?" Ian asked Izzy.

She nodded. "This is Luca. Luca, this is Mom's editor and his daughter, Violet."

"Luca, would you mind helping Violet put her plate together?" Ian asked. "I need to join the others in the den."

"You're leaving me?" Violet asked, her voice small.

Ian squatted down. "I'll be in the other room, love. If this nice boy helps you, then you two can join us in just a few."

Izzy was grateful for a job to give Luca. When he felt useful, he tended to be nicer. "You good with that?" she asked him.

"Sure, I'm okay with helping." As hoped, he stood a little taller and seemed a little older.

Izzy and Ian made their way together to the den.

Harlan and Forrest owned the elegant estate located in Boulder's prestigious Chautauqua Park. Harlan had earned his wealth in the concert industry, and Forrest's real estate development career had made him one of the richest men in the state. However, as Izzy settled into the plush leather couch across from Forrest, the raw pain reflected in the man's face spoke to how meaningless money and fame are when hearts and bodies are shattered.

The spacious living room hosted a crowd of stunned mourners, but Forrest had invited only a handful to share his private space. Izzy sat between Erin and Dylan, and as she searched all the faces in the room, she understood how such a quick funeral could be a blessing to those left behind. Most everyone was still in shock, and this connection would help ease the transition as harsh reality came into focus.

"Are you really going to represent Maisie Mae Marchand?" Forrest asked Julia.

She shook her head. "The only reason I offered was to give her a lifeline so we could resolve the crisis. Given my love for Harlan, I couldn't represent her well. After Mrs. Marchand's arrest, I referred her to one of my colleagues. However, I learned this morning that an attorney from Rocky Mountain Patriot Church galloped in and seized the reins. Now I'm concerned about whether justice will be served. With Pastor Tobias's political connections, anything is possible."

Forrest's eyes widened with alarm. "We can't let them cover this up."

"Agreed," Julia said.

Forrest stood, closed the glass French doors that separated the den from the rest of the house, and reclaimed his seat. "I'm not going to allow Harlan's work to die with him. Moving forward, I'll be taking over his position as the *Maverick*'s publisher. I understand that right before the shooting, a decision was reached to put *The North Star* to bed for a while and focus on getting the alternative news out there via recordings. I'm going to stick to that plan. In fact, I'd like to put you, Miss Tavano, on the payroll as producer of those recordings."

Izzy wasn't expecting that. "Um, well, you don't have to pay me. I'm happy to help."

"Nonsense, you should be paid for your expertise. As our payroll records could be examined because of Sasha's troubles, we'll formally hire you as a research assistant. However, you'll receive pay and benefits commensurate with all of your talents."

Although it was an amazing offer, Izzy was torn. "You don't know how much I would love the opportunity, but with Andrea's arrest I can't abandon my friends. They need me at the restaurant."

"I don't see a conflict with that, do you?" Forrest asked.

Izzy considered. "If you're okay with it, yes I can absolutely do both."

"Good. We'll welcome your contribution to our mission."

"Speaking of Andrea Night, I still can't find out what's happened to her," Julia said. "But I have all my investigators working on it."

Dread filled Izzy. Maybe Dante's Resistance cell would be able to find answers.

"Has anyone else wondered what John Yates meant when he said of Andrea, 'He is an abomination but still has the equipment he was born with, so we'll fix him?'" Erin asked. "I mean, it's obvious they are going to try to transition her back, but what if her transition had already been complete and she no longer possessed male genitals? Would they have executed her?"

"I had those same thoughts," Dylan said.

"Holy hell," Izzy said.

A knocking on the door captured their attention. It was Luca and Violet.

"No more talk of clandestine issues," Forrest said before letting the children inside.

Luca and Violet settled themselves on the floor in front of the low coffee table and began eating.

Ian cleared his throat. "I have an announcement, too. I met with Sasha this morning and we made the decision that I'm to return to England with Violet. She and I will move in with my mum. As dangerous as being a journalist here has become, we can't take the chance that Violet will lose both of her parents. I'm sorry to leave everyone at such a critical time, but I simply must."

A shock wave rolled through the room.

Alarm crossed Luca's face. "I thought the guy was killed for being Jewish, not because he was a reporter."

"He was," Ian said. "But American reporters are increasingly in the crosshairs, too. After what happened to Sasha, I can't keep risking arrest or death."

Izzy wanted to smack Ian upside the head for being the most insensitive person on the planet.

Luca looked at Erin. "Is that true, Mom? Is your work dangerous? Could you be killed?"

"I'm not going to die," Erin said, but the lack of confidence in her voice was clear. She had never been a very good liar.

Violet started to cry. "No more blood! Harlan's blood splattered all over. And Maise Mae said Mommy's blood is going to splatter, too. Everyone is going to die." Her weeping morphed into wails.

"Sorry," Ian muttered before scooping up Violet and leaving the room.

Luca set his fork down and continued to stare at Erin.

"Julia, would you consider taking Ian's place as Editor-in-Chief of the *Maverick*?" Forrest asked. "You've got a solid background in journalism, and you support our work."

Julia shook her head and opened her mouth to answer, then stopped and looked at the others in the room. Finally, she said, "Actually, I would be incredibly honored to work with all of you."

Izzy should have been elated by this turn of events, but her spidey sense told her in no uncertain terms that something was on the verge of going hellishly wrong. Perhaps it was because Ian couldn't look anyone in the eye, and it occurred to her to wonder if he might have made a deal with the authorities to turn them in for Sasha's release. Or maybe it had something to do with the recordings they were planning. Her rational mind told her they were less of a risk than *The North Star* had been, but her sense of unease was profound. Internal alarms warned her of danger ahead. Despite fear threatening an emergency shutdown sequence, Izzy forced herself to stay online, determined to override the panic and successfully execute the mission.

CHAPTER TWELVE

"If you are listening to this recording, stop now if you are afraid of hearing unpleasant truths. And if you have the CD, know that the authorities would love to get their hands on it, so guard it well."

Erin began each recording with the same warning. Then came the signature intro music. After picking Conor's brain about Vietnam War era protest songs, Izzy decided to open each episode with "All Along the Watchtower" by Jimi Hendrix and to close with "Gimme Shelter" by the Rolling Stones.

Jimi also helped to define Erin's new rebel identity: Watchtower.

Izzy masked Erin's voice in two layers. The top layer, the person the listener thought they were hearing, was a young woman with a slight South Carolina drawl. Beneath that, should anyone manage to unmask the narrator, was a man with a distinct Chicago accent.

As Izzy always liked to say, she had mad computer skills.

For the episodes Izzy released on the Dark Web and via YouTube channels outside the country, Izzy added photographs and video of the subject matter, often shot by Dylan. For the CDs, she designed the covers for a band named Watchtower. Titles given to the individual recordings were created with the hope they would easily blend in with other music CDs.

Erin and Izzy recorded each episode in Izzy's computer cave. It was the most electronically secure space they could find, and the small, well-insulated outbuilding was surrounded by a copse of trees that helped to muffle ambient sound. Erin sat at the desk with her notes and a microphone that was connected to Izzy's laptop. Izzy and her computer worked from the bed. They timed the sessions for when Luca was out of the house, either at school or at Meg's ranch, and told Conor and Kelly they were working on a research project and couldn't be disturbed. Erin needed to minimize distractions—lacking confidence, she had never felt more out of her depth than she did now. However, she garnered strength from partnering with Izzy. They made a good team.

***

The recording labeled *Sister Songbird* was based on an interview Erin had with Dante. It involved revelations made by his Resistance cell in partnership with another. As Erin sat down to record it, her emotions threatened to undermine her poise. This was one of the most difficult pieces of investigative journalism she had so far tackled.

At Izzy's signal, Erin introduced herself and launched into Sister Songbird's story. "This is Watchtower with the American Resistance coming to you from deep Underground. Today, I want to tell you about Rose Washington.

"Rose was born to an impoverished Black family in Georgia in 1945. Determined to do something meaningful with her life, she joined the Navy and became a nurse. During the Vietnam War, Lt. Washington served on the hospital ship USS Repose, which operated in the South China Sea. Rose's nursing skills were excellent, but it was her compassion that gained the most respect."

Erin studied a photograph Izzy had found of Rose in her Navy dress uniform. Every time Erin looked at it, the delightfully mischievous expression the pretty young woman wore caused Erin to smile. The sparkle in her eyes and playful grin on her lips spoke volumes about the nature of her spirit. Erin imagined that just her mere presence would offer comfort to those she ministered, but Rose had given them so much more.

"Rose could sing. *Really* sing. Trained in gospel as a child, she used her voice to comfort wounded soldiers. What made her style unique among those touched by her musical gift was her choice of songs. Although her powerful renditions of 'Amazing Grace' and 'Summertime' were always welcome, her acapella repertoire also included contemporary favorites such as 'California Dreamin',' 'Hit the Road Jack,' and 'Ain't No Mountain High Enough'—songs which brought smiles to the faces of pain and despair. And when she learned that one of the favorite songs of in-country troops was Nancy Sinatra's 'These Boots Are Made for Walkin',' she sang that, too. Sometimes her patients would even sing along with her.

"It was when she returned stateside and was assigned to San Diego's Balboa Naval Hospital that her singing took on an edgier tone. Working with wounded soldiers embittered by their experiences, the songs that had brought comfort on board the Repose were not well-received by those in transition at Balboa. Meeting the moment, and much to the chagrin of her superiors, Rose's songs changed: 'Eve of Destruction,' 'Blowin' in the Wind,' 'All Along the Watchtower,' and Nina Simone's 'Backlash Blues' connected her with patients in a way no one else in her position had before. Among the wounded warriors Rose cared for she became known as Sister Songbird, and they considered her their champion.

"My research team managed to locate several audio recordings of Rose singing at a private party when she would have been about forty years of age. To understand just how ... um, I'm searching for an adequate word to describe this woman's voice ... *magnificently* Rose sang, here she is accompanying herself on piano, singing 'Feeling Good.'"

Izzy cut the mic, and the song came on over the stereo system. Even though it wasn't necessary to treat this as a live broadcast, it helped Erin's focus to do so.

Izzy looked at Erin's trembling hand. "Nervous?"

Erin took a deep breath and tried to relax. "Shaken. I haven't pushed through the horror of this story yet. It's ... too much."

"Want to take a break?"

"No." Erin examined her feelings. "I'm experiencing this urgent need to get my stories out there as quickly as possible. Every single moment counts now, like it never has before. There's so much we need to do, and we need to do it faster."

Izzy sat up straighter. "That's what he said, too."

"What? Who?"

"Uncle Brian. He's been appearing to me in my dreams. Last night he said, 'Hurry. Get it done faster,' and when I tried to ask him what I should get done faster he disappeared."

Erin's mind raced as she inventoried all the stories they were working, all the prisoners they were trying to free, all the leads they had yet to chase, and all the mysteries they still needed to solve. "Did you get any sense what he was referring to?"

"Not really. Personally, I'm juggling so many projects. Besides producing and distributing these shows, I'm still trying to take down Pastor Christian. And the bounty hunting assignment I'm doing with Shiloh is super time sensitive. Dante needs my help with that new concern his cell uncovered about double agents in the Underground. Plus, I'm working so damn hard to find Sofia's sister." Her arms flailed wildly in the air as her voice mimicked an explosion. "My world is on fire, and I'm dancing in the flames as fast as I can."

The final notes of "Feeling Good" faded, so Erin forced herself to focus once again on Sister Songbird. She returned to the microphone.

"Rose never married, but she did bear a son. Charles Washington became a commercial pilot and eventually moved to Denver where he was based with Frontier Airlines. Following her retirement, Rose relocated to Denver to be close to him and his family."

Erin picked up another photo—one of a sweet, young girl—and studied it.

"Rose's youngest grandchild, Mercy, had Down Syndrome. Rose took Mercy under her Songbird wings and taught her to sing, which helped Mercy not only learn to speak more clearly but also boosted her fragile self-confidence. Once again, Rose's compassion and kindness carried the grace of healing."

A rush of grief flooded Erin's heart at what was about to come, and for a moment … just a moment … her voice betrayed her. She summoned all her strength to continue.

"Then Chimera struck the Washington family

down. Charles, his wife, and their two sons died, leaving Rose and seven-year-old Mercy as the only survivors. Financial reserves went fast, and the family home was foreclosed. Rose—elderly and battling numerous age-related illnesses—and Mercy found themselves out on the street but felt blessed when the new government extended a hand. Officials told Rose and Mercy that there was a place for them high in the Colorado Rockies near the town of Fairplay. Butted up against a thick forest of bristlecone pines, a state-of-the art camp for the old and infirm had been constructed in a grassy valley near the Middle Fork South Platte River. They told Rose that the former mining town of Fairplay was the trout fishing capital of Colorado, and that they would be happy there."

Erin glanced at Izzy. She thought about when their home had been foreclosed and considered how—if it were not for the kindness of her grandfather—she would have welcomed help from the government. She suppressed a shudder and closed her eyes. Erin didn't need to refer to any more notes to remind her of what came next.

"Because of its artist, Rose had no reason to doubt the idyllic picture that was painted for her. Rose had worked for the government her entire life. In a very real sense, it had been her family.

"Rose and Mercy eagerly allowed themselves to be taken to Camp Fairplay. Immediately upon arrival, they were escorted to a stark, haunted chamber. Before the door closed, Rose turned to the guard and asked, 'Will it be done with gas, son?' Startled by the bold question and her unflappable strength of character, the guard replied, 'Yes, ma'am.' Rose didn't panic or beg or cry. Instead, she led Mercy to a bench in the middle of the room, gathered her into her arms, and sang 'Summertime' while the hydrogen cyanide gas was released. Sister Songbird Lt. Rose Washington died as she had lived, with immeasurable grace and nobility."

A gasp escaped Erin. "Hell is empty, and all the devils are here," she whispered. Grief seized her and wouldn't let go. "I … I need to stop."

Izzy pulled off her headphones and stood just as Erin got up and fell into her arms.

Anguish filled Erin to overflowing. "It's all too much," she managed to say before uncontrollable sobs stole her breath.

Izzy hugged her tightly. "I'm so sorry, Mom. I should never have encouraged you to do this. It's too hard on you. Your heart is too sweet. I am so horribly sorry." She also began to cry.

Erin pulled back, grasped Izzy's head between her hands, and looked deep into her eyes. "You have nothing to apologize for. I made the decision to work with the Resistance, and I've grown so much because of this journey. I always felt being a wife and mother was my purpose in life, but this work has completed me. My soul is … bigger. Richer. No matter what happens, thank you for helping me to be more and do more. I mean that."

"I love you so much, Mom."

"No matter what happens," Erin repeated.

After a long moment, Izzy nodded. "No matter what happens."

"Okay, let's finish this." Erin pulled herself together as much as she was able, retook her seat, and continued.

"How, you may ask, do we know all this? The American Resistance is a force to be reckoned with, my friends. Two separate cells were involved in discovering the fate of Rose and Mercy. After tracking their journey from Denver to Fairplay, members of the Underground embedded themselves in the community of Fairplay, befriended employees of the camp, bugged their homes, recorded private discussions, took photographs, tracked large shipments of hydrogen cyanide to the camp, and gathered other damning evidence."

She picked up a vial of ashes and studied it.

"Included in that evidence were copious amounts of cremated human remains scattered in the mountains around Fairplay and the forest adjacent to the camp. I'm told that birds no longer sing in that forest. Longtime locals who don't know the truth about Camp Fairplay can't figure out why the birds deserted them, but we know. The new Patriot government of the United States, in its obscene effort to Make America Strong, is systematically murdering everyone who doesn't fit in with its grand plan. It is inhumane, criminal, and evil.

"These facts and their supporting evidence have been smuggled out of this country and are destined for The International Court of Justice, in The Hague, Netherlands. It is only one of many cases the American Resistance is taking to the World Court. We need help and are asking—no begging—the world to help us.

"In the meantime, what can we do? Storming the many portals to Hell in this country will only get us killed. At this moment in time, no amount of violence we could bring to the problem will correct it, and in fact would be counterproductive. We need to gather what damning evidence we can, get it where it needs to be, make connections both here and in friendly countries, and devise a coordinated, constructive plan. But most of all in the here and now, we need to help each other. Embrace what Rose Washington's life taught us. Be noble and kind and extend grace to all who need it.

"I'm going to close this episode of Watchtower in the usual way, with the song 'Gimme Shelter.' However, this time it will be sung by Rose Washington. Personally, I don't believe it was a coincidence that we found this song among those party tapes. Rose was famous for giving people exactly what they needed when they needed it.

"The storm is here and threatening our lives today, people. Give shelter to those you can. And choose love. It's just a kiss away."

Erin blew her trademark closing kiss into the microphone and allowed the magnificent voice of Sister Songbird to carry it into waiting hearts.

CHAPTER THIRTEEN

On Easter Sunday, Ruby decided to close Café Paris at noon and not open The Underground that night. Restaurants and bars rarely closed on Easter, and this was a first for them, but with everything they had all endured over the past few weeks there was a longing for family, and safety, and time to heal.

Ruby had stepped into Andrea's role as manager of the café, but it was taking a toll on her because she also managed the club. So, Karma's parents were poised to take over management of Café Paris.

And another surprising change was that Karma emerged from hiding. She said baring her face in public was nothing compared with what Andrea had endured when her top had been ripped away, and she was tired of living in fear. To that end, beginning that morning, Karma waited tables alongside Izzy and discovered people weren't as unkind as she imagined they would be.

Izzy had never been more proud of her friend.

After all her customers had paid their breakfast tabs, Izzy took a break and slid into Luther's booth next to him.

He was still eating the Easter special that Mei Ling had made him.

"Your eggs Benedict and lyonnaise potatoes look better than the eggs Benedict and lyonnaise potatoes everyone else was served today," Izzy said.

"That's because I'm special," Luther said with a wink.

"Yeah, well, there is that." Izzy snatched a potato off his plate and popped it into her mouth.

"Are you doing anything Easterish today?" Luther asked.

"I went to Easter Mass with my dad this morning."

"Surprising. You're not religious, are you?"

Izzy shook her head. "But I love Dad and it was important to him. No one else would go with. He's trying hard to be, you know, better."

"I do know that. We've become close friends. He's a good man."

"Yes, he is." Izzy snagged another potato. "What are you planning for the rest of your day?"

"I'm going to take Karma home. She said I don't need to escort her anymore, but of course I will. After that, I'll take a long nap." He gestured to the thick curtain of snow coming down outside the window. "Later, given the wicked weather, I plan to get dinner from your dad and share it with my crow friend. He's getting old. I want to make sure he gets a good meal today."

Izzy noticed Luther wore the red garnet teardrop earring that a crow had gifted him years ago. "Is it the same crow who gave you that earring?"

Luther nodded.

Izzy found it amazing that they had a relationship after all this time. "Still haven't named him?"

"Not mine to name."

"How long do they live?"

"Not long enough."

Izzy's fingers rubbed the warrior stone on her wrist. Luther had given her the bloodstone when he received the garnet, and she found a jeweler on the mall who had used it to make the bracelet. As with Lili's Cross of

Lorraine, it was something she wore every day. "Being a warrior is hard. Mom broke down and sobbed in my arms the other day. She's never done that before."

Luther pushed his empty plate away and picked up his coffee cup. "It's a hard life, what we do. I also think that she now sees you as the woman you are and no longer as a little girl. She met you as an equal. You should be honored."

Izzy hadn't thought about it like that.

"Speaking of being a woman, have you made a choice yet between your two men?"

"What? How do you know about Dante?" She waved away the question. "Oh, never mind. You're just spooky. Truthfully, they're both great guys and there's a whole lot of electricity sparking wild all over the place, but neither. Not now."

"When the time comes, how will you decide?"

Izzy spent a few minutes sorting her thoughts before replying. "Well, I'm from a family of people who love big. Really big. Papa and Nana. Brian and Mark. Mom and Dad. Because of that I have high expectations. I asked Uncle Brian what their secret was, and he quoted something Charlie Chaplin had supposedly told his daughter: 'Your naked body should only belong to those who fall in love with your naked soul.' And, yeah, I think that's what it is. Exactly that. The big lovers in my family all fell in love with who their partners were, not how they looked or how they made them feel because those things change all the time. In fact, growing up around all these passionate lovers, I came to the conclusion that they got off more on connecting on the soul level than the physical one. It's subtle, but powerful. A shy sort of magic."

A rare smile crossed Luther's face.

"What?"

"You may have just taught me something."

That genuinely surprised Izzy. "And what about you? Are you loving anyone right now?"

He shrugged and his smile faded.

"What about your bass player, Yanah?"

"Yeah, I've heard those rumors, too."

Izzy waited.

"I think I've been approaching her in the wrong way. Perhaps I need to get to know her soul better."

She slugged him playfully. "You're a fast learner."

"I try."

Izzy lowered her voice. "So, on another subject, I have an idea. We now have DNA proof that John Yates and that Ukrainian prisoner Sofia Kostenko are the parents of the baby John's wife claims is hers. And Mom believes he murdered Sofia to steal the baby. Do you think we could use that information as a bargaining chip to get Andrea released?"

"You mean blackmail him?" Luther grew thoughtful. "In the Before Times, yes. Now, no. His people control the news and the law, so how could it impact him? It would just get more people arrested and likely executed."

That's what she was afraid he'd say. "I know your spidey sense is kinda like mine. Have you been feeling more intense niggles of doom lately?"

"It's almost unbearable."

Yes, Izzy agreed. it certainly was.

***

Erin slept in on Easter morning, and when she finally

stumbled into the kitchen looking for coffee, she found her mother wrestling with a huge standing rib roast.

"Who's winning?" Erin asked.

Kelly used the back of her wrist to swipe wild red curls away from her face. "The cow."

Erin poured a cup of coffee for herself and settled at the kitchen table to watch the spectacle. "You've never cooked Easter dinner for us before. What's up?"

"I'm suddenly feeling maternal. I wanted my children ... my incarnated children ... together today. I'm missing Brian. And I'm missing you."

"Me?"

Kelly turned to face her. "I don't understand it either. There's a disturbance in the Force."

Erin found that unsettling because she, too, had been inexplicably feeling a shadow of unease. Rather than explore that line of thinking, she changed the subject. "Wherever did you find a roast that big, let alone afford it?"

Kelly washed her hands. "It's from Meg. When I told her I wanted to do this, I guess they butchered some poor unsuspecting soul." She wrinkled her nose. "Frankly, I don't want to think about that part of it. Anyway, I drove to their place this morning and picked it up. Luca wanted to go to Easter services with them, so I dropped him off. They'll bring him back when they come for dinner."

Anger ripped through Erin like a bolt of lightning. "You did *what*? How dare you do that without my permission!" The thought of Luca being exposed to the poison of Pastor Christian horrified her.

All the color left Kelly's face, and her eyes widened with alarm. "What? What did I do wrong?"

"I don't want him anywhere near that church," Erin said. "Ever."

"I'm sorry. I didn't know. Please don't be mad at me." Kelly once again swiped away errant locks of hair, but this time her hand trembled.

Erin was taken aback by her reaction. This was the first time her mother had ever demonstrated remorse or been apologetic about anything. Forcing herself to calm down, she said, "Just don't do it again."

Kelly nodded, then busied herself rubbing salt and pepper into the roast.

"Is there anything I can do to help?" Erin asked.

"Your father's name is Rory Gallagher."

The non-sequitur hung in the air, and Erin struggled to wrap her mind around it. "What did you just say?"

"Your father's name is Rory Gallagher," Kelly repeated.

The twins had spent their lives begging to know who their father was, but Kelly would never reveal his identity. This moment felt so fragile that Erin was afraid to touch it. "What ... why tell me now?"

"Because I wish I had told Brian before it was too late. I don't want to make that same mistake with you."

Erin didn't know what was happening. "Please tell me." Her heart raced with anticipation. "Tell me everything."

Kelly spent a few more minutes seasoning the roast and wrangling it into the oven, then she poured herself a cup of coffee and took a seat across the table from Erin. "You didn't know me before you were born, but I was different. I was a boring, vapid, stupid girl. Meg's father was the star of the football team, and I was the prettiest cheerleader. Meg was conceived the night he and I were crowned prom royalty. I couldn't have been more of a cliché if I had tried."

Erin couldn't imagine a moment in this time/space continuum when her mother was anything close to a normal human being.

Kelly scooped a heaping spoonful of sugar into her coffee and stirred it with a vengeance. "Erik Nygaard never wanted anything to do with Meg, even though he's always lived right here in town. I think that's a big part of why she's like she is." A sad expression crossed her face, but after a moment she shook her head and continued. "Anyway, after she was born, I went to college, majored in business admin, and was determined to be the best single parent in the known universe. My graduation present was a trip to Ireland. My folks wanted to give me a break from parenting and all things practical, and I'm sure because of how it changed me they always regretted that. But it was the best thing that ever happened in my life ..." Her voice died off.

Erin tried to be patient while her mother's wistful expression indicated she had become lost in a universe of internal memories. However, in truth she felt like a child at Christmas impatient to receive long-awaited gifts.

Finally, Kelly continued. "The trip was advertised by the travel agent as 'A Midsummer's Night Dream in Ireland,' and it promised a tour of all the hot spots where the pagans held their Midsummer fire festivals to celebrate the light and invoke an abundant harvest. The Hill of Tara, the Carrowkeel Cairns, the Grange Stone Circle at Lough Gur. Something inside me thrilled at the idea, and that's what I signed up for.

"You and Brian were conceived on the Hill of Tara. A large group of us camped out there the night before the solstice so we could greet the sunrise. There was this absolutely gorgeous man there, playing a *bodhrán* drum and singing the most haunting songs. He had us all completely mesmerized. It was a cold, windy night. At one point, I went to my tent to put on warmer clothes, and the Irish bard followed me. One thing led to another and suffice it to say that I experienced the most magical night of my life. When I woke shortly before dawn, he was gone. No one seemed to know where he had come from, and no one saw him leave. All I knew was his name. I tried to track him down, but every road was a dead end."

Erin and Brian always wondered if their mother had let their father know about their existence.

"After that night the world was different. I was different. I'm convinced that I had an encounter with the supernatural and that you and Brian are special souls. From the moment that you two started to dance together in the sacred cave below my heart, I knew that reality had shifted, and nothing would ever be the same again." She looked at Erin with a fierce expression of love. "And nothing has been. I am the luckiest woman in the world to have known you two." She reached across the table and grasped Erin's hand.

"Why did you make him such a big secret?"

"Think about it. If I had said that you two were fathered by a supernatural being, how would that have affected your lives? Think about the ridicule. No, it was best that I kept that secret to myself. Except now I ... well, things are different now and so it all needs to be said."

A supernatural being? Erin had always accepted that her mother was eccentric but until that moment hadn't considered that she was also mentally ill.

"And I knew that you would think I was insane, which is what you're thinking now."

"I don't think you're insane," Erin said.

Kelly laughed. "You're *such* a terrible liar. But what really matters is that I know the truth. Please believe me when I say that your otherworldly roots are why you and Brian were born with such incredible creativity, finely tuned intuition, and the ability to love so purely. And from what I've seen so far, Isabelle has also inherited those special genes. The seed of my Irish Bard continues to flourish in this world in beautiful and unexpected ways."

A lifetime of resentment Erin had held toward her mother for being embarrassingly kooky and emotionally unavailable faded away in an instant. Perhaps a broken mind had been responsible for the irrational behavior all along. In that moment, Erin felt only compassion and tenderness. It was a profound moment of healing, and for that gift she would be forever grateful.

***

Springtime along Northern Colorado's Front Range was the snowiest time of the year, and the storm that hit the area on Easter morning worsened by the hour. By the time Izzy left work, a thick shroud of snow and ice covered the roads, and traffic crawled. When she finally made it home, the warmth and tantalizing cooking smells that embraced her swept away the haunting doom niggles. For the first time all day, she relaxed.

Izzy kicked off her boots, hung up her coat, and joined Diva on the fireplace hearth. She tried to pet the sleepy cat, but a guttural growl dissuaded her. "You've become such a bitch since Uncle Brian left us."

Conor rolled his chair closer to the fire and stared into the flames. "She's never gotten over the loss. People who say cats are too independent to bond, don't know what the hell they're talking about."

"You're right," Izzy said. "Sorry, Diva. Grief is the bitch, not you."

Diva gave her the stink eye, then turned her back, curled up in a tight ball, and went to sleep.

"I miss him, too," Izzy whispered. She looked up at Conor. "So, Aunt Meg and Uncle Beau are coming to dinner? How do you feel about that?" They hadn't been to the house since Conor had ordered them to leave Brian's wake.

"As long as they behave decently, I'm willing. It's important to Kelly, so I'm trying to go with the flow."

"Yeah, what's with Grandma lately? She's been so … nice."

Conor grinned. "I've never understood her many moods, but I'll take this one."

Erin came upstairs and settled on the couch. Dressed casually in blue jeans and a scoop-neck sweater, her only concession to the Easter holiday was a string of Nana's pearls around her neck.

Izzy had worn her own late grandmother's pearl rosary as a necklace all day. She considered the fact that although neither of them was religious, they independently chose to honor the women from whom they descended. Like mother, like daughter. As Izzy was learning, they were more alike than she had ever before understood. She found that remarkable.

The front door opened, and a bitter wind chased Luca, Meg, and Beau inside. Excited, Mojo greeted them with a uniquely Australian Shepherd-style song and dance involving a wildly wiggling butt and a medley of happy yaps.

Before hanging up his coat, Beau pulled a big chunk of dried jerky from his pocket and gave it to him. "From the Easter Bunny."

Mojo snatched it and celebrated with an excited burst of zoomies around the room.

Kelly emerged from the kitchen. "Happy Easter."

Meg handed her a colorful bouquet of flowers. "Something to brighten up this ugly day."

Kelly clutched them to her chest. "Thank you, but having my girls together brings me even more delight."

Meg gave Erin a quizzical look and Erin shrugged.

It seemed that no one knew what to make of Kelly's pleasant side.

Beau offered a hand to Conor. "Happy Easter, sir."

Conor accepted it, and they shook.

Beau gave him an expensive bottle of Cabernet Sauvignon. "It goes good with prime rib."

"Appreciated," Conor said.

Izzy was thrilled to see the respect. No one seemed to be themselves today. It was awesome. Even Luca, who had been nothing but sullen lately, bounced around with a big grin on his face.

"What's with you?" Izzy asked him.

"I did something exciting today. I'm the man of the family now. Told you I'd take care of all of us."

"What does that even mean?"

"Mom's not gonna have to be a reporter anymore, and you can go to college. Everything's about to change. You'll see." He stuck his hands deep into the pocket of his jeans and strutted away.

Izzy looked at Beau. "What's with him?"

"He's been really upbeat since church," Beau said. "I told everyone a solid religious experience would do him good."

"Right." Izzy knew her brother well enough to easily dismiss that theory. Something was off, and her spidey sense went into overdrive. She looked at her mother, whose expression revealed alarm. Izzy stood up at the same moment Erin did, and just as they both came to attention, a violent pounding hammered on the front door. Before anyone could respond, the door was kicked open and a half dozen Homeland Security officers charged in with guns drawn.

Amid frantic screams and shouts, Izzy became acutely aware of Mojo's angry barking and Conor's desperate pleas for him to stand down. Ignoring the officers' commands for everyone to freeze, Izzy boldly intercepted Mojo, grasped him by his collar, and angled herself into the line of fire of a Glock pointed right at him. She defiantly made eye contact with the officer wielding that gun, and the man gave her a curt nod before lowering it.

After one of the agents yelled, "Clear!" Special Agent John Yates strode into the house and greeted them with an ingratiating smile. "Ace reporter Erin Tavano, we meet again," he said. "Did we stumble into an Antipat meeting?"

Erin shook her head. "We're a family having Easter dinner. What the hell do you want?"

"Actually, I want you." John held up a CD of Watchtower's *Sister Songbird*. "Your son helpfully turned this in to me today at the church's Patriot Bounty Office. Thanks to his admirable little bounty hunting patriotic spirit, I'm here to arrest you for treason."

Horror swept the room, and every eye fell onto Luca.

"What?" Luca said. "You didn't say you were gonna arrest Mom. You promised me a bounty for turning in the CD."

"Well, little man, you told me that you found it in your mother's briefcase, which makes her guilty of treason. Don't worry, you'll get your money. And in exchange, we get to execute an enemy of the state."

Execute? The word struck Izzy's heart like a spear. She fought to breathe.

John looked at the heavily laden coat rack by the door and the mountain of boots beneath it, then waggled his fingers at Erin. "Which are yours?"

Her voice strangled, she managed to say, "Jean jacket, brown boots."

The agent standing closest to the door grabbed the sherpa-lined denim jacket, examined its pockets, then tossed it to Erin.

She glanced at Izzy before putting it on. Her eyes overflowed with terror.

A moment later a pair of brown cowboy boots landed at Erin's feet. "No, these are Meg's. Mine are—"

"Just put the damn things on," John said.

Erin complied.

Izzy released Mojo and threw herself into her mother's arms. Anguish stole her words, however Erin managed to whisper, "Take care of Luca, and please remember that resistance is *not* futile."

An agent yanked Izzy out of Erin's arms and pushed her away, then cuffed Erin's hands behind her back. Roughly, she was shoved toward and out the front door.

"Mom!" Luca cried. "I didn't mean it."

Special Agent John Yates smiled again and said, "Enjoy your Easter dinner." He walked out and the last officer to leave did his best to close the damaged door behind him.

"I didn't mean it!" Luca shouted again.

Izzy spun to face him. "What did you do?"

Tears streamed down his face. "Last night, I went to ask Mom something, but her phone rang and when she answered it, I saw the CD laying in her open briefcase. I thought it was music, so I grabbed it to listen to while I was playing Xbox."

Izzy still couldn't understand. "Did you listen to the whole thing?"

Luca shook his head. "Just to when the lady said the government would want it. I was trying to help us."

"Are you stupid, boy?" Beau asked.

"You did this to one of your own?" Meg said. "You don't betray family, no matter what."

"I didn't betray her," Luca said, sobbing. He rubbed his eyes with his fists. "I was scared she was going to get killed for being a reporter and wanted to save her."

Kelly sank to her knees. "I knew it. I knew she was going to die."

Luca started to howl.

Izzy understood that she should comfort him but couldn't bring herself to do so.

Mojo whined and nuzzled Luca. Conor rolled over to rub Luca's back.

Izzy tried to process all of it. She fought the urge

to throttle Luca. She wanted to turn on Meg and Beau and scream that it was their preacher who made this possible. She was furious with herself for not having already ruined Pastor Christian. She considered gathering a posse of resisters, storming Homeland Security gates, and going all Sarah Connor on their asses. However, in the end, she decided to do the logical thing and call Julia. And then she broke the news to her father.

***

John sat behind his desk across from Erin and held up the CD. "Want to comment?"

Erin rubbed her wrists where the cuffs had chaffed. "It was sent to me anonymously. A note said it was a lead for a story."

"Presuming that's true, were you going to write a story about it?"

"How? Where would I be allowed to publish it?"

"Exactly." His eyes narrowed. "Why didn't you turn it in to us immediately?"

"I just got it. My publisher—to whom I usually turned for advice—was recently murdered. It's Easter. I hadn't really had time to think anything through yet."

He dropped the CD onto his desk and shook his head. "You're beautiful, smart, and talented, but Mrs. Tavano you do not lie well. I don't believe a thing you've said." He smiled. "That's okay because we have ways of learning the truth that involve torture and drugs. By this time tomorrow, believe me when I say that you will reveal everything you know and everyone involved with your subversive activities. Those activities that you will end up confessing to include the Antipat act of sabotage you and your photographer committed at Patrick Henry Primary School. You can take comfort in the fact that you won't be executed alone."

The burn of nausea rose, but Erin swallowed hard and breathed as deeply as she could to cool its fire. She didn't want John to witness her depth of terror. As Erin's body submitted to her will, so did her frantic mind, and the glimmer of a plan started to form.

"In the meantime," John said, "it is indeed Easter and I have family up from Texas to meet my newborn son and share the holiday with us. So, I'm going to go home. We'll resume this conversation in the morning." He signaled to the guard standing at his door. "Take her to the women's quarters."

Erin understood she had never been a good liar, but because of Brian's influence she had absorbed a few acting skills. She invoked his spirit. Casually, she gestured to the pack of cigarettes on his desk. "Well, I had quit, but it appears as if I won't live long enough to worry about my health. Can I bum a cigarette?"

John tossed her the pack. "Keep them, but you have to ask a guard for a light." He stood and stretched. "Have a lovely Easter, Mrs. Tavano. It'll be the last one you'll ever see."

"May God forgive you for the evil you do," she said.

"God?" John laughed. "God answers to me now."

***

Erin took two cigarette breaks outside in the women's recreational area so that she could become familiar with procedure. The most useful thing she learned was that the guards changed shifts at eight o'clock, so shortly before eight she took her final cigarette break. It was her hope that the incoming guard wouldn't know that she was outside because she needed as much time as possible to complete her plan.

The idea had come to her because of the story Harlan shared about his friend, Danny, who tried to commit suicide by freezing to death. Harlan said it was a relatively painless way to die. Curious, she had researched it, and the consensus was that following some initial discomfort one simply went to sleep and died.

The thought of death terrified Erin, but the idea of betraying her family and colleagues under torture was even more horrifying.

Sofia had told her that the bench in the far northeast corner was in a camera blind spot. Light from the yard's two overhead poles didn't fall in that corner either, so it was an ideal place to hide.

The snow still fell, but not as heavily as earlier in the day. After sunset, the fat fluffy flakes transformed into a lighter snowfall whipped into a frenzy by brutal northern wind. As she prepared to die, the wind's howl resembled that of a banshee. She thought it was an appropriate soundtrack for her death scene.

Erin snubbed out the cigarette and put it in her pocket in case she was discovered too soon and needed the prop. Then unbuttoning her jacket, she braced for the uncomfortable part of the plan. However, she had been unprepared for how much pain would be involved before the numbness set in. Her feet, in Meg's oversized and under-insulated cowboy boots were cold to begin with, and the colder they got the more pain she endured. She had no gloves so shoved her hands into the coat's pockets. Having cold extremities wouldn't kill her; it was the core temperature that would do her in.

Violent shivering signaled that her core was dropping, and she fought the urge to remove her coat entirely to expedite the process—if someone did come out into the yard, she didn't want her plan to be obvious. She needed this to work.

As the misery increased, Erin tried to shift her attention away from her body and escape into her inner world.

She never thought Luca would betray her. The possibility had never crossed her mind. The profound shock of it was breathtaking.

Would she do it all again? Yes, of course she would. Heroism was a family tradition, after all.

Did she help to change history? She believed what she did had made a difference. However, she certainly hadn't done that alone. She had worked with a noble group of resisters.

As she contemplated her own death, she wished there was more time to live, to love, and to grow.

And as the great unknown loomed, she wondered how the hearts of her loved ones would hold her memory.

"You do what I think you do?" Sofia asked.

Erin's eyes flew open to see Sofia sitting on the bench next to her. She didn't feel the cold any longer. In fact, she seemed quite warm. "Am I dead?"

"Not yet, but you close. Why you do this thing?"

"John promised they would make me give up fellow members of the Resistance—and confess to things we haven't done—and I believe they will. I can't let that happen."

"*Slava heroyu*, Erin Tavano. Glory to the hero. You

brave woman."

"No ... just pragmatic."

"I not know that word, but if you say so."

Erin studied Sofia's face; she looked even more beautiful than she had on the day they met. "Why are you still hanging around here?"

"Things not fixed yet. My son. My sister."

"Isabelle, my daughter, is working on fixing all of that. She will. I promise you."

"She hero like you?"

Erin smiled. "Oh, much more than me. She's extraordinary."

"Good legacy to leave."

"I'm so damn proud of her."

"So, she make sure son of bitch bastard not get away with my son?"

"Her goal is to find your sister, free her, and somehow place your son in her custody. I'm not sure how she will accomplish it all, but if anyone can pull it off, she can."

Sofia grew pensive. "*Slava heroyu*, Isabelle Tavano." After a few minutes of silence, Sofia pointed toward the other end of the yard. "I think he here for you."

Erin looked up and saw Brian, who stood in the midst of an unearthly light. Of course he would be there to meet her. They were two halves of one soul.

CHAPTER FOURTEEN

Izzy had been paralyzed by grief since the family was notified of her mother's death. She hadn't left her cave for a week; in fact, she barely left her bed. Everyone had tried to lure her out, but she resented the efforts of each and every one of them. The only soul she had admitted into her room was a very insistent Diva who clawed at her door incessantly until granted entry.

"I think Uncle Brian must have sent you," Izzy told the surprisingly affectionate cat, and she felt in her soul that was true. Her uncle also seemed to be present, which upset her more than it helped because she couldn't feel her mother's presence at all. Perhaps, despite Erin's previous protestations to the contrary, she really did blame Izzy for encouraging her involvement in the Resistance. Or maybe she was mad at her for not understanding that Brian's warnings for Izzy to hurry had been about shutting down the bounty program. That had to be it, she decided, and it deepened her despair even more.

Kelly put an insulated cooler containing food outside Izzy's door twice a day, then texted to let her know it was there. Mostly, Izzy ignored it, except in those rare moments when the hunger in her belly overrode the anguish in her heart.

Dante dropped by with marigolds harvested from his garden. He left them in a bag on her doorknob and messaged her that in the Mexican death tradition the flower was believed to entice spirits of the dead to visit. Izzy immediately brought the flowers inside, put them in a bottle of water next to her bed, and hoped her mother would find their glorious smell irresistible.

The only phone call she answered was from her father, who had taken Luca to stay with him and Uncle Nick. They were working hard to help him come to terms with his guilt and grief. Apparently, the plan was for their dad to eventually move into their mom's old room and live here with them. Izzy was proud of him for stepping up.

Tony had decided that, for the time being, there would be no memorial service. Izzy couldn't face it, Luca was too broken, Kelly was in denial, and Papa was just so damn sad.

They were told that Erin died trying to escape. Besides that, the government had provided no details. The bodies of state enemies were never returned to their families. Sometimes bullets from the firing squad were sent to family members—as they had been to Dante's family—but Erin wasn't formally executed. Izzy's imagination visited horrible places as she tried to guess what truly happened in her mom's final moments.

On day seven, Izzy sent a text message to Dante: HOW DO YOU DEAL WITH YOUR GRIEF?

Dante replied: I USE IT TO FUEL MY FIGHT FOR JUSTICE.

And those were the magic words that Izzy needed to hear.

***

In early June, Dylan came into Café Paris during Izzy's breakfast shift and pulled her aside. "I need to talk to you privately."

Izzy shook her head. "Can't it wait until I'm in the

office later?" *The North Star* had resumed publication, and she now worked as Julia's research assistant.

"No, it can't."

There was a sense of urgency in Dylan that Izzy had never before witnessed.

"Is there a safe place we can talk?" he asked.

Izzy thought about it. "Well, it's unlikely the walk-in is bugged."

"Now," Dylan said.

"Follow me." Izzy stopped to tell Karma she was taking a break and then led Dylan back to the kitchen and into the walk-in refrigerator. Before she could close the door behind them, Luther muscled his way inside.

"Bodyguard," Luther said to Dylan.

Dylan yanked off his sunglasses, and the two men stared at each other for a long moment before Dylan shook his head in defeat. "Fine." He pulled a CD from the pocket of his long black coat. "This disc just arrived at CU in the latest Highway to Hell traffic." He handed it to Izzy.

It looked like a music CD from a band called Watchtower. The title was *The Freedom Train.*

Izzy exploded with anger. "What the hell? Someone is impersonating her? How dare they!"

Dylan produced a small CD player and handed her the ear buds. "Listen to the closing messages."

"Whatever." Izzy inserted the ear buds and firmly placed her hands on her hips in a defiant pose.

Dylan hit play.

The woman's voice said, "Before I seal this show with a kiss, I have a few messages from the Underground for the Underground."

Izzy fumed. "If they were going to imitate her, they

at least could have gotten the voice right. That is *not* a South Carolina drawl, it's a Georgia drawl. And—"

Dylan hit stop and grinned at her. "You need to slow down and pay attention."

Izzy slugged him hard. "How dare you smile."

"Settle down, wildcat. Just listen."

Dylan hit the play button again.

The woman with the Georgia drawl was saying, "... and this message is from Ziggy Stardust to Caffeinated Crone: 'The key is under the mat.' From Maltese Falcon to Our Lady of Perpetual Chaos: 'Take the cake with a file baked into it to Persephone's Prison.' From Lady Hooligan to Subversive Sally: 'The drop is at Lazy Ass Ranch.' This one goes out to Taylor Swift's Shadow: 'Renegade One is on his way to you.'

"And these four very personal messages are from White Rose. To Grandpa: 'I still have Nana's pearls.' To Webmaster: 'Here's looking at you, kid.' To Agent 99: 'I'm still in the fight.' And finally, to Maquis: 'Resistance is not futile.'

"In closing, I will leave you with 'Gimme Shelter.' And please remember y'all that love is only a kiss away."

Izzy ripped out the earbuds and fought for breath. She looked at Dylan. "She's alive?" She looked at Luther. "She's alive?"

Luther produced one of his rare smiles. "Go talk with your father." He put his hand on Dylan's shoulder. "Not you. There are some things you can't know about."

Izzy snatched the CD case from Dylan's hands, took off running, and didn't stop until she burst through the back door of Tony Tavano's. Her dad and Uncle Nick were in the kitchen cooking. Breathless, all she could do was hold up the CD case.

Tony nodded and told Nick they were stepping out back for a few minutes. He took Izzy's hand and led her outside to the picnic table within the small, covered alcove where employees often took breaks.

They sat close together on one side of the table. Tony took the CD case from her hand and laid it down. "I received a copy this morning. I was going to share it with you tonight at home."

Izzy's mind was processing data at quantum speed, and she struggled to organize the threads of her thoughts into a coherent sequence. "How long have you known she was alive?"

He leaned into her so he could speak softly. "When you called and told me she was taken, I immediately contacted my Uncle Gino in Philly. He made arrangements with his associates in Denver. Luther filled us in on the information you had uncovered about John Yates and the baby. You couldn't blackmail him, but the mob sure knew how to use the information. They made him go back to the prison that night to turn Erin over to them, however they found her almost dead —she tried to kill herself so she wouldn't be forced to betray you and the others she worked with."

"How did she—"

"She tried to freeze to death. Came away with some bad frostbite to her feet, but they got her outta there in time."

Izzy struggled with a profound sense of betrayal. "Why didn't you tell me?"

"I did what I was told. That's the way it works with these guys. Erin said she would find a way to let you know when it was safe. When she was safe."

"Is she Watchtower?"

A smile played at his lips. "That would be my guess. I believe I would know her voice in whatever way she chose to sing."

"Have you been in contact?"

He shook his head. "Not since that first night. I'm not allowed to know where she's at."

Izzy considered the big picture. "Now that the local mob knows you're here are we in danger?"

"Yeah, we could be in for some trouble. But to save her … " He shrugged. "I'm good with that. You?"

"Absolutely." She thought about the rest of their family. "Who do we tell?"

"Erin made it clear in that message that Conor, Dylan, Julia, and you are the only ones she wants to know. We gotta respect that."

"Not Luca? Not Grandma?"

He shook his head. "I wouldn't trust them with the secret either. They're not … well, you know."

Izzy did know. "What do we do now?"

"What would your mother want you to do?"

"Take care of Luca and continue fighting the good fight."

"Then that's what we'll do, Bella." He hugged her hard. "That's what we'll do."

***

On Independence Day, Julia threw a party at her home for all the resisters in their immediate circle.

Izzy was excited about the gathering; it represented a welcome experience of camaraderie that buoyed her up as she faced an uncertain and frightening future.

After everyone arrived, they congregated in Julia's parlor for a champagne toast. Shiloh bustled around the room with a tray of what she explained were hand-painted Perrier-Jouët champagne flutes filled with Perrier-Jouët Grand Brut.

"I know you don't drink, girlfriend, but seize the moment," Shiloh told Izzy. "Julia says the official line by the company on this firewater is, 'a wonderfully rounded, generous champagne whose *joie de vivre* makes every moment more special.' Besides, ain't those pink flowers pretty?"

Joie de vivre? It felt like a sign from Lili that her spirit was present, so Izzy accepted a glass with the hand-painted pink flowers.

Shiloh winked at her, leaned close, and whispered, "See you tonight for the takedown."

They had an apprehension scheduled for later that evening. Izzy raised her glass to her. "Looking forward to it, as usual."

After everyone had gathered, Julia stood before them with a glass in one hand and her trademark cigar in the other. "Let us toast to our commitment to reclaim American independence from tyranny, and our pledge to work together to manifest liberty and justice for all. We cannot let the dream of this nation die. Not on our watch."

"Not on our watch," Izzy echoed with the others, then took a sip of the sparkling wine.

"I remain committed to doing everything within my power to liberate our friends who remain in government custody," Julia said. "Andrea Night, Sasha Swan, Eve Cooper, as well as eleven-year-old Abby Mahoney and her mother, Mary, who await their executions. Nor have I forgotten Keith and Autumn Evans, the owners of the Bookmark Bistro, or their missing children. I also made a promise to Ian that I would try to discover the fate of his brother. And I'm fiercely determined to find justice for Harlan Weismann's murder." She threw a meaningful look toward Forrest.

Forrest nodded. "Thank you. I intend to keep his work alive. I like to think he's proud of all of us for the extraordinary work we're doing."

Izzy looked around the room and considered the many missions represented by those in attendance—and the enormous challenges they faced.

Luther had teamed up with Yanah, and they were working with their respective Nations—Northern Cheyenne and Navajo—to assist the Resistance. Their stated goal was to offer safe houses and humanitarian aid to those in need. The irony of that didn't escape Izzy, given how the United States had historically treated the Native people. The nobility of their mission touched her heart deeply.

Rafael and Rita remained active players in the increasingly dangerous women's healthcare Underground network.

And Karma—always a cheerleader of the Resistance but never before a player—took on a role previously held by Harlan in the Underground entertainment community. Inspired by the events surrounding Casablanca Night, she began coordinating clandestine showings of banned movies and live musical events, leveraging her past as a local celebrity to make the necessary connections.

Dante handed Izzy an envelope. "It's from Joplin."

Izzy put her glass down and opened the envelope's flap, which had a wax seal imprinted with Joplin's initials. "Fancy."

"She's creative."

The enclosed card read, "*In gratitude for the gracious GoFundMe campaign you organized that changed our lives, Joplin and Jagger Winters would like to invite you to a housewarming party at our new home on August 1st at six o'clock in the evening. A fine buffet of Cantonese Cuisine shall be served. Please RSVP ASAP. And you may not bring a date because ... Dante.*"

Izzy burst out laughing.

"What does it say?"

She couldn't tell Dante about Joplin's determined matchmaking efforts, so tucked the invitation away in her pocket before his curious eyes caught a glance. "Please tell the hostess that I will be honored to attend."

"She's excited," he said. "Mei Ling is teaching her to cook. Watching her bloom has been ... amazing." With Julia's help, Dante had taken legal custody of the children, and the three of them moved into an apartment together.

"You're good with all that new responsibility?" Izzy asked.

His face lit up. "Oh, I'm good. I love those kids."

Izzy thought about how Joplin and Mei Ling had bonded when they first met. Besides learning Cantonese cooking, Joplin now exclusively wore the retro hippie clothing the older woman had given her. "Maybe when all the madness ends, and Joplin grows up, she and Mei Ling will reopen The Buddha Belly together?"

"Joplin would shine at restaurant management. She's got bossiness down to a fine art."

And Izzy knew that was true. "Where are the kids today?"

"Conor took them fishing at Golden Ponds, along with Luca and Mojo. They were excited about the whole adventure. Tonight, I'll take them to see the fireworks."

"Oh, would you consider taking Luca, too? He's having a real hard time." Witnessing Luca's guilt and grief tore Izzy's heart to shreds. She didn't know how to come to grips with the fact that she possessed the power to lessen his pain but couldn't do so.

"Of course I will. Yeah, I understand how hard it is to lose a mother, but to have been responsible for her death would be beyond bearing. I definitely feel for him." After a moment, he asked, "Do you want to join us?"

"Shiloh and I have a work thing later, but if we get done early enough, I'd love to. Text me with the details."

His smile returned. "I'd like that." The sounds of instruments tuning up from the backyard drifted into the house. "But for now, I guess a bunch of us are going to jam."

"I'll be out in a few minutes." Izzy retrieved her champagne glass and returned it to the kitchen. As she poured a glass of ice water, she thought about her epic takedown of Pastor Christian and how well that had turned out. Now her greatest challenges remained finding Sofia's sister and changing the fate of Sofia's baby. The mafia's involvement in blackmailing John Yates complicated everything. Dancing with the mob, as she and her father now had to do, was what frightened her the most. The lives of her entire family were at stake.

However, today Izzy refused to dwell on that. Instead, she found refuge in the backyard where Karma, Luther, Dante, Shiloh, Rita, Rafael, and Yanah were jamming. When she wandered outside, the song they were playing was "The Devil Went Down to Georgia."

"I still can't believe they gave her a Georgia drawl," she said with disgust.

Dylan sidled up to her and slipped a companionable arm around her shoulders. "Settle down, wildcat. Not everyone has mad computer skills as fine as yours."

***

On the Fourth of July, Erin cooked for the young women's holiday party. It was a labor of love for what had become her surrogate family. She had absorbed many of Tony's recipes through the years, and it turned out that she was a damn good cook. The appetizer trays she created included toasted ravioli, pepperoni rolls, caprese bites, and stuffed portabella mushrooms. As Tony had always said, cooking was the language of love, and it brought her joy to speak it.

She was now known as Rory Gallagher. When she had been asked to pick a new identity, her father's name came to mind, and it felt comfortable.

As she worked in the spacious kitchen, she saw a flash of colorful fireworks out of the window over the sink. Limping, she made her way across the room to get a better look. She had been told that prior to the new government, fireworks had been outlawed in Ann Arbor. However, tonight she was grateful for the sight. She wondered if her own family was looking up into the same sky, also longing for liberty.

God, how she missed them.

Rory Gallagher was the House Mother of the Athena sorority in Ann Arbor, Michigan. Comprised of university students committed to academic excellence and championing the rights of women, the independent sisterhood was formed when Roe versus Wade had been overturned. Little did they know then that their mission statement would have far-reaching application when the Patriot government came to power.

Erin had quickly grown to love the diverse, remarkable group of young women. Someday when sanity returned to the nation, she hoped to introduce Izzy to them—most especially, to Aria D'Angelo, who was Tony's Uncle Gino's granddaughter. Aria reminded Erin of Izzy. Besides a familial resemblance, they shared the same fire.

Aria, a medical student at the University of Michigan, had founded Athena. The sorority house, a stately 1908-built mansion near the university, had been owned by her family for generations. During Prohibition it had hosted a popular high-end speakeasy, and the underground cellars and tunnels had been part of a complex network used for bootlegging and smuggling. Now the home operated as a station for the Underground Railroad, utilizing its hidden rooms and underground labyrinth as part of a well-organized network that smuggled enemies of the state into Canada. The conductors of Athena Station helped travelers create new identities and provided necessary documents to facilitate their journeys to safety. When their forging efforts weren't enough, they assisted in literally smuggling travelers across the border. In mythology, Athena was not only a goddess of wisdom but also of war. The women of Athena were fearless.

The fact that Erin had landed in a house of brilliant women with superb cyber technology skills and a commitment to the American Resistance was a fortuitous situation about which her mother would have attributed all kinds of cosmic significance. However, Erin understood that a group of intelligent young women with high ideals who chose to defy tyranny really wasn't all that surprising.

When the sisterhood found out that she was Watchtower, they wasted no time in producing her shows.

Her first recording was *The Freedom Train*, which featured the activities of the new Underground Railroad. And for subsequent shows she collected the stories of those passing through Athena Station. The enemies of the state whom they helped included notable politicians, authors, journalists, military leaders, scientists, professors, and celebrities who had defied the status quo. At times Erin felt she now lived within the very heart of the Resistance.

"Rory, there's someone here who wants to talk with you," Aria said.

"Okay, give me a minute." Erin was finishing up making the caprese bites by skewering the grape tomatoes, mini mozzarella balls, and basil leaves onto the bamboo cocktail picks. As she worked to complete her task, she marveled at how the food selection was so much more plentiful here than it had been at home. Finally, when she was done, she drizzled them all with balsamic glaze.

"Those look amazing. May I try one?" The woman had snuck up on Erin, who had been too engrossed in her task to notice.

"Of course." She picked up the serving dish and extended it to her guest.

As the woman chose one, Erin looked up at her and gasped. "Governor? I thought you were dead."

The former governor of Michigan smiled. "We'll let them go on thinking that, okay?"

"Sure. Absolutely. Of course." Erin was, as Ian had always been fond of saying, utterly gobsmacked. Supposedly, this popular leader had been assassinated by a militia during the Patriot takeover.

"Quite a few state officials and members of the U.S. Congress who are presumed dead, aren't," the governor said. "After getting our families safely out of the country, we banded together to work on a plan to recover our nation." She flashed her beautiful smile. "All is far from lost."

That news evoked an unexpected flood of grateful tears from Erin. There really was hope, after all. She had been wracked with doubt.

The governor embraced her in a tender hug, then handed over a cocktail napkin to dry her tears. "I wanted to meet you, Watchtower. I've been wondering if you know just how powerful your voice has become in this country. You're helping to change the world. Please keep up the good work."

Erin recalled Brian's words to her that day she had dozed in his room. *You, my dear sweet older-by-four-minutes sister, are going to change the world.* She hoped they were both correct in their assessment of her efforts.

Suddenly, all the courageous souls she knew who were fighting the good fight tumbled like a colorful kaleidoscope through her mind. There were so many uncommon heroes. She finished drying her tears. "As my daughter is fond of saying, 'All that is necessary for the triumph of evil is for good men—and women—to do nothing.'"

AUTHOR'S NOTE

Of the many books I've written over the course of my long career, none have been so challenging for me as this one. When events in my fictional universe started to come true, I felt it would appear as if I was jumping on the headline bandwagon, so I ended up discarding multiple drafts. Eventually, after years of false starts, I simply returned to my original outline and wrote it as the Muses had inspired me to do.

As of the time of publication not all the events in my story have come to pass, but the way things are unfolding they still might. We stand at the crossroads.

I hope *Resistance* speaks to people whose hearts and minds are open, and that it successfully conveys the message that each of us has the capacity to be heroic. None of us need be superheroes. Izzy demonstrated that courage is not the absence of fear, but a decision to act. Joplin understood that one must do what's right even if it's not easy. Conor did what his heart asked him to do, despite the cost. And Erin used her talent to help change the world.

Each of us can make a difference, if we try.

Please don't let evil triumph.

Glory to all the heroes.

ACKNOWLEDGEMENTS

The beauty of many souls is reflected in this project, and I am thankful for their light.

For the perfect book cover, I'd like to thank Aeryn Havens.

Julie Campbell and Matt Klauza, PhD, provided invaluable editorial assistance.

My beta readers Jane Firebaugh and Matt McMullen gave excellent feedback.

Jenna and Joey Young's research assistance helped immensely.

And Gordon Kennedy's input was critical for developing a key plot element.

Life has taught me that you simply cannot do epic things without phenomenal people. My friends are highly intelligent, wildly creative, fearlessly bold, and incredibly sexy. Knowing them has made my own life infinitely richer, and their help with *Resistance* meant the world to me.

ABOUT THE AUTHOR

Devin O'Branagan weaves stories of souls who find themselves capable of much more than they ever imagined possible. She showcases her love of uncommon heroes across many genres including dystopian fiction, paranormal thrillers, young adult urban fantasy, science fiction, chick lit, and erotic romance.

In addition to being a novelist, Devin spent five years as a humor columnist for TAILS Pet Magazine. A passion for animals often shines through in her work, with colorful animal characters frequently appearing in her stories.

Throughout her decades-long career, Devin's publishers have included Simon & Schuster's Pocket Books, German publisher Heyne Verlag, Turkish publisher Dogan Egmont, and indie publisher Cornucopia Creations Press. Her books are available in print, ebook, and audio formats.

Explore Devin's diverse body of work and find a hero to inspire you!

www.DevinWrites.com

ALSO BY DEVIN O'BRANAGAN

Threshold

With Brave Wings She Flies

Incarnation

Glory

Pretty Sacrifices

Genesis

Witch Hunt

Of the Blood of Witches

Witch Hunt: Of the Blood (Anthology)

Red Hot Property

Red Hot Liberty

Show Dog Sings the Blues

The Twilight Bone